Paul Bennett was born i
tising and market researc
own agency enabled him
Money Race is the fourth r
and follows *Due Diligence,*
which are also published by Warner Books. The author is
a three-star bridge master, and lives in Essex with his wife
and two daughters.

THE
MONEY RACE

Paul Bennett

WARNER BOOKS

A *Warner* Book

First published in Great Britain in 1999 by Warner Books

A CIP catalogue record for this book
is available from the British Library.

ISBN 0 7515 2555 3

Set in M Janson by M Rules.
Printed and bound in Great Britain by
Clays Ltd, St Ives plc.

Warner Books
A Division of
Little. Brown and Company (UK)
Brettenham House
Lancaster Place
London WC2E 7EN

'Confound their politics,
Frustrate their knavish tricks.'

God Save The King Henry Carey

CHAPTER ONE

Day One

Tuesday. No ordinary Tuesday (although I would come to wish otherwise), but a bright, shining, brand-new-day-dawning Tuesday. A hang-out-the-flags, break-open-the-champagne, shout Hallelujah Tuesday. I'd finally done it. I had my first case.

It was the third week of September. An uneventful – non-eventful – September intent on leaving in its wake the short scuff marks of time dragging its heels rather than the burnt rubber of rapid progress. The advertisements had been placed three weeks ago. We'd taken a scientific approach, set them up so that we could monitor the response for future reference. Two matching samples: half said *forensic accountant*, half said *fraud investigator*. If we could have thought of a third option we would have tried that too. Until today the score had been neck and neck – a nil-nil draw. But now I had my first case.

'Detective Inspector Walker gave me your name,' he said.

I suppressed an inner groan. Reminded myself that it doesn't pay to make assumptions. Downgraded my initial assessment. *Probably* my first case. Walker may well have given him my name, but I doubted that a glowing reference had accompanied it. More likely a sneer, a withering look and a character assassination.

Nick Shannon, I reprimanded myself, where's your magnanimity? Give her the benefit of the doubt. Not even

1

Walker would go as far as telling a complete stranger all about you.

'She told me all about you,' he said.

The groan became more difficult to stifle. Better make that *possibly* the first case. I had the feeling it was going to be one of those days when truth was relative and nothing was for certain. Pretty much the same as normal really.

Hell, don't panic, Shannon. The man is here, isn't he? That meant that either Walker had given him an abridged version of my incident-filled biography or he was desperate. By the look of him, my money was on the latter. Not that Ladbrokes would have quaked in their boots at the thought.

Mr Khan sat opposite me, kneading a pudgy left fist into his right palm and staring down at the polished floorboards in the hope that they might provide inspiration. He was wearing a bright white shirt which had the effect of emphasising his walnut-brown skin, a striped tie (red, white and blue, would you believe?) and a pale grey suit of some lightweight material, which shimmered like a coat of chain mail on a mediaeval knight about to stand single-handed against a fire-breathing dragon. I put him at late forties by the silver streaks running along the sides of his neatly trimmed glossy black hair. He was short, and the excess twenty pounds of weight he carried gave him an air of solidity. Despite the coolness of the morning, he periodically dabbed at his forehead with a handkerchief. It was the only discordant note in the otherwise very English, loud and enthusiastic rendition of 'Land of Hope and Glory' his outward appearance was singing *fortissimo*.

Khan had telephoned late the previous afternoon, pleading urgently for the first appointment in the morning. To the exaggerated rustling sounds of the blank pages of my diary, Arlene had agreed to squeeze him in at nine o'clock. On hearing his name I'd held out hopes it might be someone famous – Imran, perhaps. The way business was going I'd have settled for Kublai, Genghis even, although what

2

any of them would have wanted with a fraud investigator (or forensic accountant – how could we decide?) I didn't know. Especially since the latter two were long dead and the former was carving out a new career in politics. On second thoughts, maybe it was Imran after all.

Picture the scene ten minutes earlier: Norman, Arlene and myself standing open-mouthed at the window as the shiny black Jaguar pulled up alongside the short wooden jetty to our premises in Docklands; the three of us taking mental notes of the *chauffeuse* in her navy blue suit and peaked cap and the practised grace with which she respectfully leapt from the car to open the rear door; Norman – whose ill-gotten gains had bankrolled the company and whose patience was wearing thin at the imbalance between overheads (large) and income (nil) – smiling as greedily as it is possible to do while simultaneously licking one's lips; Arlene dashing through to the kitchen, slamming the jar of instant coffee back in the cupboard to the accompanying sound of a singularly American curse, followed by the rattle of our best arabica beans tumbling into the electric grinder.

She had led Mr Khan into the office, where I sat at the deliberately untidied desk with its carefully propped collection of files – all stuffed with old newspapers, unused notepads and anything else we'd been able to lay our hands on – trying to look distracted and important. Her long auburn hair had been swept back and secured with a plain dark-wood clip into a practical no-nonsense style. She was wearing a floppy-collared cream silk blouse under a tan suit, beige and blue correspondent shoes with low heels, and a pair of clear-glass spectacles to add the finishing touch of serious professionalism. If you were looking for fraud, I thought, you didn't have to step outside this room. She winked at me proudly with a hazel eye and went off to get the tray of coffee.

I'd shaken Mr Khan's damp hand, gestured at Norman and introduced him simply as 'my associate', omitting the

3

non-essential information like 'one of the country's best embezzlers, reformed – more or less'. And now we sat waiting for Mr Khan to pluck up the courage to speak. My outward air of patience was betrayed by the index finger of my right hand tapping out a staccato rhythm on the desktop. Norman frowned at me, but his hand drifted in a similar exercise of displacement activity towards his scrawny neck to adjust the tie which he found he wasn't wearing. My old friend, who had a habit of changing his *persona* about as frequently as most people do television channels on an average Sunday evening, had carefully planned his outfit to mirror that which he had assumed our potential client would wear. Norman, open-neck collarless shirt teamed with loose-cut trousers, looked like he was auditioning for the title role in the remake of *Gandhi*. I flashed him a smile and sadistically let it grow wider as he flushed.

'I am Ali Khan,' our visitor said. His manner of speech had that very precise, perfectly enunciated phrasing of those who had mastered English and now put us more natural and idiomatic (i.e. slovenly) speakers to shame. His tone implied that there should have been a *the* before his name. Maybe he was famous after all.

I nodded knowingly, hoping that his next line would begin, 'As you know . . .'

No such luck.

'I shouldn't have come here,' he said, shaking his head sadly. His dark eyes drifted away from me and roved around the room as if trying to find something that would provide him with an excuse to leave. How would he judge the unadorned white walls of the recently converted warehouse? The long black table I used as a desk? The matching low coffee table and black leather chairs positioned with a view of the river? The white anglepoise lamp shining down on the spotless keyboard of the computer? Would he see it all as Norman calculatingly intended – 'minimalist, uncluttered, prosperous without

4

being profligate' – or would it simply seem like the indulgent fix of a Habitat junkie?

It must have passed muster, for Ali Khan turned back to me and said in a cracked voice, 'I need your help, Mr Shannon. There is no one else to whom I can turn.'

Whatever the guy was famous for, it wasn't graduating top of the Flattery class. The coffee arrived before I was tempted to switch into sarcasm mode with an ill-timed 'Well, thank you *very* much'. As far as client service goes, I still have a lot to learn. I poured three cups of the thick aromatic coffee, passed two across the desk, gestured casually towards the jug of cream and sugar bowl, and smiled reassuringly.

'Why don't you tell us all about it,' I prompted, Samaritan-style. 'Start anywhere you like. The beginning is usually a good place, but sometimes the unconventional works better.'

'As you know,' he began – now, this was more like it – 'I am leader of the Council for the London Borough of Oldbrook.'

I carefully put down my cup. Concentrated hard on stopping myself from flinching. Fought the instinct to reach into my pocket for the comfort of a cigarette.

The very last sphere I wanted to get involved in was politics, where the only thing you could rely on was that you could trust nobody. Still, at least with politicians you could always tell when they were lying – if their lips were moving, they were lying.

And the last place on earth I wanted to go to was Oldbrook.

Oldbrook.

Whoever had thought of the name had obviously experienced the same problem of nomenclature as ourselves. For one thing it wasn't old; for another, as far as I knew, there wasn't a brook in the entire borough – rivers of blood, maybe, if the media were to be believed (but *their* word was pretty much on a par with that of politicians).

Under the last reorganisation of local government, Oldbrook had been carved out of the worst areas of three adjoining boroughs in a misguided mixed-metaphor principle of putting all your curate's eggs in one basket where the chickens wouldn't hatch out and come home to roost. Or something like that. Oldbrook was rarely referred to by its proper name: it was the 'ghetto borough', a troublesome infernal triangle of land with signs at its borders saying 'Abandon hope, all ye who enter here.'

'I was informed yesterday,' he continued, 'that there is a large sum of money missing from the borough's accounts.'

'And what exactly do you consider to be large?' I asked.

'Four hundred thousand pounds,' he replied.

Yep, I thought with a gulp, that's large. Nothing like jumping in at the deep end for your first case. 'So, Mr Khan,' I said casually, as if I encountered such sums every day of the week, 'I assume you would like me to find the money?'

'That is part of the job,' he said, nodding his head slowly.

'And the other part?'

Ali Khan's eyes narrowed, his forehead creased in pain. 'Find my daughter, Mr Shannon. She is missing too.'

'Coincidence or connection?' I asked, more for confirmation than information.

'I don't know,' Ali Khan said, his hand drifting to his forehead as if subconsciously supporting the weight on his mind. 'I really don't know.'

'If we rule out coincidence, Mr Khan, then what do we have left?'

'It seems to me that there are only two possibilities. Either my daughter is a thief or she has been abducted.'

'And you don't want to believe the former?'

'No,' he said. 'Well, yes.' He gave a long, helpless sigh. 'What I mean is, neither do I want to believe the latter.'

CHAPTER TWO

'This is my daughter, Nadya,' Ali Khan said, extracting a photograph from the inside pocket of his jacket. He held it protectively, looking down at the subject with watery eyes. With reluctance, he relinquished it into my possession.

We had decamped to the other end of the room, where I hoped the view over the slow-running Thames to Greenwich, where the sun was casting long thin shadows from the masts of the *Cutty Sark*, would relax him and make it easier for the story to flow. Arlene had brought more coffee. I'd surreptitiously slipped her a note which I knew would raise her eyebrows, and probably her hackles too. Now Ali Khan leaned heavily back in the leather chair and gazed out of the window while I studied the picture.

It showed a girl with straight black hair hanging down to her waist. She might have been pretty, but it was hard to tell. The hair covered the sides of her face like partially drawn curtains, reducing it to a narrow rectangle, the dominant feature of which was a pair of thick-rimmed spectacles. Behind the sparkling glass, dark doe-like pupils looked down, shyly avoiding the lens of the camera. She was wearing a short-sleeved T-shirt underneath a traditional sari. Both were virginal white. One end of the sari was wrapped around her tiny waist, the other so loosely draped over her shoulder that it hid any femininity that might have lurked beneath. I estimated her age as seventeen, going on twelve. Daddy's little girl.

'When was this taken?' I asked.

'About a month ago,' he replied. 'On her twentieth birthday.'

Okay, so I underestimated a little. I'm not infallible, I admit it. But being wrong about her age made me even more convinced of her role.

'Tell me all about her, Mr Khan. What is she like? What does she do?'

For the next thirty minutes Ali Khan talked about his daughter with a mixture of pride and shattered faith. Distilling out the detail from the irrelevancies, the facts went like this. Nadya was the product of a mixed marriage, Ali Khan (Muslim) and his wife (Hindu). The family had moved to England when she was two years old, and over the years Nadya had successfully assimilated the differing cultures of her parents and, less so it seemed, that of her new country. She was bright, kind, cheerful, polite – and all the other adjectives from that long rose-tinted list fathers use to describe their daughters. And now she was about to start her last year at the London School of Economics, majoring in accountancy – and bolshevism too no doubt, unless the place had changed.

Ali Khan, whose dictionary didn't include the word *nepotism*, had pulled strings to fix her up with a temporary job in the borough's Treasury Department during her long summer vacation. It was an arrangement that presumably suited both father and daughter. Some sorely needed experience and pocket money for the girl. And for the father? Well, she was under his watchful eye. But not watchful enough, it seemed.

Yesterday morning, Ali Khan had departed early on business and the girl had left their house to make her own way to the office. She had never arrived.

No one thought anything of it until the Head of Treasury inspected the daily bank statements. And saw the jaw-dropping debit for four hundred thousand pounds.

That was the start of the long and winding trail that had brought Ali Khan to my office. Luckily for him, the Head of Treasury (experienced in putting two and two together) says not a word to his staff but hotfoots it straight to the Chief Executive. Chief Executive breaks the bad news to Ali Khan. Discreet hunt goes on for the money and the girl. No success on either front. Ali Khan pleads for time before anyone else is informed of the disappearances. Chief Executive agrees to a stay of execution of two weeks – of which only thirteen days now remained. That was how long we had before the half-yearly audit commenced. If the money could be replaced before then, the whole matter would be put down to a clerical error. If not, it would be officially reported to the Fraud Squad. And Ali Khan would be expected to tender his resignation.

'So that is all I can tell you, Mr Shannon,' he said.

Can or will, I wondered. Something didn't make sense.

'Very thorough, Mr Khan,' Norman complimented. 'Now, I'm afraid, we need to discuss the indelicate subject of fees. The rate for the job,' he said, watching his prey like a hawk preparing to swoop, 'is one thousand pounds.'

I could sense what was coming. It was going to be a variant of the old optician's trick. You know how it goes. Someone, with blurred vision and a distinct need, selects a pair of glasses and asks, 'How much?' 'Fifty pounds.' When they reach for their credit card the optician adds, 'For the frames.' Then, with the punter hooked on the line, the optician reels him in slowly, but steadily, by following up with the price of the lenses – each. Then the protective coating. Then the tint. Then . . .

Ali Khan didn't blink at the figure.

Norman added, 'Per day.'

Still no reaction.

'Plus expenses, of course.'

'Of course.'

'Plus VAT,' Norman said, talons buried deep in Ali Khan's wallet.

'Agreed,' Ali Khan said, reaching for his cheque book in anticipation of the next request – a hefty non-returnable deposit.

Norman smiled benevolently. 'Or,' he said, 'we will work for nothing.'

'For nothing?' Ali Khan said, voicing my surprise.

'For nothing,' Norman repeated, 'but a ten per cent commission on the value of any frauds we may discover in the borough's accounts. Excluding the original four hundred thousand, of course.'

Ali Khan's face brightened. In his eyes, the roles of predator and prey had been reversed: this, he was thinking, was as good as getting a freebie. 'I'll need to clear it with the Chief Executive,' he said, nodding excitedly to himself, 'but I don't foresee that there will be any objections.' He paused and looked across at me. 'You have experience of this kind of investigation, Mr Shannon? You think you can do it? Find the money and my daughter? And all within two weeks.'

The money maybe, I thought. That I'd done before. The daughter was a different matter. And two weeks?

I opened my mouth to give an honest reply. Well, someone's got to set a good example.

'Don't worry, Mr Khan,' Norman leapt in. 'Money, daughters, whatever. We specialise in everything.'

I winced. But our client seemed unsuitably impressed.

Still, maybe his mind was too focused on his daughter to notice the paradox. Or perhaps he was distracted by the soft chirruping coming from beneath his jacket.

'Excuse me,' he said, taking a mobile phone from a holster on his belt and flipping open the mouthpiece.

Now, attitudes towards mobile phones are either black or white: it's impossible to feel ambivalent about them. Either you think they are the best thing since sliced bread (*sliced bread?*) or you regard them as a bigger nuisance than double yellow lines, shrink-wrapping and corned beef tins all put together. Norman had issued us all with one as part of our hi-tech battle against crime. Mine didn't bother me. I kept it out of sight and switched off. Simple solutions are always the most effective.

10

Ali Khan frowned, asked questions of how, when and where of the caller, shook his head gravely as he listened to the answers. 'Give me thirty minutes,' he said. 'Meanwhile, just pray it's not starting all over again.'

'Bad news?' Norman asked, fearing the worst for the daughter and our contract. 'Is it Nadya?'

'No, not Nadya,' Ali Khan replied. 'A fellow Muslim. Beaten to death last night. The police have just found his body hidden behind a row of dustbins.'

'Did you know him?' I asked, immediately feeling foolish. Just because they were both Muslims didn't mean they had to know each other.

'We attended the same mosque,' he said, making me feel better. 'And I saw him around the building from time to time.'

'The building?' I echoed, the skin on the back of my neck beginning to prickle.

'He worked at the council.'

'Isn't that a bit of a coincidence?'

'Mr Shannon,' he said patronisingly, 'the council is the biggest employer in the borough. And if you count our sub-contractors and suppliers then one in nine people in Oldbrook works directly or indirectly for us. This, I'm afraid, was a racially motivated attack. The fact that he was a council employee was irrelevant.'

Ali Khan stood up to leave.

Not so fast, Mr Khan, I thought.

'What department?' I said.

'Sorry?'

'In which department did this man work?'

'Treasury,' he said. Then added quickly, 'But that has nothing to do with anything. He just happened to be in the wrong place at the wrong time. And met the wrong sort of people.'

Maybe.

It seemed like an apposite time to examine the second possibility.

11

'Mr Khan,' I said, 'if we assume your daughter did not steal the money, then why would anyone want to abduct her?'

'To get at me, Mr Shannon.'

'And why,' I said, suppressing a sigh, 'would anyone want to get at you?'

'Not anyone,' he said. 'But OWN.'

'OWN?' I repeated, none the wiser.

'It's an organisation with its headquarters in Oldbrook. OWN stands for One (White) Nation. It's a sad collection of bigoted fanatics who broke away from the National Front because they considered it had gone soft.'

'Slightly to the left of Hitler?'

'No, Mr Shannon. Occupying the same low ground. But that's bad enough.'

'And what do OWN have against you?'

'Apart from the obvious, you mean?'

I blushed.

'Our MP died a week ago – nothing sinister, he'd been suffering from cancer for the last couple of years. In the forthcoming by-election I will stand as the Labour candidate.'

'And will you win?'

'That is what the members of OWN are afraid of. To them it would be like having a fishbone permanently stuck in their gullets if the constituency were to be represented by a non-white MP. OWN would like to see me stand down. That is what they would hope to achieve by kidnapping Nadya.'

'*If* that is what they did,' I pointed out. 'Have you received any threats, any demands since Nadya went missing?'

'No, not as yet. But I see your point. And now you must see mine. I am in a cleft stick, Mr Shannon. If OWN is not responsible for Nadya's disappearance, and she did in fact steal the money, then I would still have to withdraw my candidacy. That is why I am relying on you.' He stood up;

offered his hand. 'I must go,' he said. 'You understand, I hope? And thank you, Mr Shannon. Thank you very much.'

'Don't thank me yet, Mr Khan. You see, there's just one problem. I'm not sure if I can take this case.'

Ali Khan stared at me. Norman glared.

'But why not?' both asked.

'But you must,' Ali Khan added pleadingly.

I shook my head, sucked air through my teeth. 'It's not that simple, Mr Khan. I have to see if I can reschedule my other assignments. I'll know better by three o'clock. Ring my Personal Assistant then. *If* I accept your case, I'll be round to look at your daughter's room this evening.'

'Why do you want to see her room?' he asked.

'Trust me, Mr Khan,' I said. 'I have my reasons.'

CHAPTER THREE

'Reasons, eh?' Norman said, the instant Ali Khan had departed. 'I'm glad you mentioned reasons because I'd like to hear some. If you don't mind, Mr Nick-Picky-Picky-This-Job-Isn't-Good-Enough Shannon, *I* would very much like an explanation.'

'Me too,' said Arlene, brandishing my scribbled note and waving it accusingly at me. 'And it had better be damned convincing.'

I had reasons. Good ones too. Some I didn't want to voice for fear of worrying everyone – including myself. Others could not be mentioned without opening up wounds, some so fresh they were guaranteed to bleed. I played for time; lit a cigarette and blew a thoughtful stream of blue-grey smoke towards the open window.

'Well?' challenged Arlene. She placed her hands on her hips, spreading her fingers wide, and pouted her full red lips. It was supposed to signal resolution, yet somehow managed to come across as seductive. I fought the inappropriate urge to blow her a kiss. 'We're waiting, Nick.'

I poured the remains of the coffee jug into my cup. Added two heaped spoonfuls of brown sugar. Slowly stirred the lukewarm mixture. Took an experimental sip. 'Disgusting,' I said with a grimace. 'How about a bargain, Arlene? A fresh pot of coffee in exchange for the answers to all your questions?'

'You are not in any position to bargain.'

'I am the boss,' I reminded her, 'and you are the Personal Assistant.'

'In that case I have grounds for sexual harassment.'

'You stole my line,' I said. 'How about it, huh? Coffee, that is.'

'I wouldn't mind another cup,' Norman said supportively.

Arlene heaved a sigh. Flounced off towards the door. Turned her head back towards me. 'When I return we talk reasons, okay? And job descriptions.'

'Right, Nick,' Norman said when we were alone. 'Why the pantomime?'

'Cast your mind back, please. To a little over a month ago.'

'I think I can manage that,' he said. 'Anything in particular? Or is this just a nostalgic meander down Memory Lane?'

'Future Assurance,' I said.

'Ah,' he said. 'I think I get it now.'

For a period of eight months I had been seconded by Jameson Browns, the firm of accountants for whom I was then working, to the Fraud Investigation Group, a loose-knit collection of so-called experts attached to the Fraud Squad. In my case, to be precise, 'C' Squad, headed by Detective Superintendent Collins, a man with a deep respect for the rules of police work – but only as long as they didn't get in the way of a 'result'. Which is how I came to go undercover into Future Assurance to investigate the company and find a motive for the murder of its Financial Director. And how, as a consequence of my recklessness, Arlene had been placed in a position of danger that, ultimately, resulted in the loss of our baby.

Arlene was thirty-seven, her biological time clock ticking away in an inexorable countdown. Before the climax of the Future Assurance débâcle she'd had dreams: dreams of the two of us (the soon-to-be three of us) settling down in her little old home town of Redemption, Massachusetts, midway along Cape Cod; dreams that I'd shattered through a mixture of carelessness and impetuosity.

I'd learned my lesson – the hard way – from Future Assurance. My well-intentioned friends had made sure of that. They had sent me to Coventry (thankfully, only figuratively speaking – they weren't that heartless) in order to drum into me the consequences of my cavalier attitude. So, this was a changed me. In the language of washing-powder commercials, this was the new improved Nick Shannon, who looked before he leapt. And who had made a solemn promise never again to endanger himself or others by thoughtless action. Promises, in my book, can't be broken.

'You told me,' I said, 'and in no uncertain terms, if you remember, not to act on impulse or blindly follow my instincts. That's what I'm trying hard not to do now. And that's why I couldn't accept Ali Khan's case there and then.'

'This is not simply a childish way of getting your own back?' Norman asked.

'Since when have I been childish?' I replied, sticking my thumb in my mouth.

Arlene chose that precise moment to return. She shook her head and sighed. 'Is this what happens when I leave the room? I know smoking is bad for your health but, frankly, when it comes to image, it licks sucking your thumb any day.'

I lit another cigarette. Not as a delaying tactic this time, but to aid concentration. And to show Arlene I wasn't too proud to take advice. The fact that I was hooked didn't come into the reckoning. Pure coincidence.

Arlene placed the tray on the low table, sat down in the chair facing the river and leaned back, obstinately refusing to pour the coffee.

'Reasons,' Arlene said firmly, crossing her arms over her chest.

I gave her a brief résumé of the long conversation with

Ali Khan, omitting any reference to OWN; waited till I'd received back a curt nod of comprehension, then launched into my explanation.

'Right, let's look at this case rationally,' I said, preparing to count off the drawbacks on the fingers of my right hand. That way I could go up to five: the left was only good for three. 'First, there's the problem that it's not just about finding the money. There's the daughter too. Unless I skipped that particular chapter of my correspondence course, I don't think the topic of missing persons was part of the accountancy curriculum.'

Norman, yielding no ground in the battle for profit, gave a noncommittal shrug of his bony shoulders.

'Second,' I said, quickly moving on.

'Hang on,' Arlene interrupted. She looked at me accusingly. 'You *have* to do something. What if she's in danger? What if she's been kidnapped?'

'The probabilities do favour that scenario,' I said calmly.

'Don't be so cold and heartless,' she said sharply. 'This is a girl's life we are talking about.'

'You wanted reasons,' I said, waving my hands helplessly in the air. 'Why not hear me out?'

'Okay,' she said. 'Go on. Although it won't change the way I feel.'

'Second,' I continued, seemingly pointlessly, 'there's a thirteen-day time scale. That's a trifle short. So, why should we run the risk of failing on our very first case?'

'Because we don't have any other work,' said Norman. 'And this is a limited company, not a registered charity. There are people on the payroll, mouths to feed.'

'Third,' I said, turning my green eyes to Arlene in an appeal for support, 'this case is wrapped up in politics. You know how I feel about politics. *Boring.*'

'For money,' Norman said, dismissively waving a hand in the air, 'bore me rigid.'

'Fourth,' I said, judging it was time to play a stronger card, 'it means going to Oldbrook. No one goes to

Oldbrook unless they're dragged there, bound and gagged, kicking and screaming.'

'You can't really be screaming if you're gagged,' Arlene pointed out pedantically. 'Or if you can,' she added, 'no one can hear. Ain't that the whole point of the damned gag?'

I stubbed out my cigarette with a series of short petulant jabs. Added a sigh for good measure.

'Okay,' I said, giving ground graciously, 'maybe I'm going a little overboard. But, for those of you with short memories, let me remind you that it was only a year ago when the residents of Oldbrook were running riot in the streets. How many people were killed, Norman?'

'Three,' he said grudgingly. 'But,' he continued somewhat lamely, 'for all we know, it may have changed.'

'Yes, you're right,' I replied, raising my voice. 'People only get killed in ones nowadays. Trios are out of fashion.'

'I might grant you that point,' he said reasonably.

'Gee, thanks.'

'But only in general terms.'

I looked at him blankly.

'In your specific case, however,' he said, 'I have complete faith in you. You'll be all right, Nick. You're a survivor.'

Whatever happened to the creed of staying out of trouble? Sacrificed on the altar of Mammon?

'Last, and by no means least,' I persevered, 'there's Walker. Think about it, folks. If Collins had been the one to give Ali Khan my name, then that I could have understood. But Walker? Why would *she* do me a favour? Answer me that, someone.'

'I thought you two had buried the hatchet,' Norman said.

'The only place Walker would bury the hatchet is in my back. No, she's up to something. Before I accept this case, I need to find out exactly what. Sneak a look at her hidden agenda.'

'So that's why you passed me the note?' Arlene said with relief. 'Why you wanted to see her so urgently?'

18

'My intuition tells me that Walker is setting me up,' I said. 'So, when I've spoken to Walker *then* I'll . . .'

'Wait a cotton-picking minute,' she said, her eyes narrowed, her brow creased in thought. 'What did you mean by "people only get killed in ones nowadays"?'

Oh dear. I'd let the cat out of the bag.

'Well,' I said, pausing to wriggle uncomfortably in the chair.

'You might as well tell Arlene,' Norman said. 'She deserves to know the whole truth.'

'Thanks for your support, Norman,' I said.

'Thanks for your support, Norman,' Arlene said.

'It seems there is a reason, apart from the money, why Nadya may have disappeared,' I said.

I told her about OWN, stressing Ali Khan's chosen words of *bigoted* and *fanatics* and adding a *crazy* for good measure so she would be in no doubt of the moral character of the possible opposition, and what they had to gain by kidnapping Nadya.

Arlene bit her lip and said resolutely, 'Then you have to take the case. You have no choice. God knows what these rednecks might do to the girl. Nick, you can't take the risk of what might happen if you do nothing.'

'But what about the risk of doing something? This could be dangerous. No,' I said, firmly shaking my head. 'I gave both of you my solemn word. I can't break my promise.'

'I release you from your promise,' she said.

'But . . .'

'Just this once. These are special circumstances. I want you to take this case.'

'And what about you, Norman?' I said. 'Do you release me from the promise too? For the sake of the girl? Not just for the commission?'

Norman nodded.

'You're both absolutely sure about this?' I asked.

'Yes,' they said with more than a little show of short temper. 'Take the case.'

Mission accomplished.

'Maybe,' I said, suppressing a smug grin of triumph.

'What do you mean *maybe*?' Arlene snapped at me.

'I need to see Walker before making a decision. Suss out her motives. And establish why the police aren't involved. I don't want to step into some sort of trap. I hear what you both say. I'll let you know one way or the other in a couple of hours. I promise. In the meantime, Norman, I'd like an explanation.'

'Of what?' he asked innocently.

'This no fee business. Why, short of income as we are, should we work on a commission-only basis?'

'Because I share your distaste for politics.'

'Huh,' I said, giving him the full force of my extended repertoire of repartee.

'Well,' he said, 'my basic premise is that all politics is corrupt. Are we all agreed on that?'

Arlene and I remained silent. We both knew it was better not to interrupt Norman when he climbs on a hobby-horse, let alone encourage him by giving a hand up into the saddle.

'I'll take that as a "yes",' he said. Sometimes you just can't win. 'Local government is politics. Right? Therefore, it follows that local government is corrupt. Admittedly, your average local council has slightly less scope for lying and cheating, and less imagination about the ways they go about them, but, as sure as eggs is small ovoid objects coming out of the back of chickens, you'll find some scam in Oldbrook.'

'Wouldn't it be easier,' I said, 'to concentrate on finding the missing four hundred thousand pounds and the girl rather than complicating matters by widening the search?'

'Of course it would,' he said. 'But it wouldn't be anywhere near so lucrative. And anyway, look at the potential. If – sorry, make that *when* – you discover a fraud in Oldbrook, we can use that as a case history to approach other local authorities. Councils will be beating a path to our door, falling over each other in the rush to avail themselves of our services.'

'Wow, that's really wonderful news, Norman. You've made my day. I'll hardly be able to get to sleep tonight for thinking of all that excitement to come.'

'Ah, dear Nick,' he began, 'but . . .'

'I know,' I groaned, 'think of the money.'

'Excuse me, boys,' Arlene interrupted, 'but if you've finished your Tweedledum and Tweedledee act, may I make a comment?'

'Yes,' I said uncertainly.

'It strikes me, Nick, that, albeit out of good intentions, you've got yourself into a classic no-win situation. If you take the case then you condemn yourself not only to terminal boredom, but also a money race along the mean neo-Nazi patrolled streets of this God-forsaken Oldbrook place.'

'And if I don't take the case?'

'You know what Ali Khan will think, don't you?'

'That I'm too busy. Seems quite simple to me.'

'Naïve, more like it.' She shook her head at me. 'The danger is that Ali Khan, rejected in his hour of need, will see the workload argument as the convenient excuse it is. He's gonna think you don't like the colour of his money. Or, more pertinently, the colour of his skin.'

'Ah,' I said. There were other monosyllabic words going through my brain that were more expressive of my sentiments, but none of them could be verbalised in the presence of a lady.

'Believe me,' Arlene said, frowning, 'if you turn him down you will have made a powerful enemy. You'll be up in front of the Race Relations Board before your feet hit the ground.'

'Preposterous,' I said, preparing to lighten the mood. 'I have the perfect defence against any charge of prejudice.'

'And what might that be?' Arlene said.

'Because, my darling,' I said straight-faced, 'I'm employing an American woman.'

The punch on the arm hardly hurt at all.

'Haven't you ever heard,' she said, 'that silence is a virtue?'

'You wouldn't want me if I were virtuous.'

'Maybe I like a challenge,' she said, stroking my arm.

Norman coughed politely. 'I don't mind being a gooseberry – with you two, I've become quite used to that – but right now I'm an unsatisfied gooseberry.'

'Tautology,' I said with a smile.

'I'm still after reasons,' he said. 'Why did you say to Ali Khan that you would want to see Nadya's room?'

'Oh, that's an easy question,' I said with maximum disdain. 'I've read all the books, you see. It's what private eyes always do.'

CHAPTER FOUR

At what point on the spectrum does the personality dimension of single-mindedness become selfishness? If you asked Walker that question, all you would get in return is a blank look of incomprehension. Or one of her withering looks of derision, more like it. She was good at those. The honed-to-perfection icy stare coupled with a lowering of the eyelids and the shake of the head that I knew so well. Walker and I understood each other totally – and not at all.

Detective Inspector Cherry Walker met me in the cramped and unwelcoming carpet-tiled reception area of the stained-concrete and smeared-glass building in Richbell Place. On its lower levels was Holborn Police Station: above, in what I would have liked to have described as the rarefied atmosphere, if truth could be corrupted for the sake of a fine-sounding turn of phrase, was the headquarters of the Fraud Squad. Walker had absolutely no reason to make the journey down just to escort me back up again. And I knew what that no reason was.

'Shannon,' she said, breaking off her conversation with the desk sergeant, 'I'd like to say how good it is to see you again.'

'I know, Walker,' I replied, 'but lying in front of a witness is against the Metropolitan Police Code of Conduct.'

She gave me a half-smile – progress – and gestured towards the lift. I obeyed her instruction, pressed the call button and waited for the cage to descend. 'You're looking good, Walker,' I said unnecessarily.

'I already know you want something, Shannon. You don't have to make it blindingly obvious.'

The lift door opened with a creak. It was my turn to wave an arm. She gave a full smile this time and stepped inside. I followed and concentrated on studying her reflection in the mirrored back wall. Cherry Walker was tall, slim, beautiful and black. No, make that very tall, very slim, very beautiful and skin like coffee with a dash of cream. She was wearing a dark grey pinstripe suit, skirt cut an inch above her shapely knees – but then everything about Walker was shapely so why was I singling out the knees for a special mention? I picked a piece of lint from the collar of her jacket.

'Still have trouble with lifts, Shannon?' she asked so considerately.

'Hell, no,' I said, feeling a bead of perspiration beginning to form on my forehead. 'The trick with any phobia is simply to harness the full power of the mind in a counter-attack against the irrational fear.'

'Yeah,' she said. 'You always did talk a load of bullshit.'

'And I'd always thought that was the source of my fatal attraction. Must be the green eyes, the high cheekbones and Kirk Douglas dimple after all.'

'Huh,' she said, turning her face away from me to hide the blush which would have been impossible anyway to detect against her Nubian-princess skin.

The lift doors slid open, signalling the end of Round One – Shannon slightly ahead on points and trying hard not to commit the sin of overconfidence. We stepped from the lift to be greeted by a fine cirrus cloud of cigarette smoke drifting languidly towards us. Don't ever tell a policeman that smoking damages your health. 'Being a copper bloody damages your health,' he'll reply with scorn. Thirty pairs of eyes moved up from desks littered with the remains of lunchtime sandwiches, cold pizza crusts and paradoxically empty beakers of undrinkable coffee, and shifted in our direction. They passed quickly and dismissively over me with a fleeting bad-penny expression and settled longingly on Walker. She strode purposefully to the far end of the long open-plan room, trying to keep the pneumatic sway from her hips and failing miserably.

I approached her desk and prepared to sit down.

'Un huh,' she said.

What was this? International Monosyllable Day?

'Huh?' I replied, just in case.

'Times have changed, Shannon. Come into my office, won't you.'

Her office! This was Collins's office. Always was. Always would be. Hadn't it been specially created for him in an every-expense-spared token effort at privacy? Every detail custom-built with Collins in mind, right down to the thin slabs of plywood partitioning in their badly positioned frames: designed on the principle that it is the tree that bends that withstands the wind, they rattled and shook with the force of his constant desk-thumping explosions of incredulity against the actions of his superiors. But still they survived.

Walker took three paces to cross the length of the room. She sat herself down behind the desk, leaned forward, interlocked her long fingers and smiled up at me smugly.

I looked away and around the little office. Where was the spider plant that had suffered the daily abuse of being 'watered' only with dregs from Collins's whisky-tainted coffee mug and yet impossibly thrived? Where were the piles of routine paperwork that overflowed the in-tray, imprisoned in some clerical stasis, destined never to make the short trip across the desk to the empty wastelands of the tray marked 'Out'? What was with all this neatness, the vase of anemones, their sweet smell vying for supremacy with Walker's sensual perfume? And, the key question, where the bloody hell was Detective Superintendent Collins?

'Where's Collins?' I said, fearing the worst.

Walker screwed up her lips. 'Leave of absence,' she said.

'Suspended?' I said, decoding the *copspeak*. I shook my head, more in sorrow than in surprise. Jesus, I'd only been gone for a few weeks and, left to his own devices, Collins had followed his kamikaze nose into trouble. An icicle of guilt stabbed at my conscience. Please let it not be connected to the favour that Collins was doing for me. 'What exactly did he do this time?' I asked with trepidation.

'Can't say,' she lied. Walker was the Commander's ears and eyes. She knew, all right. Hell, she was probably responsible for the demise of the late unlamented Collins. 'But the important point to bear in mind, Shannon, is that, in the unfortunate absence of Mr Collins, I'm in charge.'

'Congratulations, Walker,' I said. Another step up the ladder. Another rung climbed by standing on somebody else's shoulders. Today 'C' Squad; tomorrow, who knows? The one thing that was certain was that Walker's ambition would not be thwarted. One day she'd be the first black woman to make Chief Constable. That was her ultimate aim – and what Walker wants, she gets. And woe betide anyone who stands in her way – including her own daughter, conveniently parked while still in her swaddling clothes on Walker's mother lest the knowledge that she'd had a baby should mar the image of absolute dedication to the job. To this day, the little girl still believed that Cherry was her sister. That was my hold over Walker.

'Ali Khan,' I said, pulling out the chair as far as it would go and squeezing myself contortionist-style through the narrow gap and into the seat. The edges of the desk jammed up against my knees. Being six foot three has its disadvantages, although in this tiny office even a person of restricted growth would have suffered the same fate. 'Thanks for the recommendation.'

She shrugged. 'It's the least I could do.'

'In that case,' I said, 'presumably you wouldn't mind doing a little more.'

'Like what?' she asked suspiciously.

26

'I'm interested in the chain of events,' I said. 'How Ali Khan happened to come to you. And why you couldn't help him.'

'It's a long story, Shannon.'

I glanced at my watch. 'I've got till three.'

'But I haven't.'

'Just give me the edited highlights then.'

Walker let out a long exaggerated sigh of inelastic tolerance being stretched. But I'd heard it before – many times. She'd have to do better than that.

'Ali Khan sits on the local Police Liaison Committee,' she said. 'He approached the Chief Superintendent, tried to enlist his help to find his daughter.'

'And to find the money?'

'The money, of course, was secondary.'

'Of course.'

'Don't be so damned prejudiced, Shannon.'

'I couldn't if I tried, Walker. I've experienced too *damned* much of it myself, don't forget.'

'As a direct consequence of your own actions,' she reminded me, 'not as a result of the colour of your skin.'

'Aren't we drifting from the point?'

'No, Shannon. We're concentrating on the point. The Chief Super said he wouldn't help.'

I raised an eyebrow. 'Even with a possible kidnap and a probable OWN connection?'

Walker looked at me questioningly.

'Ali Khan mentioned it.'

'The Chief Super dismissed that line of reasoning out of hand,' Walker said.

'And how about you?'

'Not the way that OWN operates. Too subtle. That was what *he* said. Reckoned that Nadya has simply gone AWOL with the loot. Then, out of vengeance or bigotry, he took great pleasure in stressing how overstretched his force was, how lacking in resources. And that, anyway, it was a virtually impossible task; that hundreds of young kids go missing every day in London and only a handful are ever traced. He said he'd do what he could, but left Ali Khan in no doubt that it was going to be very little.'

'You haven't answered my question,' I pointed out.

She shrugged. Took some time to weigh up the pros and cons of her response. 'I wouldn't rule out a kidnapping. But I also wouldn't jump to the conclusion that OWN is behind it.'

Nicely worded. Take the girl's disappearance seriously, she was saying, but don't worry too much about any danger. If only I could believe her. She knew my weaknesses. Dish out responsibility and reassurance in equal measures, the former to prick my conscience, the latter to pre-empt any doubts.

I shrugged back, hoping to draw her out.

'It suited the Chief Super to assume that Nadya had taken the money,' she continued. 'To play Pass the Problem. He suggested to Ali Khan that he contact the Fraud Squad. Maybe we could trace her through the money, rather than the other way round.'

'So that's how he came to you. And how did he get from you to me?'

'Ali Khan spoke to the Commander. The Commander and I agreed that it would be expedient if we were not to become officially involved. So I, in turn, suggested you as the next best alternative.'

'How come when the Chief Superintendent won't help, it's prejudice: when you won't help, it's expedience?'

The world-famous withering look shot across the desk like a poisoned dart. 'Oh, Shannon,' she said, 'don't you see?'

'Nope. Better spell it out for me.'

'If we, the Fraud Squad, make it an official case then there are rules that must be obeyed.'

'Collins wouldn't have played by the rules,' I pointed out.

'Collins isn't here, Shannon. You'd better get used to

that fact. Now, may I continue?' I gave her a suitably chastened nod. 'If it's an official inquiry, it has to be followed through to the end. And the outcome made public. On the other hand, if you investigate and somehow manage to stumble across a way of finding and replacing the money, then no one need ever know. Ali Khan's reputation is unsullied.'

'And why should that be so important?'

'Because he's a good man, Shannon. Doing good work in bloody difficult circumstances.'

'Since when has that counted for anything in the blindfolded eyes of the law?'

'Since there were race riots in Oldbrook, that's when.'

'But,' I pressed, 'why is Ali Khan so pivotal?'

'Because, due to him, we are winning the war in Oldbrook. Ali Khan is gradually uniting all the opposing factions in the borough. Getting them to see the sense of fighting the system rather than each other. Each group – black, Muslim, Hindu, Sikh, whatever – burying their differences in a common goal against prejudice and all its ills.' There was a passion in her voice that I'd never encountered before – at least, not when talking about something other than herself. She paused for breath, or maybe it was for emphasis. 'Ali Khan,' she continued, 'has damned near capped the volcano. If there is any smear of corruption on his spotless person, everyone loses faith in him – he's just another politician using the people to further his own ends. Or, perhaps even more dangerously, it's seen as a frame-up by those bastards who hate and fear what he stands for. Whichever, the lid blows off the volcano. And the resulting lava flow will destroy everything in its path. Now do you understand?'

'There's no need to shout.'

'Yes, there is, Shannon. I want you to realise exactly what we have entrusted you with.'

'Thanks, Walker. Pile it on. Don't worry about me. I can stand the pressure.'

'I'm glad to hear it, Shannon. You think you have thirteen days, right? Wrong. You only have eleven days. That's when the Festival of Oldbrook starts.'

'The Festival of Oldbrook?' What the hell did Oldbrook have to be festive about?

'It's their equivalent of the Notting Hill Carnival. Ali Khan's idea. A weekend of "fun and frolicking". Create a relaxed and friendly atmosphere. Cement the whole community together. If it works, Ali Khan will walk the by-election. If anything should go wrong – and that means you not getting the money back where it belongs before the first firecracker goes off – then Ali Khan goes down the tubes. And with him goes everything he has worked for. Do you want to be responsible for a riot, Shannon?'

'Strangely, Walker, it' s not on my list of lifetime ambitions.'

'Glad to hear it. Now, is that all? Can I get back to work, please?'

'Not quite,' I said. 'This man who was killed in Oldbrook last night. What do the jungle drums say? What were the circumstances?'

She laughed. 'Not scared are you, Shannon?'

'Just prudent, Walker. I'm told the man worked in the Treasury Department. Now, you can call me the world's most lateral thinker since Edward de Bono if you like, but . . .'

'Relax, Shannon,' she interrupted. 'Don't let your imagination run the marathon in record time. The man was systematically beaten and kicked to death' – that was meant to relax me? – 'and then a fork of lightning was carved on his forehead. I think the message was pretty unmistakable. The logo of OWN is a big O with the letters W and N running together inside so that they look like a lightning flash. This killing was obviously their handiwork. Of that there can be no doubt.'

She consulted her watch pointedly.

'One last thing,' I said.

'Jesus Christ! What now?'

'Ali Khan said you'd told him all about me.'

'Correct.'

'Can you be more specific?'

'I told him you were a wisecracking pain in the backside. But that you were good at your job. I also told him you'd killed your sister, spent seven years in prison and that I'd slept with you once. Satisfied?'

I stared at her, knowing it had to be a bad joke but cursing her lack of sensitivity. I couldn't speak. Could only think of my sister, mowed down in a hit-and-run incident that had killed her boyfriend and left her a pitiful paraplegic. Until the day I'd reached the centre of the moral maze and administered the fatal dose of morphine that had put an end to her misery. I thought of Collins and his favour – digging his bulldog nose into the old case, sniffing at the cover-up that smelt to high heavens of police involvement in the hit-and-run. I thought of the long years, the wasted years, in Brixton and Chelmsford, and the truth of the old adage – you can take the person out of prison, but you can't take prison out of the person. How, no matter how hard you try (and, by God, I'd tried), the nightmare experience haunts you – and not just when you're asleep. I looked down at the gap on my left hand where the two fingers had been sliced off in the cell door. I felt the sweat break out all over my body and bile rise in my throat.

'Sorry, Shannon,' she said gently. 'I didn't say all that.'

Snatching a cigarette from out of the packet, I manoeuvred it into my mouth and lit it with shaking hands.

'Really?' I said disdainfully, drawing heavily on the comfort of the smoke.

'I missed out the bit about sleeping with you.'

'Thanks,' I said, regaining my composure. 'I wouldn't want him to think ill of me.'

'Hah, bloody hah.'

'How,' I began seriously, 'did he react to the knowledge that I'd killed my sister?'

'Seemed to take it in his stride,' she shrugged.

'It's just that I didn't know how Muslims felt about mercy killing.'

'I don't suppose you know much about Muslims full stop.'

'That's something I'll have to remedy, I suppose.'

Now that I was taking the case, that is.

The Money Race was on.

CHAPTER FIVE

I drove back to Docklands with the stereo blaring. It's the only way to drive.

Don't get me wrong, I'm not one of those geeks who wind down all the windows and play *Born To Be Wild* at ninety decibels so that the world and his wife can't fail to appreciate that they're in the presence of a cool cookie. In this car, unless the stereo was blasting out at a level a fraction below the pain barrier it was impossible to drown out the thunder of the engine. If you couldn't avoid having your eardrums assaulted, then it might as well be by some decent music rather than the constant raspy roar of two litres of throbbing metal.

I'd kind of inherited the car, and I loved it for itself and what it stood for. A two-seater mid-engined Lancia Monte Carlo with a monsoon of style and a drought of practicality. A free spirit, reckless and difficult to control. Yes, I'm still talking about the car. Remember, I've turned over a new leaf.

On a day like today when you lifted out the roof panel and stowed it in the front 'luggage compartment' there was just enough room left for Arlene's handbag – if she didn't mind leaving the contents at home. The car was approaching its twelfth birthday, that automotive equivalent of advanced senility. Each time something went wrong – which seemed to be happening with increasing frequency – Jimmy, the car's mechanic-cum-nursemaid, had to set out on a treasure hunt of breakers' yards to locate the necessary parts to keep the internal organs functioning. And as far as the bodywork was concerned, it was only the rust molecules holding hands that was preventing the poor old thing from falling apart. Pulling away from the traffic lights by the Tower of London I gunned the engine, determined the car should enjoy its last days to the full.

Arriving back at my office and home, I claimed the only parking place not appropriated by the builders who were restoring the adjoining properties. I could have complained to the developer, but then that was Norman. And he'd only tell me that you can't make omelettes without cracking eggs, and to think myself lucky that ours had been the first of the properties to be tackled. So, sandwiched between a truck loaded with essential construction materials and a skip that confusingly seemed to have virtually the same contents, I sat there for a while anxious not to cut off Teddy Wilson in his prime. His fingers were gliding over the piano, caressing the keys like an Italian gigolo on a productivity bonus: in the background, the steady supportive beat of Jo Jones on the drums and Gene Ramey's strong bass line holding the improvisations together. It was a 1956 recording – goes to prove that some things last – seven years before I was born. Teddy was playing 'As Time Goes By'. You could close your eyes and see Bogie standing in the Casablanca sun with a cigarette dangling from his lips. When the final chord had drifted away, I climbed from the car and walked with an impressionistic swagger towards the door.

Arthur was waiting inside, blocking the hallway with his six foot five of massively built frame. He was hopping from one size twelve shoe to another, unable to contain his excitement. A broad grin lit up his face. 'I've got you your first case,' he said triumphantly.

Arlene appeared behind Arthur. She flashed me a conspiratorial warning which I understood perfectly, but didn't need.

Arthur 'Dangerous' Duggan, as he was known in his

days as a professional wrestler, was as tough as an ox and as trusting as a goose destined for *foie gras*. That's how he had come to be in Brixton – through collecting a debt that turned out not to exist. Arthur had taught me how to survive. Without him I'd have suffered a fate worse than death, swiftly followed by a death worse than fate. If anyone deserved the glory of bringing in the first case it was Arthur, not Walker.

'What shall I say if Mr Khan phones?' Arlene asked.

'Get his home address, please, Arlene. Tell him I'll be there at five o'clock.'

She smiled at me. Work at last. Something to keep her occupied and me out of mischief.

'Well done, Arthur,' I said, slapping my old friend on the back. 'Tell me all about it.'

'Better get it straight from the horse's mouth. The lady's waiting in your office.'

The lady's waiting in your office. I could picture the scene. The titles slide from the top of the screen. Cut to Marlowe's office. *The Big Sleep.* Pan across to pouting long-legged redhead in a tight blouse, pencil skirt and stilettos. I jammed a cigarette into the corner of my mouth. Lit it – the cigarette, not my mouth – and let it dangle from my lips at a rakish angle so that the smoke curled mysteriously around my eyes. Suitably prepared, I opened the door to my office and stepped inside.

'Put that cigarette out, young man.'

It wasn't *The Big Sleep* after all. It was *Farewell, My Lovely* instead.

'This is Mrs Dorothy Crabtree,' Arthur said

More crab than tree, I thought. 'Pleased to meet you,' I said, extending my hand for the ritual business greeting.

Mrs Crabtree rose from the chair by my desk. She was wearing a green and brown speckled tweed suit, the hem of the skirt brushing her calves, thick support stockings and a pair of highly polished brown brogues. There was a plain gold band and a diamond eternity ring on one of her weather-beaten fingers, a simple string of pearls around her lined neck. Her hair was silver-grey and anchored in a tight perm. She was what you might call generously built: a size sixteen or eighteen with one of those large, low-slung bosoms that a whole Girl Guide troop on summer camp could have used as a pillow in an emergency. She took my hand in an iron grip and shook it vigorously. 'Shall we get down to business, Mr Shannon? Take a seat, please.'

Hang on a minute. Whose office was this?

I sat down anyway and completed my initial Holmesian assessment of my visitor. Seventy-odd years old, active (probably gardening, judging by the state of her hands), widowed (or where was the husband?) and used to giving orders (ex-schoolmistress or high-ranking officer in the Waffen-SS).

'This is most embarrassing, Mr Shannon,' she declared.

'In my line of work, Mrs Crabtree, that's not unusual. I am unshockable. I've heard it all before.'

'Really?' she said. 'Arthur told me that this would be your first case. And I'm inclined to believe him. Especially since all the files on your desk are empty.'

'I must have misheard,' I apologised. 'I thought your name was Crabtree, not Marple.'

'I have learned recently that it is wise to take nothing at face value.' She looked at me reprovingly. 'And, may I say, Mr Shannon, that you and I will get along a whole lot better if you would kindly moderate your flippancy. Serious matters demand a serious attitude.'

'Yes, Mrs Crabtree,' I said. It wasn't cowardice on my part. It was just that with the tight schedule of the Money Race I simply didn't have time for a couple of hours of detention. Or to write out 'Let Mr Flippant always remain a stranger' five hundred times in my best copperplate.

'What is your experience of fraud, Mr Shannon?'

36

'I'm a fully qualified accountant,' – as of last month – 'and I've worked with the Fraud Squad.'

'And Arthur works for you, I understand.'

'Yes, Mrs Crabtree.'

'The combination of the two of you should suffice then,' she nodded.

'Mrs Crabtree's got a problem,' Arthur said.

And here was I thinking she had dropped by because my advertisement for 'naughty boy needs strict disciplinarian' had been misinterpreted.

'May I, Mrs Crabtree?' he asked politely.

'You start, Arthur, and I'll come in at the appropriate point.'

'You see, Nick,' he began, 'I was down in Chingford this morning . . .'

'What were you doing in Chingford?' I asked.

'Helping out Lenny Malone.'

'Jesus,' I said, bringing forth a scowl of disapproval from Mrs Crabtree, '– sorry – is he still alive?' I hadn't seen Lenny Malone for nine years and he had looked like Methuselah's grandfather even then.

'Well, he's not very well,' Arthur admitted. 'That's why I was helping him out with his window-cleaning round.'

'Window cleaning?'

'Well, I was getting bored sitting around here, so when Charlie called I thought it wouldn't do no harm. A bit of folding money and a spot of fresh air in the country.'

'In Chingford?'

'Mr Shannon,' Mrs Crabtree said with a frown, 'we might progress a little more quickly if you could bring yourself to desist from making constant interruptions.'

Arthur gave me a little smile. 'Anyway,' he said, 'I was cleaning the conservatory windows of the retirement home and overheard Mrs Crabtree and the other ladies talking. So I said you'd help.'

Well, as Arthur was prone to say, everything was crystal clear after that full explanation.

'One of our fellow guests died last week,' Mrs Crabtree said.

'Murder?'

'Don't be so melodramatic, Mr Shannon. If it had been murder, I would have gone to the police. Not come here to talk to an accountant and an ex-bouncer.'

'Door steward,' Arthur corrected.

'Bouncer is as bouncer does, Arthur.'

I returned Arthur's smile with interest.

'Poor Emily,' she continued, adopting suitably respectful tones, 'passed peacefully away in her sleep.' I didn't understand where this was leading, but didn't dare to interrupt. 'The problem concerns the funeral,' she said.

I was beginning to feel that I'd been kidnapped and was at this very moment being held prisoner in a *Monty Python* sketch. That meant there wasn't even any guarantee of a punch line.

'About two months ago,' Mrs Crabtree explained to my relief, 'we were visited by a most charming man. Too charming, it now transpires. This man – this smooth-tongued lizard of a heartless charlatan – talked to us about the wisdom of providing for our future. Specifically, our funerals.'

The light was dawning at last. It wasn't the most original of scams.

'Don't tell me, Mrs Crabtree. Let me guess. He told you that by paying in advance for your funerals you could save a considerable amount of money. And be less of a burden on your next of kin. A kind of insurance policy? Is that how he put it? When the inevitable happens, someone gives him a call and all the arrangements are made according to your previously laid down specifications. No worries. No bills to be paid.'

'Exactly, Mr Shannon.'

'Except that when poor Emily passed away, the man had done a runner.'

'He had not, in your terminology, *done a runner*. The

business, however, had been placed in the hands of the Official Receiver. Who informs me that we stand very little chance of recovering a single penny of what we paid. Legally, that is.'

'Ah,' I said.

'I am hoping that a visit from yourself, accompanied by dear Arthur here, might persuade this man of the error of his ways.'

'No problem,' Arthur said, as if afflicted by a severe case of myopia.

'Our fees are normally a thousand pounds per diem,' I said. Arthur blinked. And I doubted that it was the *diem* that had caused the astonished reaction.

'That is out of the question, Mr Shannon. We shall have to reach another agreement.'

'I was about to add, Mrs Crabtree,' – if you had not interrupted, I was tempted to say – 'that, since this is our first case, we would be prepared to work on a percentage of the money we recover.'

'That sounds more reasonable,' she said, nodding her head.

'Roughly how much is involved?'

'There are twenty-four of us. We have each lost a thousand pounds.'

'Then let us say ten per cent.'

'No,' she said, 'let us say five per cent.'

'Seven and a half.'

'Six.'

What was I doing, haggling with *her*? I wasn't going to win. And what did it matter? I was only taking the case as a favour to Arthur and out of sympathy for the little old ladies of the Bide-a-Wee Rest Home, or whatever it was called. 'Agreed,' I said, sighing. 'I'll have the contract brought in for your signature.'

'That won't do, Mr Shannon. In your own interests, bearing in mind my age and the uncertainties of life, I believe there would be insufficient safeguards in that arrangement. And, to be perfectly frank, I would rather there was no misunderstanding among my fellow residents. Better, I think, that each of us has our own individual contract.'

'Twenty-four contracts,' I said, my voice rising an octave and my hand moving up to support my head. Arlene was going to love this. Norman too. We would be running at a loss before we started.

'If you would kindly have them prepared right away, we can take them with us when you drop me back home. The sooner everything is signed and sealed in black and white, the sooner you can start.'

'But I have another appointment at five o'clock.'

'Whereabouts?'

'Oldbrook.'

'Most inconvenient, Mr Shannon.' I was about to nod my agreement when she said, 'I shall just have to come with you.'

My mouth dropped open.

'Come along,' she said, clapping her hands. 'Chop, chop.'

CHAPTER SIX

Oldbrook wasn't all bad. It just smelt that way.

Mrs Crabtree had started the journey happy enough, making little 'vroom, vroom' noises and singing along with great gusto to some old standards played by Earl Hines. Now she tutted away like a hyperactive Geiger counter as we crawled along narrow streets lined with row upon row of indistinguishable dirty-yellow brick council houses or shivered in the shadows of graffiti-daubed tower blocks. We had the sun roof out. Big mistake. The smell from overflowing dustbins in the postage-stamp-sized front gardens and the giant hoppers at the bases of the flats was overpowering and all pervading. I'd yet to find out if the place fitted Norman's corruption theory, but there was certainly something rotten in the state of Oldbrook.

'Did you see that rat, Mr Shannon?' Mrs Crabtree asked in astonishment.

'No,' I replied, concentrating hard on weaving through the wafer-thin gap left by an *Antiques Roadshow* collection of cars parked on both sides of the street. 'But don't tell me. Stick a saddle on it and you'd have a good chance of winning the Grand National?'

'Do you always exaggerate?'

'Usually,' I shrugged. 'Even though I've been told millions of times not to do so.'

'Next left,' she said, shaking her head. 'Then the first on the right.' She closed the A–Z street atlas, looked around

the cockpit for somewhere to stow it and, finding no compartment designed to hold anything bigger than a book of
matches, settled on the glove box. An avalanche of cassettes
slid on to her skirt. 'I can see I'm going to have to get you
organised, Mr Shannon.'

I was about to protest, tell her in no uncertain terms
that if I were any more organised I'd be awarded the Anal
Retentive of the Year Silver Trophy (previous winners all
having been tipped over the edge of sanity by the heavy
responsibility of the extra dusting and polishing): it was just
there wasn't any bloody room in the car. But I could pre-
dict her response – a long lecture about bad workmen
blaming their tools. Sulkily, I swung hard left then right:
Mrs Crabtree's bulk, wedged into the sports seat, disappointingly did not shift an inch.

Number 27 was halfway up on the left. The *cul-de-sac*
was a little enclave of private dwellings built, so the
plaques above the front doors said, in 1921. The plaques
also proclaimed them to be 'villas', so maybe the date
wasn't accurate either. Nevertheless, the houses were a
whole lot better than anything else we'd seen so far. Each
was detached (well, separated by a narrow alley from its
neighbours), had a short driveway to a garage (single, and
with one of those up-and-over doors that scrape your shins
if you're not careful) and two large bay windows at the
front with both net *and* heavy curtains. For Oldbrook, this
was an oasis in a cultural desert.

'I'll try not to be gone long, Mrs Crabtree,' I said, opening the car door. 'Would you like me to leave the radio
on?'

'That will not be necessary, Mr Shannon.'

'A cassette then?'

'No. That will not be necessary either.'

Please yourself.

'Because,' she added, 'I shall be accompanying you.'

'But, Mrs Crabtree,' I stammered.

'But me no buts, Mr Shannon. You can't expect a frail

42

old lady to sit all alone, helpless and vulnerable, in the back streets of Oldbrook.'

Frail? Helpless? Vulnerable? And she had the gall to lecture me on the sin of exaggeration.

I shut the car door again. Told her as little as possible about the case – daughter gone AWOL – so that she wouldn't put one of her large brogues in her mouth. Laid down the law on client confidentiality. And made it very plain that from the moment we entered the house to the moment we left she was to say nothing. Not one word.

'Of course, Mr Shannon,' she said. 'I promise.'

Never work with children or animals, they say. Good advice, but woefully inadequate. Old ladies should also be included. In pole position.

Mrs Khan took a long time to open the door. But this was Oldbrook, after all. Mrs Crabtree and I looked at each other with raised eyebrows as a series of keys turned in locks, bolts slid back and finally a little crack appeared where the chain remained in place. 'Yes?' she said suspiciously.

'Nick Shannon,' I announced. 'And this is Mrs Crabtree.'

'May I see your identification, Mr Shannon?'

Her accent was very different to her husband's, much less anglicised. The word *identification* came out with the accent on the first syllable and the rest in one long fast stream.

I selected a business card – one of the variety with forensic accountant on it – from my wallet. Passed it through the slit in the door.

'You have nothing with a photograph on it?' Mrs Khan said, unsatisfied.

I shrugged helplessly. I find that usually works.

Mrs Crabtree, unused to the awesome power of the Shannon shrug, brushed me aside. And proceeded shamelessly to break her promise. She leaned close to Mrs Khan and spoke secretively. I still heard every word, but didn't understand a single one of them. She was speaking in Hindi. Or maybe it was Urdu, Bengali, Gujerati or any one of a dozen regional dialects. Hell, it could have been Greek for all I knew. Although, admittedly, the odds were against it.

At the end of this short but paranoia-inducing conversation, Mrs Khan giggled girlishly, bowed her head and waved us ceremoniously inside with an accompanying instruction of 'Please to be going to the left.'

Mrs Crabtree smiled smugly at me. I gave her the full force of the Shannon glare. She bustled inside, impervious to my secret weapon. 'Come along, young man,' she said. 'Don't dawdle. If there's one thing I can't abide, it's dawdling.'

I'll add that one to the list, I thought as I followed in her wake.

We entered a large room, square except for the bay with its bench seat covered in powder-blue satin. There was a three-piece suite in deep blue with scatter cushions of the same shade as the seat in the bay. One of the armchairs, the one facing the large-screen television, bore the impression of many nights' suffering under Mr Khan's weight. The walls were that heavily bleached blue of the sky on a hot summer's day. The floor was covered by a large and frighteningly expensive hand-made Turkish rug. The air smelt sweetly of attar of roses.

Mrs Khan gestured to the two armchairs and stood while we seated ourselves. She was wearing a lime-green sari over a dark green scooped-neck T-shirt. Her straight black hair was scraped off her face and held in place at the back by a wide elasticated band embroidered with white flowers. She wore little make-up; a touch of lipstick, some kohl eyeliner and, in the middle of her forehead, a red spot of, as I was later reliably informed by the font of all knowledge, Tilak.

'Tea, Mrs Crabtree?' Mrs Khan offered.

'Assam, Mrs Khan?'

'Of course, Mrs Crabtree.'

'Perhaps,' I suggested hesitatingly, 'Mrs Crabtree and I

could look at your daughter's room while you are making the tea?'

'I was intending to stay here and chat with Mrs Khan.'

That was precisely what I was afraid of. 'I'd really appreciate your help, Mrs Crabtree,' I said fawningly. 'Your knowledge of the language might prove invaluable.'

'Very well, Mr Shannon. Tell us where to go, Mrs Khan. We can find our own way.'

'What did you say to her?' I whispered as we made our way up the stairs.

'I simply explained,' she said, 'that you had a brain like a sieve and even if you *had* remembered to bring a proper identity card you almost certainly wouldn't have been able to find it. Like all men, I told her, you shouldn't really be allowed out on your own.'

And I thought I was the one with a lot to learn about client service. 'Thanks, Mrs Crabtree,' I groaned.

'I hope that is not a hint of sarcasm I detect in your voice. The lowest form of wit, you know.'

'I have been told that, yes,' I said.

'Frequently, I imagine.'

'How do you speak whatever it was anyway?'

'Hindi,' she said. 'My husband was in the Colonial Service in India immediately after the war. When partitioning came in '47 he was offered the position of manager of a tea plantation in Assam. We stayed there for twelve years – until the Chinese swept across the northern border and made life a trifle difficult.'

'And your husband?' I asked tentatively, thinking back to my original deductions.

'Ran off with a go-go dancer in '69.'

Whoops, that explained his absence.

'He died,' she continued, 'a very happy, and very exhausted, man three months later.'

'And did you ever teach?'

'Taught the locals English whilst out in India. Why do you ask?'

'Just background,' I said, self-satisfied.

'You should be careful about asking so many questions, Mr Shannon. It could be construed as plain nosy.'

'It's my job, Mrs Crabtree.'

'And a very strange one for a grown man, if I might say.' And if you mightn't? 'Seems to me,' she said, 'only one step removed from playing cowboys and Indians.'

'I would prefer cops and robbers. Especially under the current circumstances.'

'As you wish, Mr Shannon. Now, let's look at this room, shall we?'

Mrs Crabtree opened the door, stepped inside and sighed wistfully. 'What a lovely room,' she said.

'I don't like it,' I said instinctively, as the first impressions washed over me.

'Then you have no taste, young man.'

'Maybe not,' I said, studying the detail now: the predominant shades of pretty pink on walls, bedclothes and furniture; the chintzy curtains complete with contrasting tie-backs. 'But doesn't anything strike you?'

'Like what?'

'The dressing-table, for instance.'

'Mahogany. A lighter wood, rose perhaps, would blend in better with the rest of the room, I suppose. Be somewhat less intrusive.'

'But where are the face creams, the cosmetics, nail varnishes, perfumes?'

'She took them all with her. Wherever she went.'

'All of them?' I said, shaking my head. 'And where is the sprinkling of powder left by blusher? The tissues discarded after blotting lipstick? Those funny little communion wafer pads of cotton wool used to remove make-up? This is supposed to be the room of a twenty-year-old girl. The dressing-table, like everything else here, is too neat, too tidy. Where, Mrs Crabtree, is the personality? Did she take that with her too?'

'Maybe Mrs Khan cleans up after her daughter. I don't

suppose that is an unusual task for a mother.'

'And has Mrs Khan removed the posters of pop stars or film idols from the walls? If so, there are no tell-tale marks. And did she clear out the back issues of . . .' I faltered for a moment, my knowledge of young women's magazines being nine years behind the times, '. . . *Cosmo*, or whatever is the style bible nowadays?'

'There are books in the bookcase,' she said, evading the question.

'Textbooks,' I said dismissively. 'Looking at this room, what can you deduce about its occupant? Nothing. Absolutely nothing. Apart from seemingly having a penchant for baby pink and a Lady Macbeth complex.'

I walked over to the built-in double wardrobe that ran from behind the door along to the wall with the window overlooking the rear garden. Mrs Crabtree was unusually silent. 'You take the dressing-table,' I said, assuming command for a change. 'See what you can find. An address book and diary would be useful.'

Behind the first set of doors was a long line of saris, including the white one from the photograph, some baggy but obviously tailored trousers, long blouses and short jackets. All very traditional, very conservative, and very disappointing when you're searching for clues. There was, at least, a full-length mirror fixed to the inside of the door, indicating, assuming it was used, some degree of vanity.

The second compartment was equally unrevealing. It was half-empty, the clothes that remained representing Nadya's English collection. There were sensible skirts, all with hems about a foot longer than the current fashion, high-necked blouses, a special-occasion trouser suit in black. No jeans. No leggings. Although I supposed she could have taken them with her. On the floor of the wardrobe were four pairs of shoes (low-heeled, dull colours), two pairs of flat sandals (to go with the saris) and a pair of black calf-length boots. I picked up the boots and examined them. They were about as far removed from kinky boots as you can get – fleecy-lined with ridged soles designed for stomping through the snow on a winter's day. As I was replacing them, something that had fallen inside the right boot sparkled as it caught the light. I pulled out the item and, after one brief glance, quickly stuffed it into my jacket pocket.

'And what have you found, Mrs Crabtree?'

'No address book, I'm afraid. Or diary. Just some things for her hair. And some, er, lingerie.'

'You must be more specific,' I said. 'Let me have a look.'

'*Really*, Mr Shannon.'

I ignored her expression of old-fashioned prudery and peered into the front of the drawers. The left-hand one contained tights, mostly of the thick and woolly genre; the shallow middle drawer over the padded stool some hair bands, 'scrunchies', slides and even an Alice band; the right-hand one, a dozen or so pairs of knickers, none of them likely to shock or titillate. 'Deductions, Mrs C?'

'I wish you would stop treating me like Dr Watson to your Sherlock Holmes. And don't call me Mrs C. I'm old enough to be your grandmother, young man. Kindly show some respect.'

'I apologise, Mrs Crabtree. And, as a show of sincerity, I'll give a clue. Observe how everything in the drawers is piled at the front.'

'Therefore,' she said, 'she has taken with her those items that were at the back.'

'Your answer is correct, as far as it goes. The supplementary question to ask yourself is "Why?"'

'Perhaps,' she said peevishly, 'you would put me out of my misery, if that self-satisfied smile on your face allows you the ability of speech, that is. What is the solution?'

'The ten per cent solution, possibly,' alluding back to Holmes and his darker side.

'You really can be most infuriating, Mr Shannon.'

'Any genius must be allowed his eccentricities, Mrs Crabtree.'

She rolled her eyes.

'Nadya packs her suitcase. She takes some clothes from the wardrobe, and knickers and such from the dressing-table drawers. One would expect what remained in the drawers to be spread randomly along the bottom. In this case, it is obvious that she only removed items from the back of the drawers. The most suitable place, don't you think, for concealing what you don't want to be discovered?'

'Pure speculation, Mr Shannon,' she replied scornfully. 'And, if I might say so, more than a little ungenerous to a girl who would appear to be a much-needed shining example to the youth of today.'

'Ah, but all that glitters is not gold, Mrs Crabtree. To wit,' I said, producing my discovery from my pocket with a magician's flourish, 'this.'

'And what, pray, is that?'

'This, in the vernacular of the fashion industry, is called a boob tube.'

Mrs Crabtree stared at the five-inch-wide elasticated band of sparkling sequins with a mixture of horror and astonishment. I held it up to my chest in case the terminology or purpose were unfamiliar.

'Surely you don't mean that girls wear a thing like that to cover their important places,' she gasped.

'Or not, as the case may be,' I said with a nod and a burgeoning smile.

'My God, Mr Shannon, I think I rather need that cup of tea.'

'And how will you take it? Sweet, like Nadya appeared to be? Or just hot?'

CHAPTER SEVEN

The house had four bedrooms. I looked in all of them. Maybe Mrs Crabtree was right, it was a job best suited to those whose inquisitiveness verged on the downright nosy. I'd waited till I'd heard the clink of bone china, a good indication that Mrs Crabtree was partaking of the cup that cheers – Hip, Hip, Hooray – and keeping Mrs Khan occupied at the same time. Meanwhile I finished searching Nadya's room, peering under the bed, lifting the mattress and pillows. Then I crept along the corridor. I didn't know what I expected to find, so I wasn't disappointed.

One bedroom was primarily for guests; taking up the majority of the limited floor space was a double bed, a single wardrobe, a bedside table with reading material carefully chosen to suit most tastes without risking offence (one Dick Francis, one Trollope – Anthony not Joanna, *The Pickwick Papers*, *Pride and Prejudice*, a New English Bible and a copy of the Koran). Beneath the window was a long rectangular table, its top bearing a state-of-the-art sewing machine, reels of cotton and various bolts of fabric, mostly silks and satins.

The main bedroom was like a scene from *1001 Nights*. There wasn't a surface that hadn't been covered in Mrs Khan's handiwork, unless you counted the floor, and I suspected that was only because heavy-duty Teflon-coated do-it-yourself silk carpet material hadn't been invented yet. Or if it has, no one's told me. Anyway, the room was dominated by a four-poster bed draped with indigo silk curtains and scattered with cushions of white silk with blue ribbons at each corner. Circular tables, their glass tops placed over floor-length cream silk, were positioned on either side of the bed. On one was a radio/alarm clock, on both a box of tissues in hand-crafted satin-covered containers that added a whole new dimension to the word twee. There were books on each table – individually monogrammed copies of the *Kamasutra*, I presumed – but I made a swift exit before my brain exploded through sensory overload

The final bedroom was a welcome relief. One might have said a breath of fresh air were it not for the smell of sweat that rose like steam from a dung heap from the shirts and socks strewn carelessly over the carpet. The bed was unmade, the duvet, half off, spilt on to the floor. Both wardrobe doors were open, as were the top drawers of the dresser. In one corner of the room was a desk with a computer. The desk might have been mahogany, it might have been pine: it was hard to tell since it was perfectly camouflaged under a layer of papers and books. A Manchester United rosette was pinned to the wall. Above the bed were four grease spots where blobs of Blu Tack had once held in place a poster (extrapolating from its absence, presumably a large picture of which Mrs Khan disapproved – the Page Three girl who had been flavour of the month at that time?). I rooted around in the dresser and found a Polaroid of a scrawny, embarrassed-looking teenager wearing a headband improvised from the garter of an underdressed and overweight stripagram 'girl' pushing forty. There was a perfect red lipstick imprint on his cheek. I pocketed the photo and took one last look around the room.

I reckoned I'd seen enough, and certainly smelt enough, for now.

'Mr Shannon,' Mrs Khan said as I entered the sitting room, 'you *have* been a long time. Please sit, and I will pour your tea.'

I sat in one of the armchairs and looked across at Mrs Crabtree who was lounging back in the other, completely recovered from her shock judging by the way she was popping bright green cubes in her mouth. 'You must try the halva,' she said, almost swooning with ecstasy. 'I'd forgotten just how heavenly it tastes.'

Mrs Khan passed me a cup of dark tea and gestured to a rapidly vanishing selection of sweets on a gleaming brass platter on the coffee table. 'Pistachio,' she said, pointing to one of the green cubes, 'carrot' – orange – 'or almonds and semolina' – an ultra-rich creamy colour. Mrs Crabtree possessively scooped up one of each while I was deciding which of the options to risk. My experience of Indian cuisine was mostly limited to the standard fare of Brighton restaurants during my undergraduate days and these meals had never included dessert – neither my wallet nor my stomach having been able to cope with anything more than onion bhaji and chicken bhoona. I chose the carrot halva – you never know when you might need to see in the dark – and took an experimental bite.

'What do you think, Mr Shannon?' Mrs Khan asked. 'It's my own recipe.'

'Amazing texture,' I replied with honesty and extreme difficulty. My lips were barely functioning, locked in a titanic struggle to break free from the cloying sweetness. Christ, these weren't sweets, they were contact adhesive in cube form. I reached hurriedly for my tea, placed the uneaten piece of halva surreptitiously in the saucer where I might absent-mindedly forget about it, accidentally on purpose, and took a large gulp from the bone-china cup. The strong tannic brew rinsed away the shreds of carrot that had stuck to the roof of my mouth, and probably half the enamel from my teeth too.

'Your daughter,' I said, when I had fully regained the power of speech, 'do you have any idea where she might have gone?'

'No, Mr Shannon,' she said, lowering her eyes as if in

shame. 'She has never done anything like this before. It is so out of character. So worrying, in all respects – why she did what she did, where she is, and how she is.'

'What about friends?' I asked. 'Is there someone with whom she is especially friendly? Someone she could confide in?'

She shrugged ominously. 'Nadya had lost touch with her school friends. If there was anyone, then it would have to be someone from university. One of the girls on her course, perhaps.' She shook her head. 'I really don't know.'

'Can you give me any names and addresses?'

'I'm sorry, Mr Shannon, but I don't know any of their names.'

This never happened in books. By now I should have had a whole directory of people to interview, each one acting as a signpost on the trail that would eventually lead me to Nadya.

'You could try her tutor, I suppose,' she said. 'He might be able to help.'

'His name, Mrs Khan?'

'Mason,' she said.

At last. Something concrete. A place to start.

'Or,' she continued, 'it might be Burton. Or was it Cooper? I know it reminded me of an old *fillum* star.'

I didn't groan. Not out loud, at least.

'Would Mr Khan know?'

'No,' she said. 'What with the council and running the business he didn't have much time to talk to Nadya.'

'What sort of business is that?' Mr Nosy strikes again.

'Supermarkets, Mr Shannon.'

'And how many does he have?'

'Ten,' she said. 'Or it might be eleven.'

Tutor's name, number of shops, this was a woman who raised the word *vague* to Everest heights. Or should that be K2? Christ, she'd got me doing it now.

'Well, if that's all you can tell me, Mrs Khan, I ought to be taking Mrs Crabtree home.'

She answered my question by standing up.

I took a last sip of my tea.

Mrs Khan stood there, running her hands over the waist of her sari to smooth away creases that were undetectable to the human eye.

'This is very good tea, Mrs Khan,' I said. 'Assam, did you say?'

She nodded and glanced at the tiny watch on her thin wrist.

'Okay, Mrs Crabtree,' I said, 'time to hit the road.' I watched her prise herself slowly from the chair, take one final lingering look at the two remaining cubes of halva and move reluctantly towards the door. 'One last thing,' I said to Mrs Khan, placing my fingers on my forehead Columbo-style.

'Yes?' she said, more in irritation than enquiry.

'What about your son?'

'What about him?' she said defensively.

'I was just wondering if he would know the tutor's name.'

'It is possible.'

'When will he be in?'

'I really could not say,' she replied.

Now why wasn't I surprised?

'He tends to come and go,' she explained. 'You know what these young people are like.'

The chance to find out would be good.

'Please give him my card,' I said. 'Ask him to ring me as soon as he can.'

'Of course, Mr Shannon,' she said. 'You can rely on me.'

Possibly, I thought.

'She wasn't very helpful, was she?' Mrs Crabtree said as we pulled away from the house.

'You noticed,' I replied, surprised that anything bar halva had impinged on her consciousness.

'Mr Shannon!' she said in her here-comes-a-lecture voice.

'I meant,' I said quickly, seeing a repeat of the lowest form of wit around the corner, 'you noticed too.'

'I'm very glad to hear it, Mr Shannon.'

'Look,' I said, 'I'm not used to all this Mr Shannon business. Why don't you call me Nick from now on.'

'Very well,' she agreed.

'And . . .'

'And you can call me Mrs Crabtree.'

I gave a little sigh and headed north towards Woodford, from where I would pick up the road to Chingford.

'So, Nick,' she said, 'why wasn't she very helpful?'

'Either it was accidental, a result of a disorganised mind, or it was deliberate.'

'That's only half an answer. Which do you opt for? And why?'

It reminded me of those awful examination questions they set for A level. 'Richard the Lionheart was a good king but a bad ruler. Discuss. Write on only one side of the paper at a time.'

'Pass,' I said, the demands of client confidentiality getting the better of my desire to show off my powers of deduction. And my knowledge of Sherlock Holmes – especially what he had said about the curious incident of the dog that didn't bark.

So, Mrs Khan wasn't helpful. But that wasn't all she wasn't.

CHAPTER EIGHT

It wasn't called the Bide-a-Wee Rest Home. Silly guess really, although I wasn't far out; certainly captured the flavour of the imagery. A large sign said, 'Honeysuckle Hall – A Haven of Tranquillity for Retired Gentlewomen'. No wonder Mrs Crabtree hadn't found the halva sickly sweet.

Honeysuckle Hall! It looked more like Dotheboys Hall. Or the workhouse from the film *Oliver*. An imposing – no, make that off-putting – Victorian monolith of dark brick in need of high-pressure cleaning and grey slate tiles with a covering of green mildew. The location was convenient though. Set back off The Ridgeway, it was within hobbling distance of the park, only a two-minute ambulance drive to the hospital and a similar distance (but a longer drive) to the cemetery. And the smell from the refuse disposal works was hardly noticeable. Or perhaps, after Oldbrook, it was just relative.

'We walked up the gently sloping ramp to the huge front door. It swung open with that slow creak you usually only hear in third-rate horror movies. Which was fitting.

'Where *have* you been, Mrs Crabtree?' a Countess Dracula lookalike said.

Her face was pinched, her expression severe: the former naturally acquired, the latter, I suspected, a result of dedicated practice in front of a mirror. She was tall, thin as a model for an anatomy wallchart, pushing sixty, with long straight black hair – straight out of a bottle, that is. I wondered if she'd come with the house, part of the fixtures and fittings.

'Business,' Mrs Crabtree replied; It was a good answer. Part explanation, part admonition, with the 'None of your' omitted. 'I would like all the ladies assembled in the conservatory, Miss Beale. And tea would be welcome.'

'Tea is not served till seven-thirty, Mrs Crabtree,' Miss Beale said with an air of triumph. 'You know the rules.'

'But we have a guest, Miss Beale. Am I not correct in thinking that the rules permit tea to be served at any time to a resident when in the presence of a guest?'

Miss Beale stared at me as if I had *troublemaker* tattooed on my forehead. 'Very well,' she sighed. 'Two teas.'

'Twenty-five teas,' Mrs Crabtree corrected, savouring every moment of a battle decisively won. 'Mr Shannon has come to talk to all of us ladies. So that means we may *all* have tea.'

Miss Beale's brow furrowed and her eyes narrowed into an I'll-get-even-with-you expression. If I were Mrs Crabtree, I'd make sure all my windows were shut tight tonight. And I'd be wearing my best crucifix and smelliest clove of garlic around my neck.

'Some of those shortbread biscuits you hoard for special occasions wouldn't go amiss,' Mrs Crabtree added, sadistically rubbing salt into the wound. 'And the best china service, don't you think? Not those ghastly pottery mugs. Like drinking out of a cheap commode, in my opinion.'

Times must have been really hard in Assam, I thought. It seemed you had to make do with whatever was handy.

Miss Beale stalked off, muttering in a low voice to compensate for the accompanying high dudgeon.

'This way, Nick,' Mrs Crabtree said, leading me along an ill-lit corridor. 'Don't mind her. Huh! The woman acts as if she owns the place.'

'Who does own the place?'

'Well, actually, she does,' Mrs Crabtree admitted. 'But that doesn't mean she runs it.'

57

At the end of the corridor were three doors. The further one on the right was slightly ajar and, from the unmistakable smell of boiled cabbage – no institution is complete without it – led into the kitchen. The nearer one led into a dining room, its square tables arranged with geometric precision and set with waxed tablecloths and white plastic cruets. The door on the left opened into a large room with a high ceiling. This room housed a collection of dark green vinyl-covered high-back chairs that you couldn't have given away at a car boot sale in Russia. An upright piano, so battered that even an East End pub would have thought twice about allocating it valuable space, stood against one wall. Mrs Crabtree strode to the exact centre of the room, clapped her hands to gain the attention of (i.e. waken) the occupants and said in a loud authoritative voice, 'Conservatory, ladies. Residents' Meeting. Now.'

There was a gathering up of walking sticks and zimmer frames, followed by a shuffling of slippered feet as the old ladies complied with their general's request. In a long line, Mrs Crabtree's arthritic infantry trooped slowly after her.

The conservatory was light – a shining tribute to Arthur's newly acquired window-cleaning skills – and airy. Several residents, foregoing the pleasure of staring at the faded magnolia walls of the main lounge, were already there. They were seated in unsuitably low wicker chairs, nattering in creaky voices while watching the sun creep ever lower in the sky. From the small but well-maintained garden, in response to Miss Beale's clarion call, came the few remaining stragglers. Mrs Crabtree took a seat in what was obviously 'her chair' – larger than the rest, two thick floral cushions, prime position – and ushered me to sit beside her. She looked at her watch and announced proudly to the gathering, 'Tea will shortly be served.'

A buzz went round the room. One woman turned to her neighbour and in a loud and anxious voice asked, 'Is it half past seven already, Lily? Am I missing *Coronation Street*?'

Then, a little more quietly, added unconfidently and mistakenly, 'It is Wednesday, isn't it?'

While we waited for the tea to arrive the residents eyed me suspiciously. I didn't blame them. The last time someone had spoken to them *en masse* they had been swindled out of a thousand pounds each. Not the kind of incident to engender trust in strangers.

A heavily laden trolley trundled in, cups – not mugs, mind – rattling as the wheels bounced on the tiled floor. The trolley was guided erratically by a gangly girl in trainers and jeans who looked as if she was straight out of school – and who proceeded to justify my first impression by pouring cups of tea with all the finesse of a gangly girl straight out of school. She passed the first cup with shaky hands to me as the honoured guest, and the next to Mrs Crabtree. As if the girl wasn't nervous enough already, Mrs Crabtree, in a performance of Oscar-winning magnitude, poured the contents of the saucer into the cup – very slowly and with the extreme care normally reserved for defusing a bomb. The girl blushed, backed away almost curtsying, clamped her top teeth on to her bottom lip, and went about what was now the even more harrowing task of passing round the rest of the tea and the plate of biscuits.

Mrs Crabtree rose from her chair and walked round the room distributing contracts. 'Attention, ladies,' she called out, her voice raised to carry over the crunching of shortbread. 'This is Mr Shannon. He is going to get our money back for us.'

Well, that was that sorted then.

Just a matter of time, really.

In theory.

'We're all upstairs,' Arlene said when I finally arrived back from *chez* Crabtree, clutching an armful of shakily signed tea-stained contracts.

'Whose upstairs?' I asked.

59

'Norman and Arthur,' she replied, after a slight hesitation.

'No,' I said. 'Not *who's* up stairs, but *whose*. Norman's, or ours, or everybody's.'

'Oh, I see. Everybody's.'

There was no shortage of space in the old warehouse: that made life unduly complicated at times.

The building was on six floors. The first was occupied by the business: my office on the left, as you look from the jetty, the reception-cum-general office (Arlene's den) on the right at the front, and a kitchen behind that. The second floor was a communal area ('everybody's') – a large sitting/dining room directly above my office and another kitchen and a bathroom on the right. The third floor was Norman's, used during those periods when staying in England didn't jeopardise his tax exile status. The next storey, although renovated and redecorated like the rest of the building, had been left purposely empty: Norman called this his 'firebreak', a discreet 'heatproof' and sound-proof barrier between his accommodation and the two top floors where Arlene and I lived. We had our bedroom on the fifth floor. There was also a kitchen/diner and a bath-room – although those didn't require the 'firebreak'. Well, not the kitchen anyway. The top floor, built into the slop-ing eaves and opened up into one massive area, was our sitting room.

As I said, a lot of space. And very little furniture. At least not on those floors that were the responsibility of Arlene and me.

I'd persuaded her that we should buy only the bare minimum. It was an argument based on impeccable logic and old-fashioned pride. The logic went that, since she was now on a six-month work permit without any guarantee of automatic renewal, no major expenditure should be com-mitted until the long-term future was clearer. The pride angle, unexplained but I suspect understood nevertheless, was that what little contribution I could afford to make to furnishing the place would represent only a small proportion of the total costs – particularly when one takes into account Arlene's expensive tastes.

There was also the other unspoken little matter. I was still 'on trial'. Remember? Hard for me to forget, I can tell you. Or, should I say, be allowed to forget.

Before Future Assurance blew up in our faces, Arlene and I had been going to get married. That was now on ice until I had proved beyond unreasonable doubt that I was a changed man – and, I suppose, done my penance for not taking better care of Arlene while she was carrying our baby and for passing up my chance of a permanent residence visa for the States. And she had lost one husband already (heavily insured Cy had died before the age of forty of a heart attack). She probably wanted to make sure the second didn't shift her, according to Oscar Wilde's categorisation, from misfortune to carelessness.

Arlene was waiting for me at the top of the first flight of stairs. She had changed out of her Miss Moneypenny outfit into a sleeveless V-necked dress in a sunset-red colour and matching high heels. Her auburn hair was loose and flicked under so it just brushed the top of her shoulders. She looked tanned, and fitter than I'd seen her for a while. She'd lost weight: I reckoned at least seven pounds in the last month. Maybe it was all the stairs.

'You must need a drink, honey,' she said, raising herself on to her toes to kiss me on the cheek. There was a disquieting hint of tentativeness in her voice. 'White wine? Red? Or how about one of my Unwinders?'

Arlene's Unwinders were famous – notorious? – in this house. The recipe was simple, but effective. Take a large tumbler; throw in three ice cubes; add a very generous measure of vodka (preferably Polish, but anything with a high-proof rating would suffice). Then threaten the glass from a safe distance with a bottle of tonic.

'Sounds great,' I said. Mind you, after all the tea I had drunk today Sanatogen and cranberry juice would have sounded great. Well, maybe not the cranberry juice.

'You wait right here while I get it, honey,' she said. 'I've got a surprise for you.'

Six words to send a chill through any man's heart.

If it's a good surprise, people just spring it on you. They do *not* tell you in advance. But 'I've got a surprise for you' invariably means 'Prepare yourself'.

I stood on the landing, more desperate than ever for the drink, a long list of ever more dreadful outcomes running through my brain. What was waiting behind the door? Customs and Excise hit squad in a pre-emptive strike against Norman's creative accounting on our first VAT return? Detective Superintendent Collins looking for a volunteer to infiltrate the French Foreign Legion? Oh, God, I thought. Please let it not be Mary Jo. I'll settle for both the above as long as it isn't Mary Jo.

Mary Jo is Arlene's eighteen-year-old daughter. Queen of the spoilt brats. Founder member of the 'Nick Shannon Is The Devil Incarnate Club – special interest groups: gold-digger and mother-stealer', or something like that.

Arlene interrupted my panic attack by pressing a glass into my hand. 'Okay, honey,' she said, 'we can go in now.'

I took a fortifying swig of vodka and stepped bravely inside the room.

Arthur raised a glass of beer in my direction. Norman nodded and smiled. I looked around. No one else in sight. Unless Mary Jo was hiding behind one of the four three-seater sofas, waiting to jump out like the villain of a Hitchcock movie, it seemed as if I was safe. Still, I might skip a shower tonight, just in case.

'Where's this surprise?' I asked Arlene.

She consulted her watch ominously. 'Give it another ten minutes, I reckon.'

I crossed the room to the sofa with the best view of the river, bent down to pick up Arthur's coat where it lay in a heap and sit down in its place. 'Not there,' Arlene said as if my panic were catching. She put her drink on the coffee table, took up a seductive semi-reclining position on the sofa at ninety degrees to the windows and patted the cushion invitingly . 'Come and sit by me, honey.'

Four 'honeys' in a row. Red-alert situation: Klingons on the starboard bow; Romulans on the port; Tribbles on every deck.

I lit a cigarette. Inhaled deeply while examining each of their faces in turn. Sat down, still clueless.

'How did it go with Mrs Crabtree?' Arlene said, snuggling up to me.

'Let's just say my task for her is akin to providing dinner for all the residents – using only five loaves and three fishes.'

'She doesn't appreciate the difficulties then?' Norman asked.

'She doesn't even listen to the difficulties.'

'"But me no buts,"' Arthur chipped in, nodding his head. I nodded back.

'I've started to run a check on this funeral business,' Norman said unenthusiastically. 'Not that it will do much good, what with the company in receivership and all. List of creditors as long as your arm, I'll wager. Little old ladies to the rear.'

'Let's wait till we have more information,' I said. 'There are more pressing problems.'

'Ali Khan phoned,' Arlene said, reading my mind. 'You're to meet him at some shop at half past eight in the morning. Then he'll take you to Oldbrook, give you a guided tour of the council offices before you start work in the Treasury Department.'

'He managed to get approval for the commission deal then? That doesn't sound promising. The Chief Executive must be confident that I'm not going to rattle the bones of any financial skeletons in the closet.'

'Not confident,' corrected Norman, still holding firm to his General Theory of Corrupt Government. 'Overconfident.'

'Time will tell,' I said.

'The question is whether *we* have enough of it,' Arlene pointed out.

'Half past eight?' Arthur said, as if suffering from a bad case of conversational jet lag. 'Good. It gives us time for a run in the morning.'

'It will take at least forty minutes to get to Oldbrook in the rush hour. How does it give us time for a run in the morning?'

'It does if we leave here at six.'

I groaned. 'And why should we go for a run?'

'Because all this sitting around is making you soft. You need to get back in shape, Nick.'

'Mrs Crabtree wants to get me organised; Arthur wants to get me back in shape. Anybody else want to stake a claim on changing me or my lifestyle?'

'Well,' said Arlene and Norman in unison.

'Huh,' I grunted.

'Be prepared, Nick,' Arthur said gruffly, still hammering away at his argument.

'I am not a Boy Scout.'

'You do a bloody good impression of one at times,' he said. 'So, six o'clock then.'

I gave up on the groans and grunts. Simply sighed.

'Any luck with the search of the girl's room?' Arlene asked, changing the subject, or maybe she was reverting to it. With Arthur's interruption I'd forgotten where we were.

'You'll never guess what I found.'

Five pairs of eyes turned toward me.

Yes, five.

Two pairs belonged to little bundles of dark brown fur emerging from beneath Arthur's coat.

'This is the surprise?' I asked with relief.

'Present from Brother James,' Arlene said. 'For what you did for Rhiannon.'

Brother James was a former monk and leader of an unorthodox religious community who had got caught up in the whole Future Assurance business. Rhiannon had been one of his followers and had helped me obtain the evidence against Prospekt, the biggest drugs cartel in the country. She was now safe from their clutches, somewhere in America – courtesy of my visa.

Arlene sat up straight; searched my eyes for a reaction. 'Do you approve?'

'You do know my record with cats?' I asked.

Of the last three I'd met, one had been nailed to a door, another had finished up in the firing line between me and a psychopath. The third, I presumed, was the lucky mother of these kittens and, along with Brother James and his followers, previous occupant of our premises.

'Arthur told me,' she said sadly. 'Does that mean you want me to get rid of them?'

'Of course not,' I said, pulling her closer to me.

'And you don't think I'm being silly? You know . . .'

Kittens as substitute for baby, she was trying not to say.

'Hell, no,' I said. Arlene, with the help of Brother James and, it seemed, a few pills I'd discovered tucked away at the back of the bathroom cabinet, had adjusted well to the loss. I was proud of her. 'Cats are supposed to be a great aid to relaxation.'

The more adventurous of the two kittens gave a little leap, landed on the coffee table and began to investigate my drink, sniffing the contents, then testing the glass with its paw. The tumbler slid towards the edge of the table. I jumped up and caught it just before it toppled over.

'I think,' Arlene said with a smile, 'the relaxation only comes from stroking them. Doesn't apply to watching them. Or clearing up after them.'

'What are you going to call them?' I asked.

'I thought I'd leave that up to you.'

'No thanks,' I said. 'I'm under enough pressure as it is. You decide.'

'I've got an idea,' Arthur said.

We all looked at him with heavily disguised expressions

of astonishment. Ideas was not Arthur's *forte*. Thinking, *per se*, was not Arthur's *forte*. Unless you were in no hurry – to celebrate the millennium after next, for instance.

'Yes?' Arlene asked dubiously.

'How about,' Arthur said very slowly, building up the suspense, 'Laurel and Hardy?'

Arlene closed her eyes and slapped the side of her head with her hand, as if testing that her ears were not sending random messages to her brain. 'Laurel and Hardy?' she repeated.

'Well,' Arthur began to explain, 'there are two of them.'

'You've been watching *Numbertime* again,' I said.

'I hadn't finished,' he protested. But he didn't deny it. 'The thing is,' he continued ponderously, 'Norman is always saying to Nick, "Another fine mess . . ."'

'Thank you, Arthur,' I said, shaking my head.

'Laurel and Hardy it is then,' Arlene said. 'At least that's one problem solved.'

'Hang on a cotton-picking minute,' I objected.

'Shall we vote on it?' she said. 'All those in favour?'

Three hands shot up in the air.

'That's the trouble with democracy,' I said, shaking my head. 'Oh, for a benevolent dictator.'

'In that case,' Arlene said, 'I name these kittens Laurel and Hardy.'

'Have it your way.'

'Promises, promises,' she cooed.

'But they are not sleeping on our bed,' I said, laying down the first of the ground rules.

'Of course not,' she agreed. 'Not when they're grown up, that is.'

Sulkily, I lit another cigarette.

'You know what I've never understood,' Arthur said from the world of his own.

There goes the whole evening, I thought. 'What's that?' I enquired politely.

'Democracy,' he announced.

How could I best explain the concept? Probably skip the Greek origins and the Roman era, ignore the issue that neither believed all people were equal, try not to use complicated words like *suffrage*.

'What I want to know,' he said, 'is how can they call it democracy when you can only vote for politicians?'

'Good question,' I said, relieved and stunned in equal measure.

Laurel – well, the one who'd nearly spilt my drink *had* to be Laurel – crawled on to my lap and nuzzled his head against my free hand, subtly demanding attention.

'So what did you find?' Norman asked.

'Sorry?' I said.

'When you searched Nadya's room.'

'Oh,' I said, remembering where I had been before those damned cats had made their appearance. It seemed like hours ago when I'd started this story. 'A boob tube,' I continued, stroking Laurel under his chin. 'Mrs Crabtree nearly fainted on the spot.'

'A bandeau,' Arlene said, with emphasis. 'Not Miss Sugar and Spice after all then?'

'More like Miss Schizophrenia.'

'Miss what?' asked Arthur.

'Split personality,' I explained. 'Nadya would seem to have been two separate people, or have worn two different masks according to the company she was in. One persona – the serious student, the dutiful daughter dressed in virginal white – while in the presence of her parents; another – Disco Queen or scantily clad seductress – for the second life she's leading.'

'And what did Mrs Khan say when you showed her your discovery?' Arlene said.

'I thought it best not to. And, anyway, she wasn't telling me anything useful. Seemed only fair to withhold my information.'

'She wasn't helpful then?' Norman said.

'Ah,' I said, 'but that wasn't all she wasn't.'

'Do what?' Arthur said.

'The curious incident of the dog that didn't bark in the night-time,' I said, playing my trump card.

'In Arthur's words,' Arlene said, 'do what?'

'Sherlock Holmes,' Norman explained. 'Conan Doyle's *Blue Carbuncle*.'

'Sounds painful,' Arthur commented with a reinforcing grimace.

'The blue carbuncle was a precious stone,' I said patiently.

'That explains everything,' Arthur replied.

'And, actually,' I said smugly, 'it wasn't *The Blue Carbuncle*.'

Arthur shook his head as if experiencing a bad dream.

'It was *Silver Blaze*. A horse. Remember, Norman?'

'So it wasn't a precious stone, it was a horse?' Arthur asked tentatively.

'No, forget the horse, Arthur,' I said, beginning to regret using the analogy. 'The whole point of the story is the dog.'

'I submit,' he said, banging his hand three times on the sofa.

'You see,' Norman interjected, determined to win back the Brownie points lost on misnaming the title of the short story, 'the dog did nothing in the night-time. That was the curious incident.' He turned to me. 'Anyway, what the hell has all this got to do with Mrs Khan?'

'What would you do,' I said to Arlene, 'if Mary Jo went missing?'

'Stop you ordering a crate of champagne,' she replied perceptively. Then she thought about it a little more. 'Jeez, I'm not sure what I would do. Panic probably – that's usually the first reaction of any human being in a crisis. I doubt if I'd be able to think straight. I'd be at my wits' end. Out of my mind with worry.'

'Exactly,' I said. 'Or, should I say, exactly not. Mrs Khan didn't show the slightest sign of being worried. Okay, she was pretty vague. But I think that was just an act. I saw plenty of evidence of her meticulous handiwork

68

(beautifully crafted curtains, cushions and so on) – odds-on favourite for Seamstress of the Year, I reckon – to believe she is a person for whom details matter.'

'And your conclusion, Mr Holmes?' Norman said, preening an invisible moustache.

'She wasn't worried, Watson,' I replied, 'because she thinks her daughter is safe.'

'And is that what you think?' Arlene asked.

'I go with the odds,' I said. 'When I first spoke with Ali Khan there seemed to be only two alternative hypotheses: either Nadya disappeared because she stole the money or, coincidentally, she was abducted. Fifty-fifty bet. Now Nadya's double life raises a third possibility.'

'Ah,' said Norman, nodding his head wisely.

'Huh?' said Arlene.

'The third possibility,' I said, 'is that she stole the money and *then* was kidnapped. By someone she knew and trusted. Knew too little, and trusted too much.'

'So it's not just a case of find the money and *cherchez la femme*. It's *cherchez l'homme* too.'

'Why does it have to be a man?' I asked.

'Because only a man could be so duplicitous, of course.'

Arlene needed another drink. Arthur and Norman needed food. The kittens, apparently, needed to run up and down the sky-blue curtains and to test the durability of the beige and dark blue Regency-striped sofas with their fledgling claws. I needed a plan.

Two hours later everyone was fully satisfied. Except me. The good news was that I had at least devised a strategy. The bad news was that it only covered the next day – not exactly the Nostradamus view of the future. Tomorrow, Norman would concentrate on gathering and collating information on the prepaid funeral confidence trickster in preparation for a personal visit that would appeal to his better nature or, alternatively, ascertain his attitude to having Arthur's fist planted on his lying lips. Arlene and Arthur were to stake out the Khan residence, Arlene tailing Mrs Khan, Arthur taking Nadya's brother, in the faint hope that one or both of them would lead us to the missing daughter and missing money. Meanwhile, I would begin to dig around in Oldbrook's accounts and try to find some time to track down the quasi-anonymous tutor.

Now it was half past eleven. Arlene was giving Laurel and Hardy their last feed of the day, I was standing at the window in the bedroom, staring out across the river to Greenwich, deep in thought. 'Stuck in the middle' was the phrase that kept going round in my head.

While I was working in the Treasury Department, Ali Khan wanted me to concentrate on finding the missing four hundred thousand pounds: Norman was more interested in me investigating all other areas of the accounts in order to find scams that would justify his choice of a commission-based fee structure.

Ali Khan wanted his daughter found: Mrs Khan, it appeared, did not.

Stuck in the middle. Not a good position to be in.

Confucius he say, 'Man who walk in middle of road get hit by cars coming from both directions.'

I felt Arlene's arms wrap around my waist.

'Pretty, isn't it,' she said, 'the way the lights twinkle like stars and the moon dances on the water. We're very lucky.'

I nodded and placed my hands on hers.

'I've been thinking back,' she said, 'to something you said earlier.'

'The third possibility?'

'No, not that.'

'Not the dog that didn't bark, I hope? Please don't ask me why it didn't bark. No one remembers the reason.'

'Nope.'

'What then?' I said, wondering what other words of wisdom I had uttered.

'How did it go?' she said uncertainly. 'Oh, I know. "Have it your way."'

70

CHAPTER NINE

Day Two

'How do you feel?' Arthur asked, as we completed our ninth lap of Island Gardens. The words came out in synchronisation to the fast pace he was setting. And, for a man of fifty years, irritatingly easily.

'Gritty,' I panted.

There are few worse ways to start a day than going for a run at six o'clock in the morning. However, one is stepping barefoot into a tray of cat litter that has unexpectedly appeared outside your bedroom door.

'See,' he said smiling – how could he run and smile at the same time? – 'I told you this would do you good. Yesterday you were going soft, and now, after only twenty-five minutes of running, you're already feeling gritty.'

He was dressed in a grey tracksuit, a towel round his neck, and a pair of trainers so large I could probably have had the rubber soles recycled and made into a new set of tyres for the Lancia. As we jogged along side by side, he jabbed at the air like a heavyweight contender. Very professional.

In contrast, I was wearing a pair of maroon Lycra cycling shorts that Arlene had bought for me after watching (many times and in slow motion) Linford Christie run the hundred metres, a T-shirt with 'Boston Red Sux' emblazoned on the front, which Norman had brought me back as a souvenir from the States, and a pair of battered old tennis shoes I'd found lurking at the back of the wardrobe. I was desperate to get this bloody run finished before anyone saw me and took blackmail pictures – or someone with ginger hair from Boston arrived on the scene.

'You don't mind about the kittens?' Arthur asked tentatively.

'No, of course not,' I replied as best I could. 'If it makes Arlene happy . . .'

'I didn't mean that,' he said, his face reddening with embarrassment rather than the exercise. 'I meant about the names – Laurel and Hardy. It was only meant as a joke. I didn't think anyone would take me seriously.'

'We always take you seriously, Arthur.'

'Trouble is,' he said gloomily, 'I'm not used to that. Too many years as a bouncer. Too many insults. Too many cheeky kids speaking dead slow and saying "Watch my lips."'

'All that's changed,' I said, forcing a smile through teeth clenched against the stitch that was burning in my side. 'Now you're chief assistant to a fraud investigator. Or, if you prefer, Head of Field Operations to a forensic accountant.'

'Wow,' he said, impressed at his own position. 'Wait till I tell me old mum.'

We started another circuit. I looked longingly at the wooden hut that was the cafeteria, willing it to open so that we might have an excuse to stop.

'We'll make this the last lap,' Arthur said

'If you say so,' I replied casually.

'Build up gradually,' he said, nodding his head wisely. 'That's the best way. We'll go for fifteen laps tomorrow, twenty the day after that, and so on.'

My anticipation knew no bounds. Mainly because it didn't exist.

'Two things,' Arthur said when we'd finished.

He was standing over me breathing easily as I lay on the grass catching my breath and cursing Lycra shorts. Bloody fashion designers. Where were you supposed to put your cigarettes and lighter? Unless, of course . . . I never knew Linford smoked.

'Yes?' I said, raising myself on to one elbow.

'First, buy yourself some proper trainers. Otherwise you'll finish up with blisters and bad knees.'

'Tell me about it,' I said. 'And number two?'

'Watch yourself in Oldbrook, Nick.'

'Hell,' I said, collapsing back down. 'What are you worried about? I'll probably be dead before I even get there.'

The supermarket was quadruple-fronted and sat in the exact centre of an insalubrious island site surrounded by rows of run-down council houses. On its left was a charity shop, a chemist's that looked as if it probably did a roaring trade in methadone, and a newsagent/tobacconist: on its right was a betting shop; a place selling second-hand furniture, all apparently once owned by people whose lack of taste was equalled only by their carelessness; and one of those shops that sell everything you don't really need at such low prices you're actually tempted. Shopping Mall of the Year it wasn't.

Ali Khan was standing outside, supervising a young black lad who was vigorously scrubbing away at a wall with a hard brush. The white lightning flash was receding gradually under the combined attack of hot water and stiff bristles. The large encircling 'O' would offer sterner resistance.

I climbed out of the car, locked my briefcase (mobile phone inside) safely out of sight in the boot, and walked towards Ali Khan. At my approach he looked away from the wall and gave a helpless shrug. Extending both hands to greet me, he shook my hand and simultaneously clasped my right arm firmly just above the wrist. 'Mr Shannon,' he said, 'I am very glad to see you. So very glad you have accepted my case. Please, come inside my humble shop.'

He was glad, and so was I. Glad that I hadn't brought

Norman. Norman would have tried to make amends for his past sartorial *faux pas* by coming in his three-piece suit. And he would have been caught out again. Ali Khan was wearing a black long-sleeved collarless coat and wide trousers.

'I hardly recognised you,' I said. 'You look so different today.'

'Ah, the *isar*,' he said, looking down at the trousers and pulling at the sides so that they flapped about like sails on a yacht, 'and the *jamah*. When I am in one of my shops I dress traditionally for my customers. When at the council I like to appear more formal, more businesslike – more English, I suppose.'

'All things to all men?'

'No, Mr Shannon. Merely a matter of selecting the clothes to suit the job in hand. I imagine you do very much the same.'

'Of course,' I agreed, 'you should see me when I go running.'

'Exactly,' he said, opening the door and waving me inside.

The supermarket was a denial of the old saying that you couldn't squeeze a quart into a pint pot. The shelves were so tightly packed it seemed as if the first purchase would cause a landslide of tins or packets, the aisles so narrow that only those who had passed their Advanced Driving Test could negotiate them without difficulty. In the few spaces where it had proved physically impossible to fit more shelving, large squat dump bins stood: they were full to the brim with 'special offers' for those, I suspected, who were not too fussy about 'best before' dates.

Even at this relatively early hour there were customers at each of the three checkouts. One was manned by a plump lady in her mid-forties, another by a young and attractive girl of nineteen or so, the third by a thin woman of about twenty-five. All three were either Indian or Pakistani by birth. They each smiled up at me, the plump one in motherly fashion, the young girl flirtatiously and the thin woman either out of politeness or for no better reason than to show off her perfectly white teeth. Ali Khan snapped at them in Hindi and they returned to their monotonous tasks with heads bowed low.

'This way,' he said, leading me past the checkouts towards the back of the store. As I passed the thin woman I noticed a pile of boiled sweets – orange, lemon, lime and strawberry – by the side of her till. I restrained myself from taking one. Didn't think she'd appreciate it somehow.

At the far end of the supermarket were three doors. One led out to a loading area and refuse storage; one to a store-room where an old man was lethargically sweeping the floor with a broom that looked as if it had been inherited from his grandfather; the last to a tiny office. Ali Khan stepped to the far side of a desk littered with invoices, delivery notes, till rolls and the like, and sat down in one of a pair of wooden straight-back chairs that would have fitted in well with the ramshackle collection of furniture up the road. He motioned me to sit opposite him. I did so, cautiously testing the strength of the chair by pressing down with my hand before daring to lower myself into it.

Ali Khan leaned forward, placed his elbows on the desk and steepled his fingers in that superior and supremely confident manner adopted by schoolmasters prior to issuing a rebuke on past behaviour or, if there was no just cause, a warning for assumed future transgressions. It had to be the latter – unless his wife had taken umbrage at the unfinished cube of carrot halva. He opened his mouth to speak.

'Mr Khan,' I said, jumping in to throw him off balance, 'a question, please.'

The steepled fingers intertwined. A frown crossed his face. 'Very well,' he said.

'From what I've seen and heard, you seem to have carved out for yourself a nice little business empire. You have a wife and family. All that would be enough for most people. Why get involved in politics?'

'Because someone has to, Mr Shannon. We can't all sit on our backsides like professional critics, running down every move a government makes. Someone has to put his head on the block and actually create – form policy, take unpopular decisions for the good of the general population of this country.' He forced a smile to his lips to ease the tension – his, not mine. 'And where would the British be without us politicians? Conversation would be reduced to only two topics – the weather and religion.'

'To put one's head on the block,' I said, 'unless one is extremely foolish or the altruistic hero of a Dickens novel, needs a damned good reason. What was *your* motivation, Mr Khan?'

'Would you accept to right wrongs?'

'No,' I said. 'That's a goal, not a reason.' Believe me, I might have added, I know only too well. 'So?'

'You're very persistent, Mr Shannon.'

'A quality that will serve you well over the coming days.'

I settled myself ostentatiously in the chair, crossed my left leg over the right, ankle resting on knee, prepared to wait him out. He'd crack soon enough. The one thing politicians can't stand is silence.

Ali Khan gave a wry smile and shook his head. 'Very well,' he said. 'You shall have your reason.'

He unbuttoned his jacket, then the shirt beneath; pulled the material apart; thrust his chest at me; brandished the scar. Three inches long. And one lucky inch from his heart.

'It was eighteen years ago when I came to this country, full of hope and clutching a degree certificate for a B.Sc in Electronics. The hope stood me in good stead in the years to come: the degree certificate was a waste of paper.' He paused, leaned back in the chair and looked reflectively up at the ceiling. 'The word *khan*,' he said, 'originally meant a lord. Nowadays it has come to denote any property owner. My family had a big estate in what was once East Bengal, then East Pakistan and now Bangladesh. They farmed mostly jute and tea for export, bananas for home consumption. We were rich, especially by local standards. Until 1970. That was when the cyclone hit. Five hundred thousand people were killed, including every member of my family.'

'I'm sorry,' I said, knowing his sense of loss. The only family I had left was a seventy-year-old grandfather in County Cork, and he, a devout Catholic, hadn't spoken to me since I'd killed my sister and started a chain of events that had resulted in the deaths of both my parents. 'Very sorry.'

Ali Khan shrugged, maybe seeing my words as polite sympathy rather than genuine empathy. 'Being away at university saved me from sharing my family's fate. Or maybe, as you Christians say, I have a guardian angel. I finished my degree — what was the point of going home? — and then was immediately conscripted into the army. Somehow I survived the ravages of the war against Pakistan which led to the formation of Bangladesh. A new country, a new life, I thought. I returned to the estate, married my childhood sweetheart and started to rebuild the farm. By 1974 I was winning the battle to restore our fortunes. Then the flood came. Everything I had achieved in three hard years was wiped out in a matter of hours.'

In my first lesson in his language he'd told me that *khan* meant lord: what he'd omitted, it seemed, was that *Ali* was the Bengali equivalent of Jonah.

'I'd had enough,' he said. More than enough, I would have thought. 'It took me two years to sell the estate. Even then I had to settle for a rock-bottom price — the country was under martial law at that time and no one was very keen to buy land which might be confiscated. So, my wife and I, and young Nadya, packed our bags and tried another new country, another new life. Only to find it wasn't any easier.'

'You couldn't get a job,' I said, remembering his bitter comments on the degree.

'What I got was a lot of excuses. Some companies said they didn't recognise *overseas* degrees – especially those from the Indian sub-continent – where there was no guarantee of the quality of teaching. Others said that the five-year gap between the end of my course and deciding to enter industry was far too long – electronics is a fast-moving field, they claimed, where knowledge becomes out of date almost as soon as it is acquired. Then there were those who, after receiving my application form, suddenly realised there were no vacancies after all. Need I go on, Mr Shannon?'

'As Shakespeare might have said, "Discrimination by any other name would still smell as rank." So you decided to become part of our nation of shopkeepers?'

'Eventually,' he said. 'But only after I'd travelled the length and breadth of the country for abortive interviews. And only after being set upon in Manchester by a gang of youths carrying combat knives, chips on their shoulders and hatred in their hearts. That was the last straw. Almost my last breath, actually. So I swore two oaths to myself: I would confound the racists by becoming rich,' – and famous? – 'and I would do everything in my power to prevent others from suffering the same treatment as I. The first oath was the easier – I used the money from the sale of the farm to buy my first shop. The second, I soon came to appreciate, was virtually impossible to do if one was operating from outside the system. It had to be changed from the inside. Hence politics. The rest, as they say, is history. That, Mr Shannon, is the long, and painful, answer to your short question.'

'In my business, Mr Khan, it's a case of "if you never ask, you never learn." Unfortunately, it's a maxim that is not without drawbacks. I apologise, most sincerely.'

Ali Khan looked down at his watch, then across the room where his business suit hung on the handle of the top drawer of a filing cabinet. 'Before we leave for the council,' he said, 'I wish to stress certain points. I trust you will not take offence.'

I nearly told him that he needn't worry – the one thing that ex-cons and politicians have in common is that both need the hide of a rhinoceros. But, diplomatically, I nodded instead. I was getting the hang of client service now.

'Finding the money and my daughter must take priority,' he said sternly. 'I understand perfectly well the conflict of interest our commission agreement must create for you, but searching out any other malpractices – which, incidentally, I am assured you will not find – must take second place. Is that clear?'

I gave him another nod. Not because I agreed – distrustingly, I had a strong feeling that as soon as I had found the money Oldbrook Council would drum up some excuse for terminating the contract – but because he expected it.

'Second, you must tread as if on eggshells.' Makes a change from cat litter, I thought. 'You must remember that the only people in the council who are aware of the missing money are myself, the Chief Executive and the Head of Treasury. You must do nothing to arouse the suspicions of the staff. Nor, for that matter, will you do anything to upset them.'

Tricky. This was going to be a whole new way of working for me. I could cope with not arousing suspicion. But not upsetting people . . .

'I will do my best, Mr Khan,' I said.

'And I hope that will be good enough, Mr Shannon.'

'You must have faith in me,' I said, feeling my hackles rise. 'Believe me, I am very good at what I do.'

'Time will tell,' he said with a non-committal movement of his shoulders.

Not exactly a phrase that bolsters one's confidence.

'Okay,' I said. 'Let me give you proof. If I were you, I'd keep an eye on the thin woman at the checkout. She's short-changing your customers.'

'How can you possibly say that?' he scoffed. 'You haven't even seen her handle any money.'

'I don't need to,' I said. 'She keeps a pile of sweets by the side of the till.'

'So what?' he said dismissively.

'It's one of the oldest tricks in the book,' I said. 'I'm surprised you're not aware of it.' I shook my head and tutted. 'The big problem with short-changing a customer is what to do with the money. You can't keep slipping your hand in your pocket to stash away the loot. That will only arouse suspicion.' I stressed the last word, but I doubted whether the little dart pierced his armour. 'So, the easiest way round the problem is to put all the money – the amount that appears on the till roll plus the amount by which the customer was short-changed – in the till. Then, just before the end of your shift, you create a distraction – drop the customer's change on the floor, for instance – and, while no one is watching, you take out the money that you have been salting away.'

'I fail to see what this has to do with sweets, Mr Shannon.'

'You have to keep track of the total amount of all the short-changing, otherwise you might remove too much or too little from the till – either could set alarm bells clanging. And you can't very well write it down on a notepad – bit of a give-away, that. So you use a home-made abacus – the sweets. Different colours represent different amounts: orange is a pound, say, yellow is fifty pence. By innocently fiddling with the sweets and moving them around, you keep track of the total without anyone tumbling to what you're up to.'

I waited expectantly for the round of applause.

Instead, I heard the sound of glass shattering. Then the high-pitched squeals of women screaming.

I jumped up and started to run from the room, Ali Khan hard on my heels. Then I had to screech to a halt at the door as the old man came out of the stockroom, dropped his broom in my path and set off to the front of the store. I felt Ali Khan's bulky body bump into me, sending us both sprawling against the wall of the passage-way, heard an almighty crash; turned to see the back door fly open in an explosion of splinters; smelt the distinctive aroma from the dustbins enter the corridor, followed closely by two very large men dressed all in black with balaclava helmets covering their faces. One was carrying a jack-hammer, its heavy metal head catching the light as he raised it menacingly; the other was slapping a long wooden cosh against the thick padding of his yellow-gloved hand.

'Get the bastard,' Jack-hammer shouted to Cosh.

I don't know why I did it. Just wasn't time to think, I suppose. It was act now, or see Ali Khan smashed to pulp. And I've never been too keen on the sight of blood, even when it's not mine. I grabbed Ali Khan by the shoulders of his coat; yanked him back, ignoring the sound of expensive cloth ripping, threw him bodily into his office and slammed the door shut. I shouted, 'Block up the door', then swivelled quickly to face the threat.

Time was on my side, I told myself encouragingly. Surely Ali Khan's next move, once safely barricaded inside, would be to call the police. All I had to do was hold off the two men until the cavalry arrived. Jesus, what was I saying? *All I had to do . . .*

The corridor was narrow. That, at least, was in my favour – only one of them could attack at any time. I bent down and scooped up the discarded broom; balanced myself on the balls of my feet; took up a general all-purpose defensive position, body slightly crouched and ready to uncoil like a spring, hands on the broom, stave-style. Jack-hammer looked directly at me, gave a sickening gargling-with-gravel laugh and shook his head contemptu-ously.

Impressed, huh? Pretty good judge, I thought. The broom wasn't an ideal weapon in these conditions: the dis-advantage of the narrow corridor with its low ceiling was that I couldn't use the handle horizontally to block their blows. Forward jabs and short sideways sweeps were the limit of my freedom to manoeuvre.

Maybe I could draw them back into the main part of the supermarket. No, that wouldn't work. They would merely abandon the fight with me and switch back to their main objective — batter down the door of the office in order to get to Ali Khan.

Jack-hammer pushed Cosh forward.

'I must warn you,' I said, causing him to pause, 'that I used to be a Boy Scout. I breezed through the test for my Stavemanship badge. In my hands, this broom is a lethal weapon.'

Cosh, obviously hard of hearing, advanced.

Now, a cosh is a handy object to have in a fight — but only if you can get in close. I jabbed the tip of the broom into his chest, bringing forth a cry of pain and causing him to take a step backwards. I followed up my advantage by taking a pace forwards, jabbing repeatedly at his left shoulder, then the right. He waved the cosh in the air like a man swatting at a troublesome wasp. I switched my target to the soft flesh of his stomach and, when he moved to parry this, hit him on the heart. He gave a gasp and took another step back.

I sensed I had him licked. It was easy then.

Stomach. Heart. Stomach. Heart.

A nice steady predictable rhythm.

The sound of cosh on broom beating out like a jungle drum.

He was gaining confidence as he warded off each blow, his defensive movements speeding up as his brain became conditioned to the sheer predictability of my attack. That was when I let him have it. Instead of switching from heart to stomach, I jabbed the broom higher; hit him smack between the eyes.

He dropped the cosh, clutched his forehead with both gloved hands, staggered back dizzily, groaning loudly like a wounded animal. Which, I suppose, is exactly what he was.

One down, one to go.

Jack-hammer pushed Cosh behind him, then advanced on me. The heavy metal head swung from side to side. Sadistically, he let it thud against the walls. Large chunks of plasterboard dropped on to the floor.

I tried to repeat the same series of jabs that I had used so effectively against Cosh. Didn't work. The jack-hammer was a lot more difficult to get past. Each time I thrust forward, the head clubbed the broom handle aside. I had to struggle to keep my grip. My hands rung with the force of the blows.

I backed away, used the full length of the broom and stabbed down on to his toe. No reaction. No heartening wince of pain. No retreating step backwards. Either he was wearing steel toe-caps or it was a case that where there's no sense, there's no feeling.

He swung the hammer low, aiming for my knees. I thrust the tip of the broom on the floor. Pressed down hard to block the shot. The metal head struck the handle of the broom, smashed right through it. Eighteen inches of useless wood went spinning away. And my balance went with it. I tumbled forward, caught a glimpse of the jack-hammer being raised high.

There was no way I could regain my feet. At least not before my skull had been caved in by ten pounds of solid steel. So I chose the only option left: dropped the broom; spread my hands, palms down, on the floor; used my forward and downward momentum to complete a somersault; converted it into a handstand; kicked up with all my strength. The heels of my shoes connected just under his chin. The resulting yelp of agony was music to my ears – 'I Got You, Babe', I think it was.

He stood there, swaying. But I knew from bitter experience not to let up now. Had to capitalise on my winning position before he regained his senses and came back at me more fired up, more dangerous than ever. As he stumbled backwards I jumped to my feet, grabbed the jack-hammer from his loosened grasp and prepared to strike.

He swore loudly, questioning my parentage, implying I was currently indulging in sexual intercourse and likening me to a certain part of the female anatomy in one continuous stream that made up in emotion what it lacked in eloquence. Then, his limited vocabulary exhausted, he and Cosh made meaningful eye contact through the holes in their balaclavas, turned and bolted out the back door.

I heaved a huge sigh. Felt my heart beating fast. Heard a cheer and an enthusiastic burst of applause from behind me. Turned to see the staff gathered in a circle, at a safe distance, behind me.

I knocked on the door to the office. 'You can come out now, Mr Khan.'

Furniture scraped on the floor inside as his hastily erected barricade was dismantled. The door was opened, somewhat gingerly. Ali Khan's head appeared and took a swift inventory of the scene. Satisfied that the coast was clear, he stepped out. And threw his arms round me.

That was the moment the police chose to arrive.

Whatever questions they asked me, I knew one thing for sure: I would need to answer them in a voice as deep and gruff as Arthur's.

We drove to the council offices in my car. Ali Khan had wanted me to accompany him in the chauffeur-driven Jaguar, but I didn't want to leave the Lancia outside his shop all day. I reckoned the chances were that I'd come back and find it either gone or stripped of everything that could be resold easily – that probably meant only my jazz cassettes would be left.

The police hadn't stayed long. What was there to tell them? One front window smashed by a brick – partly a diversionary tactic, but also a vehicle for the message wrapped around it: 'STAND DOWN', it said in clumsily scripted capitals. Two thugs, both dressed in what was presumably the uniform black of OWN, wearing thickly padded yellow gloves, balaclava helmets and probably boots with steel toe-caps. One (Jack-hammer) had a north, or possibly east, London accent, which was very useful since with the knowledge of the OWN connection we could all safely assume the culprits to be local anyway. The only positive thing to come out of their presence was that they agreed to provide us with an escort on our journey, pending arranging more permanent protection for Ali Khan.

'I owe you my life, Mr Shannon.'

'I'd rather have your ear,' I said.

'I'm sorry?' he said.

'How important is this political career of yours?'

'I am on the brink of entering Westminster, Mr Shannon. From the House of Commons I can influence the thinking of the whole country, not just Oldbrook. This is more than just a career. It is a crusade.'

Just as I had feared.

'And you understand,' I said, 'the dangers of not acceding to the unsubtle request to stand down from the election? The danger to yourself? And perhaps to Nadya, too?'

'The note said nothing about Nadya. If OWN had her then surely they would have used that as their ultimate bargaining weapon?'

'And then the police would have no option but to get involved in the disappearance of your daughter. Implying, but not stating, is a safer strategy for OWN.'

'I will not stand down, Mr Shannon,' he said. 'Not unless there is no other alternative. The message changes nothing. Your priorities are still the same.'

'Then let me give you your second piece of free advice for the day, Mr Khan. Listen carefully. You would be wise to prepare a fall-back position, in the event that I can't find your daughter and the money in time. Visit your bank manager. Go down on bended knee. Plead for the loan of four hundred thousand pounds.'

'It would do no good, Mr Shannon. You see, I am committed to the hilt with the bank as it is. I borrowed every last possible penny only a month ago in order to buy another shop.'

'In that case, you should put some shops on the market. And do it right away. For one thing, we haven't much time. For another, any more bricks through windows – or bombs, for that matter – and their value will start dropping like a stone.'

His face fell.

'Look,' I said, sensing the need to lighten the load, 'why don't you make a list of your shops, their locations, floor space, turnover, profit and your estimate of approximate value – allowing for the fact that in the time available it will be a buyers' market. I'll get Mr Timpkins to put some feelers out. He has experience of putting deals together.'

Ali Khan went all quiet on me while he brooded on my words. As we approached Oldbrook Town Hall, he turned to me and said decisively, 'I will heed your advice, Mr Shannon. About the shops. And about the checkout girl. From now on, I place myself – my future and my daughter's, my career, my crusade – entirely in your hands.'

I glanced across at him. He beamed back at me like a puppy dog.

'You could have run,' he said. 'Instead you chose to defend me. Why?'

'Ask me another,' I said, shrugging.

'You are too modest, Mr Shannon.'

I shook my head. 'Just impulsive,' I said. 'And anyway, I can't answer your question because there is no easy answer. Life, in my experience, is usually about shades of grey. It's rarely black and white.'

'You should tell that to OWN.'

'I'd be wasting my breath. Some people just won't listen.'

'Then I shall have to shout even louder, Mr Shannon. So that the message cannot be ignored.'

'Only one problem, Mr Khan,' I said. 'There are those who, if they don't like the news, still favour shooting the messenger.'

CHAPTER TEN

Available building land was scarce in Oldbrook. That's why the council had committed sacrilege: cobbled together their administrative headquarters by taking an eighteenth-century baroque mansion and stapling on a modern five-storey wafer-thin greenhouse.

Perhaps I was being a little unfair. The new structure wasn't really stapled on to the old; it was connected by two pedestrian bridges (one at second-floor level, the other at the vertigo-inducing top) running across a central atrium. The old building had started life as the country – how times change – residence of a Lombardy banker, one of the influx of rich noblemen from that region who settled in the City of London to revolutionise the British banking system and give us our monetary units (lire, soldi and denarii), place names like Lombard Street and dishes such as veal Milanese – or maybe that came later. Compulsorily purchased by the Government during the Second World War for use as a training centre for officers, the house was subsequently abandoned and fell into decline in the fifties and sixties until, as a means of disposing of a potentially expensive white elephant, it was generously donated to Oldbrook on its formation.

The word baroque stems from the Portuguese *barroco*, a term originally used to describe a pearl that was not perfectly round: it came to mean anything that was odd, strange or bizarre. Are you getting the picture? Three storeys (two with very high ceilings and one very low for servant accommodation); wide, multi-pillared frontage set with narrow-paned curved-top ecclesiastical windows; short sides running back at an angle of sixty degrees; a tower tacked on at one end to house a secondary staircase; pagoda-style roof dominated by an ornate Italianate monogrammed crest and a flagpole from which now hung limply the red ensign of the London Borough of Oldbrook.

Ali Khan and I entered by the glass doors leading from the car park at the back of the tripartite building and stepped into the middle section, which served as the terminus for traffic, the reception area and a test bed for the hydroponically nurtured greenery. Or, more accurately, brownery, since the assortment of trees and plants seemed to be thriving about as well as everything else in the borough. There was an unpleasant smell in the air, a combination of damp gravel with artificial nutrients at floor level and decaying foliage above. Maybe it was all a set-up, an exercise in positive discrimination, the creation of an environment that would give unequal opportunities to the nasally challenged.

I was issued with a visitor's pass by an efficient glamour girl who looked as if she would have been more at home behind a department store cosmetics counter – but presumably her efficiency had counted against her in the selection process – and taken on a lightning tour by Ali Khan. The tour was meant to acclimatise me, but merely served to confuse. I began to wish I'd brought along a ball of wool and had spent my early morning practising wrestling bulls rather than running. The old building was a Cretan maze of indistinguishable corridors, the new a series of identical floors of glass-fronted open-plan offices, and, to make matters worse, we seemed to zigzag from one to another at every available opportunity.

All I concluded from this peripatetic disorientation was that the Treasury Department was on the fourth floor of the new building – although it might have been the third – and that the decadent splendour of the old building had been appropriated by the councillors (ground floor) and high-ranking officers (upper floors), while the workers had been relegated to the multi-layered fish tank.

'Eleven o'clock,' Ali Khan said, consulting his heavily jewelled watch. 'Time to meet our Chief Executive.'

Time to get down to some serious investigating, I thought. But you have to follow procedures. All government functions on protocol and I didn't want to start off by putting noses out of joint – there was plenty of time for that. Meanwhile, it seemed, I was destined to endure some old codger in a grey suit droning on in an unnecessary repetition of Ali Khan's ground rules.

We crossed the second-floor bridge for the umpteenth time and snaked our way to the right and left until, I guessed, we were at the front of the mansion, somewhere near the centre. A large, heavily panelled door with a brass plaque saying merely 'Chief Executive' – must make the occupant feel really secure in his job – led into an outer office guarded by a Cerberus creature with two heads. Well, actually, it was two black women wearing white blouses, their heads bent very close together as they scrutinised a single sheet of paper, but the image took a moment to interpret. Disentangled, the optical illusion revealed a girl of around twenty and a middle-aged woman. The former left the office on an errand of mercy – black with two sugars for me – the latter opened a door to the inner sanctum and waved her arm ceremoniously. As I stepped inside I let out a heavy sigh and donned my standard accountants'-issue invisible anti-boredom suit.

The suit melted.

My jaw dropped.

She was beautiful.

Okay, beautiful is an overused word. And there's the ongoing discussion about the difference between being beautiful and attractive. But she *was* beautiful, I swear. And attractive too. I could see how men, less strong than myself, could easily fall in love with her at first sight.

She was standing by the window, staring out reflectively, the sunlight catching her blond hair. It was cut in that style favoured by newscasters – not the big-haired ratings-pulling bimbo type, but the serious professional – low-maintenance length, centre parting, sides swept back. As she turned to greet me her blue eyes sparkled like the morning dew. Her skin was pale, but not unhealthily so, just that Scandinavian type of complexion that needs a liberal coating of Factor 24 before venturing out into the sun. She was somewhere around forty, I guessed, but a young forty. Very well preserved, the only signs of age being little laugh lines around the eyes and at the corners of her small, lightly lipsticked mouth. She was tall, slim and immaculately dressed in a tailored suit of Cambridge blue.

'Helen Ripley,' she said, extending her hand and smiling naturally.

Helen. The face that launched a thousand ships.

'Nick Shannon,' I replied slowly, reluctant to let go of the hand or the smile.

'I'm very pleased to meet you, Nick. Although, I must say, I was expecting someone older.'

'You don't exactly fit my stereotype either, Miss – or is it Ms or Mrs? – Ripley.'

'Just call me Helen,' she said. 'I'm not a great believer in unnecessary formality.'

'Nor I,' I said, instantly cursing myself since it sounded so formal. Then I consoled myself by wondering how she got on with Ali Khan, who acted as if unnecessary formality were a contradiction in terms.

'If you do not mind, dear lady,' Ali Khan said – *dear lady*, that's a lynching offence most places nowadays – 'I will leave you now. Meeting of the Equal Opportunities Committee in ten minutes.'

'Of course, Ali. Lunch, perhaps?'

'Please accept my apologies, but I have promised to officiate at the opening of the new Youth Centre. Duty calls, you understand?'

Plus, I thought cynically, the whirring motor drive of a press photo opportunity.

'In that case,' Helen said, 'I shall make it *my* duty to introduce Nick to the delights of the staff restaurant.'

'That is most considerate,' Ali Khan said ingratiatingly.

'Only if you can spare the time,' I said, giving her the chance to back out on her offer and hoping she wouldn't.

'One o'clock, shall we say, Nick?'

'Sounds good to me.'

'Then that's settled. Now, off you go, Ali. Mustn't be late. A chairman's prerogative, I know, but one that should only be exercised infrequently.'

She watched Ali Khan leave the room. I thought I detected a small sigh of relief escaping from her lips, but maybe she was just panting at the prospect of being alone with me. 'Do sit down, Nick,' she said.

Easier said than done. Not the actual sitting down, but the choice of seat. There were three separate possibilities. At the old-fashioned partners' desk where she undertook her paperwork; the long mahogany table set meeting-style with eight chairs, pads and pencils; or the two wingback leather chairs either side of the central window. I hovered until she solved the problem for me. Wingback chairs, it was.

The younger of Helen's aides entered with a tray, set it down on the oval, intricately veneered table between us, poured two cups of coffee and diplomatically left, shutting the door behind her.

The room was rectangular, twenty feet by twelve. The walls were barley-white up to the dado rail, brilliant white above and extending across the ceiling with its two decorative roses which must have once circled chandeliers. A wide bookcase, six feet high, and crammed with thick volumes of reference works, stood against the wall directly behind her desk. On the desk itself were two telephones (one red and one grey), an impressive maroon leather blotter and, the gentle touch of femininity, a single red rose in a thin long-stemmed vase.

'So, Nick,' she said, leaning attentively forward in the chair, 'tell me all about yourself.'

What was this? Role reversal? I ask ze questions.

I sipped the coffee – Viennese blend by the aftertaste of sweet fig that lingered on my tongue once the brown sugar had deigned to depart – and studied her face.

'I've already undergone the third degree from Ali Khan,' I said. Not to mention, I thought, the lecture on discretion being the better part of upsetting the apple cart. 'You know, qualifications, experience, all that stuff.'

'I'm more interested in the person underneath,' she replied.

I gave her one of my puzzled looks – I like to practise at least three times a day.

'In the Treasury Department,' she began to explain, 'you will gain inside knowledge of our systems – and be privy to some extremely sensitive, and potentially highly valuable, information. What are you like as a person, Nick?'

'You mean, can I be trusted?'

She gave a shrug.

'I came recommended by the Fraud Squad. Good enough?'

'And how did that recommendation come about?' she asked.

'Well . . .' I said.

She smiled at me again, tilted her head to one side and looked up at me in that coquettish manner which is supposed to be disarming. Why do women think that men are such feeble creatures?

Before I knew it, I was telling her all about how I came to study accountancy, my subsequent involvement with Collins, the undercover jobs in Glenshield and Future Assurance, the fraudsters caught, the wrongs righted. Came close to divulging collar size, favourite colour and star sign. She made it very easy for me: she was a good listener, didn't interrupt, nodded her head encouragingly whenever I paused to consider omitting something. She seemed approachable and genuinely interested.

'I'd like to meet this Collins,' she said, when I was sapped dry.

Me too, I thought.

'He seems,' she continued, 'to have a very pragmatic approach for a policeman.'

'I'm not sure pragmatic is the right word, but I know what you mean. He believes in justice and that can't be bad. Even if the ends justify the means a little too often.'

'And how,' she said, signalling a change in tack, 'was your first taste of Ali's little empire?'

'Sorry?'

'You were going to meet him at one of his shops this morning. What did you think of our local entrepreneur on his home territory?'

'Hard to say. I spent much of the time trying to defend it. Or, rather, him.'

I explained about the attack on the premises and the two thugs from OWN out for Ali Khan's blood, modestly playing down my role in frustrating their objective. Who needs hero worship? Put your hand down, Shannon.

I looked at my watch. We were drifting effortlessly towards lunchtime. No work done, no progress made. But she didn't seem to mind. But, then again, she was paying by results, not by the hour. There was a question I wanted to ask while we were still on our own. An inconsistency that needed to be resolved if it were not to prey on my mind and impede my concentration.

'May I ask you a question now?'

'As long as it's not the predictable one. The one that's the standby of all the journalists.'

'And what's that?' I asked hesitantly.

'I paraphrase,' she said. 'It goes something like, "What's a nice girl like you doing in a dump like this?"'

I blushed. Predictably.

'Oldbrook, Nick,' Helen said, settling back in the chair, 'is the land of opportunity.'

'And pigs have been given clearance to land at Heathrow,' I replied.

'The land of opportunity,' she repeated, brushing aside my interruption. 'Not for the people, the voters, the taxpayers or the businessmen. But for the public servants.'

The bureaucrats, she meant. Public servants aren't in the job to serve the public – well, only the genuinely altruistic, and there aren't many of those. They are in it for the money, the power, the prestige, and the gong from the Queen that comes with the inflation-proof pension.

'Take my case,' she said. 'I joined the Local Government Service directly after university; worked hard in the day, studied long hours in the evenings, crawled my way up the ladder through various junior then increasingly senior executive positions until I was running a department. Then my head hit the glass ceiling. I applied for several Chief Executive posts across the country – one rejection after the other. The competition was stiff, I grant you, but I was more experienced, better qualified than those who were successful.'

I ought to introduce her to Walker. She could pick up a few tips on how to play promotional leapfrog. Maybe not – one Walker on the planet was bad enough. The thought of two was bloodcurdling.

'And then,' Helen said brightly, 'just as I was beginning to despair about ever reaching that final rung of the ladder, God – or, rather, his earthly political disciples – created Oldbrook. The ghetto borough. The hornets' nest of racism. Now, Nick, tell me, who in their right mind would want to work in a place like this?'

'I plead the Fifth Amendment.'

'Nobody,' she said, 'except the desperate. Those who, like me, stood not a cat in hell's chance of promotion. Those who had blotted their copybooks in the dim and distant past and were stuck with superiors long on memory and short on forgiveness. Those who, for whatever reasons, were searching for the local governmental equivalent of the

French Foreign Legion, who were running away from a present so dark that even a future in Oldbrook seemed bright in comparison.'

'You make the people here sound like the Dirty Dozen.'

'We are, Nick. Without a doubt, Oldbrook has the biggest collection of misfits outside of a train-spotters' convention. But that is not to say we are all bad. On the contrary, we all desperately want to see Oldbrook prosper. If one can succeed here, the world is one's oyster.'

Not a pleasant thought: a lot to chew on; difficult to swallow; and, above all, slimy.

CHAPTER ELEVEN

They say that people with ginger hair should restrict themselves to as little of it as possible. Myself, I don't subscribe
to the theory. Neither, evidently, did Stuart McCready,
Head of Treasury. Head of hair too. And beard. And moustache. The man was positively smothered in long red coils;
a piece of human blotting paper for the sprouting cress
which covered his face and even poked out from his ears
and nose. But that wasn't the only thing that struck me
during that first meeting. The other was how appallingly
bad he was at concealing his emotions.

Helen had walked me along the corridor and into
McCready's antechamber, nodded at his Personal Assistant
and entered the room after only the most peremptory of
knocks. As we stood in the doorway, McCready looked up,
gave a little start, and stared long and hard at me.

'Have we no' met before?' he asked eventually.

I'd encountered this red-face-saving ploy many times
before; from people who had seen my photograph in the
newspapers or watched me on TV as I stepped outside the
Old Bailey handcuffed to a policeman. But what did I care?
Would it have been any easier if they'd come straight out
with it? 'Aren't you the Nick Shannon who . . . ?'

'I don't think so,' I said politely.

'Are ye sure?'

'I doubt if our paths would have crossed.'

He shook his head as if to flick aside the nagging

thought. 'Sorry,' he said. 'What am I thinking of? Do take a seat.'

To be perfectly honest, he actually said, 'Will ye no' tak' a sit?', but if I reproduce exactly his every word then we're going to need the services of an interpreter. So, in future, I'll try to forget about the glottal stops, the heavily rolled 'R's and the vowels that sounded like a throat being cleared.

Helen and I sat down opposite him. Screening out the impact of the camouflage of hair from my overloaded optic nerves, I noticed that his face was ruddy-complexioned, his nose and cheeks flecked with blood vessels broken by the repeated punching of the heavy hand of alcohol. His powerful shoulders – the result of a misspent youth tossing cabers over heathered glens, or enemies over the Clyde? – were swathed in a mustard and brown tweed jacket as pleasing to the eye as the aftermath of a pitched battle in a condiment factory. He was pushing fifty – back from the wrong side; the sort of age when evenings are passed in contemplation of one's pension and spending it on coach tours of the bulb fields of Holland, a lifetime subscription to *The Oldie* and a bulk purchase of tartan slippers. It was a shame that the days were spent at Oldbrook.

From the cluttered appearance of his desk, McCready didn't seem as if he was winding down for retirement. Spreadsheets, colour-coded manila folders, internal memos, outgoing letters for signing were spread liberally across the rosewood top. A desk can say a lot about a person. This one proclaimed that he was coping heroically with a Herculean workload – or that he was just plain disorganised.

McCready started to rearrange the jumble into, well, a rearranged jumble. I felt a fidget coming on. I glanced at his bookcase with its mind-numbing collection of *The Municipal Year Book*, outdated textbooks on accounting and public administration and the ten binders of bank statements arranged like soldiers on parade, and sighed. Valuable time was ticking away. Okay, Rome wasn't burning while he fiddled non-productively, but the trail was growing colder.

'Mr McCready,' I said, 'I'm anxious' – bloody anxious, do you ken? – 'to make some progress on the missing money. Ali Khan couldn't tell me exactly how it was stolen – all he could say was that the sum involved was four hundred thousand pounds. Perhaps you could fill me in on the details?'

'Are you familiar,' he asked, 'with the principle of zero balance?'

What the hell was he on about? A Glaswegian at the end of his stag night?

'Not by that name,' I bluffed.

'Let me explain,' he said. 'If you are overdrawn – have a negative balance – on your current account, you pay interest. If you have a positive balance, then that money is lying idle when it could be earning for you. The optimum position is, therefore, to have a zero balance. Not a penny more, not a penny less.'

It could only take a Scotsman to come up with a principle like that: watch every last penny – and miss the odd four hundred thousand pounds. Still, I nodded back at him knowledgeably.

'We in Oldbrook strive for a zero balance at the end of each and every working day. Any excess funds that would otherwise be lying dormant in our accounts, we place on the overnight money market.'

'Good housekeeping,' I said. 'A similar discipline to that of most large companies. They tend to watch their cash flow very carefully.'

'Aye,' he said, 'but no' as carefully as us.'

Matter of opinion, I thought.

'You see, Mr Shannon, to achieve true zero balance you have to compensate in your forecasts for the type of payment you are making and precisely when each individual cheque or credit transfer – and deposits too – will be cleared. That's no' as easy as it sounds.'

I didn't think it sounded easy, full stop. 'So what *is* your method?'

'We have a number of different bank accounts.'

'It being a simpler task,' I said matter-of-factly, 'to reconcile several smaller accounts rather than one massive account.'

'And to adjust for the different clearance characteristics. For example, we have a Salaries Account – we pay our staff by credit transfer and these clear next day. Then we have an account for Commercial Services, that's our main procurement arm – the cheques on that account take three days to clear. Then there's the main income accounts – Government grants, rates, cash received (instant clearance, of course) from rents, libraries and so on. Need I go on?'

'I get the picture,' I said.

The more complicated you make a system, the more holes there are in it. In the complex and highly technical terminology of accountants, this was a string-vest job.

'Not forgetting,' he said, – I thought we'd agreed he didn't need to go on – 'internal transfers from the income accounts to the expenditure accounts, both current and capital.'

I nodded again, more in impatience than acknowledgement.

'So,' he continued, 'during the course of the day we calculate the expected balance on each account. Then make one telephone call to the bank to give instructions as to how much to take from each account to place on the overnight money market, and how much to transfer back to each account – invariably different since money must go from income to expenditure – at the start of banking in the morning. As you . . .'

'Hang on,' I interrupted, 'you said *one telephone call*. Who makes the call?'

'Whichever member of my staff is least busy. We believe in staff empowerment,' – I thought I detected a slightly contemptuous wrinkling of his red nose at this point, but among all that hair it was difficult to tell – 'allowing people to take decisions.'

'That's right,' Helen chipped in. 'Give someone responsibility and they respond to it. Motivationally speaking, it has a lot going for it.'

Security speaking, it had a lot going against it.

'Presumably,' I said, 'during the course of this telephone call you use some codeword for authentication purposes.'

'We will do in the future,' Helen said, sighing.

Jeez. Every time one of them opened their mouth my opinion of the system was sinking lower in a sea of flawed procedures. Any moment now I'd need boots weighted with lead and a compressed-air pipeline.

'We do send written confirmation by fax,' McCready said defensively.

'Simultaneously?' I said. There was a pregnant pause. I relaxed the criteria a little. 'Or at least just after?' Another pause. 'Within the hour?'

'Well,' he said. 'That's no' always possible. Depends on the workload. But the fax is always sent the next day. Well, generally.'

I closed my eyes in utter disbelief; clutched my forehead in exasperation.

'I think you will find, Mr Shannon,' McCready said, a hard edge to his voice, 'that the same system is operated by virtually every local authority in the country.'

'In the same way?'

'Aye.'

It was all I could do to stop myself from banging my head on his desk.

'So what happened?' I asked. 'How was the money stolen?'

'Quite simple, really,' McCready said.

'You surprise me,' I grunted.

'As I said earlier,' he sighed, 'we have several accounts. These are all designated by sequential numbers – Number One Account, Number Two, etc. – right up to Number

Nine. Nadya Khan, while making the daily call to the bank, set up Number Ten.'

'Just like that?'

'With an account our size the bank strives to be helpful,' he shrugged. 'Then, in a second call five minutes later, she said there had been a mistake; too much had been allocated to the overnight market. Four hundred thousand pounds was needed urgently for the new Number Ten account for the payment of the first in a series of development grants. The bank was very understanding; transferred the money to the Number Ten account, and from there, according to the details she'd given them, wired the money directly to the recipient.'

'Mr McCready . . .' I began.

'I know,' he said, cutting off my John McEnroe 'I-cannot-believe-it' impression, 'we need to tighten up.' No, I thought, you need to be strung up. 'But,' he added lamely, 'it's the way things have always been done.'

Bad habits die hard, I thought, craving a cigarette. 'But not in the future, I hope?'

'Not in the future,' Helen said firmly. 'Soon we'll operate a new completely watertight system.'

'Soon?'

'Well,' she explained, 'we didn't think it wise to start straight away – not with Nadya missing, and you arriving to go through the accounts. We didn't want to alert the staff that anything might be amiss.'

'So you're still wide open to fraud?'

'The bank manager is now required to ring Stuart to confirm each set of instructions before making the day's transfer.'

'So as long as the bank manager is on the ball,' – and as long as you trust Stuart here – 'you are safe.'

'And if the bank manager isn't on the ball,' McCready said, 'we'll sue for compensation.'

Rather you than me. Clash of the bloody Titans that would be. Lawyers on both sides hitting the jackpot.

'How can you be sure it really was Nadya who made the phone calls? Set up the new account? Authorised the transfer?'

'Primarily,' McCready said, a wee patronising tone in his voice, 'she announced herself as Nadya Khan, Councillor Khan's daughter – that's another reason why the bank was so helpful. And, of course, Nadya is missing.'

'It might have been someone impersonating Nadya,' I said, playing devil's advocate. 'And her disappearance might be purely coincidental.'

'Do you really think so?' he scoffed.

I shrugged. 'That's what I aim to find out. What information did the bank provide on the recipient of the four hundred thousand?'

'The money was wired to a company called Megacom Films and Videos.'

Something about the name tickled at my brain, but I couldn't recall where I'd heard it before, or its significance. It would come, and then the scratch would be very satisfying.

'I'll run a check through Companies House,' I said. If McCready had been on the ball he would have done that already. And a lot more besides. 'Shouldn't be too difficult to find out the names of directors and shareholders. And I'll need to speak to the bank manager to get details of Megacom's account. It might be possible to freeze their assets, although I suspect that will be shutting the stable door after the horse has bolted. Still, can you set up a meeting for me this afternoon?'

'Aye,' he said, stroking his beard. 'So I take it you won't be wanting to waste any time looking through our books?'

'No,' I said. 'But unfortunately that's the only way I can generate any income from this case.'

'We thought you might say that,' Helen said. Had I at last met someone as cynical as myself? 'Stuart and I have come up with an explanation for your presence in Treasury. A *raison d'être*.'

'A legend,' Stuart said, bravely trying to correct his boss. 'Isn't that how it is known in your business?'

'I think you'll find that only applies in the spook game.' Or maybe that was how he saw me: a spy in his midst.

'Whatever,' he said. 'This is the story. In preparation for a change of external auditors, you have been sent by your firm to examine our systems and procedures in order to provide an accurate quotation. As far as the staff are concerned, you're here merely to cost out the job.'

'Won't anyone think that strange? Changing external auditors is a pretty rare event.'

'Things are different in local government.'

You're telling me.

'You see,' Helen said, 'as a council, we have very little freedom of action in the appointment of our auditors. It's supposed to be a security measure – no cosy relationships to develop between council and auditor; no chance of conspiracies. The Audit Commission largely dictates both who we use and when we change. The closest we get to exercising any degree of choice is to select from a shortlist – three or four private firms plus the District Audit Service – that the Audit Commission compiles and presents to us as a *fait accompli*.'

I nodded my approval; not just of the *modus operandi*, but the alibi too. I'd had a lot worse excuses in the past for an undercover operation.

'Over lunch,' Helen said, 'we will talk through the areas on which you would be best to focus; point you in the right direction.'

Or the wrong one, I thought suspiciously. I'd listen to their suggestions, and then go my own way; follow my nose and my instincts.

McCready gave a long world-weary sigh. 'We could well do without this problem right now. So much to do in so little time. What with the interim audit about to start, I mean. And I'm short staffed as it is.'

'I dread to think,' Helen said, fingering her lips pensively, 'what might happen if Ali is forced to resign just before the Festival. It could destroy everything we've achieved of late. That's why we had to give him – you – a chance to find the money.'

'We'll just have to trust to luck,' I said.

'And we haven't had much of that,' McCready said dourly.

'Really?' I said. 'Tell me, how much money did you place on the overnight market on that fateful day?'

McCready consulted one of the spreadsheets on his desk.

Wasting time again. A guess would have been sufficient to prove my point.

'Well,' he said, 'we'd just received another tranche of our grant from central government – they come every fortnight, you know.'

'I didn't,' I said, my impatience growing afresh. 'Mr McCready, how much was placed overnight?'

'Close to eight million pounds.'

'I rest my case,' I said.

'I don't understand,' he said.

'Consider yourself extremely lucky that they didn't take the whole lot.'

CHAPTER TWELVE

Egalitarianism in Oldbrook was suspended at meal times. The councillors, taking full advantage of their status as 'Members of the Council', enjoyed the luxury of a private dining room in the splendid isolation of the baroque mansion: on the top floor of the new building, the staff (technically, the 'Officers') had their very own replica of a motorway service station cafeteria.

The omens were not good.

As I walked through the door, my senses became the victim of a three-pronged attack. A noxious cloud bearing the aromas of fried food and pungent spices bushwhacked my nose. The saxophonic treacle of Kenny G – more omnipresent than God nowadays – oozed from a multiplicity of wall-mounted speakers, sticking cloyingly to my ears and worming its way inexorably into the most vulnerable reaches of my brain. The sound level, against a low background hum of chatter, was almost subliminal and absolutely irrelevant, for I knew that for the rest of the day I would be breaking uncontrollably into *Da daa da daa* as if my power of self-determination had been surgically removed. The three external walls were painted from floor to waist level in that shade of bright yellow-green which you normally only encounter in the science lab when experimenting with fluorescine. From waist level to the lemon emulsion of the ceiling the room was glassed, so that those who were lucky enough to have a table on the perimeter could look out over the wonders of Oldbrook.

And after that fifteen seconds, I suppose you just had to make polite conversation.

Helen, McCready and I had collected trays at the door and split up to cruise round a number of island sites representing a caterer's abridged version of the cuisine of the world. Some were copper-domed, offering a variety of dishes bubbling away on hotplates under the harsh glare of spotlights: chicken tikka masala, rice and poppodums; battered cod or grilled minute steak and chips; fried chicken, sweet potatoes and plantains; pizzas; kebabs; sweet and sour pork and noodles; apple pie, rhubarb crumble and custard. Others were enclosed in refrigerated plastic cases where salads, sandwiches and cold desserts could be extracted – just – through front-opening flaps.

Knowing that we would all be dining out at Toddy's tonight and therefore not wanting to blunt my appetite for the most delicious food in London, I chose what looked like a surprisingly authentic salad Niçoise. In truth, I would have been happiest with a cup of thick black coffee and a cigarette (or two or three) while tapping keys at a computer console in Treasury. But fate (and Helen and McCready) seemed to be conspiring to keep both work and nicotine at bay. I added a can of caffeine-rich cola to my tray, picked up cutlery and napkin and rejoined my companions at the cash desk.

Except it wasn't.

Oldbrook Council, so I was about to learn, was a virtually cashless society. Every member or officer was supplied with a smart card. By inserting one's card and a bank note into one of the machines outside the canteen, the card was primed and ready to use. Even the coffee machines functioned only when swiped by a card. The theory was that no one needed to carry more than the minimum of cash, making the picking of pockets an unlucrative enterprise. What the staff were supposed to do if they wanted to hit the shops at lunchtime or after work I didn't know. Like many a good theory, it foundered on the rocks of reality.

Helen gestured at our three trays and handed her card to the woman behind the 'till'.

'Is that all you're having, Nick?' she asked.

By my side McCready wrinkled his nose at my namby-pamby French la-di-da salad.

'I'm eating out tonight,' I said in self-justification as we headed past long communal Formica-topped refectory tables to a relatively discreet table for four in one corner. McCready moved the reserved sign to one side as I unloaded my tray and looked around vainly for some-where to stow it. Helen shook her head. 'You keep your tray till you've finished,' she explained. 'Then you simply place it on that conveyor belt as you leave. The belt feeds all the dirty dishes directly to the washing-up area of the kitchens.'

'I hadn't expected *Star Trek: The Generation After Next*,' I said.

'Joe's Caff, was it?' McCready said, mimicking a Cockney accent with less success than Arlene – but more than Dick Van Dyke, it has to be admitted.

'Must save on labour costs,' I said, trying to cover my *faux pas* by lapsing into accountant-speak. 'Cuts down on the payroll.'

'Not our payroll,' Helen said. 'The contractor's payroll. In-house catering was the first of our operations to be pri-vatised. Central government regulations, you see.' She waved both hands downwards and bowed her head in the your-wish-is-my-command manner of a genie. 'Councils have to justify the use of their own direct labour. Which effectively means that our DLOs must tender against out-side contractors.'

'The polemic of public choice theory,' I said, remem-bering the little Economics that was part of my correspondence course. 'Each individual rationally seeks to maximise his own self-interest. Build up a department and the person in charge, because of the added responsi-bility, gets a pay rise and improved chances of promotion.

Providing services as efficiently as possible doesn't enter into the bureaucrat's equation.'

'I wouldn't have put it quite like that,' Helen said, hand drifting to her lips to hide a smile, 'but there's no denying that's the essence of the Government's thinking.'

'It's a policy,' McCready said, 'that has had only partial success nationwide – private contractors have won only about twenty per cent of contracts – but nevertheless the cost saving is estimated at six per cent of local government expenditure.'

'That's worth about eighty million pounds across the country as a whole on refuse collection alone,' Helen chipped in, putting the meaningless percentages into perspective. A strange perspective though.

'It's a figure we're familiar with,' McCready said as if reading my mind, 'because refuse collection and disposal is currently up for tender. In nine days' time,' he smiled with self-satisfaction, 'we will have completed our programme of privatisation of Oldbrook's main services.'

Should I spoil his lunch? Let him in on the secret strategy that an unscrupulous operator – no names, no pack drill, Norman – might well adopt? Winning that very first tender is the most difficult, since you are up against an outfit (the council's DLO) which is already in place – doesn't have any start-up costs to cover. So you underprice to secure the contract. The DLO is shut down (because it now has no function, no reason to exist) and then isn't in a position to compete when the contract comes up for renewal. And that's when you jack up your price and make a killing.

'Eat up, Shannon,' he said, knife and fork already beginning to attack a mountainous plate of steak, chips, mushrooms, deep-fried onion rings and petits pois. 'You'll find it's really very good.'

Oh, well. Ignorance is bliss, I suppose. And privatising refuse collection in Oldbrook couldn't make the service any worse. That was a physical impossibility.

I brushed the appetite-suppressing vision and associated nasal flashback from my mind, took a forkful of salad and popped it in my mouth. McCready was right. It was good – decent dressing, potatoes cooked so as not to be either rock hard or like lumpy mash, crisp lettuce, egg yolks of free-range orange, good-quality tuna and anchovies, even garlicky croûtons. Not up to Toddy's standards, I hasten to add, but a whole lot better than any other staff canteen I'd been unprivileged to eat in.

'Well?' Helen said, cutting a tuna mayonnaise sandwich into quarters.

'I'm impressed,' I replied.

'You wouldn't have been a few years ago,' she said.

'When we ran the catering ourselves,' McCready said in a rare pause between mouthfuls, 'the food was completely inedible. Which was probably a good thing since the standard of hygiene was such that our Environmental Health Officers were in a permanent state of apoplexy. We were simply pouring money down the drain. Most of the staff resorted to eating out or bringing packed lunches. Now look at them.' He waved the point of his knife in the general direction of the body of the room.

Certainly there was none of the apathetic pushing of food around plates that I'd encountered at Future Assurance. Here, the eating followed a stage direction of *with gusto* – although in McCready's case *gutso* would have been more appropriate. Yet the atmosphere just wasn't right. Okay, so one of their number had very recently been systematically beaten to death, but that wasn't it. Nor was it the garish decor, the hard chairs or our man with the honeyed saxophone. It was the underlying ambience of a culture based on cliques that was the problem. At the long tables where most of the staff were forced to sit, gaps had been deliberately left between groups. Those on the flanks of each group had angled their chairs slightly so that their backs signalled an exclusion zone. And, within this emotionally ring-fenced barrier, heads were turned

110

conspiratorially inwards and down. This was not one united workforce, it was a collection of individual competitive units compelled through necessity to occupy the same space and hating every minute of it.

'I've prepared you a wee list,' McCready said, interrupting my uncomplimentary thoughts on Helen's management style. He passed me a sheet of paper and proceeded to concentrate on a complex manoeuvre that involved transposing the positions on his tray of one empty plate and one large bowl of rhubarb crumble in a sea of custard. 'Areas for possible investigation,' he added as an explanatory afterthought.

I looked down at his barely legible scrawl, concluded that his writing was as difficult to decipher as his speech, and ventured a hopeful 'Perhaps you'd talk me through it.'

'Housing,' he said. 'You can check the rents-received account. Architects and Building – take an inventory of stock of materials, make sure nothing is missing. Payroll – establish that all those on it actually exist. Then there's Social Services . . .'

I could feel the onset of brain death and McCready still wasn't anywhere near finished. Just wait till I get my hands on Norman.

'What about Commercial Services?' Helen asked.

'Aye,' he said, 'it's on the list. There.' He leaned across the table and pointed to a longer than average squiggle at the bottom of the sheet.

A number of questions crossed my mind.

What, I wondered, was so special about Commercial Services that Helen should pinpoint its importance by checking its inclusion on McCready's list of the Top Ten Most Incredibly Boring Tasks in the World? And what, I wondered more suspiciously, was it doing at the very bottom of the sheet? Was Helen trying to steer me towards Commercial Services and McCready steer me away from it? Or was it some extremely devious double bluff – Helen assuming that I would perversely not follow her lead, or

McCready, making a similar judgement of my character, knowing I would go for the area of seemingly least importance?

Hell, Shannon, why do you have to think in such a convoluted fashion? Now what have you achieved? Confusion not only reigns, it pours.

I lifted an eyebrow in what I hoped was a Roger Moore expression of quizzical interest rather than a transmission of my state of mental muddle.

'Commercial Services,' Helen began, in the slow, patient tones of one used to dealing with the absent-minded, 'as we said earlier, is our procurement arm – the equivalent of a central buying department in the private sector. Pretty much everything the council purchases is ordered by Commercial Services. The staff there scour all relevant market sectors – computers, say, or office furniture or stationery – decide which products meet our specification and then use the muscle of one large buying unit to obtain the best possible price. The system produces significant cost savings over a less structured purchasing function. We're very proud of Commercial Services.'

Pride. We all know what that does, don't we? Goeth before a fall. Well, not quite actually, as Brother James once pointed out, to my annoyance. 'Pride goeth before *destruction*,' he had corrected me, 'and an haughty spirit before a fall.' My version was snappier – hadn't he heard of sound-bites? And who uses a phrase like *an haughty* – it sounds so, well, haughty. And hell, it's all the same. Especially when, like now, the only words that really mattered were payola, backhander and bung.

'Then that's where I'll start,' I said. 'Which floor are they on?'

'All in good time,' McCready said to my dismay. 'You need to know how Treasury operates first.'

'And you'll need help,' Helen said. 'Someone to share the load of the mountain of paperwork. And to give you the introduction that will be necessary if you want full co-operation. Assign Adam to Nick, Stuart.'

It was McCready's turn to raise an eyebrow. He didn't do it with quite the same effortless panache as I had, of course. But, then again, his eyebrows were so bushy he probably had to do weight training three times a week in order to move them at all. They did, however, have the advantage of emphasising his puzzlement.

'Adam needs to broaden his experience,' Helen said in justification. 'Working with Nick will do him good.'

Yes, I thought. But would working with Adam do Nick good?

Somehow I didn't think so.

I had the sneaky feeling I was being manipulated; and lumbered with a biblically named junior who probably couldn't even add up.

Look on the bright side, Shannon. If it came to multiplying, then Adam would be your man for the job.

CHAPTER THIRTEEN

Auditors are regarded by accounts staff with suspicion bordering on the paranoid, and treated with the strained rigor mortis smile of polite – but damned near zero – forbearance. They are blown spies – there to dig the dirt, and everyone knows it – and disruptive of the normal working routine of those they are investigating. I wasn't expecting a ticker-tape parade to welcome my first entrance into Treasury. Which was just as well.

'So *you're* Shannon,' said the girl at the desk just inside the door, a nanosecond after McCready had introduced me.

She was nineteen or twenty, Kate Moss thin but without the counterbalancing bone structure of natural beauty, cropped-haired, and visibly piqued. 'We've been looking all over for you,' she said, her pale eyes narrowed into an accusing stare.

I refrained from pointing out that if she had really been searching so diligently then how come she had missed the obvious lunchtime hiding place of the staff canteen. Instead, I smiled and said, 'Is he in heaven? Is he in hell?'

She looked at me strangely.

Good.

Experience has taught me that in the long run it never does any harm to be underestimated.

'The Scarlet Pimpernel,' I explained, back-pedalling a little. Underestimated, yes. Taken as the accounting equivalent of the village idiot, preferably not. 'You know: "They seek him here, they seek him there. Those Frenchies seek him everywhere." I thought it was appropriate in the circumstances.'

'But I'm not French,' she said, mystified.

That's modern education for you. Still, she could probably name in chronological order the complete works of Oasis and Blur – what an onomatopoeic name – and quote from the collected pearls of philosophical wisdom of Eric Cantona – or should that be pearl?

'Anyway,' she brayed, the final syllable coming out as if she were reading from a script where a distracted typist had forgotten to take the right index finger off the *y* key, 'your office rang. They asked me to tell you to turn on your mobile phone.'

Bit louder, I thought. There might be someone at the far end of the office who didn't quite catch it. Although that was unlikely, seeing that I seemed to be the focus of attention. A dozen or so heads were turned in my direction, eyes critically moving beyond suit, shirt and tie to conduct a brain scan and an X-ray of soul. A lad of around twenty-one years with long blond hair smirked. I won't bother to give you three guesses as to his identity.

'Adam,' McCready called, simultaneously beckoning and wiping the grin from my new assistant's face.

One shouldn't make snap judgements. But, hell, that was what everybody else was doing right now. So I submitted to the one-word message that was being transmitted by the prejudiced electrical currents of my synapses. Himbo.

Adam was six feet tall, slim and dressed in a hand-stitched jet-black suit that Versace had decided not to include in his autumn collection because it was just too expensive. The blond hair was straight, short at the sides, long on top. It fell across one eye as he strode casually across the room. He tossed his head in a vain effort to bring the hair back under control, or maybe he was being sponsored by a brand of two-in-one shampoo and conditioner and had to complete so many head-tosses each day as part of the contract.

'Nick Shannon,' McCready said formally, 'meet Adam Schroeder.'

I was tempted to say, 'How do you spell that?' but wouldn't have been able to cope with the expected response of 'My brother helps me.'

'Hi,' Adam said, extending a hand.

'Hi,' I replied. No one outcools Shannon. Competitive? Who, me?

'Nick's going to be with us for a couple of weeks,' McCready said. 'You've read my memo about the potential change of auditors, I take it?'

'Yes, Stuart.'

I saw McCready flinch at the over-familiarity. Adam didn't seem to notice, or maybe he didn't care.

'I want you to look after Nick,' McCready said with an avenging smile. Adam's face dropped, the classic Aryan features sagging, the piercing blue eyes glazing over at the thought of how his popularity rating would plummet. 'Tell him how we operate. Explain the systems. Take him wherever he wants to go. Do whatever he asks. And, Adam,' he sighed, 'try to be helpful.'

'Sure,' he replied. 'I always do.'

'Yes,' McCready said dubiously. 'Oh,' he added, 'Nick will need a smart card for the restaurant and coffee machine. Organise it.'

'No sweat.'

McCready shook his head, and decided that a swift exit was the best strategy to avoid bursting a blood vessel.

Adam watched him depart then turned to the girl behind the desk.

'Becky,' he said, smiling sweetly.

'Yes, Adam,' she said breathlessly.

'I'm a bit pushed at the moment. Sort out this card for Shannon, will you?'

'Yes, Adam.'

'Give Becky a tenner, Shannon, and she'll charge up your card. How do you take your coffee?'

116

'As black as it comes. Two sugars.'

'And the usual for me, Becky.'

'Yes, Adam.'

Three bags bloody full, Adam.

'There are seventeen of us in Treasury,' Adam said. 'Sixteen if you exclude Greedy McCready, since he spends most of his time in the old building. Well, fifteen, I suppose, now that Rashid has . . . And Nadya is off sick – probably the same bug that had me off work yesterday – so that makes fourteen at the moment.'

He made it sound like the setting for an extended version of Agatha Christie's *Ten Little Indians*. And here was I nonchalantly drinking my coffee without having forced Becky to try it first.

It was three o'clock. We were sitting side by side at Adam's desk. He was telling me all he knew. Should be finished by ten past, I estimated conservatively. The desk was one of the favoured few facing a window. The bulk of Treasury was behind us. And that suited me fine.

The large open-plan room was painted in a drab shade of beer-bottle green. The floor was covered in those ultra hard-wearing industrial carpet tiles that feel as if they have been woven from porcupine quills, their highly singular colour resembling the sea at Southend after a thunderstorm. The partition wall abutting the next department was just visible above a long line of six-feet-high steel storage cabinets. Staff sat on slate-grey typists' chairs at desks with veneer tops in what office furniture catalogues call 'sapele', which is a way of avoiding using the more accurate but less appealing description of dark brown. The desks were arranged in seemingly random clusters of two, three or four, with no screening between them to provide even a semblance of privacy. It was the kind of environment that could turn a newly appointed well-adjusted clerk into a manic-depressive within the first few hours. And, after a year or two, voluntary euthanasia must have seemed a whole lot more attractive than the long featureless road to an inflation-proofed pension. I couldn't wait to meet the sadists in Commercial Services. Unless I was doing them an injustice. Maybe they were just obeying the orders for bottom-of-the-range furniture and dour choice of colouring which was part of McCready's Celtic gene structure?

'We're divided into six sections,' Adam said, beginning to count them off on his fingers. Thank goodness it wasn't eleven sections otherwise he'd have to slip off his loafers and silk socks. 'They're all pretty self-explanatory,' – something else to be thankful for – 'payroll. Payment of accounts. Receivables – the largest section, deals with rents, rates, grants, letting and licence fees, superannuation interest, sales of council houses – well, in theory, not that there's any in actual practice. Now, who,' he switched into a Loyd Grossman imitation, 'would want to live in a place like this? Computer. Accounting – that's monthly and final accounts, budgets, financial control and such. And internal audit. Which is just me and Mrs Monk now.'

He gave a small sigh, either for the loss of Rashid or the gain of a bigger slice of the work pie.

I sipped my coffee – bitter as a jilted lover – and gave Adam a moment to reflect. 'I think I understand the set-up,' I said.

'But what you don't understand, Shannon, is local government. And the prevailing culture of distrust.'

'Not a bad thing for internal audit,' I said.

'I'm not just talking about internal audit,' he said, 'but the whole way of operating.'

'Which is?'

'The principle of double-check.'

'Which is?' I said again, no wiser than the first time.

'The accuracy, and honesty, of every person's work is checked by someone else. Then it's checked again. For instance, someone from receivables will balance the rates account. Then someone from accounting will make sure

118

there are no mistakes – either accidental or deliberate. Know what I mean?'

I nodded quickly, staving off the expected wink and nudge in the ribs which normally followed that phrase.

'And then,' he continued, 'Mrs Monk, Rashid or I would go through it all again as part of our ongoing audit. Come to think of it,' he said, 'I suppose you could say it's really triple-check, since you external auditors will examine everything with a fine toothcomb at the interim or full audit.'

'So whose idea was this system? McCready's, or Helen Ripley's?'

He studied my face slowly, as if reading the word ignoramus on my forehead, then gave a laugh. 'I knew you wouldn't understand local government, Shannon. No one invents a new system. We follow the tried and tested ways. Tread the paths walked by men with spats over their shoes.'

'Even though it may be a misuse of time and resources?'

He shook his head pityingly. 'Look,' he said, 'it's the Rank Xerox syndrome. No one ever got sacked for buying a Xerox machine, did they? But go for a different make – worse still, something brand new to the market – and your neck's on the line. If it turns out to have been the wrong decision, you can't justify it, can you? So it's bye-bye, Mr Innovator. Exit PlaySafeVille, USA.'

'But,' I protested, 'you and other councils *have* embraced the new philosophy of privatisation.'

'Only because we were forced to by Westminster.'

'What about computers then?' I persisted. 'There's not a person here without a terminal on his or her desk.'

'Sure,' he said. 'But the procedures are exactly the same. Double-entry bookkeeping on screen rather than in leather-bound ledgers. Twenty-first-century technology handling nineteenth-century arithmetic. Beautifully word-processed tender documents generated by laser printers, but packed inside *with parties of the first part, whomsoevers* and *be it known thats.*'

Call it a wild hunch if you like, or a flash of inspiration that brings total enlightenment, but I was getting a feeling – only slight, mind – that he didn't like it much here.

'Okay,' I said. 'Local government is unique. I give in.'

'I knew you would, Shannon. Why should you be different to the rest of us?'

I shrugged. *He* wouldn't understand.

'So who checks whose work?' I asked.

'It doesn't work like that.'

'Now why am I not surprised?' Would be too bloody simple, that's why.

'You can't have fixed pairings,' he replied with undisguised scorn. 'Hardly much better than each person working on his own. No. Accounting and audit float. That way the risk of collusion between checker and checkee is cut to the minimum.'

Checkee. And he was the one criticising legal documents for their arcane language.

'Let me get this straight,' I said. 'By float, do you mean that everybody checks on everybody else?'

'Got it in one, Shannon.'

'And when you say everybody's work is double-checked, does that include McCready?'

'What little he does, yes. The bank reconciliation is his sole contribution to alleviating tedium among the troops. That's subject to audit, naturally. But Greedy is an admin man – runs the department, steers the ship. And a strategy man, of course. Must be bloody hard work, strategy.'

'Talking of work,' I said, and that seemed to be about the closest anyone got to it round here, 'I'd like to start by looking at Commercial Services.'

'I hope you know what you're letting yourself in for,' he said, shaking his head. 'Although I very much doubt it.'

'And what is that supposed to mean?'

'Commercial Services is the biggest generator of paper in the council. Auditing their work is like trying to walk on quicksand. You're likely to sink without trace.'

'Then it's lucky I have you, Adam,' I said, feeling just the opposite. 'You can lead the way and I'll follow in your footsteps.'

A look of horror spread across his face as he saw hard graft looming over the horizon.

His agony was to be postponed. The telephone rang. It was McCready for me. The bank manager would see me in fifteen minutes.

'We'll have to leave Commercial Services until tomorrow,' I said to Adam, as I rose to leave. 'I have to see . . . a man about a dog.'

'Who you go out with, and who makes the arrangements, is your own business, Shannon.' He rolled around in the chair, fit to burst.

'Adam,' I said, bending over him and pressing my face close to his, 'you and I are going to be working together for the best part of the next two weeks. It may come as some surprise to you, but I relish that prospect even less than you. Now, either we can make the best of it and try to get along with each other during that time – which means you suppressing the more annoying traits of your personality, i.e. all of them – or . . .'

'Or what?' he said defiantly.

'Or I will unleash my secret weapon. Set upon you someone who will strike fear in your heart and have you screaming for mercy.'

He shrugged.

Hell, it was his funeral.

Come to think of it, I rather hoped he would transgress. Then I could carry through my threat. And I would savour every moment of him crumbling under the onslaught.

Mrs Crabtree would make mincemeat of him

CHAPTER FOURTEEN

'I was wrong,' I admitted to the entire workforce of Shannon Investigations Limited. 'Nadya didn't steal the money.'

We were gathered at Toddy's, seated at Norman's proprietorial corner table where he could watch the door, the customers and the till with one economical movement of his head. The place, as was the norm nowadays, was packed, tonight's privileged diners having booked at least a couple of weeks earlier. Toddy's had been 'discovered'. Over the past month it had been reviewed by every restaurant critic worth his salt, and Michael Winner too. Only joking, Mr Winner, sir. The praise, rare for him, that he had lavished on Toddy's angels on horseback, herb-crusted rack of lamb and bread and butter pudding had carried more weight than a Sumo wrestler on steroids. The accompanying photograph of a smiling Winner with arm draped round Toddy's shoulder had managed to capture the friendly atmosphere and old-fashioned charm of the place. In the background was the long bar, to one side one of the wooden tables laid with thick trencher-style place mats instead of tablecloth, heavy cutlery and sparkling crystal glasses. The oak panelling on the wall evoked solidity and signalled that Toddy's was a place you could trust.

I had returned home to find the building empty. The mobile had rung – wouldn't you believe it – when I was in the shower, washing the smells of Oldbrook from my hair. A smug-sounding Arlene had told me that she would meet me at the restaurant, and then proceeded to give me a list of instructions about emptying and replenishing litter trays, filling up bowls with fresh food and water, and how to tie a knot in a piece of string for use in *quality time*. She forgot about putting each cat over my shoulder and burping it, but I did that anyway, just in case. With time now running short, I threw on a pair of jeans, a T-shirt and a leather jacket (all in black) and set off at a brisk pace for Island Gardens station. As I passed the shop selling souvenirs I caught sight of my reflection in the window and did a swift double-take: it looked as if I had seen the dark and become a fully paid-up member of OWN. I gave a shudder, entered the Asian newsagent's for a pack of cigarettes and, through a discussion with the owner about the paucity of good leg spin bowlers, reassurance that I was still a normal human being. Or as normal as a cricket fanatic can be. At least no horns had magically appeared with the donning of the black.

'No, you were right,' Arlene said. 'She did it. Nadya stole the money.'

I shook my head in a mixture of disbelief and puzzlement. 'But you were the one who first suggested that Nadya was innocent and had been abducted.'

'I've changed my mind,' she said. 'If you can change yours, then why can't I? It's supposed to be a woman's prerogative, after all.'

'Do you have a reason?' I asked. Does a woman need a reason? 'Or is this simply that world-beater of all logic, female intuition?'

Arlene smiled, the hazel eyes twinkling mischievously. 'All in good time,' she said. Hell, she was going to make me sweat; drag it out till the last moment when she revealed the vital clue with a magician's flourish. 'Why don't you go first, Nick? Tell us the reason for your *volte-face*.'

'Okay,' I agreed, willing to play her game. Not that there was any point in doing otherwise.

'Hang on,' Arthur interrupted.

'It means *about turn*,' explained Norman.

'I know that,' Arthur protested. 'Did you think I reckoned it had something to do with half-dressed people running in and out of doors and jumping over settees? I was going to say I wouldn't mind us ordering first, that's all. I've had nothing to eat today but a bleeding sandwich.'

'You should specify your beef well done,' I said.

'It was cheese,' he said. 'And bloody cream cheese to boot. On that dark bread that tastes like cardboard and has little bits inside that play havoc with my fillings.'

Norman, with a barely perceptible movement of his hand, summoned one of the attentive waiters, waved aside the menus we knew by heart, and let him recite tonight's mouth-watering specials. As I listened I felt Arlene's hand on my knee and glanced over to absorb her playful wink. She was wearing her 'trailing incognito' outfit – a dark blue suit of long, immaculately tailored jacket and boot-cut trousers, with pointed-toe, spiked-heel ankle boots – which would have blended in perfectly in Bond Street, but in Oldbrook was about as easy to spot as Ian Paisley in a whispering contest.

When the waiter departed I reached for my glass of wine, took an appreciative sip of Norman's favourite Pomerol, and said with a heavy sigh, 'It's been a helluva day.'

'We know,' they chorused to my surprise.

'What is this?' I asked. 'The annual dinner of the Psychic Society?'

'You were mentioned on the radio,' Arlene said with pride.

'Ali Khan?' I groaned, remembering the media opportunity of his opening of the new Youth Centre.

'Quick-thinking hero saves equal opportunities campaigner from brutal racist attack.' She squeezed my hand.

'I wish Ali Khan was as quick thinking,' I said. 'I am trying to be as inconspicuous as possible within the council. What the hell are the people in Treasury going to think?'

'It's good publicity,' Norman said.

'For Ali Khan.'

'And for us. Ali Khan told the media that you were an accountant, at his shop by happy coincidence for a meeting when the mob smashed their way in, baying for his blood.'

'Mob! Baying for his blood! And what did Ali Khan and I do, fight them back-to-back?'

'No, he gave you all the credit,' Norman said, then frowned. 'I wish he'd said *forensic* accountant though.'

'Or why not fraud detective?' I said. 'That *really* would have blown my cover.'

Norman nodded. 'I suppose so,' he said with exaggerated reluctance and a burgeoning grin. 'Still, maybe we can make something more of the incident when this Oldbrook case is over. Might be a good slogan in it: "If you're faced with fraud or an angry mob, Nick Shannon's the man for the job."'

'Norman!'

His grin erupted.

'Now stop it, Norman,' Arlene said, trying not to snigger. 'Nick's had a hard day. Don't wind him up.'

'Did Ali Khan say anything else in this interview?'

'Like what?' Norman said. 'Oh I see, you mean apart from how you caught the bullets in your teeth?'

'Ignore him, Nick,' Arlene soothed. 'He's just jealous, because he can't leap tall ledgers at a single bound.'

'Huh,' Norman said disdainfully. 'I favour brains over brawn any day.'

'Thank you,' I said.

'Thank you very much,' Arthur added menacingly.

'Sorry,' Norman said. 'Bad joke. It takes all sorts to make a world. Horses for courses, and all that.'

'In fact,' said Arlene, moving on quickly before Norman could dig himself deeper inside the hole, 'Ali Khan made quite a speech.'

'You surprise me.'

'He said that violence was not the way; that the attack

would not sway him one inch from his determination to rid the country' – the country, note, not just Oldbrook any more – 'of the evil of racial prejudice. Then he stressed that he wished for no retaliation.'

'Well then, that's his victory in the forthcoming by-election cut and dried.'

'He did mention that too,' she said. 'The by-election, I mean. Didn't presume to claim winning was a foregone conclusion though.'

'Following in the footsteps of John Major,' Norman said paradoxically. 'Seems that he started out in politics as a local councillor. What odds do you give, Nick, on Ali Khan one day living in Number 10?'

'Long at the moment.'

I explained about the imminent resignation from the council and withdrawal of his candidacy from the by-election if the money wasn't replaced by the newly reduced deadline of Festival Friday.

'Which brings us back,' Norman said, 'to you and Arlene and your pantomime act. "Oh yes, she did. Oh no, she didn't." What made you change your mind, Nick?'

The first course arrived. I looked longingly at my smoked eel with fresh horseradish sauce, took a piece of paper out of my pocket and placed it in the middle of the table. 'Practise saying that to yourselves while we eat. Then I'll reveal all.'

Normally Arlene wouldn't have been able to resist coming in with a seductive, 'Promises, promises', but the words I had written down reduced her to silent puzzle-ment. The three of them stared blankly at the paper, shrugged their shoulders and, under the irresistible pressure of the sight of food and the tantalising aromas rising up from plates, did as I asked.

'This is what Nadya is supposed to have done,' I said, my plate cleared and my glass replenished. I described the principle of zero balance, the placing of surplus money on the overnight market, the setting up of the new account and the subsequent transfer of the four hundred thousand pounds. 'The money was wired to the account of Megacom Films and Videos.'

'And?' they asked.

'I met the borough council's bank manager. He gave me the full details of the transaction. Megacom's account is in the Isle of Man.'

Norman groaned, as I had done a few hours earlier. 'Then that's the last anyone will ever see of the money,' he concluded.

I nodded.

'What's so special about the Isle of Man?' Arlene asked.

'Witches and motorbike racing,' Arthur said.

Arlene shook her head at the vision. 'I suppose the broomstick had to go out of fashion one day.'

'What Arthur says is true,' I said. 'But the Isle of Man is also one of the few places where you can form a bearer-share company.'

'Is this going to be complicated?' Arthur asked anxiously. ''Cos, if so, then another bottle might help.'

'It never has in the past, Arthur,' I pointed out.

But Norman took pity on him and waved our near-empty bottle in the air.

'In fact,' he said, 'it's all very simple. A bearer-share company can be formed with no names, no pack drill. It's just a company with one share issued. Whoever has the certificate for that one share in their possession (hence, bearer share) has simply to show it at a bank. Legally, in the Isle of Man, this is all the evidence required that the bearer has complete control of the company and its assets.' He turned to me. 'So, what is your thinking? That Nadya, as a mere student, wouldn't have got as far in the textbook as the chapter entitled "All you ever wanted to know about money laundering but were afraid to ask"? Is that it, Nick?'

'No. Read out what is written on the piece of paper.'

'"Megacom Films and Videos,"' they chanted.

'Exactly right,' I said. 'The woman who made the telephone call to the bank said it in precisely the same way as you three.' Although in a slightly higher key to Arthur, I imagine. 'Which is how I know it wasn't Nadya. Because, like her mother when talking about the tutor's name reminding her of an old film star, Nadya would have said Megacom *Fillums* and Videos.'

'Is that it?' Norman said derisively. 'The whole foundation of your conviction that Nadya is innocent is the pronunciation of one word?'

'The letter combination of *lm* is alien to the language of an Indian or Bangladeshi. It is impossible for them to say. Believe me. I tried it out on some of the Asian staff at the bank. They just couldn't do it.'

'Maybe Nadya was an exception to your rule,' Arlene said, against a distracting background of Arthur repeating the word *film* over and over again. 'She was brought up in this country, after all.'

'But taught to speak by her mother and father. Speech patterns learned during those early formative years are almost impossible to change. No, Nadya did not make that phone call.'

'Oh yes, she did,' Arlene said.

'This is where we came in,' said Norman, shaking his head. 'I think we ought to give Arlene a chance to air her theory. It can't be any more flimsy.'

'Oh, damn,' she said.

'Having second thoughts already?' I asked impishly.

'No, Mr Wise Guy, I am not.'

'Then what's the problem?'

'Here comes my *confit* of duck. And it looks delicious.'

'The tutor's name was Burton,' Arlene said, dabbing the napkin lightly on her lips. 'I went to see him this morning.'

'Excuse me,' I said, 'but wasn't your allotted task to follow Mrs Khan? Arthur, why didn't you stop her?'

'Don't blame me,' he grunted irritably. 'I was following

128

the son, wasn't I? Can't be in two places at bleeding once.'

'It's not Arthur's fault,' Arlene said. 'Nor is it mine. In fact, it's your fault, Nick.'

'Me? What did I do?'

'Caused a flurry of cops around Ali Khan. And his home.'

'I'll try to remember that in future. The next time I'm confronted by two thugs armed with a cosh and a jack-hammer. Don't cause a flurry, Shannon.'

'You know what I mean,' she said. 'I'm very proud of you.'

'Gee,' I said, feigning embarrassment – but not too hard.

'But,' she said, 'with the cops swarming around, if I'd hung around the Khans' house any longer I would have finished up in the cells. And I tried to phone you to tell you what I was going to do, but you had your mobile switched off.'

'I forgot to switch it on,' I said.

'Huh,' she replied scornfully. 'Let that be a lesson to you.'

'Yes, Miss.'

'So, since I couldn't follow Mrs Khan, as per my lord and master's instructions, I decided I might as well do something useful instead. I phoned the LSE from my mobile and got them to give me the name of Nadya's tutor. Went to see him down at the Aldwych – do you remember the Aldwych, Nick?'

Of course I did. It was how we had first met: Arlene coming out of the back door of the Savoy en route to the Aldwych, turning the wrong way, ending up on the Embankment, prey to a mugger with a flick-knife. One well-placed kick from me had been enough to deal with him. Arlene and I were the only people who, when hearing a cry of pain, could say, 'They're playing our song.' It had been the only time in our relationship where she had been the magnet for trouble, not I. Yet she coped; stuck with me despite my fatal attraction. I reached across, pulled her hand towards me and intertwined my fingers with hers. We didn't need to be married to be locked together for better, for worse.

'This Burton guy,' she continued, gazing into my eyes, 'was surprised when I told him that Nadya had disappeared. She was a model student – intelligent, diligent, polite and respectful. He had high hopes for her; expected her to graduate top of the class and be the subject of an auction among the big accountancy firms.'

'So she would have been familiar with bearer-share companies,' Norman stated.

Arlene shrugged. 'Seems that way, I guess.'

But that couldn't be the basis of her conviction that Nadya had stolen the money. The topic had only just been raised. It could not have come up in their conversation.

'What else did he tell you?' I probed.

'Nothing. Nadya was a very private student. She never spoke to him about her home life or mentioned any problems. He did, however, give me the name of Nadya's best friend.'

'Who was obviously your next port of call.'

'Girl called Claire. Lives in Highbury.' Arlene pronounced it *Highberry*, as if saying hello to Chuck. 'It's kinda nice there. Big old houses. Smart shops and restaurants.'

'Used to be a real dump,' said Arthur, a contradictory hint of nostalgia in his voice. 'But since the yuppies have moved in, everything's changed. Even the Arsenal football team doesn't send you to sleep any more. Can't rely on nothing nowadays. Bleeding fashion has a lot to answer for.'

'I think we're straying from the point, Arthur,' I said, sounding more like Mrs Crabtree than I had intended. 'So, Arlene, what earth-shattering fact did Claire reveal?'

'She told me where to look for Nadya,' Arlene said, her hazel eyes sparkling with girlish self-satisfaction.

'Where?' we cried, from the edge of our seats.

'Gretna Green.'

CHAPTER FIFTEEN

'You do know where Gretna Green is?' I asked. 'And why people go there?'

'What is it with you Limeys?' Arlene said, her voice raised. 'All Americans are dumb or something? You know, I guess you English are just about the most prejudiced nation on the face of this planet.'

'I'm only three-quarters English,' I said defensively.

'Then you're only three-quarters prejudiced,' she replied. 'Remind me – how does it go? All Scots are mean; the Irish are stupid; the Italians are cowards – their tanks were built with five reverse gears and one forward, in case the enemy attacked from the rear; the Spanish are greasy; the French are selfish and arrogant.'

I kicked Arthur under the table. I didn't think his nodding along was likely to ease the situation. Arlene was serious, not joking.

'We are not a race of xenophobes,' Norman chipped in.

'I know,' Arlene said. 'The prejudice even extends to your own country. People from the north wear flat caps, race whippets and drink gallons of flat beer.'

'And that's only the women,' I said. It was a vain attempt at making her laugh, to defuse the bomb that was ticking inside her.

She scowled at me, and continued with her list, working closer to home. 'Essex girls are bimbos, east Londoners are crooks, Cockneys are cheerful fools, always whistling in the face of adversity.'

'And there's a bloke just down the street I'm not too

'sure about,' said Arthur unhelpfully.

'Look,' I protested, 'we all make generalisations. Mostly it's just a joke.'

'Mostly,' she said.

'And if we do, it doesn't mean that we treat an individual Scotsman or Welshman – you forgot those, singing killjoys, by the way – any different to anyone else. I can't speak for OWN, but you'll find that the vast majority of the English take people on their merits.'

She shrugged, unconvinced.

'If we've offended you,' I said, bitterly sorry, 'then it was unintended. We apologise profusely. Norman, Arthur and I are all so used to taking the Mickey out of each other we forget that others might not understand that it's just a stupid masculine non-embarrassing way of showing affection. And,' I added, genuinely puzzled, 'I never appreciated it mattered so much to you.'

'Well, it does,' she said.

'Go on, honey.'

'Two reasons,' she began somewhat reluctantly. 'First, I wasn't always called Tucker, you know. My maiden name was Martinez. I'm part Puerto Rican.'

'Ah,' I said.

'Don't you "Ah" me, Nick Shannon, as if a complex set of neuroses has just been laid bare for all to see.'

'Sorry,' I said. 'Rough time at school?'

'Yeah, well, I'd rather not talk about it.'

'Maybe another time, huh?' I said.

'Maybe.'

'But didn't you bring up this subject?' Norman said.

'Mainly because of the second reason,' she said. 'This case revolves around prejudice. It's vital you all appreciate that fact.'

'I think I had made that mental leap,' I said.

'Ali Khan's prejudice?' she said.

'But I thought he was a paragon of virtue. Equality for all men.'

'But not for women,' she said triumphantly.

We all stared blankly at her.

'That's why Nadya ran away to Gretna Green. She's eloped. See, I did know why kids go there.'

'I think you'd better go back to the beginning,' I said, struggling with the mental leaps. 'Tell us exactly what Claire said.'

'Ali Khan, in many ways,' she said, 'is a modern Muslim. He is tolerant of other religions, believes in live and let live. That all men are equal under the skin.'

'But,' I said.

'But as far as women are concerned, he is still living in the Dark Ages – adheres to the belief that when in public women should walk five paces behind. And when he's in the family home, like most men he wants his woman to be a nanny in the nursery, a master chef in the kitchen and a whore in the bedroom.'

''Ere. Hold on,' Arthur said, blushing.

'Arlene may be right,' I jumped in, before he could say that he wouldn't stand for language like that from a woman. 'I've seen the Khans' bedroom; it's like being inside a harem. And at the supermarket he didn't seem to treat his female staff with much respect – just barks orders at them. He even calls the Chief Executive, Helen Ripley, *dear lady*.'

'But what has this to do with Nadya?' Norman asked.

'Ali Khan had Nadya's whole life plotted out for her. She was due to be married; an arranged marriage. Nothing wrong with the guy, but she just didn't love him. But Ali Khan ran roughshod over her objections. The date was set, the dowry agreed. And after the wedding, Nadya was expected to give up a promising career and become a dutiful wife and mother.'

'So she decided,' Norman concluded, 'to ruin her father's career; steal the money and run off with her true love. Who is Young Lochinvar anyway?'

Arlene shook her head. 'Claire didn't know. Nadya was very secretive about him. They'd met at some party, then went out together to discos, and that led to candlelit dinners at restaurants far from Oldbrook. But whoever he is, Ali Khan would not approve. That thought left Nadya with no option but to hightail it to the Highlands with a suitcase of cash to start a new life.'

I let her theory sink in, tried to digest it, fit it in with other facts.

'You don't look happy, Nick,' Norman said.

'Because,' Arlene said smugly, 'a mere woman has proved him wrong.'

'It's not that,' I said. 'Something doesn't quite fit.'

'Like what?' Arlene said petulantly.

'For one thing, there was eight million pounds of surplus funds going on to that day's overnight market. Why didn't she take the lot instead of a measly four hundred grand?'

'Maybe, unlike some people,' she said, staring blatantly at Norman, 'Nadya is not greedy. Just took what she felt she needed to set her up.'

I shrugged, unconvinced.

'And couldn't you apply that argument to whoever the thief was?' she persisted.

'I suppose so,' I said thoughtfully. 'I told you it doesn't make sense.' I gave a heavy sigh. 'Let's look at it another way: Nadya is Top Gun of the accounting set, right?'

'Right,' she said hesitantly, not knowing where I was leading but the ring of confidence in her voice nevertheless wearing a little thin with the approach of technicalities.

'So she steals the money on a Friday,' I said.

'What the hell difference does that make? Is there some law against stealing money on a Wednesday or Thursday?'

'Yeah,' I said, 'it's called fraud.'

'Ha, ha.'

'What Nick is trying to say, Arlene,' Norman intervened, 'is that the best time to commit a fraud is on a Friday. You then have all weekend to make your escape.'

'And even better, Norman,' I said, jogging his memory, 'if there's a bank holiday. You get an extra day, or even two.'

'Yeah, well,' he shrugged awkwardly. 'The point is, if

134

Nadya is so clever and she commits the crime on a Friday then why does she wait till Monday before disappearing?'

'That's why I still reckon she didn't do it,' I said.

'Okay, Mr Wise Guy,' Arlene said, 'then answer me this. If she didn't do it, then why had she taken a suitcase filled with clothes and make-up? Who are we dealing with – New Age kidnappers who set out their victims' rights in a charter? We'd like you to be comfortable during your captivity, Miss, so please report with all your worldly goods tomorrow morning at nine o'clock? Huh! My explanation is the only one that fits.'

'Not necessarily,' I said, constructing an alternative theory. 'Let's say – as I suggested earlier – that some other woman in Treasury made the phone call to transfer the money. Let's also say that this act was planned a while ago, and in order to deflect the hunt for the culprit Nadya is allocated the role of patsy. But how can it be arranged that she disappears at the appropriate time?'

Arthur shrugged.

'A honey trap,' I said. 'What we have here is a conspiracy – a partnership. The woman who made the phone call is in league – in bed for all we know – with someone who sweet-talks Nadya. She's young, inexperienced and vulnerable. Young Lochinvar makes her fall in love with him, suggests the elopement. That would explain the suitcase. *Cherchez l'homme*, remember? Whoever the real culprits are, they have Nadya locked up somewhere.'

'And what about OWN?' Norman asked, frowning.

'Either uninvolved,' I said, shrugging my shoulders, 'or, more worryingly, the real thieves are members of OWN. That gives them a second motive for stealing the money and kidnapping Nadya – forcing Ali Khan to stand down from the election. What do you think?'

'It seems to me . . .' Arthur began slowly.

'Yes,' we said expectantly.

'. . . that we still don't have a bleeding clue.'

*

135

We did what all sensible people do when faced with an intractable problem: ordered another bottle of wine and changed the subject.

'How was your day, Arthur?' I asked.

'Terrible,' he said, reaching for his wineglass and sniffing at the contents to satisfy himself that this bottle was as excellent as the previous two – or was it three? 'I followed the kid to a sixth-form college. He spent all bleeding day there. And I spent all bleeding day staring out of the window of a poncey vegetarian "café" opposite the main gates.'

'Eating cheese sandwiches.'

'And drinking fruit tea. Jesus, whoever invented fruit tea should be strung up.'

'Or made to drink it,' I ventured.

'Yeah. Serve him right.'

'So what happened when Ali Khan's son finally emerged?'

'Nothing. Him and a gang of his cronies mooched about, took me on a tour of Oldbrook, dropped into an amusement arcade, a coffee bar and then to the pictures.'

'What was showing?' I asked, as if it might be relevant.

'How do I know?' he said. 'It was all in foreign, wasn't it? Not even any bleeding subtitles.'

'And when it was over?'

'They hung around the foyer talking to other kids. And do you know,' he said, an expression of shock on his face, 'you can't get a bleeding Drink-on-a-Stick nowadays. They don't make them any more. "No demand," the bloke said. "Well, I'm bloody demanding one," I said.' He sighed. 'Didn't make no difference though.'

'What about me?' Norman asked. 'When is it my turn on the Dear Diary slot?'

'The floor is yours,' I said.

'I know that,' he grinned. 'And the walls. I own the place.'

'Are you going to make us drag it out of you, Norman?' Arlene said. 'Not sulking because we left you till last?'

'No, my dear,' he said. 'Simply despondent.'

'You don't fancy our chances of recovering any money for Mrs Crabtree and her band of little old ladies?'

Norman shook his head.

'What did your searches reveal?'

'That he's smart,' he said, 'and operates just outside the reach of the law.'

'*Modus operandi?*'

'Very simple. Blackstone – he's our con man – has started, and subsequently closed down, twelve companies over the past three years alone. Wide range of fields – the funeral business, a building contractor's, mail-order firm, double glazing and so on – the common link being that they have all involved getting money up front from the customers. Each company has been a wholly owned subsidiary of a holding company, of which Blackstone and his wife are the sole shareholders and directors. He lets each company function for around six months: enough time to do a little legitimate business and to receive a substantial amount of advanced payments or deposits on goods and services. Then he hits the subsidiary with a huge management fee from the holding company, supposedly to cover his and his wife's services, rent and rates, marketing and the like. This fee – surprise, surprise – wipes out all the assets of the company, so he declares it bankrupt, shuts it down and starts all over again.'

'And this is legal?' Arlene asked, aghast.

'Barely,' I said, 'but yes. Blackstone's lawyers, if a case ever came to court, would put up a defence of initial poor planning, insufficient controls, downturn in the market, lack of demand – it doesn't really matter, since it would be virtually impossible to prove *intent* to defraud. He's treading a fine line, sure, but only a small percentage of fraud cases ever end up in court – and for those that do, the record on prosecutions is pretty damned poor. If the worst came to the worst, he would salt away the money some place where the authorities can't touch it and maybe do a year or two in an open prison. More likely he'd get probation or community service.'

'But that's . . .' Arlene spluttered, searching for the words to communicate her utter disgust.

'Yeah,' I said. 'That's life. Not fair, and never has been.'

Norman nodded. 'I agree,' he said, 'but there's fraud, and there's fraud. Some victims deserve to be hit – rough justice for what they've stolen from their customers. Others – the little people, the ordinary man and woman in the street – should be protected from the likes of Blackstone. According to my calculations from going through the holding company's accounts, I estimate Blackstone and his wife to be worth at least three million pounds – all taken out of the pockets of those who can least afford it.'

'Can I thump this Blackstone?' Arthur asked.

'No, Arthur,' I said. 'As much as we would all like that, you cannot thump him. If you do, then you'll be the one who winds up in court. And ends up in prison.'

'Strategy,' Norman said profoundly.

'Well?' I asked.

'We need one,' he said.

'Tomorrow,' I said, trying to sound as if I had everything under control, the many strands firmly in my grasp and merely requiring to be reeled in, 'Arthur and Arlene will visit Blackstone.'

'But,' said Arlene, 'I thought you were going with Arthur. And, anyway, what's the point? Blackstone's not going to hand over twenty-five grand.'

'We have to give him a last chance to do the decent thing. Conscience, Arlene. And I reckon our best shot is the combination of Beauty and the Beast.'

'Thanks a bundle,' muttered Arthur.

'If you lose your temper with Blackstone, Arthur, I think Arlene will handle the situation better than I. She'll be less tempted to join in for one thing.'

Norman peered at me with deep interest and suspicion.

'And in any case,' I said quickly, 'I need to spend some time in Oldbrook – suss out the staff in Treasury; immerse myself in the accounts; make some progress on finding a fraud to generate some income.'

'How's it look?' Norman asked.

'Let's just say there are some interesting avenues to explore.' I took McCready's list from my pocket and passed it to him. He squinted at it, put on his glasses and squinted slightly less. 'Once, that is,' I added while he read, 'I actually manage to get down to some work. The strange thing is that no one in Oldbrook seems to have any sense of urgency. I almost get the impression they want me to fail, and Ali Khan to fall from a great height. They've even given me an assistant who could win the Witless Himbo of the Year Contest.'

'Sounds interesting,' said Arlene. 'You must introduce me.'

'Gone off brains, have we?'

'You assume too much,' she pouted. 'What makes you think I was ever on them?'

'So you'll be starting,' Norman said, 'with Commercial Services.'

I nodded. He knew me as only a mentor could.

'How did you work that out?' Arthur asked him, impressed.

'Because it's at the bottom of the sheet. Tuck away what you least want investigated below a long list of time-consuming tasks.'

'That was my theory,' I agreed.

'Of course,' Norman said, 'there is another possibility.'

'I've already thought of that too,' I said. 'Been through the bluff and double-bluff bit till I was going round in ever-decreasing circles. But I may need to call on you.'

'That's what I'm here for,' he said.

'What about Mrs Khan and the son?' Arlene said. 'We can't follow them if we're seeing Blackstone.'

Norman can take first watch on Mrs Khan. I'll talk to the boy in the afternoon. What time did he leave college today?'

139

'Around four,' Arthur said.

'Okay,' I said, leaning back in the chair. 'Time we went home. Busy day tomorrow.'

Norman called over a waiter and asked him to telephone for a cab. 'Do you want to stay with us tonight, Arthur?'

'Makes sense,' he said. 'We can get an early start that way. Don't forget,' he said to me, 'we've got fifteen laps to do in the morning.'

And here was I thinking the day couldn't get any worse.

It wasn't the most comfortable cab ride any of us had ever had; three of us squashed together in the back and Arthur wedged in the inadequate front seat with his elbow in the driver's ribs. Nor was it the most auspicious arrival.

The front door was wide open. Lights blazed throughout the building.

'Stay here,' Arthur shouted, racing from the cab.

I extricated myself from between Norman and Arlene, and ran after him.

'Bloody hell,' I heard him say from inside the hall.

'Christ,' I said, my heart sinking as I surveyed the mess. Computers lay smashed on the floor, chairs broken or fabric slit by a knife. The still-wet lightning-strike logo of OWN dripped down one wall. The entire contents of the fridge and kitchen cupboards had been emptied and distributed liberally over every surface. There was a smell of rotten eggs – or was it just rottenness? – in the air.

'What is it?' Arlene asked anxiously from behind me.

'We've been trashed,' I said, shaking my head. 'Done over. And a bloody good job they've made of it.'

She brushed past me in a panic, blind to any danger that may still have lurked somewhere in the building.

'Laurel,' she screamed. 'Hardy,' she sobbed

CHAPTER SIXTEEN

I grabbed Arlene by the shoulders; spun her round so that she was facing me; held her very tightly, partly as an act of comfort, but mostly to root her to the spot. I didn't want her wandering around the building like the kamikaze heroine of a horror movie before Arthur and I had checked it out. It was possible, although unlikely given the late hour and the thoroughness of the trashing, that we had disturbed the vandals and that in some dark corner of one of the six floors they were hiding, waiting to jump us. My main worry, however, was what scenes we would find upstairs. The past vision of a cat nailed to a door invaded my mind and brought back the mixed emotions of revulsion and anger I had felt on first gazing on the empty eye sockets of its face.

'Stay here,' I ordered, and then, seeing the tears in her eyes, immediately thought of a better alternative. Waiting wouldn't be easy – Arlene needed something to occupy her mind.

'Norman,' I said, handing him my car keys, 'take Arlene outside. Sit in the car. Lock the doors. Use the mobile phone to call the police. After that, the insurance company – they must have either a twenty-four-hour helpline or an answering machine.' I paused; examined his face while fighting back the panic. 'Christ, we are insured, aren't we?'

'Of course,' he replied. 'With Future Assurance. I got a discount for past services rendered. Don't worry, Nick.

We'll come out of this all right. Might even make a small profit.'

Arlene stared at him wide-eyed.

'Sorry,' he said. 'I didn't mean to be insensitive. Wasn't thinking, that's all. Come on, love. Let's make ourselves useful.'

I squeezed Arlene's shoulders encouragingly, kissed her on the cheek, the salty taste of her tears lingering on my tongue and in my heart. I brushed away the thin trickle from her eyes with my thumbs, turned her towards the door, and released her into Norman's care.

'Downstairs first,' I said to Arthur. 'Then floor by floor.'

He nodded grimly and marched off to the right, entering the front office and then the kitchen. I went left to cover my office. With each step, glass from the computer screen, coffee granules and sugar crystals crunched underfoot. The table had been upturned, files lay scattered on the floor. I bent down to pick up the two marked *Crabtree* and *Khan*, hesitated and pulled back.

'Try not to touch anything,' I shouted through to Arthur, hoping that the Scene-of-Crimes Officers might pick up a tell-tale fingerprint.

The room was clear – if you can call what looked like the result of a hurricane clear. I exited at the far end and met Arthur at the back door which led to the landing stage. He shook his head, either to indicate that his search had been unsuccessful or in disbelief.

We mounted the stairs, Arthur leading the way and I following close behind. At the top he moved LA-cop style to one side of the door to the communal living area, covering me as I entered.

The devastation was less here, but only, I suspected, because they had now realised how extensive the old warehouse was. Their aim had presumably been to cause maximum damage in the minimum amount of time. The coffee table had been split in two by what I could only assume was one mighty swing of a jack-hammer; the fabric of the regency-striped sofas had been slashed; the sky-blue curtains liberally sprayed with black paint.

Arthur stuck his head round the door. 'They've smashed the bath and basin,' he grunted. 'The kitchen's a mess too. Broken every bottle of booze in sight. The floor's awash.'

'Any sign of the kittens?'

'No,' he said, looking grim. 'Or of the bastards who did this. Just let me get my hands on them. I'll tear them from limb to limb.'

'Don't make any hasty decisions, Arthur. I reckon we might be able to think of something slower and a lot more painful.'

'Yeah,' he nodded. 'I'll work on it. Come on, Nick. Onwards and upwards.'

Methodically, and with due caution, we progressed from floor to floor and room to room, trying to stay focused and not let our boiling anger cloud our judgement or slow our reactions. It wasn't easy. Norman's bathroom had received the same treatment as the one below, the acrylic bath holed in one side, one half of the basin lying on the floor, the other half hanging by the pipework to the wall; smaller items of furniture in his bedroom had been reduced to kindling, the larger pieces merely upended so that clothes and bedding spilt across the carpet. The fire-break on the fourth floor was untouched – its emptiness must have been a big disappointment to them. Bloody shame!

It was as we mounted the stairs to Arlene's and my living quarters that we heard the noise – a bedside lamp, judging by the thud closely followed by the sound of the tinkling glass. Arthur put his finger to his lips, signalled me to the left of the door, stood full-square facing it himself. He raised his size twelve boot, and kicked.

The door flew open; slammed back into the wall with such force that it would have caused permanent brain damage if anyone had been hiding behind it – and if they'd had a brain. I leap inside and to the right, Arthur broke left.

We both adopted the ready-for-anything crouch and scanned the room.

The contents of the cat litter tray had been tipped on to the bed, where, judging by the non-feline ammonia smell emanating from that direction, someone had committed the final indignity. The bedside lamp rocked slowly from side to side on the floor, its shade askew, its bulb shattered. One of the wardrobe doors was open, exposing a row of Arlene's dresses and suits – or what was left of them after a knife had been systematically drawn diagonally across each item. We padded silently to either side of the wardrobe. Arthur placed his hand on the knob of the closed door and prepared to throw it open. There was a slight movement of the hanging clothes. From the folds of a long evening dress a face peered out.

Laurel.

He looked around the room, then up at me with tilted head and an expression that seemed to say, 'It wasn't me. Honest. Well, maybe the lamp. But that hardly notices, does it?'

I scooped him up and tucked him inside my jacket. 'Where's your brother?' I asked, hiding my foolishness under the guise of anthropomorphism. If this had been a scene from *Flipper* or *Lassie* I would have received an answering mew informing me that Hardy was down a mine shaft giving mouth-to-mouth resuscitation to the local mayor's adventurous son who had been caught in a roof collapse. Probably would have told me the geological composition of the rocks too. But this was real life – God, it was real life.

On the rug next to the bed I noticed a pool of blood.

A small pool, admittedly. But Hardy was just a little kitten.

I knelt down and peered under the bed. A furry bundle was curled up unmoving against the corner of the wall. On my signal Arthur grabbed the foot of the bed and raised one side in the air, sending a cascade of damp litter against the wall. I crawled underneath and gently wrapped a hand around Hardy; slid him out until I could get my other hand under his back legs and lift him up. As he lay still in my palm, I felt the warmth of his blood trickling through my fingers – and the merest flicker of a heartbeat.

'You take him downstairs,' Arthur said, after clearing the lump in his throat. 'I'll check the last floor.'

Gingerly I climbed down the stairs, Laurel inside my jacket, Hardy pressed against my chest. There was a deep wound running along his belly and down the flank of his leg. Bloody Ali Khan, I thought. Why couldn't he keep his self-serving mouth shut? None of this need ever have happened.

'We must make a decision,' I said. 'About this case.'

The four of us were camped on the dusty floor of the partially renovated building next door, sitting uncomfortably on two tartan car rugs from Arthur's van, surrounded by bags of cement, tins of paint and planks of wood of assorted sizes. Hardy was in the safe-keeping of the local vet, Laurel was stretched out languidly on Arlene's lap. A pessimistic, seen-it-all-before-faced SOCO was going through the motions of examining the debris of our possessions for clues that would pinpoint someone within OWN. A loss adjuster from Future Assurance – Jeez, we hadn't even put in a claim yet and already they were trying to adjust our expectations downwards – was due to arrive at nine o'clock in the morning, a little under five hours' time. We were into Day Three of the Money Race. Either eight or none still to go, depending on the decision we were about to take.

'What happened tonight,' I said, 'was a warning. We have two options. Heed it – and pull out of the Ali Khan case. Or continue – and be prepared for what will be an inevitable escalation. If we stick with the case we can be sure that next time it won't be fabrics that get slashed and a kitten who gets knifed. It will be us. So, what's it to be?'

I looked at each of them in turn, wondering who would be the first to speak. Arlene, still shocked and dazed from the trauma? Norman, mentally preparing a list of invoices for the ex-forger Toddy to create as evidence for his inflated claim? Or Arthur, brow creased, head shaking from side to side?

'I don't like a job left half-done,' Arthur said. 'Let's see it through to the end.'

'To the bitter end, my friend?' I said.

He shrugged. 'If that's what it takes, yes. I'm not going to let a bunch of fascist bastards – pardon my French, Arlene – push me around.'

She nodded her agreement. 'My sentiments entirely. These hoods not only trashed our offices, they also violated my home. That's only one step removed from rape in my book. Right now, I don't know how I can ever face going into that building again. Someone's gonna have to pay for that. If we quit now, they get away scot-free. If we persist, then by setting ourselves up as targets we stand a chance of catching them. I vote with Arthur. Stick with it.'

'Norman?' I said.

'It's not going to look good if we let ourselves be bounced off our first case. The word will spread that we can't stand the heat. Give in this time and we might as well give up permanently. I'm for continuing too.' He grinned at me. 'But my vote is academic, isn't it, Nick? You've never quit on anything in your life. I can't see you starting now. Old habits die hard.'

I gave a helpless smile.

'Then we're unanimous,' I said. 'You know, I think OWN made a big mistake tonight. Now this is personal. Now this is war.'

CHAPTER SEVENTEEN

Day Three

'Morning, Shannon,' Adam said with infuriating brightness.

What was it with him? Couldn't he see the mad cast to my bloodshot eye? Still, at least he'd omitted the inappropriate adjective *good*. I must try to be objective about him. Which wasn't easy right now.

I was tired and irritable, the former the result of three hours' sleep and the latter the prospect of never catching up on those precious missing hours during the time we would be staying at Arthur's noisy Soho flat. How we would all fit in without constantly tripping over each other, I didn't know. Or, more pertinently, how we would cope with the continuous nocturnal staccato beat of five-inch-high spiked heels on the wooden stairs and the moans and groans in response to cracks of whips from the adjoining rooms. For a while, *client service* would take on a whole new meaning.

Arlene and I, in the harsh light of dawn, had salvaged a clean blouse and shirt respectively from the shredded remnants of our wardrobes – my two suits had suffered from the knife too – and set about packing a few essentials to keep us going till we could confuse economists with an upward blip in the Retail Sales figures for the month. We threw underwear, socks, stockings and shoes into a suitcase and filled a holdall with Arlene's jewellery, cosmetics and the contents of the bathroom cabinet. Then she had set off with Arthur to organise our bolt-hole. Norman had remained behind to progress – and talk up – our claim with the loss adjuster, clean up the spilt drink and food, and close up the building for the duration.

Now I was grunting a curt reply to Adam and hoping that this day would be better than the last.

He wrinkled his nose with a mixture of distaste and surprise as his blue eyes flitted over my creased black jeans, black leather jacket and white open-necked shirt. 'We're looking a bit casual today, aren't we?'

We? A right little master of irony I had as my assistant.

He was wearing a pale grey suit with the faintest blue pinstripe. The cloth was from one of those ultra-expensive bolts – mohair, alpaca, vicuña – that are kept in a back room for special customers, the jacket and trousers so lovingly hand-stitched that I suspected his tailor was a bespectacled little guy in Gloucester with a team of mice working the night shift. I'd have asked Adam for the man's name but, unless the loss adjuster had an uncharacteristic mental aberration, there was no way I could ever afford such a suit. How could *he* afford it, come to that? What was the humble pay of a clerical officer anyway? Did he supplement his income? Was he someone's toy boy? Might that explain it? Was there a Sugar Mama some place who lavished him with gifts and decked him out in finery? Why didn't I like him? What did it matter?

So many questions.

So few answers.

And then I knew.

It wasn't that he was smoother than silk, dumber than Marcel Marceau, prettier than some of the girls I'd gone out with in my pimply youth. It *was* his youth. He was twenty-one. I was jealous; envious of all he would do before responsibility grabbed him by the collar and yanked him from the shallows into the depths of a brave new world.

'Commercial Services beckons, Adam,' I said, sighing in a manner I hoped he would interpret as a world-weary reluctance to respond to his bait. 'We have a day of sifting through dusty invoices ahead of us. Let's get started. Lead the way, please.'

'But the invoices are stored here,' he said. 'We don't have to leave this room.'

'Is that the way you go about your internal audit?'

'Why not?'

'Context, Adam,' I said. Stick with me, kid, and you might learn something. 'Auditing isn't simply about checking invoices and assessing systems in isolation. You need to view the scene,' – of a possible crime – 'sniff the air, get the feel of people, put faces to names. And, hell, it helps to relieve the monotony and stops your legs from atrophying. Come on, let's go.'

He shrugged apathetically and ambled off with a singular lack of urgency in the direction of the stairs. I paused at the coffee machine, bought two cups with my plastic card – big spender – handed one to Adam and gave my system a much-needed shot of caffeine.

'What do you do around here when you need a cigarette?' I asked, thinking of the other chemical stimulant that might keep me awake.

'Chew gum,' he replied.

Such a help.

We descended two flights and entered a large rectangular office where the weak rays of the September sun filtered through the open slats of cream-coloured vertical blinds, throwing long shafts of light on the black ash desks – and the rosewood desks, and the walnut-effect plastic-topped desks, and the . . .

The office, unlike Treasury (which was not only grim but also uniformly grim), had no coherent theme or style. It was as if someone had riffled through a catalogue with the aid of a blindfold and a random pin. Every item of furniture – desks, chairs, baffle-boards, screens, filing cabinets – was a one-off. Maybe the individuals working here had complete freedom of choice, but it was hard to credit that their tastes could vary so much. Especially since most of them looked as if they'd been cloned from a Wall Street stock dealer. There were heavy-check wide-lapelled jackets over the backs of chairs, exposed braces, loud ties, button-down-collar shirts – and that was only the women. Not really. They were dressed in short skirts, sheer tops and lethal-looking stilettos. Everyone was either on the phone or tapping away at computer terminals. Some, by practised use of overdeveloped neck and shoulder muscles, were doing both at the same time.

A short, prematurely balding man in his early thirties hurried over to meet – to intercept? – us.

'Adam,' he said, a tense smile pinned to his lips. 'Good to see you. What brings you to our neck of the woods? New recruit, is it?' He nodded his head in my direction. 'Want him kitted out with the full Monty, do you?'

'No, Steve,' Adam replied. 'This is Nick Shannon. He's from an accountancy firm that's chasing the external audit contract. Wants to look around, see what systems you operate, what paperwork you generate, so he can cost out the job.'

'Accountancy firm?' said Steve, looking me up and down with a raised eyebrow.

'You know what it's like, Steve,' I said, smiling and letting his imagination create my excuse.

'Oh, right,' he said, leering and giving me a man-of-the-world wink. 'So, Nick, what I can do you for?'

'Just fill me in with what you do and how you go about it.'

'No problem. Always glad to help a mate of Adam's. Come and take the weight off your feet. And give me that,' he said, reaching for the beaker of coffee still clasped tightly in my hand. 'Let me get you a decent cup. Wouldn't say no, eh? How do you like it? Cappuccino? Espresso?'

'Espresso would be great,' I said, unable to believe my luck.

'Sian,' – or maybe it was Shar'n – he called out as we

moved towards the rosewood desk by the window, 'espresso for Nick, love, and the usual for Adam and me.'

'Well then,' he said, rocking back in a leather chair, 'don't s'pose you've come across a Commercial Services department before.'

'I've seen a few central buying departments though.'

'But this is a world apart, Nick.' Another planet, even? 'State of the art, mate. We were able to set it up from scratch when Oldbrook was created. Didn't have any inherited baggage to weigh us down. Could pick and choose the staff. The people here could out-haggle a Turkish carpet seller. Been to Istanbul, Nick?'

'No,' I replied, hoping he wasn't about to produce his holiday snaps.

'Don't bother,' he said. 'It's a dump.'

Not exactly the in-depth investigative analysis of *The Travel Show*.

'Give me Marbella any day. Anyway,' he continued, 'we can get anything – and I mean anything – cheaper than anyone else. Your eyes will stand on stalks when you see our invoices.'

One can but hope.

I cast an ostentatious glance around the office. 'But do you only get a good price because you're buying oddments?'

'*Oddments.*' He shook his head condescendingly and smiled. 'This is our showroom, Nick. And long-term test-bed. If a manufacturer or wholesaler wants to sell to us, he has to provide us – free of charge – with examples of his wares. That way we can ensure that it meets our exacting specification. And our customers here in the council can inspect the goods, see exactly what they'll be getting for their money. Of course, it also meant the department got furnished at pretty much zero cost – not that that was the intention.' He gave me a wide grin. 'Ah, here's your coffee.'

Sian – let's give her the benefit of the doubt – trip-trapped over on her high heels, her movement hampered by the tightness of her skirt and the tray she was trying to balance while concentrating all her mental energy, such as it was, on fluttering her long black eyelashes at Adam. She handed me a miniature white china cup of espresso, complete with authentic light brown 'cream' on top and individually wrapped Belgian biscuit in the saucer, passed one frothy cappuccino, lightly sprinkled with cocoa powder, to Steve, and another, heavily sprinkled with cocoa powder, to Adam. I took a sip and swooned. She just swooned.

'Good, eh?' said Steve. 'Proper stuff from a proper machine – it's got all the knobs and whistles. The machine's on trial too, in the hope that we'll persuade the catering contractor to take a couple. Before you go, Sian will give you a questionnaire to fill in saying how much you liked it.'

Seemed as if the consumer research was about as unbiased as I was to Adam.

'So, if it's not oddments,' I said, 'then how do you achieve these rock-bottom prices?'

'Power and competition, Nick. It's as simple as that. Putting all – and I mean all – buying through one central department gives us clout, makes us a force in the market.' He drank some of his coffee. A small film of froth stuck to his upper lip. 'And all the big orders – like when we installed the computer network – go up for tender. For the smaller orders, we get three competitive quotes – and then beat the lowest supplier down from there.'

Nothing he had said was new or revolutionary – it was the standard theory behind setting up such central buying departments. The trouble was that power didn't always make for fair competition.

'Tell me about the tendering system. How does that work?'

'I'll tell you what,' he grinned, 'you've got a suspicious mind, my son. You're worried about kickbacks, aren't you?'

Who, me? The thought never crossed my mind – mainly because it had taken root there.

'No chance,' he scoffed. 'The tender system here is tighter than a gnat's chuff.'

'I've heard that before,' I said. Well, not those precise words, I must admit. 'Usually just before the case comes up in court.'

'It's true,' he said. 'My life. All the suppliers invited to tender receive the same documents, stating not just the quantity required but all the terms and conditions too: performance and safety standards, delivery schedules, warranties and indemnities demanded, and the swingeing penalties for not meeting any of our requirements. They all bid on the same basis. It's a level playing field.'

'And what about the opening of the tenders themselves?'

'No room for manoeuvre. No chance of a quick job with the Snopake and pen to alter the bid price. All tenders come in sealed envelopes, signed by the supplier across the seal. They're delivered to McCready and opened by him and three other staff who are selected at random that morning from the internal telephone list. Whoever opens an envelope writes down the tender price of that particular supplier and this is countersigned by the others present. All taking place under McCready's watchful eye. Like I said, tighter than a . . .'

'Impressive,' I said. But tenders were only a part of their work. 'And for those smaller purchases that only require informal competitive quotes?'

'If a department wants to purchase, say, a couple of new desks and chairs they come along here and see what's available and get a rough idea of the cost. Then the head of that department has to give me a requisition form saying he authorises the purchase and stating the maximum budget. I allocate that form to one of my staff, spreading the work around so that one person isn't always buying office furniture and another always buying printers, for instance – you wouldn't want someone dealing exclusively with the same suppliers. I don't have to teach you about sucking eggs, Nick, but that's the scenario for palm-greasing. So all staff buy a bit of this and a bit of that. Not a problem though. We're mostly generalists here in terms of what we buy – it's how we buy that makes us specialists. Isn't that right, Adam?'

'Treasury estimates that Commercial Services saves us around twelve per cent of our total current expenditure budget, excluding salaries that is, and five per cent of our capital budget. That's good for the council and good for the ratepayer.'

But was it too good to be true?

'Do you mind if I have a look around?' I asked. 'Maybe sit at someone's shoulder? Pick up some tips. I'm in the market for some new office furniture and desktop computers myself.'

'If it's computers you're after, then Terry's your man. He knows his RAMs from his ROMs, his . . .'

'. . . from his elbow?'

'Goes without saying. And there are not many heads of department here could say that. You know something, Nick? Commercial Services is the only department – and I mean only department – in this council that is loved and not loathed by every other department. We help them maximise their budgets, see? Name of the game. Overspend and McCready has your guts for sporran strings. Mind you, if you underspend, then the Policy and Resources Committee cuts you back next year. Can't win. Not without our help. In local government, money's kept on a tighter rein than a nymphomaniac wife at the Rugby Club Christmas Disco. More coffee?'

'Thanks,' I said, struggling with his similes and non sequiturs, but appreciating his hospitality. 'I'll drink it while I'm sitting with Terry.'

'Do you need me, Nick?' Adam asked, screwing up his pretty face.

No, I didn't need him. But I thought the point was that *he* needed *me*. Oh, well. I give up.

'I'll see you back in Treasury,' I sighed. 'In the

meantime you can assemble the past three months' invoices and any associated paperwork.'

'Maybe I'll stick around after all.'

'See you later, Adam.'

He loped off towards the door, stopping only to flirt ostentatiously with Sian. For fifteen minutes! Fifteen minutes when no invoices were being assembled, no supporting paperwork gathered together and, worst of all, no espresso being dripped into my cup.

I followed Steve to Terry's desk. Or should that be Terry's cocoon? He was surrounded by bright orange hessian baffle-boards – great for the ears, but inflicting permanent damage to the colour-sensitive nerve endings of the eyes. He was leaning back in a swivel chair, gazing up at the ceiling while talking on the phone.

'I'm really sorry, Mike,' he said, smiling insincerely from ear to ear. 'I'd like to go with your quote, but . . .' – he let the pause hang threateningly in the air like the sword of Damocles – 'no can do, I'm afraid. Not even for an old mucker. Not at that price.' He winked at Steve and acknowledged my leather-jacketed presence with a widening of his predator's eyes. 'Not for this volume. But, if . . . No, I shouldn't even suggest it. Maybe next time. What, Mike?' He listened to the voice on the other end of the phone while raising his eyebrows at us. 'You'd have to come down a grand. At the very least.' He held the phone in the air. When the loud ranting had ceased, he replaced it to his ear and said, 'Yeah, I know. I'm forcing you into bankruptcy and robbing your children of their future inheritance. So, it's a deal then? Cheers, mate. Nice doing business with you.'

But not, as I was to learn over the course of the next hour, necessarily vice versa.

CHAPTER EIGHTEEN

After Commercial Services I went for a walk. I needed to buy a suit and to clear my head. The latter was the more difficult. I'd listened to Terry make a series of almost identical phone calls, each time mercilessly browbeating a supplier into submission. Maybe they did cut the best deals – Terry had quoted me prices on computers that would make Norman's jaw drop and his lips drool – but the system was a little too adversarial for my liking. I wondered what the staff were like when they arrived home each evening to the wife. Could they switch to a normal co-operational rather than confrontational personality? Or was it a case of 'I'd like to say yes to the sausages, love, but . . .'?

I found an old-fashioned tailor's shop hemmed in by high-street giants making their first tentative foray into Oldbrook; bought a dull but client-friendly single-breasted dark blue pinstripe from a limited stock of off-the-peg suits; listened to the sexagenarian lament the changing times and rising rents while he measured me for the alterations to lengthen the legs and sleeves. He promised me faithfully that the suit would be ready for collection later that afternoon, and shrugged when I thanked him. 'Well, with business as it is . . .' he said mournfully. I picked out four shirts – two white, two plain blue – because I needed them, not for the smile the purchases brought to his face nor to place a tiny pebble in the sling shot of one David against many Goliaths.

I walked back past posters – most of which had been

defaced – advertising the Festival and the multi-cultural programme of events planned, starting with the Grand Carnival Procession. Maybe, if the case ended successfully, we could all come along and join in the celebrations. But that seemed like a big *if* at the moment.

Before returning to Treasury I dropped in to see Ali Khan. I picked up his list of shops and their associated putative values and learned that he had not received any follow-up correspondence – wrapped in bricks or otherwise – issuing ultimatums or making demands for the return of Nadya. I explained my strange garb by recounting the tale of the trashing; gave him a mendacious and unspecific 'progress' report of promising leads that were being followed.

'There you go,' said Adam, smiling sadistically.

He was pointing to two teetering towers of paper.

'This one,' he said, pointing to the marginally smaller of the two skyscrapers, 'is all the invoices for the past three months. And this is the associated paperwork – purchase orders, requisition forms and so on.'

'Jesus,' I said, inwardly groaning at the hours – no, make that days – it would take to go through the lot. 'And this is all Commercial Services?'

'No,' he said. 'But they're in there.'

'So you didn't separate them out like I asked?'

'I didn't want to get them out of order,' he said innocently. 'We'd only have to put them back again when we're finished.'

'But we might have finished a whole lot quicker,' I said, raising my voice in frustration.

'Don't shout at me, Shannon. I'm doing my best.'

'Depressing, isn't it?'

I couldn't help saying it. The words – the truth – just rolled off my tongue, aided by a lubricating oil of too little sleep and too much hassle, and the supporting evidence that he was more of a hindrance than a help.

'Well, if that's how you feel . . .' he snapped back at me.

'Okay,' I said soothingly, 'I'm sorry. I'm a bit touchy today, that's all.'

'Apology accepted,' he said sulkily.

'Can we just get on with it?'

'But there's only an hour before lunch. I was hoping to . . .'

'*Adam.*'

'If that's what you want,' he shrugged. 'So what do we do?'

I closed my eyes and counted slowly to ten.

'How many invoices in this pile?' I said calmly.

'A few hundred. Give or take.'

'Give or take what?'

'A few hundred, I suppose.'

Was he doing this deliberately? Did he have shares in blood pressure tablets or a controlling interest in a cardiac arrest clinic?

'We don't have the time to go through every invoice. Not even every invoice from Commercial Services. What we will do, therefore, is an audit trail.'

He looked at me blankly.

'Right,' I said. 'In the hour before lunch, we each take half the pile and select, let's say, one in every ten invoices relating to Commercial Services. Later we will follow the trail of our randomly chosen invoices through the system from initial authorisation to their appearance on the purchase ledger.'

'Fine with me,' he said, appreciating that the workload had been cut by ninety per cent at a stroke. 'Seems like a good system.'

'Not thorough enough for a full audit, but it will do in the circumstances. And one more thing, Adam. While you are working your way through the invoices picking out your one in ten, I want you to keep an eye out for anything unusual.'

'Like what?'

'Like anything that seems to go against a pattern.'

'What pattern?'

If he was hoping that I would get fed up with his constant questioning and tell him to (for Christ's sake) leave me to get on with it on my (bloody) own, then he was out of luck. But only just.

I split the pile in two, slid one half across the desk. 'Look,' I said patiently, 'this should be easier for you than for me,' – although somehow I doubted it – 'since you are presumably already familiar with the system and the format of the invoices. As you go through the invoices, take an overview of what is normal. That way the unusual will leap out at you.'

Maybe.

'Got you,' he said unconvincingly.

For the next forty-five minutes I worked methodically through invoice after invoice, glancing over the format and detail of each and drawing my ten per cent sample for later investigation. At my side Adam sighed periodically and looked at his watch with increasing regularity, somehow managing to restrain himself from shaking the offending item in the air or placing it against his ear.

I found little of interest, and nothing that was unusual. I wasn't relishing the prospect of admitting to Adam that my scour through the records had been fruitless. Maybe he would discover something to justify the time spent. Shannon, the perpetual optimist, strikes again. Still, there was always the audit trail of our twenty or so invoices to fall back on. And I did at least come across three invoices for computer equipment at rock-bottom prices. I made a note of the suppliers' details – telephone numbers and salesmen's initials – for calling when we were given the glad tidings from Future Assurance that a cheque would be winging its way – pigeon post? – and we could set about replacing everything we had lost.

Adam turned over the last invoice and slumped back in

his chair as if he'd spent the entire morning breaking rocks on Dartmoor.

'Found anything?' I asked hopefully.

'Not a chorizo,' he said. 'How about you?'

'Here, let me have a look,' I replied evasively.

'What's the matter? Don't you trust me?'

'It's not that,' I said. 'I just want to make doubly sure.'

I took the pile from him and began to skim through.

'What about lunch?' he asked.

'If you hold on five minutes,' I said, trying hard to concentrate, 'I'll treat you to lunch. Okay?'

'Thanks,' he said. 'That's very kind of you, Nick.'

'Don't mention it.'

Ah, now here was something that broke the mould.

'Sort of gesture, is it?' he said. 'To make up for what you said earlier?'

'Yes, if you like,' I said automatically, my attention diverted.

'Great. There's a nice little Greek restaurant just round the corner.'

I really fell for that one, didn't I?

What the hell, I thought. I folded the invoice I had been attempting to study and placed it in my inside jacket pocket.

'Come on, Adam,' I said. 'Greek it is.'

Well, the world would be a poorer place if a man couldn't be selflessly generous from time to time.

And I've never – and I mean never, as Steve was prone to say – been in a Greek restaurant that played Kenny G.

'You're not really cut out for this sort of work, are you, Adam?' I said above the sounds of the bouzouki. Okay, so it didn't have the dexterity, tonal quality and innate feeling of Jean Baptiste (Django) Reinhardt, and the tape hissed a bit – well, a lot actually – but it was music to my ears.

I'd had home-made dolmades and seftalia, two large glasses of Othello and two tiny cups of black coffee so thick and sweet that I wouldn't have to worry about low blood sugar or caffeine levels for a fortnight. Towards the end of the meal I had placed the invoice in front of Adam and asked for his comments.

'It's an invoice,' he replied. 'Just a common or garden invoice.'

'And what is it for?' I said, feeling compelled to lead him step by step even if it did mean we would be at John o'Groats before he reached a conclusion.

'Ten computers,' he said. 'What's unusual about that?'

'And, in your exhaustive search through your half-share of the invoices, did you by any chance stumble across any others relating to computers? Or, for that matter, any other large items of office furniture, photocopiers etc.?'

'I did actually,' he said. 'I'm not blind, Shannon.'

But he could not see.

'And did you perhaps notice,' I continued, 'that every other invoice of said office requisites bore the identifying monogram of a purchase-enabling representative?'

'Huh?'

'They all carry a salesman's initials? For commission purposes, Adam.'

'So?'

'Look again at this particular invoice.'

He grudgingly cast his eyes down.

'No initials,' he said. 'So what.'

And that was when I had made my remark questioning his suitability for the job. Maybe there *was* nothing sinister going on; no cause for waving the flag and calling on the might of the Fraud Squad for a dawn raid. It might mean absolutely zilch. But he should at least have noticed the singularity.

'What I mean is,' I said, 'you don't seem overburdened with either the talent for accounting or the enthusiasm necessary to cope with the repetitive routine of auditing. It just seems an odd choice of career. Begs the question "Why?", don't you think?'

'You know what it's like, Nick,' he said, a slight slur to his voice from the two-thirds of the bottle of wine he had drunk. 'End of the sixth form at school, three A levels under your belt, grades not good enough to get into university, and no real idea of what you want to do. You take advice, bow to parental pressure, and finish up a square peg in a round hole.'

'So you've had, what, three years in Treasury?'

He nodded. 'And haven't passed an exam yet.'

'Don't you think you've given it a fair shot? No one can criticise you for not trying. Isn't it time for a change of direction; to do something *you* want, rather than what your parents want for you? What interests you, Adam? Where *do* your talents lie? Under what bushel are you hiding your light?'

'I'd like to be my own boss.'

'Believe me, it's not all it's cracked up to be.'

'An entrepreneur, like; buying and selling. I was pretty good at that at school. You know, pick up bankrupt stock – trainers, CDs, magazines, whatever – from adverts in the paper and sell it at a profit to the other kids.'

'Then why not Commercial Services?'

'It's a bit infra dig. Despite what Steve says about being loved not loathed, the people in Commercial Services are seen as a bunch of barrow boys. The job's boring too – same thing every day. And I told you, I don't want to stay in local government. I want to be my own boss; run my own show.'

'Then do something about it, Adam.'

'I will, Nick. I've got plans.'

But, I thought, plans by themselves are not enough. Would he have the drive and the courage to put them into action? But I didn't voice my reservations. He was mellow from the red wine. I didn't want to spoil his mood. Or the fishing trip on which I was about to embark.

'Must have been difficult for you,' I said as if musing out loud.

'What do you mean?'

'This student you have working in Treasury. The one who is off sick. What's her name? Nadya?'

'What about her?'

'It's just that I've heard she's good. Very good. It can't be easy having a mere temporary outshine you.'

'I didn't mind that,' he said, shrugging. 'You know, she was a bit like you, Nick; a natural. Errors or inconsistencies jumped off the page and landed in her lap. But I couldn't begrudge her for being lucky or gifted.'

'There are many malcontents in this world who would.'

'She was a nice kid. Had a good future ahead of her. Shame.'

My ears pricked up. 'Shame about what?'

'Hadn't we better be getting back?' he said, looking pointedly at his watch.

He was right. It was already a quarter past three, the afternoon evaporating like the wine.

'In a minute,' I said. 'Shame about what?' I repeated with persistence.

'Parental pressure,' he said. 'Or should I say paternal pressure. Nadya's father – the almighty Ali Khan – wanted her to join him in the business, keep the accountant's fees in the family.'

'And what does she think about that?'

'Not much,' he said. 'Anyway, why are you interested?'

'I'm not,' I said nonchalantly. 'Just killing time before I go to pick up a suit. And after that I have a prior engagement.'

'Oh, yeah,' he said. 'Does that mean I'm lumbered with this audit trail job?'

'No,' I said hurriedly. God knows what he might miss. I'd only have to repeat his work. And that would offend him. 'We'll follow the trail together tomorrow. After we've looked into our unusual invoice.'

'So you don't need me any more for today?'

'I'm afraid so. First you can get me a copy of the payroll. Then go and see the Head of Personnel . . .'

'Human Resources,' he corrected. 'Why should I see her?'

Mrs Crabtree would have told him that if he didn't interrupt he would find out more quickly. But he'd taken enough stick for one day.

'I need access to the Personnel – sorry, Human Resources – files. So that we can compare them against the names on the payroll.'

'But that will take ages,' he said, managing not to give a customary groan.

'Not with you calling names off the payroll list and yours truly verifying with the files. It's called teamwork.'

'So it will take fifty per cent of ages then?'

'Nowhere near that,' I said, getting up to leave. 'Have faith in my experience, Adam. Trust me.'

He nodded. 'Okay. I'll trust you.'

Good, I thought as we parted. Pity it was going to be a one-sided arrangement.

During my fishing trip I had felt the line twitch in my hand. Throughout the conversation concerning Nadya, I had been very careful to use the present tense when referring to her.

But he had consistently used the past tense.

CHAPTER NINETEEN

The sixth-form college was a large rambling Victorian building. Much extended (mostly unsympathetically) over the years, it had now lost all its original symmetry. To say it was ugly would be not an insult but an understatement. To some extent the external appearance would have benefited from high-pressure cleaning, repointing and repainting. But, judging from the collection of Portakabins used as overspill classrooms, the smart move would have been to pull it down and start again from scratch.

The students, a melting-pot of various colours and creeds, began to drift out a little before four-thirty. Unconstrained by any officious and outmoded rules on the wearing of uniforms, they had exercised their freedom of choice by dressing almost identically, becoming mirror images of their peers. The boys wore baggy trousers, designer sweatshirts and thick-soled trainers emblazoned with desirable logos; the girls had opted for crop-tops, skin-tight jeans and clumpy shoes. Both sexes had small backpacks slung over one shoulder, freeing the hands of the boys for sticking in pockets and the girls for animated, fingers-spread weathergirl-style gesticulating.

I took one last look at the photograph of Saeed Khan, climbed out of the Lancia and examined the faces as they filed through the tall wrought-iron gates. He was the central part of a group of three Asian youths who slouched along with hunched shoulders and shifty expressions. The group loitered by the gates until joined by four more young lads with the same ethnic background and body language, then moved off. I followed at a discreet distance as they turned left into the High Street, waiting for an opportunity to separate Saeed from the other six members of his brat pack.

They cruised the High Street – thankfully giving the cinema a miss today – splitting up into smaller groups to enter an off-licence, a hardware store, a charity shop and an amusement arcade. They emerged from the shops with their purchases in plastic bags, and from the arcade with three more added to their number. The enlarged group turned west, heading for three tower blocks silhouetted against the low, reddening sun.

I was beginning to get a distinctly uneasy feeling in the pit of my stomach, which had nothing to do with dolmades and seftalia and everything to do with the nervous mannerisms of backwards and sideways glances coming from the pack. I ducked into a doorway, took my mobile phone from my pocket, tapped out the two short-code digits (programmed in by Arlene, the only one of us actually to have read the user-unfriendly sixty-page handbook) to call Arthur. The comforting message LOW BATTERY shone dimly on the tiny display panel. Now it tells me! I'd never had this trouble when I'd kept the damned thing switched off.

'Arthur?' I said into the crackling ether. 'Whereabouts are you?'

'Why?' he asked perceptively. 'Where do you want me to be?'

'Head for Oldbrook straight away. I'll call later,' – bloody battery permitting – 'to give you a precise location.'

'Are you in trouble?' he asked anxiously.

'Not yet. But don't worry about fuel economy and conserving the planet's diminishing resources of fossil fuels when you're driving here. Give it some welly, Arthur,' I explained more simply. 'Roger and out,' I added professionally, disconnecting.

Leaving the shelter of the doorway, I crossed to the

opposite side of the street and lengthened my stride to catch up. Dodging prams, chocolate-smeared babes in buggies and those shin-scraping reinforced steel bags on wheels, I closed the gap and neared the concrete quadrangle which formed the unattractive centrepiece of an open square flanked by a block of flats on each of three sides. Saeed's band – I was in little doubt that he was the ringleader – turned towards the block on the right and skirted along its edge before disappearing behind the building. I quickened my pace, reached the corner and peered gingerly around it.

One of the youths was inserting a key into a heavy-duty padlock which hung across the wooden doors of a garage at the far end of a row of thirty or so. The others faced outwards, eyes cast vigilantly in all directions.

The only available hiding place for me was a cluster of large black dustbins, six feet high and, more relevantly and most inconveniently, twenty yards away with no scrap of cover in between. I waited, and wondered how long I could stand here suspiciously peering around the corner before being spotted by a member of the local Neighbourhood Watch or a nosy busybody, either of whose instinctive reaction would be to reach for the phone to call Mr Plod.

The youth finally got the padlock unlocked, wrestled with its size and weight as he freed it from the clasp, and pulled open the doors. Faces turned to look inside. I grabbed my chance with both feet and sprinted for the dustbins.

If it had been a fictional stakeout in an episode of *The Bill* then the observer would have been warm and comfortable in the sitting room of a public-spirited, glamorous housewife who lived directly opposite the place 'under obbo' and spent her time in a diaphanous negligée and feather-festooned high-heeled mules delivering platefuls of assorted sandwiches and steaming cups of tea. But it wasn't. Unfortunately. My boots squelched in the decomposing matter deposited by people who could be bothered to walk to the dustbins, but strangely not to climb the specially erected steps to tip their rubbish inside. The smell was indescribable, but I'll try.

Imagine the inside of an aircraft hangar filled from floor to ceiling with battery hens. Take three weeks' worth of the resulting guano and place it on top of the slurry pile from a pig farm. Add the concentrated essence of the entire world's Brussels sprout harvest for one year. Stir well, aerating the mixture and exposing it to the full force of the merciless rays of the noonday sun. Are you getting an impression of the magnitude of the rich nasal whiff of the festering organic stench? Right, now treble it.

I held my breath, wishing I'd trained as a diver or at least had possessed the foresight to borrow some scuba equipment. Called Arthur again, giving him the location in short bursts while attempting to conserve precious air. Squinted through a gap in the bins to see the majority of the pack entering the garage, leaving just two outside on guard.

According to Arthur it would be at least twenty minutes before he arrived. That was about nineteen minutes longer than I knew I could endure. I justified the action I was about to take by remembering the words of my grandfather as he encouraged me into some activity I had been effectively avoiding up until that point. 'A cat with mittens catches no mice,' he would say with that slow, lilting delivery of the southern Irish that added little to my comprehension of his advice. It took a good few years before I fully understood what he was on about – by which time people were confusingly telling me to look before I leaped. Well, here goes, Grandpappy.

I broke cover, emerging from behind the bins to the surprise of the two youths on lookout. One of them banged on the door of the garage with the back of his fist.

Cave.

The door partly opened. Three lads squeezed through the narrow gap and joined the two already outside. The five now formed themselves into a protective barrier stretching across the width of the garage.

As I approached, they leaned back against the wood, adopting a nonchalant air, which was totally destroyed by the trembling of fingers as they maladroitly extracted cigarettes from a pack being passed along the line. A murmur spread among them and, obviously thinking better of displaying their nervousness by trying to light the cigarettes, they replaced them in the pack.

Slowly and deliberately, displaying my left hand as a badge of courage, I took out my own lighter and cigarettes; lit one with a steady hand; showed them what casual was by exhaling a long grey plume in the air. I thought I heard a whimper. Or maybe it was my imagination. No, couldn't be. Ever heard an imagination whimper?

Up close, the youths were no more than kids really. Sixteen, seventeen at the very most. Fluffy chins. Gangly build. A mass of uncoordinated arms and legs with not a muscle to speak of. Looked like their idea of taking exercise was dispensing with the use of the television's remote control.

'Let me inside, please,' I said, lowering my voice an octave to the key of John Wayne and drawling the words from the corner of my mouth. Pondered, too, stealing a line of his dialogue – *Stick your hands up, yer bums* – but couldn't trust myself to insert the comma.

'Piss off,' one of the lads said. The wonders of a modern education. Such a wide range of vocabulary. 'We don't want your sort round here,' he added.

My sort?

Then it clicked. It was the fetching black ensemble again.

'I'm not from OWN,' I said. 'If I were,' – little grammatical lesson, *en passant*, on the use of the past subjunctive – 'would I have come alone? Would I be asking politely for entry? Nope. Don't think so somehow.'

'Then who are you, mister?' Mister? They really were showing their age. Or lack of it. 'And what do you want?'

'My name's Nick Shannon. And I want to speak to Saeed Khan.'

The boy gave a nervous giggle. Said, 'I'm afraid he's not available right at this very moment.'

Much more polite. A sign I had them worried.

'So like I said,' he continued, 'piss off.'

'Tell him his father sent me.'

'Are we supposed to be impressed?' They laughed.

'Just tell Saeed I know what you're all planning. And I'm about to call the police.'

I reached for my trusty mobile phone. Ignored the new message. NO BATTERY. Punched out the three digits on the keypad. Poised a finger over the SEND button.

Consultative glances were exchanged. One of the lads popped his head round the door. There was a pause while my demands were relayed and tricky decisions were made. Then I was graciously ushered inside.

And came face to face with Saeed Khan, who was sitting on the concrete floor pouring petrol through a plastic funnel into a row of bottles while someone else inserted screwed up rags in their necks.

'Why have you come here, Shannon?' he said, looking unwaveringly up at me. 'Want a round of applause for saving my father's life, do you? Well, we'd like to oblige, but, as you can see, we've got our hands full at the moment.'

'With taking the law into them, by the look of it.'

Saeed gave me a pitying smile. 'Someone's got to, Shannon. Or would you prefer that OWN got away with murder?'

He was a cocky little kid: big brown naïve eyes; stubborn set to his jaw; impetuous too. A dangerous mixture of personality traits. Yet for some reason I couldn't help but like him.

'They killed Rashid,' he said, in case I'd missed the import of his earlier statement. 'Beat him to death. Everyone knows that.'

'Knowing and proving are two entirely different things, Saeed.'

'Like who else could have killed him? The answer stands out a mile. No one but OWN. And what have the police done about it? I'll tell you, Shannon. Nothing.'

'It's early days,' I said, playing devil's advocate. 'They probably haven't even had the results of the forensic evidence yet.'

'And probably still won't act when they do. I wouldn't be surprised if half the local force aren't fully paid-up members of OWN. That's why we're going to do their job for them.'

'Didn't you listen to your father on the radio yesterday? He made a special plea for non-violence. Passive resistance.'

'Well he would, wouldn't he?'

'Look, Saeed,' I said, 'I'm the cynic around here. Your role is the realist. Don't you know your history? Haven't you heard of Mahatma Gandhi or Martin Luther King?'

'Remind me, Shannon,' he said with a grin. 'Weren't they both assassinated?'

'And so was that advocate of violence, Malcolm X,' I replied, having had more practice at being a wise guy – still, give him credit, he wasn't doing too badly. 'So don't bandy biographies with me. Just look up Montgomery, Alabama in your encyclopaedia and you'll see that Martin Luther King achieved ten times more for civil rights than the Black Panther movement ever did.'

'Times have changed. We're the new Black Panthers.' Seven left fists were raised in the air in answer to his salute: the two on lookout outside, almost certainly eavesdropping on our conversation, were probably making the same gesture. 'We won't make the same mistakes,' he said.

'You already are, Saeed, just by following their path.'

'Do you know why they took the name Black Panthers?'

'Yes,' I said.

'The black panther,' he said, feeling the compulsion to give me the benefit of his knowledge, or maybe it was intended to raise the morale of his comrades-in-arms, 'is not normally an aggressive animal. But it will fight to the death under attack.'

'You haven't even seen life yet, Saeed. It's too early to be talking about death.'

He shook his head at me. 'This is getting us nowhere, Shannon. Turn around. Walk out the door.' – *You're not welcome any more?* – 'And forget what you've seen and heard.'

'I can't do that.'

'Why not?' he asked with a mixture of frustration and desperation in his voice.

'For one reason because people might get hurt. For another, because it might be you lot.'

'Do you think we're going to let you stop us?' said Saeed, acting the rooster among the chickens.

'I don't see that you have any option. Unless you're going to kill me, that is. And, frankly, I doubt that. Lobbing Molotov cocktails through the windows of OWN's HQ is easy. But I don't think you have what it takes to kill someone in cold blood. No offence. It's a compliment, really.'

'Don't patronise me, Shannon,' he said, his frustration increasing with his impotence. 'Look, there are ten of us and only one of you.'

'No,' said Arthur, poking his head round the door. 'I make it two of us.'

'Wasn't someone supposed to be on guard outside?' Saeed said with a groan of accusation.

'You mean this pair?' Arthur asked innocently as he squeezed awkwardly through the gap in the door. In each hand, gripped securely by the collar, was a highly embarrassed youth, struggling half-heartedly, feet dangling a good eighteen inches from the floor. 'You been reasoning with them, Nick?'

172

I nodded. Then gave a shrug.

'So can I start thumping them now?' he asked enthusi-astically.

'Well,' I said uncertainly, 'I have been trying to teach them that might is *not* right. That the pen is mightier than the sword. But fine words don't seem to butter any parsnips round here.'

'So can I thump them or not?' he said loudly, playing up his annoyance. 'That's all I want to know. Simple bloody question, I would have thought.'

'I suppose, Arthur,' I sighed, 'as all else appears to have failed, your old-fashioned but undeniably direct and mem-orable educational methods may be more effective.'

'If that's a long-winded way of saying yes, Nick,' he said, releasing the two dangling youths and dispassionately watching them drop to the floor, 'then who do you want me to start with?'

The kids suddenly seemed to find the ceiling of great interest.

'Before you begin, Arthur, can you do me a favour?'

'Come on, Nick. I haven't got all day.'

'Just don't get too carried away. I mean, not like last time. Okay?'

'Are you never gonna let me bleeding forget it, Nick?' he said, picking up the tune I was whistling. 'Are you always gonna hold it against me? So the blood wouldn't come out. I would have thought a new shirt was a small price to pay.'

'There was the jacket too,' I said. 'And the shoes. Splattered all over they were. Ruined.'

'I told you not to wear suede shoes. Bloody impractical if you ask me.' He paused as if considering the situation deeply. 'What if I just break a few bones? Won't be *much* blood then.'

'Oh, very well.' I turned to question the group of trem-bling youths. 'Anyone here left-handed?' One shaky arm was raised in the air – fist not clenched this time. 'Try to remember that, Arthur. Break his left arm when it's his turn. Now, why not start with . . .' I waved a fickle finger of fate hesitantly in the air before letting it point to Saeed, '. . . the little runt on the floor.'

'I am not a little runt,' he said in a shaky high-pitched voice.

'No,' Saeed cried.

'One at a time, Nick?' Arthur asked as he took a giant stride across the floor. 'It's over too quickly if I do them all together. Let me spin it out a little. Eh?'

He bent down to grab his victim's arm. Saeed scuttled backwards on his bottom, all dignity finally lost.

'Shannon,' he whimpered. 'Call him off. Please. You win.'

'No,' I said slowly, 'we all win.'

I turned to survey the silent and sorry bunch. 'Are we all agreed on that?'

'Yes,' they mumbled.

'Shannon can't hear you,' I said.

'Yes, Mr Shannon,' they choroused.

'Okay, Arthur. I think they've finally seen the light.'

'Now ain't that a shame,' he said, smiling.

'Right,' I said, above the sighs of relief. 'Let's get organised.' I picked willing volunteers at random. 'You, pour the petrol back in the can. You, dump the bottles in dustbins. You, write out a list of everyone's names and addresses – and don't bother with any *noms de plume* because we shall want to see some means of identification before anybody is allowed to leave. And, Saeed, you're coming with me. I think we need to have a little chat. Arthur, I leave them all in your capable hands. See you back at the college.'

He nodded; clapped his huge hands loudly to spur them into action; caught me by the arm as I shepherded Saeed through the door.

'Not a bleeding brain cell among them,' he whispered in my ear. 'But a helluva lot of spunk.'

*

Saeed Khan thrust his hands deep into the pockets of his trousers, hunched his bony shoulders and walked by my side with an affected – but not effective – air of indifference. The gossamer-thin thread of street cred he was attempting to hang on to snapped the moment he saw the Monte Carlo. 'Cool,' he said. 'Hey, can we go for a ride?'

'Later. After we've had our little chat, I'll drop you home.'

His eyes sparkled. He anchored himself by the front of the car. 'What's under the bonnet?'

'One briefcase, one suit and four shirts.'

He gave me a puzzled expression.

'You get to the engine from the back,' I explained. 'It sits just behind the two seats.'

'Can I see?' he asked.

'Sure.' Whatever turned him on. Or helped to loosen his tongue.

I unlocked the car and pulled the handle to release the engine compartment. He had the lid raised and propped up by the time I joined him at the rear.

He gazed wide-eyed.

'Neat,' he said, his voice echoing from deep within the cramped compartment.

'You were supposed to phone me,' I said.

'Yeah, well,' he said. 'You know what it's like.'

'No, I don't. Tell me.'

'There wasn't any point. You and Dad want Nadya found. Mum and I don't. I wouldn't have told you anything.'

'Do you want to sit inside?'

'Can I?' he said, dropping the lid down and rushing to the driver's seat. He jumped in, just managing not to scrape the top off his skull. I slid into the passenger seat.

'Why don't you want her found?'

He fiddled with the tiny gear shift, ham-fistedly practising moving up progressively from first to fifth and back down again.

175

'Because if you find her,' he said, 'you'll bring her home. And then she'll be pressured into marrying that fat slob. I reckon *she* should decide her future, not Dad.'

'I agree with you. But Nadya could be in danger. There's a chance she's been kidnapped. Maybe by OWN. Maybe' – remembering Adam's remark about her being a natural – 'by someone who is on the fiddle in Treasury. She could be in big trouble. Certainly your father is.'

'He'll find a way out,' he said, unconcerned. 'That's what politicians are good at, isn't it?'

'On the grounds that if you're always getting in a hole you become skilled at climbing out?'

He nodded; transferred his attention to the steering wheel.

'Hands a little further up,' I said. 'Place the fleshy part of your palms at the quarter-to-three position, fingers at ten to two. Spread your fingers a little – that way you feel the car more. She'll communicate with you through your fingers.'

He followed the instructions. Looked very professional. Pity his feet didn't reach the pedals.

'She didn't take the money,' he said.

'Then who did?' I asked pointlessly.

I mean, I didn't have a clue. There were so many possibilities. Greedy McCready? Adam? Probably not – even if he'd managed to summon up the enthusiasm, he'd find some way to mess it up. Could be anyone else in Treasury for that matter. Maybe the unfortunate late Rashid? Then there was Helen Ripley – although she wasn't strictly Treasury and may not have been familiar with the procedures for placing money on the overnight market – so why I bothered to include her I didn't know. And after considering individuals you had the added complication of people acting in concert. It was like some complex horse racing bet: singles, doubles, trebles and so on. The permutations were not exactly infinite but near enough to make no difference. The mind boggled.

'How should I know?' Saeed replied reasonably, and unsurprisingly. 'That's your job to find out, surely.' Tough luck, Shannon. 'All I'm saying is that she wouldn't jeopardise her career. That was the other bone of contention between Nadya and Dad. It doesn't make sense for her to have stolen the money.'

He jiggled the wheel to the left, then to the right; expertly negotiated the imagined chicane; narrowed his eyes as he sped along the final straight; smiled in acknowledgement of the chequered flag, which signalled not only winning the race but with it the World Championship – for the third year in succession.

I waited until he had sprayed the champagne and said, 'Sometimes money and sense are mutually exclusive.'

He shrugged.

Being a philosopher and a Formula One driver are mutually exclusive too.

But that *was* one thing we knew already.

Arthur appeared, shepherding a flock of shamefaced kids and smiling broadly to himself. He handed me the list of names and addresses and we agreed cryptically to meet 'back at the ranch'. I drove Saeed home, showing him how to change gear dextrously and giving him tips like always being in the right gear at the right time – that was rich coming from me – in order to give yourself the option of either braking or accelerating hard.

'Will you teach me to drive?' he asked hopefully. 'Please.' A pleading note this time.

'Maybe,' I said. But not in this car. No way. 'It depends.'

'I honestly don't know where Nadya is,' he said.

'In that case, how about the name of her boyfriend?'

'I didn't know there was one. Not a special one, that is. She never mentioned a name.'

'Can you get me a copy of your latest telephone bill?'

He looked at me thoughtfully, perhaps calculating my chances of success when checking the numbers, then nodded.

'Now will you teach me to drive?' he asked again.

'It still depends,' I said.

'On what?'

'You keeping your nose clean for a start. No more vigilante groups or Molotov cocktails.' I wagged a parental finger at him. 'If I even get a sniff that you're planning something, I'll take the list of names straight to the police. From now on, Saeed, you leave OWN to those better qualified.'

'But you aren't going to let them get away with it?'

Why me?

Hell, why not?

Attack is often the means of defence. Not to mention cats and mittens.

CHAPTER TWENTY

By the time I arrived back, Soho had undergone its daily transition. The smart offices of film production companies and advertising agencies were dark and silent: the night-clubs and sex shops were neon-lit and vibrating to the rhythm of the thumping bass lines of slow seductive numbers. One sub-set of the population was outward bound, having beaten a hasty retreat against the onslaught of those who would cruise at their leisure before selecting their pleasure. The air was filled with the aroma of the Dutch-courage beer of the young lads, the nervous per-spiration of the middle-aged men and the cheap perfume of the streetwalkers hawking their trade. The grey plumes of vaporised sesame oil wafting out of the vents of the Thai and Chinese restaurants smelt pretty good in com-parison.

I pressed the button of the entryphone, announced myself to Arthur, pushed open the heavy door after the responding buzz and began the long climb up the creaky stairs to the fifth floor of the terraced building.

Arlene, raising herself on the toes of her strappy sandals, greeted me with a hug and a kiss. Hazel eyes sparkled up excitedly at me. Her auburn hair, peach-scented from her shampoo, was swept back off her ears, revealing two simple white earrings. The long white halter-neck cotton dress emphasised her tan. Or, seeing her now in a new light since the revelation of the previous night, was it partly the Puerto Rican colouring of the inherited Martinez genes?

She broke the embrace, stepped aside and walked over to the gate-leg table where a bottle of white wine was lying in a plastic washing-up bowl of ice. As she poured me a glass, I glanced around the room and tried to see it through her eyes.

It was too small; twelve feet square and usable space diminished by the sloping ceiling. Ill equipped; two chairs by the table, two armchairs (currently occupied by Arthur and Norman) in the centre of the room facing the portable TV and a low coffee table. Tacky; the dining chairs scratched, the once-brown upholstery of the armchairs stained and faded to a patchy yellow-cum-beige, the aerial of the TV a dry-cleaner's coat hanger bent into rabbit ears, the dark-wood top of the coffee table blemished by white rings from years of torture by steaming hot mugs of tea.

I sighed.

'I like it here,' she said, handing me the glass of wine.

I gulped.

'It's cosy,' she said, shrugging her shoulders.

I tilted my head enquiringly and looked her in the eye.

'I feel safe here,' she admitted.

'Who wouldn't?' I said, dragging the dining chairs close to where Norman and Arthur were sitting. 'With Arthur around it's possible to feel safe anywhere.'

Arlene tousled Arthur's hair, he blushed, and she sat down.

'How are the kittens?' I asked.

'The vet's keeping Hardy in for a few days, but he'll pull through – Hardy, I mean, not the vet. And as for Laurel, well, Arthur's spoiling him rotten.' My friend ducked his head out of reach. 'He's loving every minute. He won't want to go home.'

'And will you?'

'Not for a while, Nick.' She gripped my hand with an anxious tightening of her fingers. 'Not till our place is fixed: I want everything cleared out so we can start afresh – not a single reminder of OWN's presence. And certainly not till we're all out of danger.'

Which could be a long time. Even when the case was over there was no guarantee that OWN wouldn't continue to seek retribution for the spoiling of their plan to take Ali Khan out of the action.

'How did you get on today with Con Man of the Year?' I asked rhetorically.

Arlene screwed up her lips and frowned. 'Arthur and I,' she began, 'arrived at his home-cum-office shortly after eleven. We did a reconnaissance of the place from a distance first.'

'You should have seen it, Nick,' Arthur interrupted. 'Right little stately home it is. Long sweeping drive. Big stone steps up to this whopping great house. Garage block. Fleet of cars. Matching Porsches for Blackstone and his wife, Range Rover, Bentley and a couple of vintage jobs I last saw when Stirling Moss was winning the *Mille Milia* in Monte Carlo.'

'And,' Arlene said, 'two chauffeurs. Except they weren't, of course. Just rednecks in suits. Bodyguards, judging by the bulging muscles, low foreheads and grunts.'

'But you got past them?'

'Only because they recognised Arthur from his days as Dangerous Duggan, Terror of the Ring.'

Arthur preened himself in the light of the overhead lamp. 'Those were the days,' he sighed wistfully. 'Did I tell you about the time me and Jackie Kwango were . . .'

'Many times, Arthur. So,' I said, moving swiftly on, 'you were granted an audience with the great man.'

'A very brief audience,' Arlene said, biting her lip. 'We put our case to him; appealed to his non-existent better nature. And – how did you phrase it, Arthur?'

'Er,' he stuttered, 'we got the bum's rush.'

'And who said that life was full of surprises? Okay, tell me about Blackstone. Before we take any decisions we need to know our enemy.'

'Sonovabitch,' she said succinctly.

'I get the sentiment,' I said. 'But I wouldn't mind the odd detail. Could you be a teeny bit more explicit.'

'Kinda guy you wouldn't leave alone with your pocketbook or your daughter. Or your cookie jar, come to that. Unprincipled, untrustworthy. Sly . . .'

'. . . and slippery,' Arthur said, adding his contribution to the character assassination. 'An all-round nastier piece of work you wouldn't want to meet.'

'Good,' I said.

'I'm kinda finding it hard to see what is good about it,' Arlene said.

Norman sipped his wine, hiding the imaginative smile on his lips.

'What are we going to do, Nick? I know exactly what Mrs Crabtree will say: "He cannot be permitted to get away scot-free. Apart from the money, there is a principle at stake here. Blackstone must pay – and be taught a lesson in the process."'

'Which, she will be delighted to know, is exactly what I intend to do. Which is why I didn't go to see Blackstone; or, more accurately, let him see me. At the risk of inviting a chorus of groans, I must tell you, fellow conspirators, that *I* have a plan.'

'But will it work?' Arthur asked, thankfully stopping there and not feeling the need to add 'this time'.

'Let me put it this way,' I said. 'The plan relies on Blackstone always having an eye on the main chance. It stands or falls on Blackstone being greedy, untrusting and duplicitous.'

'It'll work,' said Arlene, nodding at me.

'And may we know the details of this plan of yours?' Norman asked, his eyes bright with interest.

'For the moment,' I said, 'just marvel at its fundamentals. This is a plan that, firstly, will get Mrs Crabtree and her ladies their money back. Secondly, it will teach Blackstone a lesson he will never forget. And, last but not least, it will rescue Ali Khan from his current predicament.'

'Sounds too good to be true,' said Norman.

'That's exactly what I'm hoping Blackstone will think.'

'So it's only you and Norman involved in this scam then,' Arthur said with obvious disappointment after I had explained the full details – and full beauty – of the plan.

'Sorry, Arthur,' I said. 'But I've another job in mind for you. It's highly specialised and, I might say, right up your street. With a bit of luck you start Monday, providing I can get the necessary cooperation.'

'Highly specialised? Right up my street? Tell me, why do I get a bad feeling about this job?'

I suppressed a grin; shrugged as innocently as possible; took three pieces of paper from my pocket.

'I've been thinking about lists,' I said.

'Sign of an anal retentive,' said Norman, the amateur psychologist.

'This one's for you,' I said, passing him the details of the computer and office furniture suppliers. 'If you contact these companies you should get the best deal around when replacing all we've lost.'

He nodded, folded the piece of paper and placed it in his pocket.

'This one is the list of names of our freedom fighters. And this is McCready's list.'

They all stared at me.

'There were ten kids in the All New Black Panthers. Right, Arthur?'

'Yeah,' he said slowly.

'But there are only nine names on this list.'

Arthur's forehead creased in concentration. I detected a slight but progressive movement of his fingers as he replayed the scene in his mind.

'I know,' he said finally. 'Saeed's name isn't on it. He

was with you when I went round taking down the details. Bleeding obvious, if you ask me.'

'Sometimes the blindingly obvious is the hardest to spot.'

'I'm tired, Nick,' Arlene said. 'Can you get to the point, please.'

'Let us assume for the present that we can trust no one in Oldbrook Council.' Apart from Helen, I added for my own benefit. It was her cooperation I needed to get Arthur *in situ.* 'Whether it is the missing four hundred thousand pounds or a yet-to-be-discovered fraud, everyone is a potential suspect.'

'Sounds fair enough,' said Norman.

'Then we should not trust McCready.'

'Agreed,' he said. 'But why single him out?'

'Because I don't like him much,' I admitted. 'And, of more import, since McCready is Head of Treasury he has the most opportunity of anyone to fiddle the books or take a little something on the side.'

'Point taken,' Norman said.

'Think back to when we first studied McCready's list. We went through the classic bluff and double-bluff bit. Was the most important item the one at the top of the list, or the one at the bottom? Was I being pointed towards one item and, consequently, away from another?'

'And, as far as I recall, we never resolved the dilemma.'

'So where on the list is the best place to hide what you don't want investigated?'

'Ah,' Norman said, making the connection and nodding wisely. 'I get you. We were being too clever. The best method of hiding an item when you're making a list is,' he paused for dramatic effect, 'to leave it off.'

'Exactly.'

'So what was missing from the list?' Arthur said.

'Tenders,' I said. 'More specifically, the last of Oldbrook's main services to be privatised.'

'Which is?' he asked suspiciously.

'Which is why I have marked you out for this very important undercover assignment.'

'Which is?' he persisted, smelling a rat.

Good man. Already in training.

'Peripatetic operative for the collection and disposal of abandoned domestic, commercial and industrial materials.'

'Which is?'

'Bin man.'

CHAPTER TWENTY-ONE

Day Four

There are receptionists and there are receptionists.

There are those who regard themselves as the modern-day equivalent of the heroic Horatius, who saved Rome by holding the bridge over the Tiber against an entire army: 'They shall not pass' is their motto. Their weaponry is a lengthy checklist of increasingly irrelevant questions which eliminates few but delays all; an ability to say in complete innocence, 'Please take a seat, sir, while I phone Mr Smith'; coupled with a temporary but (in)convenient paralysis of both arms which prevents the telephone being lifted for long periods. They are unknowing adherents to the philosophy of Buridan, whose main claim to fame was the paradoxical hypothesis that an ass positioned between two equally alluring and equidistant bundles of hay starves to death because it has no rational basis for preferring one bundle over the other. Thus, their sadistic pleasure is brought to orgasmic heights by the similar, but opposite, plight of the poor visitor, forced to choose from the available reading material either the terminal boredom of *Bifurcated Valve Monthly* or the culture shock of the more general magazines with their news that Hitler is dead or Mafeking relieved.

There are those military types who work grudgingly to supplement their army pension (invalided out on psychological grounds) and look as if they are reaching for a bayonet beneath the desk each time you make a hasty movement. They manage to imbue the word *sir* with all the connotations of a misspelling of *cur*. They are at their happiest when barking orders – 'Take the lift to the third floor, *sir*, and proceed in a northerly direction, *sir*, . . .' – or when delivering incoming parcels, since this provides an opportunity for a twenty-minute skulk and two roll-up cigarettes.

There are those who have, through constant repetition of the same phrases, achieved the ultimate aim of delivering every sentence in the same tone and at the same speed. For them, 'Have a nice day' and 'The building is on fire' are perforce imbued with the same lack of emotion.

And there are those like Jakki (that's how it was spelt on her badge). Okay, so she was single-handedly attempting to produce bumper profits for the whole cosmetics industry and, judging by the tightness of her blouse and the short-ness of her skirt, a compensatory recession among yarn manufacturers, but she was polite, efficient, and seemed genuinely interested and caring.

'You're looking very smart today, Mr Shannon,' she said with a warm smile.

'As are you, Jakki,' I replied, smiling back. 'As always, I should add.'

'Thank you, kind sir,' she chirruped.

'Please call me Nick.'

'New suit, is it, Nick?'

'Just a little something I ran up last night,' I said. 'Tell me, Jakki, how are you able to remember everybody's name? I'm very impressed. I mean, there are all the visitors like myself who come and go and . . .' I picked up her copy of the internal telephone list and scanned it, 'there must be at least a couple of hundred staff. How do you do it?'

She shrugged. 'Must be a gift, I suppose.'

'So there's no trick to it? No tips you can pass on?'

'Not really, no.'

'Shame,' I said with an exaggerated sigh. 'You see, I have this old client who simply can't get my name right. Insists on calling me Bannerman. Trouble is, it's gone on for so long that it would be embarrassing to correct him now. Oh, well.' I repeated the sigh.

'Must be a problem,' she said sympathetically. 'Oh, there's an envelope for you.'

I peeled open the seal and peered inside – Ali Khan's telephone bill. Dangerous situation: Saeed was beginning to collect the Brownie points which would make a refusal of driving lessons difficult.

'And I nearly forgot,' Jakki added, 'I've got you a new badge to replace the one you lost.'

The one still fixed to the top pocket of the slashed suit in the wardrobe, more accurately, but it was too long a story to tell her the truth. *Lost* was a little mendacious, but saved time.

'Can't have you wandering around without your visitor's badge,' she said.

God forbid, I thought. I might be mistaken for someone who worked here.

'Thanks,' I said, clipping on the badge. 'Must be going, Jakki. Nice to talk to you.'

I gave her a wink as I turned towards the door to the old building.

Before you start aiming two fingers at the back of your throat, let me simply say that today was a day for making allies. And, if you forgive a somewhat stretched and mixed metaphor, when you're building bridges you need to use a trowel to lay it on thick.

I walked along the corridor to Helen's ante-room; knocked and entered. I was asked to wait while the younger of the two black aides checked to see whether her boss was free. In *PA-speak* that didn't mean free in general: it was the guarded way of saying free specifically for me.

I was ushered inside, reluctantly leaving behind the tantalising aroma of Viennese coffee which hung in the air of the outer office, but substituting instead the not unpleasant – and, by implication, not entirely pleasant – heady sweetness of today's freshly cut single red rose, sitting as on

Tuesday in the thin long-stemmed vase on her desk.

Helen was behind the desk, her fingers clicking the top of a ballpoint pen. I smelt tension in the air as well as roses. And did I detect a little puffiness around the eyes, insufficiently masked by the light application of make-up? Think so. You sure picked a good time to ask a favour, Shannon.

'One moment, Nick,' she said brusquely. 'Lydia? Is everything ready for this afternoon?'

'Well,' the girl said, hesitating as she called up a mental list, 'I'm due to pick up the watch from the engraver's at eleven. Nibbles and drinks are all organised with the Catering Manager – I told him to send the bill direct to you for authorisation – and a few of us are on standby to decorate the restaurant as soon as it shuts after lunch. It's bound to be the usual last-minute rush, but we'll cope.'

'Thanks. Perhaps you could bring some more coffee. You will join me, Nick?'

I looked at my watch – ten past nine already – and thought of the hundred and one things that had to be crammed into the day. 'Just a quick cup, if you don't mind.'

'It's your time,' Helen said, making me feel ungallant. She leaned back in the chair, pulled the red-and-black plaid jacket tightly around her and crossed her arms over her chest. 'What can I do for you?'

'I'm trying to pursue as many lines of enquiry as possible,' I said, trying not to sound as if I was following the path of the headless chicken. 'One of those is your system for tendered contracts.'

'Hasn't Adam explained how we operate? The system is foolproof.'

How many times had I heard that before?

'The trouble is,' I said, 'most fraudsters are not fools.'

'But what do you hope to find?'

'Contracts are normally put out for tender because they involve a great deal of money. The consequence is that an unscrupulous tendering company would be prepared to pay substantial sums to get around the system.'

'Backhanders?' she said with a hint of scorn. 'Cash for information?'

'It's a possibility,' I said.

'As I said before, it's your time. If you want to waste it . . .' She shrugged. 'So what do you want from me?'

'I'd like you to fix up one of my employees with a temporary position. Starting Monday.'

'That might not be as easy as it sounds. What department? Not Treasury, surely?'

'No,' I said. 'Refuse collection.'

'You are joking, aren't you, Nick?' She took a long hard look at me; ran her fingers through her hair in one of those this-is-all-too-much gestures. 'No, I can see from your face that you're deadly serious. What do you hope to discover?'

'To be honest, I don't precisely know.' Nor imprecisely for that matter. 'But it's the last of the big privatisations. It has to be worth a shot.'

'And you have someone who is willing to join the ranks — and I use the term "rank" deliberately — of the bin men for what could very well be a wild-goose chase?'

'No. Not willing. But prepared.'

'Sooner him than me.'

'That was pretty much what he said.'

'Okay,' she said. 'Consider it done. You happen to have chosen the one area of council work — surprise, surprise — that doesn't have a long line of people queueing up for a job. I'll ask Lydia to make the arrangements when she brings in the coffee.'

'I'd rather this was kept strictly between you and me.'

She gave a small sigh. 'You do have a suspicious mind, Nick.'

'I don't like taking chances unless I absolutely have to. And I like it even less when other people are involved.'

'As you wish. I'll let you have the details — where he reports, when and to whom — at lunchtime. What's the man's name?'

'Arthur Duggan.' She didn't blink – obviously wasn't a wrestling fan, but then they are thin on the ground nowadays. 'And I'd rather that no one suspects that Arthur is being foisted on them. Can you make it sound natural?'

'You don't want me to sing it to the tune of "Rule Britannia" while I'm at it?'

'I'm sorry,' I said, taken aback by her sharpness.

'No,' she said, shaking her head in self-deprecation. 'I'm the one who should apologise. It's a bad day, that's all.'

'I've been having a few myself recently.'

Lydia chose that moment to bring in the coffee. There was an awkward silence while she seemed to take an age topping up Helen's cup, pouring one for me and placing the big glass jug of coffee carefully back on the tray.

'Do you want to talk about it?' I asked when we were at last alone.

'I thought you had things to do, places to go, people to see.'

'I like to savour my coffee,' I said. 'Talking would help to pass the time. And you know what they say – a problem shared . . .'

'. . . is two people with a problem,' she said, completing the saying as I knew it.

'My shoulders are broad,' I encouraged.

'Oh for a pair of broad shoulders,' she said, sighing.

I sipped my coffee and let the silence build until one of us broke. With luck it would be Helen.

She took the rose from the vase; twirled it round in her fingers; examined it intently from all angles and found dissatisfaction in every one. Then she placed it in the palm of her hand; closed her fist; and crushed the flower within.

'Bloody, bloody rose,' she said, her eyes filling with tears.

I didn't understand the action or the words. There was nothing I could say. Yet I had to do something. Whenever I see a woman cry, my stomach ties itself into a tight knot and my brain shouts sexist instructions to my arms: sweep her up, make it better.

I stood up, rushed around to the other side of the desk, took hold of the back of her chair and swivelled it round so she was facing me. I went down on my knees, clasped her hand and prised it open. An intense aroma of rose oil hit my nose. Blood red petals fell to the floor like a shower of confetti at Count Dracula's wedding.

Wrapping both my hands around hers, I said, 'Whatever it is, you can't keep it inside. Let it out.'

She looked at me uncertainly.

'Trust me,' I said, 'I'm an accountant.'

She gave a little snort, the nearest she was going to get to a smile.

'My husband picks the roses,' she said.

So she was Mrs Ripley, after all. And I had a hunch that was the root of the problem.

'Fresh one every morning. It's only a little thing, but it means a lot to him – a way of saying he still loves me. And, you see, it's one of the few things he can still do.' Helen closed her blue eyes. 'He has MS. Multiple sclerosis.' The knot in my stomach assumed Gordian proportions. 'He had another relapse this morning. Overstretched while picking that damned rose. Tumbled head first out of his wheelchair.'

'And was he badly hurt?' I said, drawing her hands, and with them her body, closer to me.

'No, only his pride,' she said. 'And a few cuts and bruises. That's not the problem.'

'What is, Helen?'

'It's the brutal way the disease attacks. The periods of remission when you grow accustomed to the symptoms, find ways of coping with them and start to build up your hopes that it won't progress any further. Then comes a relapse. And you're forced to realise that it will never get any better. Just worse and worse.'

'Is there nothing that can be done?'

'Oh, there are drugs he takes,' she said scornfully.

'Supposed to reduce the frequency of the attacks and the severity of the symptoms, but what relief they bring is only partial and purely temporary. Mostly you're reduced to helplessness. All you can do is watch the relentless progression. In the past ten years I've seen him go from trembling hands and slurred speech through double vision to the loss of control over his legs and bodily functions.'

'And the loss of dignity that comes with it,' I said, thinking back to my sister, paralysed from the neck down.

'I know I should be strong,' she said, looking into my eyes, 'but I just don't know how much more I can take.'

'No one ever does.'

In my experience the only time you discovered your limit was the moment when you were pushed past it. But I didn't think that was what she wanted to hear.

'The strange thing is,' I said, taking the soft option of a comforting white lie rather than the hard reality of the truth, 'there's usually a lot more in the well of courage than you ever imagine. I think you'll find that, once you've got over the shock of this morning, you can carry on drawing from that well for a long while yet.'

'Do you really think so?' she said uncertainly.

'Of course,' I replied confidently. 'You wouldn't be running Oldbrook if you lacked guts or fell prey to hopelessness.'

'But that's different,' she said, although there was less uncertainty in her voice now.

'Is it?'

'Perhaps not so very different,' she conceded.

'Do you want to hear one of Shannon's pearls of wisdom?' I asked, knowing it was an offer she couldn't refuse.

'What have I got to lose?'

'Well,' I said, 'sometimes when you're faced with an intractable problem, it helps to turn it on its head.'

'And this is a pearl of wisdom?'

'Take the coffee jug, for instance. Is it half-empty or half-full?'

'That depends on your point of view.'

'Exactly. Personally, I find it more encouraging to think in terms of half-full. Maybe you would too. Try to stop dreading the relapses and look forward instead to the remissions. Aren't they just as inevitable?'

'Accentuate the positive, eh?' she said thoughtfully.

'Eliminate the negative. "And don't mess with Mr In-Between,"' I sang.

'God, you're corny, Nick,' she said with a smile.

'Don't knock it,' I said. 'It takes years of practice. You should hear my rendition of "My Way".'

'"Regrets, I've had a few"?'

'Now you're being corny.'

'It must be catching.'

'That was what I'd hoped.'

'Very well,' she said. 'You're not going to give up, are you?'

I gave her a cheesy grin.

Helen sighed, but this time more in exasperation at me than at her own troubles. 'What was it you said earlier?' she said. '"It's worth a shot." Can't do any harm, I suppose.'

I returned to my chair. Went back to my coffee. Didn't bother with savouring it. Just tried to drink it as quickly as possible so I could make a swift exit. Always quit when you're ahead.

'There's a little party at four o'clock this afternoon. One of our heads of department is retiring. No one would mind if you came along.'

And, I guessed from her tone, she might like it if I did. I nodded. A man's gotta do . . .

CHAPTER TWENTY-TWO

I sauntered into Treasury feeling pretty damned pleased with myself. If I'd had a tail, it would have been wagging like a metronome beating out the time for the Sabre Dance. I should have known the feeling couldn't last. But you always think things are going to be different *this* time – surely Fate has enough on his hands to bother about teaching little old me a lesson in hubris and nemesis.

'Have you got the Personnel files?' I asked Adam.

'No,' he said, without a trace of contrition.

'Okay,' I said, thinking he was being pedantic just to wind me up. 'Have you got the Human Resources files?'

'Not as such.'

'Would you like to explain?' I said, wound up like a spring by now. Or, I was tempted to add, would you prefer a smack on the kisser.

'The Head of Human Resources says that the files are the sole property of *his* department. And as such, they *stay* in his department. If you want to see them, he says, *you* have to go *there*.'

'I might just do that.'

He shrugged. 'Why bother?'

Because I don't like being thwarted, I thought.

'Because it might be important,' I said.

'You could always take it up with Helen,' he said.

Not today.

'We'll pay a visit to Social Services instead,' I said. 'Check out this computer invoice.'

'And how are we going to do that?'

'Let's just make sure the computers physically exist first.'

He opened his mouth to speak.

'Adam,' I warned, 'if you're about to say, "How are we going to do that?", then please don't.'

He closed his mouth.

'Haven't you ever done an asset check before?'

'Rashid used to handle that.'

Well at least he knew what I was talking about. I'd been dreading the riposte of 'What's an asset check?'

'Okay,' I said, determined he should think it out for himself and learn more in the process. 'How might Rashid have gone about it?'

He stared up at the ceiling with a pained expression. And when he had become bored with that, he transferred his attention to the floor. Then he nodded his head, beamed proudly at me and said, 'Check against serial numbers.'

'Well done, Adam,' I said, trying to keep the patronising note from my voice.

'But,' he said, 'the invoice doesn't have any serial numbers on it.'

'Then dig out the delivery note,' I said, hoping he wasn't going to launch into a 'there's a hole in my bucket' routine.

'But,' he began, confirming my worst fears.

'Don't tell me how difficult it is going to be, Adam. Just do it, eh?'

'Give me half an hour,' he said.

'I'll compromise on fifteen minutes,' I said, turning away from him and preparing to make a run for the door before my blood pressure went into the stratosphere.

'Fifteen minutes?' he said. 'Is that how long it takes you to smoke a cigarette?'

'No, Adam,' I said disdainfully. 'It's how long it takes to smoke two cigarettes.'

And who could blame me?

*

I stood outside the old building, my back pressed up against the stone wall, sheltering from the wind. Overnight it had changed and was now blowing from the north, bringing with it a rolling mass of dark clouds that looked like a flock of black sheep returning to the fold. It wouldn't be long before the rain came. There was exactly one week to go till the Festival. In churches, mosques and synagogues people should be praying for a return to the Indian summer: weather like this would put a real dampener on proceedings.

I turned up the collar of my jacket and drew deeply on the cigarette. It didn't taste as good as I'd expected. Wasn't the cigarette's fault; it was mine. Brooding about Adam was destroying the mood and the moment.

His casual, lethargic attitude brought out the worst in me. And, as a result, I'd probably been too hard on him. Again.

I told myself I should try harder to give him the benefit of the doubt. So he seemed to know very little: well, maybe he had simply had insufficient training – could be that Rashid was one of those guys who resent passing on the secrets of the trade. And, after all, working with me was supposed to be all about broadening Adam's experience. But he'd already admitted he had yet to pass an exam. All the training in the world can't compensate for an absence of aptitude or ability.

Frankly, I groaned to myself, Adam was a liability. All he was doing was slowing me down. Perhaps Rashid had reached the same conclusion. He'd done his best to teach the uninterested and disinclined lad and reasoned that it was quicker and easier to get on with the job himself, rather than explaining every little detail to Adam in words of one syllable.

Unless . . .

I dropped the half-smoked cigarette on the grimy pavement, letting it join in comradeship the scattered stubs of other refugees from *smoke-ist* oppression; ground it out pensively with an elongated soft shoe shuffle. Then I punched out the three digits for Directory Enquiries on my mobile; wrote down on the back of my hand the number the computer-generated voice intoned. Then dialled it. Held my breath while crossing my fingers that the great man would be in.

Professor Trefor Davies was one of the most jovial men you could hope to meet. And, given the option, I preferred to meet him outside of the autopsy room of the London teaching hospital where he worked. Just one visit to the wrong side of the double plastic doors had been enough to last me a lifetime – if that isn't too inappropriate a word to use in the circumstances. Trefor is an undaunted trencher-man, being able to eat heartily ten minutes after removing someone's entrails and laying them out like an oracle for examination. He is a Rorke's Drift, sing-in-the-face-of-adversity sort of Welshman, which is just as well, I suppose. For he is also *the* foremost expert on murder. Corpses from all eight areas covered by the Metropolitan Police end up on Trefor's hosed-down stainless-steel slab.

I waited patiently for his secretary to put me though. Lit another cigarette as a means of distracting my mind from sending me a vivid flashback of the bloated body with its one staring eye. It didn't work. I could almost smell the sharp aroma of formalin drifting along the airwaves. Imagination can be a curse at times.

'Nick, my boy,' he boomed at me, managing to make the three short words sound like the final bars of the highpoint in the repertoire of a male-voice choir. 'How are you?'

I forced myself to go through the formalities rather than rushing straight in with my questions. 'I'm fine, Trefor. And you?'

'Strong as an ox, aren't I? Which is more than I can say for our friend Collins.'

'You've seen him lately?'

'Met him for lunch about three weeks ago. Looked green around the gills, he did.'

Sounded like me on the occasion I had first encountered Trefor. He'd been digging into a pink slice of calf's liver like there was no tomorrow. I'd wished there had been no today.

'Collins is on leave of absence,' I said.

'In trouble again then, he is,' he said sadly, decoding the jargon as I had done when hearing the news from Walker. 'What can I do for you, Nick? Did you want to buy me lunch?'

'Can I just send the money?'

He laughed, a rich bellowing sound that echoed around the speaker of the phone.

'Did you conduct the autopsy on a man called Rashid Sadiq?'

'And who else would they entrust with such an important cadaver?'

Cadaver.

Jesus, *corpse* was bad enough, but *cadaver*!

'Why important?' I asked, managing to focus on the relevant word.

'The theory is that a group called OWN killed him. I had two spooks from Special Branch breathing down the back of my neck all the way through the autopsy.' Rather them than me. 'Right bloody pain they were,' he added. 'How's a man supposed to concentrate when they're firing questions all the time?'

'Maybe that's their form of displacement activity.'

'I don't think so, boy. I got the impression that if I'd stopped for a cup of tea and a biscuit, one of them would have taken over.' He paused. 'What's your interest, Nick?' he said, sounding cagey.

'I've had two run-ins with OWN myself. The first time they were after a man called Ali Khan and I happened to be in the wrong place at the wrong time.'

'Now why am I not surprised?'

'The second time, *I* had the dubious honour of being the target. I need information, Trefor. Anything to help me know my enemy and stay out of their clutches.'

'Ah,' he said.

'Why "Ah"?'

'Last time was different, Nick,' he said, referring back to Future Assurance. 'You were working for Collins then. It was official. You had a right to know everything.'

'And now I don't? Why are you stalling me, Trefor?'

'I have your interests at heart, Nick. I don't want you getting out of your depth.'

'It's a little too late to worry about that. Right now I need a lifebelt to keep my head above water. Come on, Trefor. Throw me one.'

'Make me a promise,' he said. 'You only use whatever I tell you in order to stay out of trouble. And not in order to take action which will land you in it. Believe me, Nick, you do not want to get in the way of Special Branch. They are a law unto themselves. They'll trample you underfoot with less thought than the London Welsh scrum. More effectively too. And that's saying something, boy.'

'I promise,' I said. 'I'll be extra careful. Scout's honour. Now, what did you find? In layman's terms, please, Trefor.'

All deaths, he went on to explain, can be put down to one of three causes relating to the failure of one of the organs essential to life: asphyxia (lungs), coma (brain) or syncope (heart). It was the last of these that had claimed Rashid.

Syncope can be brought on naturally by many degenerative diseases, in some cases accelerated by shock or powerful emotions. Homicidal syncopes can be caused by certain poisons (but not in this case) or extensive injury to the heart.

'So the beating they gave him,' I said, recapping, 'damaged his heart badly enough to bring on one of these syncope things?'

'*That* is the key question,' he replied.

'And what, pray, is the key answer?'

'Maybe,' he said.

'That's not very scientific,' I said.

'Oh, I don't know,' he said. 'Sometimes the best that science can do is to posit opposing alternatives for subsequent investigation.'

'Like the earth is either flat or round?'

'In this particular case,' he said, ignoring the interruption, 'there was an added complication. Rashid had an embolism.'

'Layman's terms,' I reminded him.

'An embolism is usually an air bubble or, more rarely, a clot of fat in a blood vessel. Rashid drew the short straw and had the latter variety. May have harboured it for some time without noticing any ill effects. The problem is, Nick, that it's possible that the *shock* of the attack caused the clot to move and block the supply of blood to the heart. His heart *was* damaged by a large number of blows, but those injuries could have been post-mortem. Legally, I presume, the exact charge would have to be in doubt – manslaughter if death was an unintended result of the embolism, murder if due to the malice aforethought of the physical attack.'

'I bet your Special Branch boys loved that.'

'They did press me to come down on one side or the other, but there wasn't the evidence for a hard-and-fast prognosis.'

'What about physical evidence?'

'Inspector Morse stuff, you mean? Strand of albino hair? Splinter from a wooden leg? Book of matches from a strip joint, with the phone number of the criminal mastermind conveniently written inside?'

'You can but hope,' I said, feeling more than a little amateurish.

'There was a single fibre stuck to some dried blood on a head wound. I would hazard a guess,' he said proudly, 'that only someone as meticulous as I would have spotted it.'

'What was the fibre?' I asked, my interest level climbing rapidly. 'No chance it belonged to a specially woven vivid blue and gold cashmere sweater brought into this country by a small importer who has sold only three to date – and two of those were to Nick Faldo?'

'Quite right,' he said. 'No chance. The fibre was from a heavy-duty industrial glove sold in thousands across the country every year.'

'The two thugs who came to attack Ali Khan wore industrial gloves. And I suspect the vandals who trashed my place did the same – I found a yellow thread. The police sent SOCOs to both incidents. You couldn't get hold of copies of their reports, I suppose? See if they handed in any fibres. Maybe establish a match. That way, if you find the culprits for one of those two crimes, you could pin Rashid's death on them too.'

'I'll give it a shot,' he said. 'Tell me where these incidents took place and I'll get in touch with the appropriate areas.'

'Oldbrook for the first – that was on Wednesday – and Docklands for the second – probably went down in the book as early Thursday morning.'

'Give me your number and I'll get back to you if I have any news.'

I gave him the number.

'Mobile?' he said with surprise. 'Converted, are you, boy?'

'More like necessity is the mother of convention.'

CHAPTER TWENTY-THREE

'Don't shout at me,' Adam said in a pre-emptive strike.

'I am not going to shout at you,' I said calmly, wondering what the hell he'd done now. Or not done now, as the case may be.

'I couldn't find the delivery note,' he said.

'Good,' I said.

He gave me a puzzled expression. But, then again, that was par for the course.

'We now have two anomalies,' I explained. 'No salesman's name and no delivery note. I suppose this invoice has been paid?'

'Bound to be,' he said, looking at the date.

'Check, please, just in case.'

'You think you're on to something, don't you?'

'I feel it in my fingers. I feel it in my toes.'

'Comes with experience, does it?'

'No,' I said. 'It comes with perennial re-releases of old Troggs records.'

He shook his head pityingly at me.

'An accountant without a sense of humour, Adam,' I said, in self-justification, 'is like a convict doing thirty years' hard labour without any hope of parole. It *is* possible for both to survive, it's just that the time passes exceedingly slowly.'

'I'll remember that,' he said.

I doubt it, I thought.

He called up the purchase ledger on his terminal,

scanned through the list of invoices entered and paused at the appropriate point. 'Yep. Been paid,' he confirmed.

'Then lead the way to Social Services, trusty assistant.'

'Why bother?' he asked. Character, it seems, will out, even in the most auspicious of circumstances. 'How can we check if the computers exist if we don't have the serial numbers?'

'What is this?' I asked, tapping my hand on his terminal. 'A computer,' he answered.

'No, Adam. This is a bulk-standard networked slave computer, like, I suspect, the vast majority of the others here. It has few facilities of its own, since it utilises those of the host. These computers, on the other hand,' I waved the invoice at him, 'are top-of-the-range, all-singing-and-dancing stand-alone models. It will be like Kate Moss has wandered by chance into a Pamela Anderson lookalike contest. Shouldn't be too difficult to spot.'

Social Services was on the second floor of the new building. The Head of Social Services, like her peers, worked on the first floor of the old building. She set a new world record for covering the distance in between.

We had explained to her deputy the perfectly routine – hem, hem – nature of our mission; baffled him with asset checks and audit trails. In response he had hit us with the full contents of what now seemed to be the standard lecture in Oldbrook – departmental boundaries (and the transgression thereof) and formal protocol (proper channels, the ignoring of). While the deputy phoned his boss, I wandered around the office looking at a loss and doing exactly what he was attempting to prevent. It all seemed a bit pointless really.

The Head flapped in like a mother hen protecting her chicks from a rampaging fox. Her appearance was congruent with her action: short legs, dumpy body and a pair of thickly glassed spectacles which enlarged her eyes and gave them a bemused and staring expression. In her mid-fifties, she was wearing a dark brown jacket and skirt in that kind of heavy material that looks as if it has come from an inept crofter's loom and subsequently failed the washing machine 'bobble' test. The expression on her face could have frozen the lava from a volcano in mid-stream.

'Good morning,' she clucked politely to Adam. 'You must be Shannon,' she pecked accusingly at me.

I took my time answering. I wanted to delay her follow-up question of 'What do you think you're doing?' for as long as possible. I considered several ripostes; rejected all of them, including 'They call me Mr Shannon' in my best Sidney Poitier *In the Heat of the Night* voice; settled on a disarming smile and an economical nod.

'What do you think you're doing?' she said.

'Just showing young Adam here how to conduct an audit trail. We take a random sample of invoices and track them through the system. This one of yours, for instance. We started with the order for the computers and followed on from there until all we're left with is seeing the machines *in situ*.'

'Well, you should have asked my permission. You have no authority here. This is my department and I won't have my staff disturbed unnecessarily.'

'There is no disturbance, Mrs . . .'

'Cluck,' she said.

'I'm sorry, I didn't quite catch that.'

'Clark,' she repeated disappointingly.

'So . . .' I began.

'I'm afraid that this is not a convenient time,' she said, raising the word *brusque* to new heights. 'If you would like to arrange an appointment with my secretary, I would be glad to accompany you on your trail on some future date.'

Her arms swept at the air in an effort to propel us towards the door.

'That's very kind, Mrs Clark,' I said, standing my ground. 'But I'd hate to put you to any trouble. If you would simply tell us where these computers are, we'll be on our merry way.'

'They're here somewhere,' she said, waving her hand vaguely across the expanse of the department.

'No, I've just had a quick look. The machines you have here are all networked terminals. The ones we're checking on are stand-alones.'

'Oh, *those* computers. They are at our outstations,' she said, making a pair of rabbit ears with her fingers to enclose the last word.

'Outstations?' I asked.

'Social Services,' Adam explained, 'have four offices, or outstations, each sited in one of the four quadrants of Oldbrook.'

'The better to serve our clients,' Mrs Clark said, as if singing the departmental song. 'All part of our policy of striving to be more accessible to the community. Each quadrant has, in effect, its own mini Social Services. Residents are allocated to their nearest outstation and can drop in there to discuss their problems and needs. They also have a greater opportunity to form a meaningful relationship with their individual case worker, since the units are smaller and, therefore, more personal.' She puffed up her chest in pride, or maybe to appear more intimidating. Probably both, since her next words were delivered in a patronising tone. 'If you had only spoken to me first, Mr Shannon, I could have saved you from wasting your time. I'm sorry, but you have had a fruitless journey.'

'It's only two floors, Mrs Clark,' I said, smiling at her insincere consideration. 'And Adam needs the exercise. So, if you'd just tell us which of the outstations these computers are at, we'll jog on down there.'

Adam gave me a look that said 'Do we really have to?' with his customary lack of enthusiasm.

Mrs Clark fixed me with piercing eyes; carried out an X-ray of my mind and a complete psychometric test of my character; didn't like what she found. She bit her lip in a mixture of deep thought and deeper frustration; shook her head in weary resignation. 'I think we had better go to my office, Mr Shannon,' she said. 'You see, I have an admission to make.'

'These computers,' she said, when we were seated in her office, 'do not exist as such.'

'As such?' I asked. 'Surely, either they do or they don't. It's a bit like pregnancy: either you are or you aren't. There isn't any middle ground.'

She sighed at me as if I was being deliberately obtuse.

'What I mean is,' she said, 'the computers exist "on paper".' She made the accompanying rabbit ears again. I was getting the hang of the gesture now. It signified that I wasn't to take the words as her own, but as an unattributed quotation. Basically, don't hold anything I say against me.

'But not, I take it, in what we would call "real life"?' I wiggled my fingers in the air this time. The mocking gesture escaped her. In her book, I was merely adhering to the norm.

'Are you familiar with the term "virement", Mr Shannon?'

'Not as such,' I replied, after a pregnant – or non-pregnant – pause.

'Each department in the council has a budget for the financial year. As the end of the year approaches, if it appears that a department will not utilise all of its budget, the process of virement comes into play. Virement' – she almost spat out the words in disgust – 'allows the Chief Executive and the Head of Treasury, together with the Policy and Resources Committee, to transfer money from the budget of the underspending department to another which is likely to overspend due to unforeseen circumstances.'

Adam gave a bored nod of agreement with her explanation. Talk about unreliable corroboration.

'Perhaps you would like to get us all some coffee,

Adam,' she said, handing him her smart card. 'My secretary is very busy at the moment. White with one sugar for me.'

He jumped at the chance to escape the technical elements of the confession. Left the room with the air of someone anticipating a well-timed loiter that would bring him back on cue for the denouement. Was too dumb to realise that she didn't really want coffee. It was just an excuse to get him out of the way so that he wouldn't hear what she was about to say.

'What virement means to me, Mr Shannon, is that some other department gets their hands on *my* money. And, to make matters worse, *my* budget for the following year is cut back in line with the underspend. My department loses out on two counts – this financial year and the next. I simply couldn't allow that to happen.'

'So you fiddled the books,' I said, having slotted the final pieces of the jigsaw (no salesman, no delivery note and no serial numbers) into place the moment she had uttered the word *admission*.

'I merely did what any other department head here would do: played the system for the benefit of my department, my staff and, ultimately, the clients.'

Ultimately the clients. That put them in their place in the pecking order.

'At the risk of sounding naïve, Mrs Clark,' I said, 'should not the good of the whole borough override that of any individual department?'

She gave me a pitying smile. 'You are an outsider, Mr Shannon. You simply do not understand how things work in Oldbrook. Our Chief Executive, in her "wisdom",' – rabbit ears again – 'believes in the principle of "staff empowerment". All that she has achieved is for the other department heads to use their freedom of action to enhance their own power bases – build empires. I have to follow suit. Don't you see that I would be foolish if I did otherwise? I would be doing myself and my staff a grave injustice.'

'Money – or in this case budget, the ability to spend it – is power? Do I read you correctly?'

She nodded. 'I knew I would underspend this year. I was given approval to increase the staff numbers – my social workers have been working their socks off for the past year. And all for a pittance, I might add – my hands are tied by job grades as to what I can pay them. Anyway, when it came to recruiting the additional staff I couldn't find suitably qualified people quickly enough. I now have them in place, but there were four months when salaries were below budget. That ruined my forecasts.'

Adam reappeared carrying three beakers of coffee in a plastic holder. He handed them round and returned the smart card.

'So,' I said, attempting to bring him up to date, 'you enlisted the support of someone in Commercial Services in an effort to *appear* to spend your budget?'

'I did nothing wrong, Mr Shannon. I simply gave Terry, out of the goodness of my heart, a case of Scotch and per-suaded him to use his contacts to my advantage. I ordered, and was invoiced for, the computers on the strict under-standing that the full cost would be credited at the start of the next financial year. The supplier didn't mind. Didn't even have to go to the trouble of delivering the computers. Just a paper transaction. Invoice now, credit in April.'

'Very clever, Mrs Clark. If someone is going to manipulate the budget they would almost invariably do the deed imme-diately before the end of the financial year. Which is exactly what is expected by those who control the finances. They are especially vigilant at that time. But by working six months in advance you were most unlikely to raise any eyebrows.'

'Thank you,' she said, looking immensely self-satisfied.

'Only one problem,' I said, mentally poising a pin to prick her balloon.

'That you have caught me out?'

'Oh, apart from that,' I said. 'You don't understand accounts, I'm afraid. You see, staff expenses come under

209

current expenditure. Computers are capital expenditure. What you have accomplished is to overspend your capital budget and still undershoot on your current budget. If only you'd come to me first, Mrs Clark,' I said, deliberately echoing her earlier words, 'I could have saved you from wasting your time.'

CHAPTER TWENTY-FOUR

'Fancy Mrs Clark calling you a bastard,' Adam said, grinning broadly and shaking his head in amazement. He peeled off the top slice of bread from his ham sandwich and delicately picked out the salad, placing the cucumber, tomatoes, lettuce and onion in neat piles around the edge of his plate.

It was a little after twelve o'clock and the staff restaurant was already busy. There seemed to be a tacit agreement that everyone should eat early today so that the party organisers had maximum time to prepare the room. A small group from Social Services was commiserating with Mrs Clark and sending *Beano* daggers at me whenever my gaze wandered in its direction. Terry, the Scotch drinker from Commercial Services, stared down glumly at his plate, refusing to look at me in that childish belief that if he couldn't see me then I couldn't see him. How to win friends and influence people, Shannon.

The good news was that the aurally challenged person whose job it was to choose the musak in the staff restaurant had decided to spare us Kenny G today. The bad news was that in his place we had *Best of the Pan Pipes* on a continuous loop of tape. I composed a letter in my mind to whoever was supposed to take action under the Trade Descriptions Act – by rights it should have been a blank cassette.

'I suppose I did provoke her,' I admitted. 'Tried hard not to, but the temptation was too great to resist. One of my many failings.'

'You and me both,' he said. 'But why bother? Life's too short, that's what I say.'

I shrugged at the homespun philosophy; speared a piece of sweet and sour pork on my fork; raised it to my lips; put it back untouched on my plate. It wasn't because of the overzealous use of vinegar in the sauce. My mind was too preoccupied to devote the time and energy to conjure up an appetite.

'So,' Adam said, thinking aloud, 'there was no delivery note because the computers were never delivered.'

I nodded.

'And no salesman's initials because there was no commission on the paper transaction. You were clever to spot that invoice, Nick.'

'Lucky, more like it,' I said. 'What will happen to Mrs Clark?'

He screwed up his face and fingered his lips, involuntary actions that signalled his brain had locked on to the question. 'It's a minor offence, really,' he said. 'Every head of department tries something like it from time to time. She'll probably escape with a rap on the knuckles from Greedy McCready. And a public warning, which will serve as a lesson to others that you can't fiddle the books and get away with it. We've done the reputation of Treasury a power of good. Cheat, and we'll catch you.'

'I wonder,' I said, shaking my head.

'What's the matter?' he asked.

'How would you describe Mrs Clark?'

'Well-meaning, I suppose. Heart's in the right place – wouldn't be in social work otherwise. Highly protective of her staff. But underneath, and especially where other departments are concerned, she's a bit of a hard nut.' He smiled at me. 'You cracked her though.'

'Did I?'

'Of course.'

'I'm not so sure, Adam. Didn't it strike you as just a bit too easy? One moment she is all prepared to bluff it out and bully us so that we wouldn't darken her doors again. The next she capitulates.'

'You'd caught her red-handed. What else could she do?'

'Out of character,' I mused. 'She shouldn't have rolled over so easily.'

'Well, what's the answer?' he asked.

'Tell me,' I said, 'when does someone admit to a crime?'

'Pass,' he said.

'When it's a lesser one.'

I sat in the car watching the entrance to a building in the extreme north of Oldbrook. Not any old building – although even the architectural equivalent of a train-spotter would have found it hard to summon up any enthusiasm for this run-of-the-mill converted shop with its opaque double-glazed windows designed purely as a barrier against the noise from the busy street and the prying eyes of passers-by. No, this building, I was assuming, was very special – it was one of the four Social Services out-stations.

While observing Adam fastidiously eat the remains of his sandwich, I had explained my theory. Mrs Clark's change of heart – the transformation from bluff to confession – had occurred the instant I had threatened to visit whichever of the four outstations housed the computers. She hadn't wanted that visit to take place. Which was why that was exactly what I intended to do.

'Like to help you,' Adam had said insincerely, 'but I've volunteered to lend a hand setting up the party.'

So I was here on my own, the windscreen wipers flicking away the steady drizzle and providing me with an intermittent clear view of absolutely nothing. When I had arrived, a handwritten notice taped to the inside of the glass panel on the door had said 'Closed for lunch'. Must have been a gourmet meal; it was now a quarter to three and there was still no sign of life. True, a light was burning in one of the upstairs windows, but no one had walked in front of it or shown themselves by peering out at the gloom of the street below.

I could have given up and moved on to the next port of call. But giving up doesn't come easily to me. I lit another cigarette – I said giving up doesn't come easily. Blew the smoke through the two-inch gap where I had wound down the window. Watched another potential client read the notice, shake his head in frustration but not disbelief, and trudge on up the pavement.

I turned down the volume on the cassette player. Faded out the breathtaking piano solo of John Lewis halfway through 'It Ain't Necessarily So' from the *Modern Jazz Quartet Plays Porgy and Bess* album. Phoned the main switch-board at Oldbrook Council. Asked for Helen Ripley. Made an advance apology. Explained that I'd unexpectedly got caught up with something and might not make the party. 'I'll try to look at it,' she said, 'as if that means you still might.' At least I'd achieved something today.

The light in the first-floor window snapped out. A minute later a hand peeled off the notice from the glass and stuck another one in its place. The door opened and a tall man wrapped in a long raincoat, collar turned up, backed out and set about locking up. Using three different keys, he secured the premises against the most persistent of burglars – or maybe the average citizen of Oldbrook – and walked up the street looking to neither right nor left. All I could see of him as he disappeared around the next corner was the top of his head (balding), the bottom of his legs (faded blue denim jeans) and a pair of Western-style boot heels (scuffed). Not exactly the sort of description that brings forth admiring glances from a policeman with note-book poised expectantly ready to take down a few particulars.

I sat there for a couple of minutes in case I could redeem myself by spotting a raincoated balding man drive by with a blue-jeaned leg hanging out of the window. Strangely, no such luck. I climbed out of the car and ran across the road, dodging the traffic and the raindrops, to read the new notice.

'Closed till Monday morning', it read.

'Closed till Monday morning', read the identical notices on the doors or windows of the other three outstations.

Two hours of sitting in my car waiting; another hour touring the area, battling against the Friday afternoon exodus of traffic from London. And what had I learned? That Mrs Clark was taking no chances, that was all. Whatever was behind the multiplicity of locks at each building, one thing was for sure: she didn't want me to see it. Which made me even more intent to try. But that would have to wait till Monday when Social Services deigned to open its doors to the world and his wife.

The party must have been in full swing as I headed back towards the centre of Oldbrook and the shop where I had come face to face with OWN's enforcers. I had arranged to meet Ali Khan there at a quarter to five and was looking forward to the astonished expression on his face when I broke the good news.

I parked outside the charity shop and popped inside to kit myself out. For the princely sum of three pounds I bought the tattiest pair of trousers they had in my size, a baggy jumper and a pair of shoes that had probably been the height of fashion back when Bill Haley was rocking around the clock. If I dirtied the outfit up a bit, and didn't shave all weekend, I reckoned I would strike the right sartorial note when I sought out the sympathetic ear of a social worker or four.

Ali Khan was in his office, bent over a calculator and a pile of till rolls, a pair of spectacles balanced on the end of his nose. He peered at me over the top of the glasses as I entered.

'Mr Shannon,' he said, rising politely from his chair. 'You have news for me? Have you located Nadya?'

'Not as yet,' I said promisingly.

We both sat down. He looked at me disappointedly.

'It might have helped,' I said defensively, 'if you had told me about your marriage plans for Nadya.'

'That was family business. I fail to see the relevance to your enquiry.'

'It gives Nadya another reason for disappearing – apart from stealing the money. The relevance is that I could have cast my net wider from the very beginning.'

'And now that you know about the arrangements for her marriage, and presumably have cast your net wider, what progress have you made? Where is the money?'

'Good question, Mr Khan,' I said.

'And do you have a good answer?'

'Oh, yes.'

He smiled.

'Could be absolutely anywhere,' I continued, building his disappointment so he would be even more grateful when I posed my solution to his problem. 'It was paid into an account in the Isle of Man. Withdrawn in cash first thing on Monday morning. No hope of tracing it, I'm afraid.'

'And this is your news? Frankly, I had hoped for something more positive.'

'Then try this,' I said. 'We think we may have a buyer for one of your shops. By the end of the week you will be able to repay the four hundred thousand pounds. Your reputation will be saved. There will be no need to withdraw from the election.'

'A partial solution,' he said ungraciously. 'But – correct me if I am wrong – am I not four hundred thousand pounds down at the end of the day?'

'I thought one of your objectives' – and the prime one at that – 'was to save your political career; free you from any scandal that would prevent you from fighting the good fight with all your might. Not to mention stopping a riot in Oldbrook.'

'I suppose you are right, Mr Shannon,' he said grudgingly.

'And look at it this way,' I said. 'If you follow in the footsteps of that other one-time local councillor, John Major, you'll recoup the money from the sale of your memoirs.'

Ali Khan nodded thoughtfully. From the expression on his face, I wondered why he bothered with the calculator.

'And,' I said, 'you're not going to be four hundred thousand pounds down. The shop we intend to sell is this one.'

His face fell. He gave a scornful laugh. 'Just as my spirits rise,' he said, 'you dash them. Of all my shops, this one is of least value.'

'That is exactly why we chose it.'

'But the site itself has only nine years of the lease left. And I keep the profit margins here low – this is my ward, after all, I want to keep the voters sweet. Didn't you see the figure I put down. You'll be lucky to get two hundred thousand, let alone four.'

'Trust me,' I said, fingers crossed. 'I guarantee that next week you will receive an offer for this shop from a man called Blackstone. All the necessary documents will have been prepared in advance. You will sign and, in return, be handed the money in cash. And, Mr Khan, you will not settle for a penny less than the four hundred thousand you need.'

'Is this legal?' he asked with a frown.

'Perfectly.'

But only just. *And* only just, too.

'I think it is better if I don't know the details,' he said, not a hundred per cent reassured.

I nodded; rose from the chair; took two long slow strides to the door; paused, and turned back to face him.

'Mr Khan,' I said. 'If I do manage to find Nadya and bring her back, will you still insist on this marriage?'

'All the arrangements have been made; the date set, the dowry agreed. It is the Muslim way. I have given my word. I cannot lose face in the community.'

'What about gaining face with your daughter? There are

217

times when the only way to win respect is to admit that you are wrong and back down with good grace.'

'She is my daughter, Mr Shannon. Respect me and obey me. That is her duty.'

'Read any Robert Louis Stevenson, Mr Khan?'

His eyes narrowed in puzzlement. Probably wondering if *Kidnapped* had any relevance.

'Stevenson once wrote, "There is no duty we so much underrate as the duty of being happy." Mull it over, Mr Khan.'

You know it makes sense.

I drove into the car park at Oldbrook at five-thirty. Ten seconds later I spun the car round and drove out again.

I had no right to be angry. But I was.

I had no right to moralise. But I did.

If Adam wanted to stand in the shadows with his arms round someone, then that was his prerogative.

If she wanted to bury her head against his chest, then that was hers.

I thought *opposites* were supposed to attract. Maybe personal magnetism works differently. They made a fine pair, I had to admit.

Who could blame him for choosing her? Power, money and beauty all wrapped up together for the taking.

And who could blame her? When she needed more than a rose.

Good luck to you both, I should have said. But I couldn't.

Suddenly it all made sense. But, hell, I'd much preferred it when it didn't.

CHAPTER TWENTY-FIVE

We sat in Arthur's room like a quartet of dunces, each facing a corner and adopting identical statuesque poses: left hand clamped over ear to blot out the other conversations and the even more distracting sounds of heavily faked orgasm emanating through the ceiling of the room beneath at regular fifteen-minute intervals, other hand pressing mobile phone tight up against right ear. We'd been at it an hour, which, thankfully, was more than you could say for the woman below – but then again she was being paid per head rather than on commission. In terms of satisfaction though, I imagine ours was pretty much on a par with hers. We were on the final few numbers on Ali Khan's itemised telephone bill and so far not a single clue had emerged as to Nadya's whereabouts – no one who even remotely sounded like our Young Lochinvar; just a variety of tradesmen, a series of work-related calls (his fellow councillors, several to Helen, editors of local rags, his shops) and a miscellany of what we assumed were friends and acquaintances.

I watched the phones being set aside, bodies swivelling round towards me and the accompanying shakes of heads.

'You know what I really like about you all?' I sighed.

'Y'all?' drawled Arlene in perfect American – which, in my view, was only appropriate.

She was wearing tight denim jeans and a navy blue V-necked T-shirt, her hair tied back in a black scarf, a smear of dirt on her forehead. The flat was clean and tidy, carpet swept, table and chairs dusted, our sleeping bags neatly rolled up and stowed against the wall behind the TV.

'It doesn't matter what I ask of you,' I said, 'you never let me down.'

'Do I detect a touch of melancholy?' Norman asked, uncorking a bottle of red wine

'Maybe,' I said. 'It's just that with most people, all you can rely on is that you can't rely on them.'

Norman poured four large glasses and handed them around as we pulled the chairs into a circle. He watched me with a paternal frown as I sat down wearily and went through a ritual introspective manoeuvre of reaching for my pack of cigarettes, slowly taking one out, lighting it and staring at the smoke as it curled upwards. 'He's got it bad,' he concluded.

'And that ain't good,' continued Arlene.

'I know what he means though,' chipped in Arthur with a wise nod.

'We all know what he means, Arthur,' Norman said. 'It's the fact that he has to say it that's worrying. Has someone let you down today?'

'Let's just say that her behaviour has been below my expectations.'

'Was that,' Norman began, speaking slowly and deliberately, 'a problem with her behaviour or your expectations?'

'A bit of both really.'

'Tell us about the birth of the blues,' Norman said, settling himself in the armchair and stretching out his legs.

'Would you say that I was paranoid?' I asked him.

'I wouldn't blame you if you were,' he replied stoically. 'Why?'

'I told someone today that if you are faced with a seemingly insoluble problem, it helps to stand it on its head. Look at it afresh from a totally different viewpoint.'

'And?'

'Unless my imagination is running away with itself, I

think I've solved the problem. The case. Well, the money side at least. I know who did it.'

'Not the bloody butler again?' said Arthur, attempting light relief.

'Ever since we took this case,' I continued, 'it's been trouble. The attack at Ali Khan's shop; the trashing of our house. And, within Oldbrook Borough Council, a series of obstacles put in my way and no sense of urgency from anyone about when I would clear them.'

'And this is a radical new insight, honey?' Arlene said.

'I – we – have always assumed, quite naturally, that the intended victim of the thugs at the shop was Ali Khan. But what if we were wrong?'

'That would mean . . .' Norman started to say, then shook his head. 'No.'

'Yes,' I said. 'I think *I* was supposed to be the victim.'

'I can see why you talked about being paranoid,' he said.

'I believe the intention was that I should be stopped in my tracks. Before I ever had the chance to set foot inside the council.'

'But it was OWN behind the attack,' Arlene said. 'And OWN who were responsible for the destruction of my home.' She looked at me uncertainly. 'Wasn't it?'

'Yes, but not for the reasons we thought.' I drew deeply on the cigarette, exhaled slowly as I tried to find the easiest way to explain. 'The vandals who trashed our place were simply muscle, hired by someone who has connections with OWN. Think back to the state of my office. They swept everything off the table. I remember thinking about picking up the files from the floor. Now, these guys may be bigots but surely they can read. If they were *really* after Ali Khan, why didn't they take his file? There was enough in it to light a fuse under him and his career.'

'So,' Norman said, 'if the hypothesis is that you were attacked at Ali Khan's shop to stop you pursuing the case, when it failed they resorted to the trashing to persuade you to pull out. Can you support this theory with any actual evidence?'

'Unfortunately, yes.'

'Which is why you have the blues?'

I nodded.

'I know for certain that Helen Ripley, Oldbrook's Chief Executive, knew I was going to see Ali Khan at his shop – when I first met her she asked me what I thought of his little empire. *And* I had lunch with her that day. Told her I would be eating out that evening. She could assume our premises would be empty.'

'Go on,' Norman said. 'If you don't mind me saying so, it's all a little circumstantial at the moment.'

'And it doesn't get much better.' I turned to Arlene. 'Do you recall me mentioning the himbo?' I asked her.

'Adam somebody or other,' she said.

'Adam Schroeder. Well, Helen Ripley was the one who suggested that he be the person who should work with me. And he's done a pretty good job of slowing me down ever since. I think I made the grave mistake of underestimating him. He's smarter than he looks. Not much, maybe, but enough to throw me off the scent.'

'And to which particular foxhole does this scent lead?' Norman asked.

'Helen Ripley's husband has multiple sclerosis. According to her, he's little more than a wheelchair-bound cripple.'

'Aha,' said Arlene.

It wasn't just *my* imagination that was functioning on all six cylinders.

'I caught Helen and Adam together in the car park. I think they've been having an affair.'

'And,' Norman said, 'you don't think the partnership stopped at the bedroom?'

'They stole the money. That's why they didn't want me in Oldbrook. She was the woman who made the phone call to the bank to transfer the funds; the one who didn't say *fillums*. And Adam was the one who went to the Isle of Man to withdraw the cash. He gave me some cock-and-bull story about being off with a bug on that Monday. It all fits.'

'I wish it didn't,' Norman said gloomily.

'Why?' grunted Arthur. 'What difference does it make who did it?'

'Because, in this case, our client is Oldbrook Borough Council. Helen Ripley signed our contract. That makes her our paymaster. We're about to bite the hand that feeds us.'

'So what do we do now?' Arlene said.

'Sing along with me and Nick,' Norman said. 'Woke up dis mornin' . . .'

'No, seriously,' Arlene persisted. 'What do we do now?'

'Stick to the plan,' I said, shrugging. 'What else can we do? We need the unknowing cooperation of Oldbrook council in order to teach Blackstone a lesson. Without that everything falls apart. If we don't get sweet revenge on Blackstone then we don't recover the money he conned from the old ladies or raise the four hundred thousand pounds that Ali Khan needs. So we have to hang on in there. Might as well complete our investigation while we're at it.'

'Does that mean I'm still on bleeding bin duty?' Arthur asked.

'Sorry,' I said. 'You report at eight o'clock sharp on Monday morning.'

'And how can I help?' Arlene asked.

'Come with me to Oldbrook. I'll point out Adam. You take a few photographs of him. Then go to the Isle of Man. We need some hard evidence. Get someone at the bank to identify Adam as the person who withdrew the money. Shouldn't be difficult, he's not easy to forget.'

'What's my story?' she said.

'You position yourself as the rightful owner of Megacom – I'll give you the account number as some form of proof. You tell the bank that your bearer share is missing and that you suspect Adam of stealing it. But you want

223

to be sure. Because if it isn't him you need to report the theft to the police. If it is, you say, well, that's a different matter. Act all embarrassed. Add a touch of pathos too. From that point on you can play it one of two ways. Either Adam is your son, or he's your toy boy.'

'How old is he?'

'Twenty-one.'

She did a quick calculation. 'Toy boy,' she said.

'Vanity, where is thy sting?'

'Be a good boy and you might find out.'

'I don't get it,' said Arthur, frowning with deep concentration.

'It's a *double entendre*,' I said.

'No, not that,' he said. 'If this Helen bird stole the money, then why did she agree to hire us?'

'For one thing,' Norman said, 'it seems she never had any intention of letting Nick get inside Oldbrook. And even when he did, she must have been reasonably confident that she could get away with it. After all, who but Nick is going to pick up on the pronunciation of the word *film*? Without that small mistake, every finger points to Nadya.'

'So where is bleeding Nadya?' Arthur said.

'On honeymoon, perhaps,' I said. 'It could be Arlene's theory is right: Nadya eloped to avoid the arranged marriage. Or maybe she's just trying to scare her father, put some pressure on him to change his mind.'

'So you've suddenly started believing in coincidences then?' Norman said.

I flashed him a warning. Not now, Norman.

'They do sometimes happen,' I said. 'Unless, of course, Nadya let something slip about her plans. Maybe Adam overheard her on the telephone when she was making arrangements with her beau. Or, for all we know, she might have confided in Helen. Say her disappearance *is* purely for her father's benefit. She wouldn't want it to seem as if she's walking out on the job – might be grateful for a glowing reference when she's applying for a post at one of the big accountancy firms. So she goes to Helen – a more sympathetic ear than McCready – spells out the situation and asks for unpaid leave. And that gives Helen the opportunity she has been waiting for. A perfect patsy on which to pin the crime.'

'You know something, Nick,' Arthur said. 'Ever since I first clapped eyes on you, you've made my brain hurt. Life used to be so simple.'

'We've all come a long way since those days,' Norman said philosophically.

'Excuse me, guys,' Arlene said, rising decisively from the chair and putting her hand on my shoulder. 'But if you're about to go all sentimental on me, I think I'll just freshen up and change before we go out to eat.'

I sighed with relief. Then just sighed as I watched her walk pneumatically in the jeans from the room.

'Coincidences,' Norman said, pursuing his earlier theme now that the time was ripe.

'Haven't we been through that,' Arthur said, sounding bored.

'Only half of it,' Norman said. 'Isn't that right, Nick?'

'I didn't want Arlene worrying unnecessarily. After all, I might be wrong.'

'Wouldn't be the first time,' Norman said.

'Or the last,' added Arthur.

'Thanks for the vote of confidence. The problem is that I can cope with one possible coincidence – Nadya's disappearance – but not two. I think it's safer if we assume that Rashid's death may be linked to Helen and Adam. Perhaps Rashid got wind of something,' I said, shrugging. 'I don't know. Maybe he was some sort of threat. And Helen sets her thugs on him too. Let's give her the benefit of the doubt. Say that all she intended was to take him out of the action for a while. And the men from OWN get carried away. Or he dies accidentally from fright.' I explained what Professor Davies had told me about the embolism. 'And there's another point to ponder. When I spoke to Adam about Nadya he kept referring to her in the past tense. It may be nothing but . . . Well, let's keep all this to ourselves.'

'You look worried,' Arlene said when she came back into the room.

She had changed into a sleeveless salmon-pink shift dress and matching high heels. Her hair was brushed and caressed her shoulders. She stood looking down at me, clutch bag in hand, eager to leave the flat for food and respite from the groans of Sindy ('Strict Disciplinarian – just call for satisfaction') below but knowing that it was better to wait till the air had been cleared.

'Just thinking of Blackstone,' I said.

'All under control,' Norman said. 'I've got the accommodation address for the company set up, a solicitor working on the papers and have issued my invitation to Blackstone. He won't refuse – be against his nature. He'll take the bait.'

'How can you be so sure?' Arlene asked.

'Because the bait was a thousand pounds in cash; with the promise of much more to come. Who wouldn't risk a lunch with that sort of incentive? Even if it is at some Greek restaurant in Oldbrook. Blackstone has nothing to lose and everything to gain. Don't worry. Nothing can go wrong.'

CHAPTER TWENTY-SIX

Day Five

I was dozing, my breathing synchronised to the soft lapping of the waves on the sandy shore. Somewhere in the distance a cicada chirruped rhythmically. Through closed eyelids I could see the red flare of the sun directly overhead. High noon. The heat was building.

Opening my eyes, I gazed at the cool clear water. It glistened invitingly, presenting an easy solution to the increasing flow of perspiration on my body.

'Go on in, Shannon,' Adam encouraged.

He was swinging lazily in a hammock slung between two palm trees. A bevy of dusky babes surrounded him. One held a tall tumbler of rum punch from which a long straw led up to Adam's lips. He took a sip; turned to me and smiled. 'I'd go myself, Shannon, but,' he said with a lazy shrug, 'you know how it is.'

'Go on in, Shannon,' McCready echoed.

He was sitting at a table in the shade of a multicoloured umbrella. In front of him was an enormous plate of steak and chips. A waiter wandered past with a tray of spiny lobsters. McCready's hand darted out and snatched one. He crushed the shell in his fist and plucked out the succulent white meat with deft movements of his stubby fingers.

'Come on in, Nick,' Helen called. She was standing in the shallows, wearing the Ursula Andress white bikini from *Dr No*, her hair plaited and beaded like Bo Derek's. She bent down, scooped up a handful of water and splashed it over her body so that it ran in little rivulets between her breasts.

I walked towards her, breaking into a run as the sand began to burn my feet. Helen backed away into deeper water. A salmon broke the surface and leapt over her head.

I waded through the shallows. The cicada chirped out a Morse code SOS. Ignoring it, I swam in a straight line to Helen – who metamorphosed into Nadya Khan.

She clung to me, her long black hair streaming behind her in the water. 'Save me,' she said.

'You *are* safe,' I replied. 'Aren't you?' I added uncertainly.

Nadya pointed out to sea. The triangular fins of sharks were homing in on us. As they neared I noticed that the fins, like some bizarre fleet of underwater aeroplanes, were decorated with the lightning flash logo of OWN. The sharks circled us – spiralled us – closing in with each orbit. The first silvery-grey head broke the surface. Row upon row of razor-sharp teeth gleamed in a sick smile.

The cicada – Jiminy Cricket? – became more persistent. Chirrup, chirrup. Burr, Burr. Danger, danger.

'Dammit,' Arlene said loudly at my side.

The chirping stopped.

'It's for you,' she said, nudging me awake and angrily thrusting her mobile phone into my hand.

I sat up in bed. Pressed the phone to my ear.

'This is Staff Nurse Riley,' a concerned voice said. 'It's Mr Collins. You're to come immediately.'

I lit a cigarette with shaking hands; looked at my watch in the dim glow of the tip. Three o'clock.

'What?' I said, my heart beating fast. 'Where?'

'There isn't much time,' she said. 'The man's fading fast.'

She gave me the name of the hospital and the number of the ward. I repeated them back to her in the instant before she disconnected.

I stubbed out the cigarette, thinking of the fifty a day that was the norm for Collins. Extricated myself from the sleeping bag while telling Arlene what little I knew. Threw on a pair of jeans, a T-shirt and a pair of boots. Stuffed my car keys and mobile in the pocket of my leather jacket. And ran from the room.

The Monte Carlo has a theoretical top speed of 120 miles per hour. Rarely did one have the opportunity or reason to test that limit. But it was the early hours on a moonlit Saturday morning, the roads were dry and near deserted, and Collins was dying. If the conditions and circumstances weren't right now, then they never would be. Collins had saved my life – not once, but twice. Go for it, Shannon.

Once I had cleared the East End it was dual carriageway pretty much all of the way. I drove with both windows wound fully down so that the wind rushed past my face, beating on my cheeks and intermittently blowing strands of hair over my eyes. It was a price worth paying. I needed the cold jet-stream of air to blow away the last cobwebs of sleep and clear my mind of the alcohol that still lingered in my system from the evening at Toddy's. My right foot was pressed hard down on the accelerator pedal, the needle of the rev counter hovering a millimetre from the red zone. The noise from the engine growled loud and harsh in my ears. I concentrated hard on the road ahead, watchful for the ever more frustrating appearance of another round-about or set of traffic lights and alert to the threat of overtaking a police patrol car. I knew I was risking my licence, but that seemed of very little importance. I would have risked my life for Collins.

The hospital was one of several dotted along the meander of the Thames to the east of London that had been built in the mid-1850s to house the sick and wounded from the Crimean War. Perhaps fittingly, although not pleasingly, it resembled a barracks rather than a place of healing. Occupying a large and sprawling site was a central building (administration, casualty, X-ray and so on) from which fanned out lines of long two-storey brick 'huts'. The bricks, presumably once red, had acquired over the years a patina of grey from the nearby cement works overlaid with a sooty-black from the polluting factory chimneys. Or maybe it was the other way round. Whichever, it was a grim place to die.

Having circumnavigated the complex, obediently following the signs for Visitors' Parking, I brought the Monte Carlo to a screeching halt in a tarmac area which seemed miles from anywhere a visitor might actually want to go. Slamming the car door shut, I broke into a run, the words of Staff Nurse Riley sounding in my ear: 'There isn't much time.'

Ward 21A was only (!) six hundred yards from the car park. I pushed the double doors aside and entered. To my left was a sluice room complete with a giant autoclave for sterilising bedpans and the like, followed by two toilets from which emerged the strong smell of disinfectant; ahead of me the ward proper stretched out, beds barely visible in the dimness of the blue night-light; to my right was the nurses' rest room. I knocked on the door. A thin woman came to greet me. She was dressed in an all-blue uniform, her hair tucked out of sight in a stiff white disposable paper cap. She looked to be in her early thirties, although the lines around her eyes indicated the sad experiences of someone twice that age.

'Shannon,' I panted breathlessly, still recovering from the sprint from the car. 'I've come to see Collins.'

'Staff Nurse Riley,' she trilled in a soft Irish accent that took me back twenty years or so. 'This way, please.'

She led me into the ward and along the narrow middle strip. On either side, men with the grey pallor of death on their faces slumbered with mouths open or stirred restlessly in pain. Our destination was obvious. A set of curtains screened one bed from all the others in an effort to give the occupant a last moment of privacy on this earth. I heard a low wheezy groan from within. And shuddered involuntarily as the angel of death passed over my shoulders.

Staff Nurse Riley parted the curtains.

'Christ, you took your time, Shannon,' Collins said.

I stared at him.

He was sitting, as large as life, in a chair by the side of the bed.

In the bed was someone I had never seen before. A plastic tube snaked from a drip on a stand into a vein on the man's hand. The transparent bag – a mixture of glucose and morphine? – was nearly empty: the compensating outlet bag clipped to the steel bar on the side of the bed was nearly full. I was reminded of the vision of the soldier in white in *Catch-22* – when the drip on the stand was empty, the ward orderlies merely swapped it for the full outlet bag. I shuddered again.

'What the bloody hell is going on?' I said angrily.

'Have some respect for the dying, Shannon,' he said, nodding his head at the man propped up on three pillows.

'*You* were the one who was supposed to be dying,' I said.

'The message must have got a bit garbled,' he replied.

'Like hell it did.'

'Would you have come as quickly for a man you'd never heard of?'

'If you had asked, yes I would.'

He shrugged. Turned away from me. Placed his hand on the man's arm and shook him so roughly I feared that the tube would be ripped out.

'Wake up,' Collins urged. 'Shannon's here.'

A groan was the only response from the man.

Collins slapped his face.

I winced.

The man stirred.

I noticed the loose skin on his jowls flap as he shook his head to rouse himself. His eyelids fluttered as if all his will-power had to be harnessed to force them open. He stared up at me and gave a loud racking cough that made my stomach churn. His blue-tinged lips moved slowly, emitting a whisper so low as to be inaudible.

I looked at Collins helplessly.

'He wants to tell you something,' he said. '*Need*s to tell you something.'

231

Moving to the man's side, I bent my head down close to the barely moving lips. Felt his stuttering breath on my ear.

'Sorry, Shannon,' he wheezed. 'Sorry about your sister. It was an accident. I didn't mean to cripple her. Or kill the boy.'

He turned his head. His eyes met mine. A tear formed and rolled in slow motion down his cheek.

'There,' he said. 'It's over now. All over now. Rest in peace, eh?'

The eyelids fluttered again. His eyes closed for the last time. A low gurgle came from his throat. I shivered, recognising the sound of the death rattle. His head lolled to one side. His breathing ceased.

Dammit, it wasn't meant to be like this.

Nine years I had waited to savour the moment when the bastard would be caught, tried and sent to jail. And condemned to endure the same punishment – the same treatment – as I. Revenge was supposed to be sweet. How could this man deny me the pleasurable taste?

'Right,' Collins said, rising from the chair. 'Let's go and have a cigarette.'

'How can you smoke in a place like this? At a time like this?'

'How can you not?' he replied.

'Who the hell was he?' I asked Collins.

After the man's timely death, Collins had headed resolutely up the ward. I had stayed at the bedside to press the buzzer for a nurse, waited until she had shaken her head in weary resignation, and then followed in his footsteps to the day room at the far end of the building.

We now sat opposite each other on grey plastic stacking chairs, sipping black coffee from a machine which gurgled intermittently and chillingly. In an illogical vicious circle we were smoking to calm nerves shattered by the reminder of deaths past and the prospect of those to come.

'He', Collins said without emotion, 'was Chief Inspector Leyton. One-time head of CID for the western division of the Mid-Anglia Police Force. Took early retirement nearly nine years ago.'

'Around the time of my sister's death,' I said, calculating back.

Collins nodded.

'And he was the driver of the hit-and-run car?' I said.

'No,' Collins said with a sneer. 'But that's what he wants us to believe.'

'I think we had better start again,' I said. 'I don't get it. What are you doing here anyway? I thought you were on leave of absence. Under suspension was the impression Walker gave me.'

'Not me,' he said proudly. '*I* am inviolate. Unsackable.'

'For the first time in your long and distinguished career, I suspect.'

Collins smiled at me. Took a hip flask from the inside pocket of his rumpled jacket. Added a generous slug of cheap whisky to his coffee. Waved the flask in my direction. I shook my head. I still had to drive back. It would have been ironic to get stopped and breathalysed on some technicality while driving back at less than half the speed of my outward journey. He gave me a *please yourself* shrug.

'I went to see the Commander,' he said. 'Laid my cards on the table. Made him an offer he couldn't refuse.'

'Slow down,' I said. 'What cards? What offer?'

'Christ, Shannon, it's only been four weeks. Do you forget that easily?'

'I've had my mind on other things lately.'

'The file on the hit-and-run,' he prompted. 'The file that was buried deep in the archives? And guarded so jealously that even I, a Detective Superintendent, couldn't get sight of it? Well,' he added grudgingly, 'not legitimately, that is.'

He paused to light another cigarette from the stub of the one he was just finishing. A spot of ash fell on to the lapel of his jacket. He brushed at it, managing to create a long smear out of the original small dot. Collins never seemed to change. No matter how good his intentions to smarten up, either fate or a lack of commitment contrived to keep him as an adult version of Pigpen from *Peanuts*. He grinned at me as if reading my thoughts; ran his fingers through his long ginger hair in an evidential demonstration of its inability to be controlled.

'The file,' I said, trying to speed up his story, 'with the missing page from the forensic report of the scene of the crime.'

'Which Professor Davies established was an impression of the sole of a boot. A very singular boot. One issued only to police officers who have undergone special training.'

'Riot training,' I said.

'And, more worryingly, firearms training.'

'I was trying not to think about that.'

'You know your trouble, Shannon?' he laughed. 'Where guns are concerned, you always transgress the golden rule. You're supposed to stay on the side with the butt. Not stand in a direct line with the barrel.'

'Don't tell me,' I protested. 'Tell the people who keep shooting at me.'

'Why spoil the fun,' he grinned. 'So,' he continued, 'I went to the Commander. Laid the evidence – or lack of it – in front of him. Asked him if he, like me, could smell the stench of cover-up.'

'And?'

'And I told him that unless he let me investigate, I would go to the media.'

'Whose nostrils are more highly developed than your average bloodhound.'

'Exactly,' he said. 'Of course, the Commander couldn't actually go as far as formally sanctioning the investigation – not the Met's jurisdiction – but he did allow me paid leave for six weeks.'

'And while you've been away,' I warned, 'the mouse has been playing. Walker has mounted a takeover bid. By the time you get back, you might not have a squad to your name.'

'Let her have it,' he said, without a hint of generosity in his voice. 'What do I care? Good riddance. I never wanted the job in the first place. Crime, Shannon, takes place on the streets. That's where you need coppers. Not sitting behind a bloody desk all day.'

'Someone has to plan the movements of the long arm of the law.'

'Then let Walker do the planning. Or plotting, should we say?' He gave me a wink. 'We both know that's what she's best at.' He took a deep puff at the cigarette. Held it clamped tightly between two fingers as he pointed at me. 'And when I clear up the mystery behind the hit-and-run, the Commander will have to give in to my demands for a front-line job.'

'*When?*' I said. 'Not *if?*'

'I'm getting closer to the truth, Shannon. That's why I had to get you here so you could hear Leyton's phoney confession for yourself.'

'Then perhaps you could explain the little charade we just witnessed. Why did Leyton confess? And how can you be sure he wasn't the driver? Or are those inexplicable mysteries of the Orient?'

'Four weeks *is* a long time,' he said, sighing. 'Leyton bloody Orient.' He rolled his eyes towards the low ceiling. 'I'd forgotten just how bad your sense of humour was.'

'At least I have one.'

'Well,' he said. 'I haven't seen much to smile about lately. But I will. When I've cracked this case, we can both have a bleeding good chuckle.'

'Not me,' I said.

'Perhaps not,' he said. 'I see your point. Sorry, Shannon. Anyway, I know Leyton couldn't be responsible for the very simple reason that he never received special training – and the boots that go with it.'

'Are you saying he confessed to protect the real culprit?'

'Why not? Leyton had nothing to lose. Maybe he owed someone a favour – you know what we coppers are like for favours. Thought he might as well save a skin before he popped his clogs.'

'I don't exactly feel waves of sympathy rolling over me from your direction.'

'You know how I loathe bent coppers, Shannon. I hope Leyton rots in hell. My only regret is that I couldn't get the truth out of him.'

Couldn't beat the truth out of him, more like.

'How did you get on to Leyton?' I asked.

'Good old-fashioned police work' he said with a worryingly evasive shrug of his shoulders. 'But now isn't the time for all the ins and outs. Don't want to bore you with details. What are *you* up to, Shannon? What's so important that you let your mind wander from avenging your sister?'

'I'm working on a case for Oldbrook Borough Council. I seem, *en passant*, to have upset an organisation called OWN.'

Collins looked at me sharply.

'You might say,' I admitted, 'that I'm knee-deep in trouble.'

'I wouldn't say that.' He shook his head. 'Not knee-deep, at least. If you've crossed swords with OWN, I would say a much better description was up to your neck.'

'OWN,' Collins said, sighing heavily and shaking his head at me. He helped himself to another coffee from the machine. Added more whisky. Settled himself back down as if we were in for a long session. 'You sure can pick 'em, Shannon. Of all the crooked, dangerous, stop-at-nothing organisations in the world that you could have chosen, *you* have to single out OWN. The worst of the lot. If there was a Richter scale for trouble, you'd be in the earthquake zone.'

'I hate to point this out,' I said sulkily, 'but, in the past, my problems could mostly be lain at your door. Future Assurance. Glenshield, before that. It's *you* who usually gets *me* into trouble.'

'And what happens when I leave you to your own

devices?' he replied, somehow managing to sound both innocent and offended at the same time 'You step on the tender toes of OWN, that's what.'

'Look, if all you're going to do is criticise, I'd rather go home and catch up on my beauty sleep.'

'Nick,' he said soothingly, 'don't misunderstand me. I'm just concerned about you, that's all. I see it as part of my job to protect you.'

But from what? Or for what? I was beginning to get an uneasy feeling. When Collins became all sweetness and light it was generally an ominous sign.

'Why don't you tell me all about it?' he said, smiling sympathetically.

The hairs on the back of my neck prickled. But I told him anyway. I reckoned I was maybe too close to the case at the moment. An outsider's view – I wouldn't go so far as to say impartial where Collins was concerned – might help me see the wood for the trees.

He listened attentively as I went through the story from the very beginning. Not the whole story, of course: I felt it best to omit the sub-plot of Mrs Crabtree, Blackstone's scam and the fate I had in mind for the fraudster. Collins pricked up his ears at the mention of Walker. Nodded sagely at the financial and political plight of Ali Khan. Sighed wearily at my tackling of the thugs from OWN. Shook his head sadly at the subsequent trashing of our building in Docklands.

'So,' he said when I had finished, 'you don't have any actual evidence of OWN's involvement in the murder of Rashid and the attempts to keep you away from the council. Or anything concrete with which to link the missing money to this Helen lady and her toy boy.'

'Not yet,' I said. 'But I'm working on it.'

'That's good,' he said.

That's bad, I thought. Then immediately began to revise my thinking. Started going off the whole idea of getting more deeply involved.

'You see,' he continued, 'Special Branch has been trying to pin something on OWN for a good while now. Close down the organisation, put the ringleaders behind bars. But so far, so bad. No joy, I'm afraid.'

'Uh huh,' I said warily.

'OWN box clever,' he explained. 'No one even knows who spearheads the organisation. They have a PR guy who acts as their spokesman and churns out their propaganda, but otherwise they operate with the same level of secrecy as the Knights of the Ku Klux Klan. Except in OWN's case they use black balaclavas instead of pointy white hoods to protect identities.'

Collins paused thoughtfully.

Out of bitter experience I refrained from asking the obvious question of why hadn't Special Branch attempted an undercover operation, planting someone in the organisation to gather evidence. I didn't want to run the risk of being misconstrued and mistaken for a volunteer.

'What's your interest in OWN?' I asked instead.

'We – the Fraud Squad – worked on the case with Special Branch earlier this year. You know OWN's history?' he said.

'Breakaway from the National Front,' I said, repeating what little information Walker had given me. 'Bunch of disaffected hard-line ultra-radicals who thought that the Front had gone soft.'

'They evolved from the Front, yes,' he said, 'but in the process became something much more dangerous. You see, the National Front was never really a major threat to law and order. Granted, they stirred a few irrational fears among a small minority of the population. But they never actually caused much trouble. A few banner-waving rallies, a bit of incitement to racial violence, but it never led to much. They were a big embarrassment to the government, sure – that pamphlet they produced, *Did Six Million Really Die?*, stating that the Holocaust never happened, sold hundreds of thousands of copies and gave the impression for a while that Britain was a hotbed of neo-Nazism. OWN, Nick, is different. Not just because they are more fanatical. OWN can buy supporters, can hire thugs to do its dirty work. OWN has money. Lots of it. And God knows where it comes from. That was why the Fraud Squad got involved. We were asked by Special Branch to see if we could trace the source of their funds, prove its illegality and cut off the supply.'

'But without success, I presume?'

'The only bank accounts we could find were in Switzerland. The authorities there, as is their bleeding wont, refused to release any details. Our guess was that the funds were brought back into this country in cash by couriers.'

'So you hit a brick wall? A dead end?'

'I hope that is not an unfortunate phrase, Nick,' he said seriously. 'What with this Festival coming up next week. I don't see OWN letting such an opportunity pass by. I'd be willing to lay good money that they're planning something big. If you hear anything while you're in Oldbrook, let me know, eh? It would be nice to have a rain check signed by Special Branch.'

'You're all heart, Chris,' I said.

'You've got enough for both of us, Nick,' he said. 'One last thing before we leave this dump.'

'And what might that be?'

'This missing four hundred grand.'

'Yes?'

'What's your theory? Is it going straight into Helen's purse or her toy boy's back pocket?'

'That's what I assumed. What's the alternative?'

'Do you believe in coincidence?' he asked.

'Why?' I replied guardedly.

'The London Borough of Oldbrook was formed about three years ago. Isn't that right?'

I nodded.

'And so was OWN,' he said.

CHAPTER TWENTY-SEVEN

Day Seven

Monday morning. The final countdown had begun. But, unlike NASA, we had no *Abort* button to press if things got out of control.

Saturday had been spent shopping for a camera, and an outfit in which Arlene would feel at ease, and in role for her meeting with the Manx bank manager. The former item took about fifteen minutes; the latter, including the necessary accessories of shoes and handbag, around two hours – although it seemed more like four (days). In response to Arlene's question of 'How does this look?' I must have said the word *fine* more times than a weather forecaster in the Seychelles at the height of summer. And all to no avail. Arlene would shake her head, say, 'No, it's not quite right', and move back to browse the garments hanging on the rail or on to the next shop. By the end of the afternoon I knew every crack in the pavements along Bond Street. Somehow, we managed to find time to book a ferry crossing from Liverpool to Douglas (no suitable flights being available from any of the London airports now that the tourist season had ended) and a hire car for the journey – which thankfully didn't have to coordinate with the fuchsia pink of the new trouser suit.

Sunday had been a day of relaxation – a walk through Regent's Park, lunch at a wine bar opposite Camden Town tube station – and an evening of running over the final details of the planned scam against Blackstone.

'But will it work?' Arlene had asked us for the umpteenth time.

'I don't believe in making predictions,' Norman said. 'Never have, never will.'

She groaned. 'How about a serious answer to my question.'

'I think we can make it sound very plausible,' I said. 'And we have two firmly held beliefs on our side. Firstly, Blackstone, being totally unprincipled, will cynically believe that everyone else is too – he will be convinced that something crooked is being planned and want to cash in on it. The second, while we're on the subject, is that, of all local government functions, Planning is the one that has attracted most adverse publicity for underhand dealings and backhand payments. All we need to do is drop a hint here, leave something unsaid there, and Blackstone will put two and two together. It won't be our fault if he comes up with the wrong answer.'

'Well,' she had replied, 'take care, the two of you. Keep out of the range of his bodyguards. Both before and after you pull the scam.'

'By the time he finds out he's been conned, the case will be over and we'll be long gone. Don't worry. Nothing can go wrong.'

She had been convinced at the time, but her confidence must have dwindled with a night's sleep. Earlier this morning, while we sat, camera at the ready, in her hire car awaiting Adam's arrival at the council's car park, she had sought extra reassurance and reiterated the need for caution. Patiently I had repeated the benefits of the plan and stressed its simplicity. 'The best plans are always the simplest.' I didn't bother telling her that there was no alternative.

We had been in place since half past eight. Adam had not shown up, as might have been expected, until a minute before nine, but we couldn't afford to take any chances that, for once in his working life, he would be early. The photographs taken, Arlene had set off to the nearest developers that advertised a one-hour service. I kissed her goodbye, fussed about the route to Liverpool, reminded her about driving on the left and generally behaved as if she were off on safari and I wouldn't see her for three months, if ever again.

Now, sartorially correct, if not elegant, in my rag-bag collection of second-hand clothes and sporting a two-day growth of stubble, I entered the first of the Social Services outstations I intended to visit before lunch.

The door led into what had originally been the front room of a terraced house. A wall had been knocked down, increasing the size by about three feet and transforming what had been a small square room into a marginally larger rectangle. There was just enough space for a reception desk, four fold-up chairs and a coffee table. One wall had been covered in corkboard and was a patchwork quilt of notices – local support groups, fringe organisations (Save the Gay Whale, or the like) touting for members, hostels willing to provide a bed for one night, soup kitchens, the dangers of drug abuse, suppliers of free needles and so on – in more languages than I could count and in scripts where I was unsure whether to read from top to bottom and left to right or vice versa.

The girl behind the desk peered past the screen of her computer and looked me up and down – probably from side to side and inside out too.

'Yes?' she said.

I would have preferred 'How may I help you?' but maybe she assumed that anyone seeking help had a brain of equal size to their bank balance, and that monosyllables were the most effective means of communication.

'I need to speak to someone,' I said, scratching at my bristly chin for verisimilitude. 'I need a place to doss. And some money to tide me over, like.'

'Do you have an appointment?'

'I tried to make one on Friday, but you were shut.'

'Unforeseen circumstances,', she said with the matter-of-fact curtness of someone who has been taught never to apologise. 'Now, let me see.'

And me too. I craned over the desk to get a better view of her screen. A blast of citric perfume hit my nose. The smell was about as subtle as her bright orange T-shirt and lavender blue leggings. Still, when you're barely twenty you can get away with that clash of colours – or at least you think you can.

She clicked the mouse a few times and a computerised diary appeared.

'Wow, that's clever,' I said. 'What is it?'

She gave me a withering look.

'Just a diary. Allows me, and anyone else in Social Services, to see all the appointments for any of the social workers.'

'They come and look over your shoulder, do they?'

She sighed. 'We're connected,' she explained, 'by ISDN lines – a sort of cable, that is – to the main computer at the council.'

Slave models, as I had assumed. Mrs Clark really hadn't been very clever in her attempt at budget rigging; going for stand-alone models because they were more expansive.

'Mr Ngogo and Miss Gilman are out on calls,' she said, studying the screen. 'Mrs Bannerjee and Mr Hutchinson are fully booked until eleven and then they have calls to make.'

'I don't mind waiting,' I said with a shrug. 'On the off chance, like. Got nothing else to do.'

I sat down on one of the hard chairs before she could dissuade me otherwise. Picked up one of the tabloids from the coffee table. Stretched out my legs and prepared for a short read and a long wait.

Over the course of the next hour a series of clients arrived. Mrs Bannerjee (first name, printed on a badge, unpronounceable) and Mr Hutchinson (Iain) collected them from the reception area, took them into their respective rooms and fifteen minutes later, like clockwork (or Sindy), the whole process was repeated. Neither of the two social workers had the time, or maybe the inclination, to give me a second glance (avoid eye contact wherever possible, the manual probably cautioned – it only leads to trouble). Mrs Bannerjee wore a flowing sari and a fixed smile which only emphasised the stress written on her face; Mr Hutchinson wore jeans and cowboy boots. Unless this was the new trend-setting uniform of male social workers, he was the man I had glimpsed exiting the building on Friday afternoon.

I was just about blending in with the wallpaper when my mobile rang. It didn't exactly blow my cover, but it didn't do my prospects of getting a hand-out much good. I gave the receptionist a weak smile and beat a hasty retreat.

The call was from Norman.

'We're on,' he said, his voice a mixture of excitement and tension. 'I'll try to keep him busy till half past two, but you'd better stand by from two o'clock onwards just in case.'

'But it can't be any earlier,' I said, suddenly worried. 'Jakki doesn't get back from lunch till then.'

'I'll keep him plied with drink, you keep your fingers crossed,' he said. 'You know what you have to say?'

'Yes, Norman,' I sighed. 'It was my idea, you know.'

'Sorry,' he said. 'Last-minute nerves. Stage fright. It's a while since I did this kind of thing.'

'And hopefully a while before we have to do it again. Sock it to him, Norman. Act your heart out.'

'"Now",' he said, '"is the winter of our discontent . . ."'

'Wrong play,' I interrupted. 'Try "Friends, Romans and Blackstone, lend me your four hundred grand."'

'I do a good Long John Silver,' he said.

I resisted the temptation to tell him to hop it.

'Keep it simple, eh, Norman,' I said.

'No parrot then?' he asked innocently.

'Goodbye, Norman,' I groaned. 'And good luck.'

I walked back to the car and headed across Oldbrook to the next outstation on the list. En route I saw workmen making preparations for the Festival. Bunting – how very British, no celebration is complete without bunting – was being strung up and coloured lights wired in along the main streets where the procession would pass. Several shops had signs warning customers that they would be closed – and presumably boarded up – from four o'clock on Friday. Many storekeepers, I suspected, had learned from the last riots the lesson of taking precautions against looters.

The second outstation was similar to the first: a run-down property in a run-down location, but what else could one expect in Oldbrook? Instead of a wall of corkboard there was a large home-made pinboard in a wooden frame. Same notices, same computer on desk, slight variant on the receptionist front (black girl, a couple of years older than the first, long blouse, thick belt, short skirt, marginally less bored expression) but pretty much *déjà vu* land.

I was going through the beard-scratching, 'gimme hand-out' routine when Hutchinson walked in, imaginary spurs jangling on his cowboy boots.

'This gentleman', the receptionist said to him, 'would like to see someone.'

'Not today,' Hutchinson said, shaking his head at me. 'You'll have to make an appointment. I'm very busy.'

I bet you are, Mr Hutchinson.

Or is it, as your name badge now says, Mr Cartwright? Bonanza!

CHAPTER TWENTY-EIGHT

You'd think people had never seen someone shave before. Me, I'd watched Spanish lorry drivers at motorway service stations contort their bodies as if they were practising some Iberian version of t'ai chi simply to wash their feet in the hand basin and hold them under the stream of hot air from the hand drier. And all without batting an eyelid. Okay, so I was in a public convenience, and not a very salubrious one at that, but that was no reason to stare or, worse still, look at me out of the corner of one eye as if I were a professional gun-toting paid assassin slipping effortlessly from one disguise into another.

The publicly performed ablutions were a necessary evil. I couldn't really show up at the council offices looking like a refugee from a TV documentary about what can happen to a person who doesn't watch *The Clothes Show* or who lacks the important gene that makes him susceptible to all-so-convincing advertisements for those electric razors that are so good the bloke bought the company. So here I was, scraping a blade across the stubble and puzzling over the ways of the world. Think about it for a minute. The guy in the advertisement obviously had a lot of imagination – how else could he have diversified into nose and ear trimmers? – so how come he ploughed his money into razors? If *you* had that sort of cash, what would you buy? The answer's obvious. Something like the Thornton's chocolates company, a vodka brewery, or a champagne vineyard. But electric shavers?

I flinched as I nicked myself – serve me right for not concentrating, do I hear you say? – and a little trickle of blood began to run down my chin. I focused my wandering mind on the job in hand. And the fraud in Social Services. I could just picture what had gone through Mrs Clark's mind. You can't get the quantity or quality of staff. You feel protective of your existing people who are working their proverbial butts off. And all for the immutable-scale salary that makes no allowances for circumstances or commitment above and beyond the call of duty. Why not put some well-deserved money in their back pockets by inventing a full complement and sharing the pay-out? She would see it as just another paper transaction and excuse it with a pragmatic shrug of her mother hen's wings. There was still some checking to be done, the full cost to be counted, but I knew with absolute certainty that a ten per cent slice of something would soon be coming our way.

I finished my cold-water shave. Rinsed my face. Dabbed it dry on the towel from my holdall. Risked even more suspicious looks by splashing on some aftershave. Slipped into a cubicle to change into my white shirt, suit and tie. Started to rehearse the roles I would play this afternoon.

On arriving back at the council, I found the place buzzing. The reception area, rather than being quiet as I had hoped, was filled with staff crowding around several large packing cases. Two porters were working hard to create order out of chaos. Each fished around in a box, took out an elaborate costume, shouted the name pinned on the front and waited for the lucky recipient to push their way forward.

I spied Jakki examining a red-and-white striped length of fabric which looked as if it had come straight from the sands of Marbella.

'What's going on?' I asked, squeezing through the throng to her side.

'It's our costumes for the float. The council is leading the Festival procession.'

'What's the theme?' I said, wondering if it was Beach Towels Through The Ages.

'Peoples of the world,' she said, her heavily mascaraed eyelashes fluttering wildly with excitement.

'Must have taken eons to come up with such an original idea,' I commented.

'We're all wearing national costumes,' she explained, as if that was likely to change my opinion. Then she smiled at me. 'You don't get it, do you?'

'I have to admit the subtlety is lost on me.'

'We're all wearing someone else's national costume. Mine', she said, flourishing the fabric and producing about a dozen multicoloured strings of beads, 'is Kenyan. Clever, isn't it? Mr Khan says it is symbolic.'

'Really,' I said. In my experience, when someone claims something is symbolic it usually means that the explanation that follows has none of the first syllable and loads of the last two.

She nodded thoughtfully as if casting her mind back to some internal memo from the great man himself. 'It symbolises the ease with which we can all embrace another person's culture.'

'The moccasin analogy,' I said, half to myself.

It was her turn to look puzzled.

'The native Indians of America say that the only way to really understand a man is to walk a mile in his moccasins.'

'And the only way for a man to really understand a woman,' she said with a twinkle in her eye and a smile dancing on her lips, 'is for him to walk a mile in her stilettos.'

I shook my head. 'Fifty yards would be sufficient. What with the pain and the embarrassment. And talking of embarrassment,' I said, managing to manufacture a convoluted link, 'you could save me a lot today.'

'Why do I get the feeling that I've just walked into a trap?'

Maybe because you've just walked into a trap.

'It's only a small favour,' I said.

'Uh huh?' she said dubiously, as if many a man had said the same thing before.

'You know that client I was telling you about? The one who insists on getting my name wrong? Who, for some reason, keeps calling me Bannerman?'

She nodded her head slowly.

'Well, he's coming in to see me this afternoon.'

'And?'

'And I wondered if you could save both him and me a lot of embarrassment. When he asks for Bannerman, can you just play along?'

'Is that all?' she said with a sigh of relief.

'Perhaps you could phone me when he arrives? I'll be in Human Resources.' I screwed up my face and shook my head. 'Better not tell him that. It will only confuse the poor guy. Won't know what you're talking about. Maybe you could simply say that I'm in a Planning Meeting – that's easy to understand. Sounds important too. Yes, I like that. Planning Meeting. Ring me when he arrives – I'll phone you first with the number of an extension – and I'll pop down and see him.'

'I won't be back from lunch till two,' she warned.

'That's okay. He shouldn't be here before then.' Fingers crossed. 'Thanks, Jakki.'

'All part of the service.' She paused. 'Nick,' she said, 'would you like to be on our float? I'm sure we could accommodate you. One more wouldn't make any difference.'

To me it would. Prancing around in a silly costume wasn't high on my list of fun things to do on a Friday afternoon.

'Can I let you know?' I prevaricated.

'Did you know,' she said, 'that there are fifty-two nationalities speaking forty-seven languages in the borough?' She didn't wait for my gasp of surprise. 'In fact,' she said, 'we're short of someone for one of our nationalities.'

'Really,' I said, glancing ostentatiously at my watch. 'I must go, Jakki.'

'Don't you want to know which one?'

'I can hardly contain my apathy,' I said.

'Great,' she said, her eyes sparkling.

'Well?'

A smile began to break out on her pink lips.

'Zulu,' she said. 'Terrific costume.'

What there is of it, I thought. Free bout of pneumonia for every lucky wearer.

'Damn,' I said, shaking my head in self-rebuke. 'Silly me. The procession is *Friday*. I'm already committed. Otherwise . . . Well, see you later, Jakki,' I said, moving quickly towards the lifts.

'Spoilsport,' she called after me.

Human Resources was a winter wonderland. Rows of white filing cabinets lined both side walls of the large square room on the second floor; white plastic-topped desks stood back to back like icebergs floating in a sea of pale blue carpet. Even the anglepoise lamps were white. I suspected that the chromatically single-minded interior designer had gnashed his teeth in frustration at not being able to find a practical way of making everyone use white ink on white paper. The whole effect was probably intended to be clinical, *symbolising*, you can almost hear him proclaim – it had to be a man, no woman would create a room like this – the objectivity of a department that records the lives of people without comment, criticism or condemnation. But, having not known when to stop, the result was sterility. I felt as if I would have to scrub up before being allowed to touch anything.

I approached an authoritative-looking woman who was handing out a sheaf of papers to a young man with metal-rimmed spectacles and glazed eyes. She leaned over him intimidatingly – or maybe it was intimately – one hand balanced on his desk.

The woman was around forty years old, wearing a

tightly cut lightweight beige suit over a dark brown tank top. The cream high-heeled shoes had peep toes and thin ankle straps. I revised my previous estimate on the stiletto front down from fifty yards to twenty feet. The one good thing you could say about the shoes was that they drew attention away from the dimpled knees revealed by a skirt which was three inches too short for her figure.

'Shannon,' I said, extending my hand and then fighting the instinct to withdraw it as I caught sight of the long red fingernails heading in its direction.

'Velma Thorne,' she said softly. 'What can I do for you?'

'I'm working in Treasury. I was told that I could examine the personnel records if I came along here.'

'Oh, you're that Shannon,' she said, as if there were hordes of us roaming the offices. God forbid, many would say. 'Adam mentioned you. Such a charming boy is Adam.'

Are we talking about the same Adam?

'It isn't the most convenient time, you know,' she said.

'Rarely is, Velma,' I replied with a smile. 'But you'll hardly notice me, I promise. I won't disturb anyone.'

It was partly true, but only inasmuch as there were very few people here. Probably still in the throng downstairs, swathing themselves in grass skirts and bikini tops. Missing all the fun as usual, Shannon.

'Walk this way,' she said as I suppressed a grin, and she swayed her hips over to a desk in the centre of the room where I could be observed most easily. 'The files are in alphabetical order starting with the cabinet on the left. If you could replace them exactly where you found them before you leave.'

She swivelled on her heels in preparation to return to her work, then turned back to me.

'Will Adam be coming to help you?' she asked hopefully.

'Other things to do,' I said. 'You know Adam.'

'Yes,' she sighed, leaving me feeling upstaged.

I picked up the phone and called Jakki; gave her the

extension number; tapped the bar to clear the line and called Adam. I asked him to read out from the payroll all those employed in the Social Services outstations.

'I'll call you back,' he said, sounding distracted.

'Nope,' I said, not wishing to twiddle my thumbs for the next couple of hours. 'I'll hold. And I'd like them listed by outstation, please.'

'Are you on to something?' he asked to a background of key tapping.

'Maybe,' I said, unwilling to trust him any more.

Taking a pad from my briefcase, I waited, pen poised. Adam read out twenty names in four sets of five, taking trouble to spell out letter by letter the more complicated ones. I thanked him, hung up and started to move methodically along the lines of filing cabinets, pulling out drawers, extracting those records and the ones for Adam, Helen, McCready and Rashid for good measure but no good reason other than curiosity.

Back at the desk I arranged the outstation files in order of location and set about making notes on the two I had visited that morning. Apart from the lowest paid member of staff – the receptionist – the offices' complements were mirror images. The ages of Hutchinson and/or Cartwright were within two years of each other. Mrs Bannerjee had a *doppelgänger* called Bhindi (of bhaji fame, no doubt); Ngogo was Mbopo at the other office; Gilman was Gladwin. It was the same story with the other two outstations. In each case an actual real-life social worker was duplicated by a non-existent one of a similar age and background. The 'phantoms' were easy to pinpoint, all having joined four months ago, the exact time when Mrs Clark had decided her expenditure against budget needed boosting.

I was just about to delve into Adam's file when the phone rang.

'Mr Blackstone is here,' Jakki said.

'Can you put him on?' I said. 'Yes, Mr Blackstone. What can I do for you?'

'Will you come down to me, Bannerman?' a smooth voice asked. 'Or would you prefer me to come up to your office?'

'I don't understand,' I said. 'Do you have an appointment? Do I know you?'

'Not yet,' he said. 'But we have a common acquaintance – a Mr Simpkins.'

Simpkins was Norman's assumed name for the purpose of the case.

'I'll be right down,' I said, sounding very anxious.

'I rather thought you might,' he said.

'Mr Blackstone?' I said tentatively, singling out the tall, immaculately dressed man in his late thirties flanked by two huge thugs in figure-hugging dark suits. 'Shall we get some fresh air?' I added with a nervous glance around the reception area.

'Excellent idea, Bannerman,' Blackstone replied, while Jakki suppressed a knowing giggle. 'You lead the way.'

I headed towards the door. The two heavies fell in step beside me, a hand on each of my elbows, ready to scoop me up and carry me bodily from the building at the first sign of a change of heart on my part. We did a little dance at the entrance, neither of them wishing to relinquish their grip but not having the mental machinery to work out how we would get through the doorway three abreast. Which, of course, we couldn't.

A shiny black Rolls-Royce was parked on the double yellow lines outside.

'Let's take a little ride,' Blackstone said.

'Perhaps you could tell me what this is about,' I said, raising my voice a squeaky semitone.

'Don't come the innocent with me, Bannerman. You wouldn't be here now if you didn't know exactly what I want to talk to you about. Get in the car.'

I hesitated. Made out I was studying his face to sum up his resolve. Instead, took in the curling lips, the cold grey eyes, the light brown hair trimmed to perfection.

'Mr Blackstone has asked you real nice like,' one of the heavies said in a low, guttural voice. What it lacked in volume, it made up in menace. The man had an ugly scar running across the right side of his ugly face. 'Now,' he added, 'you can either do as Mr Blackstone says or . . .'

Christ, he was corny. Probably spent his leisure hours watching old gangster movies – when he wasn't biting the heads off whippets, that is.

The other bodyguard, also a graduate of the Kray School of Charm, opened the rear door and stood there running thick fingers through his long greasy hair. Which surprised me, I have to admit. I'd expected his brand of displacement activity to be scratching of armpits.

I climbed in obediently. Shuffled across to the far side as Blackstone slid in beside me. Shuffled back again as Scarface entered by the offside door and boxed me in. Very cosy.

Mountain Gorilla wormed his way into the front seat and started the engine. 'Where to, Mr Blackstone?' he asked.

'Just keep going round the block. That all right by you, Bannerman?'

I nodded.

'Answer Mr Blackstone,' Scarface said, banging his elbow into my ribs.

'Yes, Mr Blackstone,' I said quickly.

'That's better,' Scarface grunted.

'I've just had a very interesting lunch,' Blackstone announced, unbuttoning his silver-grey jacket. 'With our mutual friend, Simpkins.'

'I've never met any Simpkins,' I said, choosing my words with the utmost care so as not to say anything that was actually a lie but at the same time trying to sound shifty and unconvincing.

Blackstone rewarded me with a cynical laugh.

'I was propositioned,' he said.

'You can never tell nowadays,' I said, preparing myself for another rib-breaker. I wasn't disappointed. 'Sorry, Mr Blackstone.'

'Say *sir*,' Scarface ordered, enjoying himself.

'Sorry, sir.'

'Don't you want to hear about this proposition?' Blackstone said, as if it would make any difference what I replied.

I shrugged. But I did it with a silent 'sir'.

'Christ,' I howled as the pain shot through me.

'Simpkins asked me to buy a property for him. Said he needed to remain anonymous – didn't like publicity, even if it was only a local rag.'

'Some people are like that,' I said casually, adding instantly, 'sir.'

'Simpkins was willing to pay me handsomely for my assistance.'

I looked out of the window, pretending nonchalance.

'He said I could go up to four hundred and fifty thousand pounds for the property. And he'd buy it off me in a week for half a million.'

'Very generous, sir,' I said.

'Very peculiar, you mean,' Blackstone said. 'You see, for one thing, he couldn't tell me the name or location of the property. He gave me a full set of legal documents for the purchase, but the name and location had been left blank. Said he'd telephone me tomorrow with those details.'

'Maybe he didn't trust you.'

A throaty snigger came from the front seat.

'Maybe,' Blackstone said. 'But, you see, I got to thinking. Started asking myself questions. If Simpkins was willing to pay half a million, then what was the property really worth? What was *his* profit going to be? And, more importantly, why shouldn't it be mine?'

Scarface nodded his head.

'Now, correct me if I'm wrong,' Blackstone said, knowing I wouldn't dare, 'but no one hands out fifty grand or more just for the privilege of remaining anonymous. I smell a rat, Bannerman.'

255

Me too, I thought. And he's sitting beside me. And I don't mean Scarface.

'When Simpkins excused himself to pay a call of nature,' Bannerman continued smugly, 'I had a little peek in his briefcase. Nothing much there of interest. Except, that is, a piece of paper with the name Bannerman, and the initials OBC beside it. Let's just say I didn't need the services of a mathematical genius to put two and two together.'

'I'd like to help you, Mr Blackstone, sir, but I don't know what you're talking about.'

'How much was Simpkins going to pay you?'

'Pay me?'

He sighed. Shook his head wearily for good measure.

'I am not a man of violence. Please don't force me to ask Brian' – now what the hell kind of a name was that for a thug: no wonder the guy had psychotic tendencies – 'to break your arm.'

'But I don't . . .'

'I hope you weren't going to say "I don't know what you're talking about." I have a particularly low threshold of boredom. Bannerman,' he said, the sigh heavier now, the head shake a little more weary, 'you work in Planning, right? Don't bother denying it, that girl on reception told me.'

'What has my job got to do with it?' I said, carefully avoiding confirming what he thought he knew.

'This is a Planning scam, Bannerman. Stands out a mile. So, I repeat my question. How much was Simpkins going to pay you for the inside track?'

I looked at Gorilla in the front, Scarface by my right side, let my hand drift to my lip as if considering my options.

'Strangely,' I said, 'the figure thirty thousand pounds has just popped into my head.'

'Then I'll match it,' he said.

'You'll give me thirty thousand pounds?' I asked in astonishment.

'And you'll take it, if you know what's good for you.' He

paused to suck air through his teeth. 'Because if you don't,' he shrugged, 'we'll break both your arms. And then move on to your legs.'

'You don't leave me much choice.'

'Stop whinging, Bannerman. Whereabouts is the property?'

'I don't know,' I said.

'Break his arm, Brian.'

'No, you don't understand,' I said, doing a hasty impersonation of someone scared witless – or something like that. I cast nervous glances at Scarface and Mountain Gorilla as if reluctant to say anything in front of witnesses. 'Let's talk hypothetically. Say there's a choice of three sites for a new development. And two of those sites are owned by the leader of the council, Ali Khan. You can imagine how delicate a situation that might be. And the secrecy it would necessitate. Even Mr Khan wouldn't be allowed to know what's going on. Not until after any decision had been made. Which might be tonight, if that is when the Planning Sub-committee meets.'

Blackstone took a card from his wallet.

'Ring me as soon as the meeting has finished.'

'No,' I said.

'What?' he boomed.

'I'll meet you outside the council offices at half past nine in the morning. You hand over thirty grand in cash, *then* I'll give you an address. Otherwise the deal is off. And don't bother threatening me. You need me, Blackstone. What would developers pay for a prime site? A cool million, do you think?'

'Okay,' he said. 'Nine-thirty tomorrow. And don't even think about contacting Simpkins.'

'Simpkins?' I said innocently. 'As far as I'm concerned, he doesn't even exist.'

CHAPTER TWENTY-NINE

'A result,' I said proudly to Norman, as he sipped a glass of champagne and beamed up at me from what had become his armchair. '*I* have had a result.'

'You'd better sit down and join me then,' he said, taking the bottle from the bowl of ice at his side and producing a spare glass magically from under the chair.

I was late home, partly the result of Blackstone dropping me off about three miles from the council offices. 'Can't take any chances on being seen together,' he'd rationalised. Which was a bit rich since we were to meet outside the building in the morning. And I'd stopped en route to buy a box of chocolates for Jakki, then lingered in reception to thank her and listen politely while she talked excitedly for a good half-hour about the Festival – all the staff (even those not on duty on the float) were apparently being given the afternoon off on Friday. Not to mention specially printed T-shirts so that their support wouldn't be missed by the media.

Norman looked up at me with a smug expression on his face.

'Didn't you hear me?' I said. 'I have had a result.'

'Me too,' he said, grinning.

'BIackstone taking the bait was a foregone conclusion,' I said, waving my hand dismissively in the air. 'I'm not talking about him.'

'Neither am I,' he said.

'I think we had better start again,' I sighed, placing my bulging briefcase on the ragged carpet and taking a seat opposite him.

He finished slowly pouring the glass of champagne and passed it to me.

'So what's your result?' he asked. 'What fraud have you discovered?'

'Phantom staff on the payroll.'

I explained the background to the fraud – the underspend on the budget, the impossibility of recruiting experienced social workers to a place like Oldbrook – and how my masterly detective work had led inexorably to its discovery.

'So what's the bottom line?' he said, brushing aside my achievement – and my immodesty – and zeroing in on the aspect of prime importance to him. 'What do we stand to make as commission?'

'I haven't worked it out exactly yet,' I said. 'But I've brought all the personnel files back with me so that I can do the precise calculations.'

'Just give me a ballpark,' he said, topping up his glass.

'Well, eight non-existent staff at an average salary of around twenty-seven grand a year for a period of four months. I make that a fraud to date of approximately seventy-two thousand pounds.'

'Is that all?' he said derisively.

'It still comes to a commission for us of just over seven grand.'

'Chicken feed.'

'So nice to be appreciated,' I said sulkily. 'Thanks for all your hard work, Nick. The boy done good.'

He shrugged. 'I had a phone call from the insurance people this morning.'

'Don't change the subject.'

'They gave me the go-ahead to repair the damage to the building and to replace everything.'

'Oh, is that it?' I said. 'You've managed to con them out

of more than my seven grand's commission without lifting a finger.'

'I made some phone calls about new computers and office furniture – you remember those supplier details you gave me from the invoices to Commercial Services?'

I nodded, noticing Norman's trademark cheesy grin beginning to spread across his face.

'When I rang the first company, I asked to speak to a specific salesman. I quoted them the initials from the invoice.'

The penny dropped with a clang. Except that I had the feeling it was actually a lot more than a penny.

'There *was* no one with those initials,' he said. 'Same for the other suppliers. What do you say to that? The old man done good?'

'So the person doing the ordering in Commercial Services has freelanced his own deal with the suppliers.' I thought back to what Steve, head of the department, had said. 'If it's computers you're after, Terry's your man.' Terry, the only specialist among a staff of generalists. Anyone in the market for a computer would want him to handle the purchase. 'Terry is pocketing the commission,' I said.

'So how much do you reckon Commercial Services has spent on computers over the years?' The grin was plastered all over his face now. He tried to take a casual sip of champagne, but his contorted mouth wouldn't allow it.

'They must have a couple of hundred terminals,' I said, doing swift mental calculations. 'Plus the machines that act as servers. And then there are printers and scanners and software and . . .'

'Just give me a ballpark,' he repeated.

'Half a million, maybe.'

'We're in the money,' he sang.

'You jammy beggar.'

'Give me generals who are lucky. That's what Napoleon used to say. Don't knock luck, Nick. We all need a slice from time to time.'

'It seems like we may be on to a roll,' I said, unwisely tempting fate. 'Blackstone falling for the scam *and* two frauds uncovered. All in one day too.'

'No news from Arlene, I suppose?'

'She won't get to see the bank manager till the morning. What with the car journey and then the ferry crossing.' I took out my cigarettes, lit one and inhaled thoughtfully. 'I did have some news from Professor Davies though.'

'Ah,' Norman said seriously. 'Are we still on a roll?'

'Depends which way you look at it,' I said. 'The SOCO teams found yellow threads at our place and at Ali Khan's shop. They match the one Davies found on Rashid's body. Davies was quick to point out that it doesn't prove conclusively that the same people are involved with all three crimes, merely that the same type of glove was worn.'

'Conclusive proof!' he scoffed. 'The police may need that, but we don't. I would say that the conclusion is obvious. Unless . . .'

Norman's mouth dropped open.

I followed Norman's eyes and took in the sight of Arthur standing in the doorway, resplendent in a pair of dark green overalls, three sizes too small. The patches of dirt on the shoulders and around the many deep pockets made the heavy-duty garment look like something the army would wear for the purposes of camouflage. There was a smear of grime across his forehead, a blob of grease on his nose.

'Is that champagne?' he asked, taking two giant paces across to us.

The room filled with a pungent aroma. Unless my memory was playing tricks on me I marked it down as essence of dustbin – vintage Oldbrook. I held my nose as he reached for the champagne bottle. Norman shot up and opened the window wide. The sounds of Soho invaded the room. But it was a price worth paying.

'Well, Arthur,' Norman said, coughing and laughing at

the same time, 'you're looking particularly fetching this evening. What do you think, Nick?'

'Definitely,' I agreed. 'In fact I'd go so far as to say that he has a certain air about him.'

'Very funny,' Arthur grunted.

'Had a good day?' I asked, as Norman handed Arthur a placatory glass of champagne.

'Could have been worse,' he said. 'I won fifteen quid at poker.'

'You what?' I said.

'Is this Moët?' he asked, after an experimental sip from his glass.

Norman nodded.

'Thought so,' said Arthur. 'Still, never mind.'

'Pardon me for my parsimony,' Norman said.

'While I remember,' Arthur said inconsequentially, 'I have to take a flask of tea with me tomorrow. And some sandwiches. And something for a mid-morning snack.'

'What about some scones and clotted cream for the afternoon?' I said.

'That would be nice,' he replied. 'And strawberry jam. When I was a kid and we went to Devon for our holidays, we always had strawberry jam. Home-made, of course.' He smiled nostalgically. 'You can't whack home-made strawberry jam. Get more of your actual fruit in it, if you ask me. Nowadays . . .'

'Arthur,' I interrupted, 'if I can drag you back to the present, am I perhaps right in my impression that you haven't exactly been working your socks off today?'

'Don't get me wrong,' he said, 'we did *do* some collecting.'

'In between playing poker and breaks for sustenance?'

'You have to pace yourself. That's what the foreman said. No sense going about the job like a bull in a wassname.'

'Why not?' I asked. 'Emptying dustbins isn't exactly the most delicate operation in the world.'

Arthur shrugged. 'The foreman didn't say. But he's been doing the job for years. You got to bow to experience.'

'Especially,' Norman said, 'when you can do it sitting down with a mug of tea in one hand and a sandwich in the other.'

'It's not been a piece of cake,' he said defensively.

'Didn't expect you could find room for that too,' I said smiling.

'Don't forget the working conditions. You should see the place. It's a dump.'

'You surprise me.'

'Cooped up in a bleeding draughty old hut for half the day,' he grumbled.

'I don't understand,' I said, although I was beginning to. 'Why so little time spent working?'

'A couple of the trucks are busted,' he said. 'The council won't fork out the money to fix them, not with privatisation only a few days away. So the crews take turns at doing the collections with the trucks that are road-worthy. I reckon they don't do a bad job considering. A bit behind schedule, admittedly, but what can they expect?'

'How long has this been going on?' I asked.

'Good few months by all accounts.'

'Are you thinking what I'm thinking?' I said to Norman. He nodded his head sagely.

'Got any red wine?' Arthur asked. 'This is a bit gassy for me.'

'There's a couple of bottles breathing in the kitchen,' Norman said.

Good place to breathe, I thought.

Arthur walked past me to fetch a bottle and a clean glass, then back again. The smell from his clothes seemed to be getting worse.

'Will you do me a favour?' I asked. 'Before you sit back down, will you slip those overalls off and put them some-where out of range. The next county would do.'

He tossed his head. 'There was a time,' he said, 'when

263

you would happily have swapped the smell of my overalls for the stink of . . .'

'Don't remind me,' I said. 'I'm already struggling to enjoy this champagne as it is.'

He sighed; set the bottle and glass down on the gate-leg table; unbuttoned the overalls; tugged at the shoulders.

'Give me a hand, Nick,' he said. 'They're a bit tight.'

'Turn round,' I said, rising to my feet and steeling myself to place my hands on the dirt-covered, evil-smelling material.

Then I froze.

Sticking out of his back pocket was a pair of gloves.

A pair of yellow gloves to be precise.

I pulled them out gingerly and showed them to Norman.

'Are you thinking what I'm thinking?' he asked, frowning deeply.

'Unfortunately, yes.'

CHAPTER THIRTY

Day Eight

To say that the day presented certain logistical problems was like describing Elton John as a guy who'd made the odd bob or two by lightly tickling the ivories. As under-estimates go, it was a real humdinger. Lack of time, a woeful inadequacy of manpower and the inability to trust anyone within the council were the key constraints. If we were to achieve our objectives, then risks would have to be taken, cats deprived of their mittens.

We travelled into Oldbrook separately. Norman, who had a mission to undertake in the City, went with Arthur. I, having drawn the short straw, travelled first to Chingford and now had Mrs Crabtree as company. The best that could be said of my passenger was that she showed a high degree of adaptability: coped admirably with the absence of a second row of seats in the Lancia; managed to back-seat drive perfectly from the front.

Mrs Crabtree, when I had phoned to tell her of the scam, had insisted on being in at the kill – she wanted to physically see Blackstone hand over the money. It was an unmissable opportunity to savour the moment of sweet revenge. And, I suspected, the half-nine meeting would provide extra hours to spend on gloating. In some ways it suited me to have her along. Walking around with thirty thousand pounds in cash in my pocket would not have been wise, bearing in mind my plans for the day. I could now discharge myself of my responsibilities by handing the money straight over to her. Norman – needs must – would have to act as minder.

I dropped Mrs Crabtree off at the snack bar-cum-sandwich shop opposite the council offices at eight o'clock. Since I had a lot of digging around to do before keeping my appointment with Blackstone, she would have to pass the time in a cosy tête-à-tête with Norman and, when her patience waned, by showing the proprietor how to make a decent cup of tea and the exact thickness of butter that was necessary for the construction of a perfect bacon sandwich.

The night guard was coming to the end of his long stint. He flickered a sleepy eye at me as I stepped inside the building. I raised a hand in greeting, and walked directly to the lift as if on my way up to the fourth floor and Treasury. Which was true – in a way.

Exiting the lift at the fourth floor, I quickly descended the stairs to the lower of the two bridges spanning the central atrium. Crawled across it on my belly like a commando silently closing in on the enemy. Opened the door to the old building a fraction, intending to squeeze through. Stopped dead in my tracks as I heard the sound of a radio blaring. Paused first to curse under my breath and then to assess the situation.

Outside the second door on the left stood a cleaner's trolley. On the bottom shelf were two black plastic sacks bulging with rubbish, a dustpan and brush and a spare pair of neon-pink rubber gloves; on the top was a weird and wonderful collection of polishes, disinfectants, dusters and rags, and the aforementioned accursed radio. The door was open. From inside came the tone-deaf screech of the cleaner singing – huh! – along to some disc jockey's idea of blast-from-the-past, get-up-and-go, breakfast-time music. Under the current circumstances, 'Staying Alive' was more than a little grating on the nerves.

McCready's office was towards the end of the corridor and on the right. I tried to calculate how long I would have inside before the cleaner arrived. Would she work her way

266

down one side and then back? Or, better for my purposes, would she criss-cross along the corridor to the end? Then the thought struck me that I was just wasting time.

Moving silently – and pointlessly, I realised with embarrassment – to the open door, I stole a glance inside the room. The cleaner, polishing a desk, had her back to me. The dyslexic logo *Kleen-Rite* stood out in bright yellow letters against the background royal blue of her uniform. I sprinted past and entered McCready's office.

The room looked the same as on my first visit. The desk was still a mess, the folders of bank statements still stood in a straight line on the shelf like soldiers on parade.

I started with the papers strewn across the surface, examining the topmost and then carefully lifting these to see what lurked underneath. My light-fingered care and heavily paranoid caution were probably misplaced – unless the disorder was in fact a cleverly disguised unique method of filing, there was no way he was going to detect my prying.

The file I sought was buried halfway down a rickety pile on the right-hand corner. A clear plastic wallet contained a sheet with the names and addresses of the four companies who had been chosen to tender for the privatisation of refuse collection and disposal, together with a copy of the combined contract specification and background information. I would have loved to have stuffed the lot into my briefcase or taken it to the nearest photocopier, but I contented myself with noting down the details of the tenderers and the salient points from the document.

Next, it was over to the bank statements.

If Norman and I were right in our suspicions that someone was pulling a variant on the age-old 'backhanders for an inside track' fiddle, it was a fair assumption that the current tender was not the first time the scam had been employed. McCready's adherence to the principle of zero balance and the concomitant rigid separation of the different activities of the council by bank account should make my task simple. All I needed to do was locate the appropriate folder. The odds, *a priori*, were one in ten when I took down the first set of bank statements. Down to one in nine when I replaced that and reached for the second.

I found the one I wanted at the fourth attempt – the name of the catering company and that of *Kleen-Rite* jumped out at me from among the list of debits.

The music, louder now, closer now, changed to 'Step Inside, Love'. It was like having my own personal segue. What was next on the play list? Bloody Dire Straits? 'Money for Nothing'? What a joke!

I focused my mind back on the job in hand. And a bigger one than I had imagined. I hadn't appreciated quite how many services, or parts of services, had been contracted out. Some companies had unhelpful names that gave no clue as to their line of business, but others could be clearly linked to street cleaning, maintenance of grounds, fleet management, homes for the elderly, buses, parking and housing management. In all, there were twenty-seven names on my hastily scribbled list by the time I had finished.

And by the time the door handle turned.

'Later,' I shouted in simultaneous panic and broad Glaswegian. 'I canna be disturbed. Come back in ten minutes, woman.'

The door closed. The music receded a little as the trolley trundled one office along.

I waited until the cleaner's tuneless duet with the radio started up again. Assumed she had immersed herself in her chores – 'What chores?' 'Thanks, a large brandy would go down a treat at this very moment' – and cautiously peeked into the corridor. The coast was clear.

I turned left out of the door. Closed it behind me. Forced myself to ignore the instinct to run and instead affected an innocent and casual stroll.

Which was just as well since otherwise I would have collided headlong with McCready at the entrance to the new building.

'Shannon,' he said, reflectively fingering his beard. 'What are you doing here? At this hour, too.'

'Hoping to bump into you,' I (rep)lied. 'Thought you might be an early starter like myself. Just couldn't wait to tell you my news.'

'What news?'

'Perhaps we could go into your office.' I winked conspiratorially. 'Walls have ears, Stuart.'

'Although what they'd hear above the din of that bloody radio, I dinna ken. Mrs Kemp,' he bellowed angrily, striding along the corridor towards the source of his irritation. 'Turn off that insufferable cacophony. Instantly.'

'If not sooner,' I said to him supportively.

'Aye, if not sooner,' he shouted.

I suppressed a chuckle. Watched Mrs Kemp emerge red-faced and obediently silence the radio.

'Can I do you now, sir?' she asked, as if auditioning for a role in a sitcom.

'No, you may not *do* me now, Mrs Kemp. You should have *done* me in my absence.'

The chuckle was rapidly turning into a fully-fledged grin.

'But . . .' she stammered.

'Maybe you could leave Mr McCready today,' I suggested. 'And give him a double doing tomorrow.'

'Aye,' he agreed, opening his door. 'Anything for some peace and quiet.'

I followed him inside to the strains of Mrs Kemp mumbling to herself. 'Double doing!' she said. 'As if I've got time for double doings.'

'So, Shannon,' McCready said, depositing a large pilot's case on the floor by his desk and sitting down, 'what is this news you couldn't wait to tell me?'

'I've discovered two frauds.'

His brow furrowed into a deep frown. And from the little I could see of his jaw, I reckoned that dropped too.

'The first in Social Services,' I said.

'That's not news, Shannon. That's history. Mrs Clark has already been disciplined for her manipulation of the budget.'

'I'm afraid she has committed another, and much more serious, fraud.'

I took a stack of files from my briefcase, being careful to leave inside the ones relating to Helen, Adam, Rashid and McCready himself.

'These,' I said, placing one set of the files on the desktop, 'are the people working at the four Social Services outstations. And these,' I handed him the remaining files, 'are the others on the payroll. The only difference being that these eight do not exist. Mrs Clark has been busy redefining the phrase job-sharing.'

'Bloody woman,' he said, shaking his head. The mop of ginger hair fell across his eyes and he brushed it angrily aside. 'What does she think she is doing? How could she expect to get away with it?'

'She was getting away with it all right until I started to poke around.'

It was not immodesty on my part, but a deliberate attempt to stir the muddy waters of Oldbrook to see what – who – crawled out. I wanted to create uncertainty and fear; to prompt action – reckless action.

'And how exactly did you uncover this fraud?' he asked.

I explained in detail the thought process that had led to my investigation of the outstations. The little clues that Adam had missed – Mrs Clark's admission, for one – and would still have overlooked at the internal audit. The undercover visits that had exposed the fraud, the detailed examination of the personnel records that had proved it beyond reasonable doubt. With luck, the impression created would be of an alert and superior intelligence

(Shannon doesn't miss anything and can draw conclusions), painstaking diligence (he'll stick at a job until he has obtained the necessary proof) and pragmatic application (he can be as underhand as the fraudsters he's trying to catch). Either that or everyone would simply regard me as a big-headed, nosy sonovabitch. Every good plan has its drawbacks.

'You mentioned two frauds,' McCready said when I had finished my self-publicity.

'You'll like this one,' I said. Not a lot though. 'Very simple. Hard to spot. And a one-man operation. All the right ingredients for a successful fraud. Commercial Services, this time. Been going for years, I would think. You know Terry?'

'Aye,' he said. 'What you Sassenachs call a bit of a spiv.'

Sassenach! I had a good mind to let Arlene Tucker *née* Martinez loose on the man.

'Exactly,' I said with self-restraint. 'The spiv has been taking a cut on his purchases.'

I now explained the second fraud, gilding the lily some-what by omitting the element of luck and substituting in its place an instinct for all matters fraudulent which had led to a series of revealing telephone calls with suppliers.

'You've done a good job, Shannon,' he said. 'Such a shame you had to do it now.'

'How's that?' I asked innocently.

'The Festival. If the media hears that we've sacked or suspended staff for fraud, it will overshadow the whole event.'

'You're the only person I've told so far,' I said thought-fully. 'Maybe you should have a quiet word with Helen and decide on a strategy. It might be best not to take my action for a week or so, what with the by-election coming up too.'

He nodded his head. 'Leave it with me, Shannon. I'll let you know our decision. You'll be in Treasury, I take it.'

'I'm going out for a couple of hours. Something else to

271

check on.' I clicked my fingers in the air like a person whose brain had just kicked into a different gear and said, 'Oh, that reminds me. Could I attend the opening of the tenders on Friday morning? You know, the ones for the privatisation of refuse collection and disposal?'

'If that's what you wish,' he shrugged. 'How can I refuse?'

'Is that a pun?'

He gave me a blank look.

'Re*fuse*. Re*f*use.'

'I don't have time for puns, Shannon,' he said with a curl of his moustached lip.

'You should make time, Stuart. It's good training for the mind. Breeds a heightened level of recognition of similarities and differences. Still, each to his own.'

I spent some time over a coffee, had a long chat with Jakki, popped out to the car park to stow my briefcase in the Lancia and was still outside the building at twenty past nine. I stood a little to the right of the entrance so as to be in the line of sight from the steamed-up window of the snack bar. Watched as Norman's sleeve cleared a circular patch in readiness for the big moment. Lit a cigarette. Tried to look nervous. It was easier than I thought.

What if Blackstone had had second thoughts? What if, for some reason, he'd tried to phone me at the council and met with a nil response to his request to speak to Bannerman? What if it all seemed just too good to be true?

I need not have worried. The Rolls-Royce purred quietly past me at nine-thirty on the dot and pulled to a sedate halt fifty yards up the street. Blackstone climbed out and walked back towards me. He was carrying a canvas holdall.

Dropping the cigarette to the pavement, I ground it out slowly to give Blackstone's black crocodile-skin loafers time to reach me.

'Have you got the money?' I asked anxiously.

'All here,' he said, handing me the holdall. 'Thirty thou-

272

sand pounds. As per our agreement. Now, how about delivering on your side of the bargain? Let's have the exact address of the property.'

'You don't mind if I check,' I said, unzipping the bag and scrutinising the serial numbers on a randomly chosen bundle of brand-new fifty-pound notes.

'They're real,' he said, sighing. 'Whatever happened to trust?'

'You mean like what happened to someone who trusted you?'

The shoulders of his light grey suit shrugged back at me. I think the right one signalled disdain and the left apathy – although it might have been the other way round. Hard to tell with an obvious Savile Row suit – covers a multitude of sins.

'Come on, Bannerman,' he said impatiently, 'I haven't got all day.'

'Quite right,' I said, checking another bundle, this time from the bottom of the bag, to be on the safe side. Satisfied, I told him the address of the shop. 'If I were you,' I added, 'I'd wrap the deal up within the hour.'

'Why the rush?' he asked. And then answered his own question. 'I get it,' he laughed. 'You're going to milk Simpkins for another thirty grand. I like the way you think, Bannerman.'

It won't last, I thought with a grin, as he hurried back to the waiting Rolls.

I watched the car disappear from sight; heaved a sigh of relief; crossed the road; entered the snack bar.

'Let me take that,' Norman said considerately, one hand outstretched for the bag, the other gesturing to the seat alongside him. 'What can we get you?'

'In the absence of a magnum of Bollinger, I'll settle for a cup of hot sweet tea.'

'It's counter service, I'm afraid,' he said, nearly ripping off the zip in his haste to get the bag open. 'Put it on expenses.' He gave a broad smile. 'I think we can cover it.'

'May I look?' I heard Mrs Crabtree say to Norman as I made my way to the counter. 'May I run my fingers over it?'

The man meant to be serving stared over my shoulder.

'Tea,' I said. 'Don't mind them,' I added in a whisper. 'They're on honeymoon. Marvellous, isn't it? I mean, even at their age . . .'

'I'll bring it over,' he said.

'That's very kind. Two sugars, please.'

He nodded distractedly. Started pouring a mug of tea from the stainless-steel urn while his eyes rested on Norman and Mrs Crabtree.

I walked back to the table, grinning.

'It's beautiful,' Mrs Crabtree said with a loud sigh while peering under the table into the bag.

The man handed me a large mug of tea. A little cloud of steam rose up in the air. He placed two plates of bread pudding in front of Norman and Mrs Crabtree.

'On the house,' he said, smiling. He gave them an exaggerated wink. 'It'll give you energy. Know what I mean?'

'Strange man,' Mrs Crabtree said, gazing at him dubiously as he walked back to the counter. 'Generous, but not a little impertinent, if you ask me.'

'Well, Nick,' Norman said triumphantly. 'We did it. We bloody did it.'

Careful, I thought. Not so loud. The man will want his bread pudding back.

'Phase One complete,' I whispered. 'And as far as Phase Two goes, I think we can expect a delighted phone call from Ali Khan within the hour.'

'Not to mention the key call from Arlene,' Norman reminded me.

'Meanwhile,' I said, 'you two better get started for Companies House.' I took the two lists from my inside pocket. 'The good news is that there are only four companies to look into as far as the current tender goes.'

'And the bad news?'

'Twenty-seven who have already won contracts for pri-vatised services.'

'Twenty-seven,' he groaned. 'We'll be there all day. I was looking forward to a celebratory lunch at Toddy's with Dottie.'

Dottie! Norman was a fast worker – not even Dorothy any more.

'Good job you've got the bread pudding to keep you going then,' I said.

'We mustn't grumble, Norman,' Dottie said. 'I'm very grateful, Nick. And likewise for the rest of the residents. I shall give them the money tonight before dinner.'

'I'll take our five thousand for expenses – the lawyers and so on,' Norman said vaguely. 'Plus our commission, of course. Then the rest is all yours.'

'It's a pity you have to miss out on your lunchtime cel-ebration, Dottie,' I said. 'Still, maybe you and your ladies can make up for it this evening. Norman, I'm sure, is already planning to pick up a case or two of champagne and take them with him to Chingford when he drops you back home. Out of our share, of course.'

'That's about a bottle per person,' he said, stunned.

'You're right, Norman. Better make it three cases.'

'You're such a generous man, Norman,' Mrs Crabtree said, gazing into his eyes.

'But, Dottie,' he spluttered.

'Don't embarrass him, Mrs Crabtree,' I said. 'He's very sensitive.'

Especially where money is concerned.

I looked at my watch. Ten o'clock.

'I must go,' I said, rising from the table. 'McCready should have relayed our conversation to Helen by now. I've stirred the mixture, popped it into the heat of the oven. It's time to see what sort of cake comes out.'

'Be careful, Nick,' Mrs Crabtree cautioned. 'Don't get your fingers burnt.'

CHAPTER THIRTY-ONE

Follow your nose. Good advice. Especially when you're trying to locate the borough dump.

I didn't have to rely solely on nasal navigation. There were helpful signs too. Helpful, that is, once one had decoded the euphemism 'Civic Amenity Site'. And, as a final direction beacon, there was the white cloud of circling seagulls – what a paradoxical indictment of our modern environment that there now seem to be infinitely more gulls in cities than at the seaside – periodically dipping and soaring like synchronised yo-yoes.

My plan was simple. Other possible descriptions were 'well-thought-out' (my view) and 'ill-conceived' (Norman's). The sole aim was to show myself and then see what transpired. If my theory was correct, I would be recognised. And any show of recognition by the bin men – or a later reporting of such to Arthur – would be conclusive proof that their number included the two thugs responsible for the attack at Ali Khan's shop.

I parked the Monte Carlo alongside the grey and green units of the Recycling Centre, extricated myself from the car and took two carrier bags from the luggage compartment. One contained empty bottles, the other newspapers and magazines. Like a good citizen, I posted through the black rubber flaps my contribution to the conservation of the earth's dwindling natural resources (ignoring, of course, the inconvenient fact that it apparently takes more energy to recycle than to manufacture afresh) and looked around for a better vantage point to see and be seen.

To my right was a small wooden cabin where a sallow-faced man squinted through a murky glass window. He appeared to have one bored eye on proceedings in general – watch out, there's a thief about! – and a hawk-like one on the space reserved for domestic appliances in the hope that he might cobble together one good fridge or television set from the cannibalised remains of those abandoned. To my left was a small flight of steps leading to a combined pulping and compacting machine where larger items were deposited, minced up, compressed into neat little cubes and fed via a conveyor belt into the dark-tunnelled mouth of a long, low steel container.

I climbed the steps; stood at the top, registering the enclosing fence with its barbed-wire top and surveying the main bulk of the site hidden from public view. The tip itself was small, necessitating, according to Arthur, bulk transport of much of the borough's waste to other locations in adjacent areas. It resembled a miniature volcano, on whose treacherous slopes a bulldozer trundled up and down pushing the top layer into the crater beneath. The seagulls, conditioned to these repetitive movements, dug their beaks greedily into the decaying matter farthest away from the vehicle and close to the shelter of a ramshackle hut. Outside it, two dustcarts stood idle: inside, no doubt, two crews were sitting equally idle, passing their allotted time in countless mugs of tea and hands of poker. I wondered how Arthur's fortunes were faring today. He wasn't the world's most intuitive card player by any stretch of a highly elastic imagination, but I had managed to hammer home the basic strategies to adopt and pitfalls to avoid so that he could at least hold his own.

Surprisingly, perched as I was on the top of the steps, for all the notice anyone was taking of me I might as well have been invisible. I climbed back down to the concrete hard-standing, walked along the narrow alley between the compacting machine and the bottle bank and squeezed through a gap in the fence.

Oh, to be a seagull, unencumbered by a sense of smell, immune to the noxious gases that infiltrated the nose, journeyed through the lungs, grabbed hold of the stomach and tried to rip it out of your body via the throat.

What little breeze there was that bright sunny morning was blowing from the wrong direction. For me, that is. If you were one of the residents of the flats on the opposite side of the dump you were probably taking huge gulps of fresh air and singing 'Zip-a-dee-doo-dah' in celebration of the respite. I walked to the right, edging closer to the hut, partly in an effort to get up-wind, but also to create some sort of noticeable movement. At the first sign of trouble, I told myself, I would simply retrace my steps and make a bolt for the car.

Still no reaction. I lit a cigarette and promised myself that if nothing happened by the time I had finished it, then I would give up – on the venture, that is, not smoking. A person has to be allowed some vices: perfection can get up your nose much more effectively than the smell of a burning cigarette. I was four puffs in when a hooter on the roof of the hut gave three long shrill blasts. Probably, I thought cynically, just a lazy method of signalling to the driver of the bulldozer that a fresh pot of tea had been brewed or there was a spare seat at the poker table.

Sure enough, the bulldozer reversed down the slope, spun on a sixpence and spluttered off towards the source of refreshment.

The hut door opened. A group of men dressed in dark green overalls emerged and crowded round the doorway. I could easily make out the towering, wide-set figure of Arthur as he talked animatedly to a man wearing a black Navy watch-cap pulled down over his ears. Two of the men walked off in the direction of the broken-down dustcarts, and hoisted themselves up, one into each driver's seat. Simultaneously, the engines coughed into life, clouds of foul black smoke pouring from the exhausts and billowing up into the already polluted atmosphere. The noise was ear-splitting, making the approaching bulldozer sound as sweet as a purring kitten.

One of the trucks lumbered off in an arc to my right: the other, in what looked suspiciously like a classic pincer movement, set course straight for me. Either I was about to watch an impromptu display by the dustcart equivalent of the Red Arrows or the plan had succeeded – I had prompted the bin men into showing their hand. With my money on the latter, I turned to go.

And found that the bulldozer had made rapid progress. It had already reached the gap that was my intended escape route and was now a mere twenty yards away.

The driver pushed up on a lever. The bucket at the front rose up like a bull tossing its head. The long line of jagged-edged horns pointed at my chest. Half expecting to hear the trumpet fanfare of the *corrida*, I shook my head, dropped the unfinished cigarette to the ground and appraised the situation. Either I could take off my jacket and outwit the charging bulldozer with a matador's sharp-footed grace and mesmerising cape work, or I could run like hell and hope to outflank the vehicle.

I ran like hell. Forward and left. The bulldozer swivelled to match exactly my movement. The driver's tactics had changed. He was content to keep me penned in until the reinforcements arrived.

Which wouldn't be long now.

For trucks that weren't supposed to be capable of even starting, they were closing in on me with a surprising, and worrying, rapidity. And it wasn't just the short bursts of speed from the vehicles that was the problem. It was their length. Each time I attempted to run round the back of one of the dustcarts, it reversed up so that I was forced on a wider course – which took me into the path of another approaching vehicle.

Slowly the net closed. I was being skilfully manoeuvred into an ever-decreasing circle – the centre of their web.

The men outside the hut decided it was time to join the

hunt, add Shannon-coursing to their list of sporting pursuits. They formed themselves into a line, bridging the gap between the two dustcarts. Now there was nowhere to run, nowhere to hide.

It was time for the last stand.

I stood my ground; looked at the faces of the men; saw their sick smiles; heard the jeers of derision; smelt, I was convinced, that singular variety of sweat that comes from the unique mixture of animal aggression and adrenaline. Towards the middle of the line and a pace behind, Arthur's gigantic figure was stiff and immobile, his eyes glazed with indecision.

'Why are you doing this?' I shouted. 'What's your problem?'

'*We* haven't got a problem,' the man in the watch-cap said with a wide grin. 'But I reckon you have.'

'So brave,' I sneered. 'Eight of you, and only one of me.'

They responded with a mocking schoolgirl chorus of '*Ooh.*'

'I could take you all,' I said.

The response was predictable. Terror? Fear? Second thoughts, even? No, they fell about with laughter. Well, at least it was one way to cripple them.

'Right,' I said, snapping out the word as if my temper had finally been stretched too far. 'One at a time. Who's first? You,' I pointed to Arthur.

He stared at me.

'Yes, you,' I said. 'The gormless one. Come on, Lurch. Try your luck.'

He took a pace forward. Hands slapped him on the back and propelled him towards me.

I waved a finger, beckoning him on.

As he approached, a mindless chant broke out: 'Kill him. Kill him.'

Keep it up, I thought. Lots of noise.

I ran straight at Arthur.

And straight past. Spun around and jumped on his back, my hands around his throat.

280

'Make it look good, Arthur,' I whispered in his ear. 'They want blood. You're going to have to give it to them. Which means giving it to me.'

'But I can't, ' he whispered back. 'What if I hurt you?'

I knew what was going through his mind. Arthur had been forced to give up wrestling – progressively boycotted by his intended opponents until there was no one left prepared to take the risk of fighting him – because of the injuries he had caused by forgetting the prearranged moves or failing to pull his punches sufficiently.

'I'll understand,' I said, pretending to strain and tighten my grip. 'Okay? Right now, Arthur, you're my only chance of getting out of here alive.'

He reached up and behind him. Grabbed me round the waist. Heaved me over his head. Threw me to the churned-up earth. Followed up by diving on top of me and pinning me to the ground.

'That's better,' I encouraged. 'Ready? Knee in the groin.' He kneed me in the groin.

'Not you,' I groaned. 'Me. You roll over and then come after me.'

I kneed him gently but theatrically, holding back on the blow at the last moment.

He gave a howl and rolled off me.

I leapt to my feet. Set off towards the bulldozer and the blocked exit by the compactor. Stumbled elaborately when ten yards away.

Arthur caught me up. Grabbed me from behind.

'Turn me to face you,' I said, through a mouthful of grey clay soil. 'Make like you've lost your rag. Gone berserk.'

He manhandled me effortlessly around so that I was gazing up into his anxious face.

'Forearm smash,' he warned, before hitting me across the windpipe. 'Left jab.'

I let out a cry of pain.

'Sorry,' he said, seeing the blood trickle from my split lip.

'Don't worry,' I mumbled. 'Keep going.'

He let me have a series of blows – the weight better pulled with practice – a combination of left jabs and right hooks.

'Do you see the compacting machine?' I said.

He nodded.

'I want you to pick me up, hold me above your head, and throw me on top.'

'But . . .'

'It's my only way out, Arthur. Get mad. *Loony Tunes* time.'

He gave a loud roar. Behind him the chanting stopped as the men appreciated that something special was about to happen.

I stared up at Arthur as he rose to his feet, leaned down and placed one hand on the lapels of my jacket, the other on the fly of my trousers.

Careful!

He jerked me up weightlifter-fashion and held me triumphantly above his head. Twirled me in the air to the excited shouts of encouragement from the crowd. Lowered me slightly so that I could feel his muscles flex for action. Took careful aim at the roof of the compactor. And gave a mighty heave.

It was a good job that I suffered from claustrophobia and not fear of flying. I sailed through the air with such force that I thought I might actually overshoot the target. I hit the far end of the steel roof with a loud echoing thud, thrusting my forearms down at the moment of impact to break the fall. Raising myself unsteadily to my feet, I looked at the now silent crowd. The realisation had struck them that I was going to escape.

The bulldozer driver was rushing to his cab to unblock the gap as I jumped from the roof. I ran to the car; pulled the keys from the pocket of my dirt-stained jacket; jiggled them in the lock; flung the door open and threw myself inside. As I turned the key in the ignition, the first of the

pursuing bin men came into sight. He was squeezing sideways through the narrow gap.

The engine fired. I pulled away, gunning the accelerator and receiving from the tyres a screech of complaint.

I left behind an angry mob, shaking fists at thin air,
shouting blue obscenities into the distance, and choking on
a black cloud of burnt rubber.

But at least they hadn't turned on Arthur. They had
bought the act.

Mission accomplished.

I drove back to the council, feeling my split lip, and pretty
damned pleased with myself. My sense of euphoria was
taken to new heights when Arlene phoned. The bank manager, either buckling under her relentless pressure or
succumbing to her feigned helplessness and embarrassment,
had identified Adam as the person who had withdrawn the
money by producing the bearer share.

And then, to cap it all, the mobile rang a second time.
Ali Khan. Much relieved. And eternally grateful.

'I've sold the shop,' he said. 'It was just like you said.
Well, almost.'

'What do you mean, *almost*?' I asked, my heart sinking.
Don't tell me Blackstone had pulled some flanker. 'You did
get the money? In cash? All four hundred thousand?'

'Even better,' he replied. 'Four hundred and twenty-five
thousand actually.'

'Considering your weak position, you drive a hard bargain.'

'It wasn't difficult,' he said modestly. 'Why didn't you
tell me you had lined up a second bidder?'

'What are you talking about? Second bidder?'

'Someone telephoned this morning. Offered me four
hundred thousand. That's why I was able to push
Blackstone to up his price.'

Oh, God!

What the hell did I ever do to deserve this

CHAPTER THIRTY-TWO

Pear-shaped. It had all gone horribly pear-shaped. I'd seen bottoms at the All England Champion Doughnut Eaters' Step Aerobics Class that were less pear-shaped. Christ, for that matter, I'd even seen pears that were bloody less pear-shaped than this operation. And all because I had made two little mistakes. One an error of commission, the other of omission. I could even have got away with the first, if only I had asked Ali Khan one simple question.

I parked at the council. Couldn't face going inside. Trudged across the road, back to the snack bar. Sat in the same window seat trying to gather my thoughts and resist the temptation to drop my head into my hands and cry, '*Mea culpa*.' I ordered a coffee – very black and very sweet. Lit a cigarette. Stared despondently out of the window.

Hell, I said to myself, bloody pull yourself together, Shannon. Kick off your self-disgust. Store your anger for another time, another place. You need a plan – another bloody plan. It's damage-limitation time.

I took the personnel files from my briefcase; opened the one marked Ripley; confirmed my suspicions. Saw that her last job (her glass ceiling) before Oldbrook had indeed been running a department, just as she had said. But she'd omitted to tell me that it had been a Treasury Department. So very economical with the truth was our Helen Ripley.

Adam's file was a whole lot thinner. It would have been slimmer still if the annual appraisal reports from McCready had not been couched in long flowing terms to water down the negative opinions into a Sargasso Sea of ambiguity.

Rashid, by contrast, had received a glowing report. He'd been unselfishly recommended to apply for promotion, even if it did mean the borough losing his talents.

And as for McCready himself, one had to read between the lines. A career path that seemed straight and narrow until he upped sticks, left his posting at a county council in a managerial Siberia somewhere north of Watford, and emigrated to South Africa. There he had spent seven cushy years in the sun (while I was incidentally languishing in the gloom of prison) as Finance Director to a township council in the Transkei. And, just as suddenly as he had left these shores, he returned to join the Dirty Dozen of Oldbrook on its foundation.

An hour ago I had been congratulating myself on effectively wrapping up the case with nearly three days to spare. Now, as the plan took shape in my mind, it seemed as if I would need every last moment. With a big slice of luck — and didn't I deserve my fair share for a change? — I might just do it by three-thirty on Friday — a whole half-hour before the Festival procession took its first step. Talk about cutting it fine.

I ordered another coffee, borrowed a telephone directory from the man behind the counter and set about making the first of a series of telephone calls. Chain-smoking nervously, I booked — in another's name — a large conference room for the afternoon and evening at a hotel on the fringes of Docklands. Calculating travelling times, I phoned Arlene and Norman, gave them the details, told them to meet me there as close to six o'clock as they could make it, and to relay instructions to Arthur if he phoned. Next on the list was Collins. I asked him to flash his warrant card, pick up a passenger in Oldbrook and drive directly to the hotel. Then I downed the last of my coffee, resolutely stubbed out my cigarette, and set off unashamedly to browbeat and blackmail the pivotal figure into completing the issuing of the invitation list.

'We have a conference room booked,' I said to the smartly dressed woman behind the oak-panelled reception desk. 'Name of Khan. Mrs Khan.'

'Will you require refreshments? Tea? Coffee? Drinks? Sandwiches, perhaps?'

I looked at the sheepish figure of Mrs Khan at my side.

'I doubt that anyone will have the appetite for food,' I said. 'But to cover all the other eventualities, we'll have flasks of tea and coffee, two bottles each of red and white wine and cups, saucers and glasses for twelve people.'

'I'll have them brought up right away,' she said, handing me a plastic security 'key'. 'Fifth floor, to the right when you come out of the lift.'

I took Mrs Khan by the elbow and escorted her to the room. I placed the key-card in the slot just inside the door, the lights blinked on and the air conditioning cut in with a low rhythmic hum. A long honey-coloured table had been arranged for twelve: burgundy fake-leather blotters, notepads, pencils and water glasses had been laid out with a considerate precision and immaculate symmetry. A matching sideboard stood along one wall. Heavy floral curtains were drawn back to reveal full-width windows. Outside I could see a panoramic view of the Tower of London, where, unfortunately, traitors are no longer imprisoned.

'Can I use the bathroom?' Mrs Khan asked.

They were the first words she had spoken since we had left her house. In the car she had sat staring directly ahead through the windscreen. Part of her mind, I imagined, was coping with the shame, the rest working out how she would explain everything to her husband. She needn't have bothered. That would have to be my job.

I shrugged an apathetic reply, milking the situation for the moral advantage it gave me. But nevertheless I watched her like a hawk as she walked towards the en-suite bath-room. While she was inside, I went round the room turning on the three standard lamps. It was time to shed all available light on the subject.

Room service came with the refreshments. Mrs Khan continued to skulk in the bathroom while the young man in black trousers and white shirt set everything in neat little sub-groups: tea at one end of the sideboard, coffee at the other, wine in the middle. I checked my watch. Collins should be here soon.

It was ten minutes before the knock on the door came; ten minutes during which Mrs Khan sat bolt upright at the table, obstinately refusing with a shake of her head all my offers of something to drink. I opened the door. Collins raised his eyebrows in greeting and ushered before him a puzzled Saeed. Outside his own environment the boy seemed even younger and more vulnerable.

'What's going on, Mum?' he said, looking past me to the statuesque figure at the table.

'We couldn't have you going home to an empty house,' I explained. 'And I suspect we are going to be here quite some time. All will be revealed in the fullness of time.'

He took a seat next to his mother and wrapped an arm comfortingly around her.

Collins's professional eye roved around the room, surveying the situation. He examined especially the heavily laden sideboard; gave a little disapproving click of his tongue; walked over to the phone; punched out a number.

'Bottle of Scotch. Room 501,' he said. 'One tumbler. No ice, no water.'

He turned to me.

'Well?' he said, in defiant challenge. 'If I'm to be stuck in this room for the next few hours listening to you post-rationalising your heart out, there's no sense suffering the additional agony of thirst.'

Over the course of the next hour the remaining players arrived: Norman and Mrs Crabtree, to all appearances very pleased with themselves; Arlene, more than a little weary and strained from her long drive down the motorway, but not tired enough to forego giving me a welcoming hug and a very public kiss; Arthur, enquiring anxiously of my health and, on being reassured, immediately stripping off his overalls for the benefit of the other occupants of the room; Ali Khan, unsure now of whether to look jubilant or downcast. And then came the final knock on the door. More tentative than the others. And rightly so.

'Come in, Helen,' I said, to her surprise. 'Come in, Adam. And, last but by no means least, come in, Nadya.'

CHAPTER THIRTY-THREE

'Where to start?' I said, pacing the room dramatically while addressing the gathering of heroes and villains, and those lying somewhere in between. 'Introductions, maybe?'

I went clockwise round the table, deliberately using first names only, apart from the whisky-imbibing Detective Superintendent, who permitted only a highly privileged few to address him by anything other than Collins or sir, and the tea-drinking Mrs Crabtree, who would not have thanked me for the over-familiar use of Dottie among so many new faces. By some tacit agreement, the participants at the meeting had divided into two main camps: Arlene, Norman, Mrs Crabtree, Arthur and Collins on one side of the table; Mrs Khan, Saeed, Helen, Adam and Nadya on the other. Ali Khan, either because he was accustomed to taking the role of Chairman or through doubts over which of the factions most deserved his allegiance, sat at the end opposite where I would sit when my theatrical perambulations had run their course.

'No, now I think of it,' I said, 'perhaps I should return to one very special person.' I moved behind Arlene, placed my hands on her shoulders. 'To give the lady her full title, this is Arlene Tucker, *née* Martinez.'

Arlene turned her head to look up at me. Her hazel eyes narrowed in puzzlement.

'You see,' I said, 'Arlene and I have been having an ongoing difference of opinion concerning Nadya.'

I moved around the table and stood beside the girl who

was barely recognisable as the same one as in the photograph. The long hair had been cut powerfully short, revealing a fine bone structure and drawing attention to mesmerising dark brown eyes accentuated further by the liberal use of eyeshadow, mascara and kohl pencil. She was wearing a tight-fitting black top (which answered unequivocally my previous unspoken question on what sort of figure lay beneath the enveloping sari) over a free-swinging short skirt in a sheer material of white printed with large blue flowers. Her legs were bare; on her feet were black, thick-soled 'attitude' boots. A beige canvas shoulder bag was open on the table. I could see a mobile phone inside. Thanks for your help, Saeed!

'Our discussion,' I continued, 'centred around the theft of the four hundred thousand pounds. Did she or didn't she steal it? That was the nub of the argument. Well, Arlene, I can now tell you that you were right and I was wrong.'

She knew me better than to smile in self-satisfaction.

'Or, do I mean,' I said, pausing for effect, 'that I was right and you were wrong?'

Collins suppressed a groan and reached for the whisky bottle.

'We were both nearly right,' I concluded. 'And oh, so wrong.'

Mrs Crabtree couldn't restrain herself. 'I think we would progress more quickly, Nick, if you were to ...'

'Indulge me, Mrs Crabtree,' I interrupted. 'Just this once let me talk in riddles and at length.'

She nodded. 'I owe you a measure of indulgence,' she said, 'after what you have done for myself and my friends.'

'But at what cost?' I said enigmatically, before resuming my place in the script. 'It's a funny old world. On the one hand you have someone like Arlene who can't wait to get shot of her maiden name. And on the other hand, you have Helen, who has clung on to hers all these years. Was it purely for convenience, Helen? Or did you not like the sound of Schroeder?'

From the side of the table seating my camp I could hear the sound of brains whirring.

'Ripley,' she said dismissively, 'was the name under which I started my career. Everyone knew me as Ripley, so I simply retained it when I married.'

'I made two errors,' I admitted. Then I remembered the smell of attar of roses and the evidence of the calls from the Khan household to Helen. 'Two types of error,' I amended. 'One of commission and one of omission – that was the one of commission. I assumed the obvious: that you were who you said you were. I even logically progressed the assumption to the point of believing, when I saw you and Adam locked together in the car park, that the two of you were having an affair. It never crossed my mind that you were mother and son. Although, with hindsight, it jolly well ought to have done.' I looked pointedly at both of them, with their blond hair, blue eyes and lightly coloured Scandinavian skin – the beauty and the himbo. Prejudice had clouded thinking once again. 'The similarities in appearance between the two of you; the deference that a young and inexperienced Adam received from the sharks of Commercial Services, the toleration of him in Treasury, not to mention assigning him to work with me – or was it to spy on me? Your relationship was such common knowledge that it had long since gone past mentioning in the council.'

I walked over to the sideboard and helped myself to a glass of red wine. All this talking was making my throat dry.

'I blame myself more though,' I said, after a large sip, 'for my error of omission. There was Nadya, her future mapped out by her father, arranged marriage, dowry set aside and everything.' I turned to Ali Khan. 'I blame myself for much of what has unfortunately transpired. But I ask you now the question that should have occurred to me a week ago. Strapped as you undoubtedly were for money – borrowed up to the hilt at the bank – where were you going to get the dowry?'

'I was going to give Nadya and her future husband the shop.'

'The shop that we sold this morning?'

'You what?' Helen cried out in amazement. 'Oh, no.'

'Yes, I'm afraid so,' I said, looking her in the eye. 'Despite *your* generous offer, we were able to obtain a better price from another bidder. It is signed, sealed and the money banked. The shop has been sold. Or should I say *the* shop? The one that has been at the root of your elaborate deception.'

The Nadya camp exchanged meaningful glances. Then seemed to settle *en masse* on head shaking, eye rolling and any other expressions of despair they could think of.

'As I said, I blame myself. But I acted as I did from the very best intentions. As indeed, I suppose, you too would claim. You' – I cast a condemning finger along the far side of the table – 'must take the lion's share of the blame. Saeed, I exonerate' – he looked down at the table in shame rather than embarrassment – 'although he could have spared us the wild goose chase of checking a lengthy telephone bill. I don't believe he was ever privy to your plan. But I blame you, Ali Khan, for your talk of opportunities and freedom while at the same time treating your daughter as a chattel to be sold.'

Saeed looked up and stared at me in a confused mixture of shock and admiration – no one had ever spoken to his father this way.

Nadya glared at her father, emboldened by my support; took Adam's hand and clasped it defiantly.

'Don't think you're going to escape my anger,' I said to her. 'Or your co-conspirators either. Helen, Mrs Khan, if these two young people really loved each other so much, then what did the dowry really matter?'

'We wanted them to have their due,' Helen said.

Mrs Khan nodded in agreement. 'Just because Nadya chooses to go against her father's wishes, and Adam is not a Muslim, why should they lose out?'

'Because you should have talked it through as a family – as an extended family, reached some sort of agreement. Or begged to differ and gone your own way. Instead you act like a bunch of financial vigilantes.' Saeed cast his eyes down again as I uttered the last word, reminded of my lecture in the garage. 'And last, but by no means least, because of all the bloody trouble you've caused.'

'Why did you have to interfere?' Nadya asked accusingly. 'We had it all worked out.'

'Don't try to pin this mess on me,' I said angrily. 'I was doing my best to unhook your father from the horns of a dilemma; to save his political career so that he can make his dreams a reality – make the world a better place. And, at the same time, I was taking revenge on a common swindler to recover money that Mrs Crabtree and her elderly friends could ill afford to lose.'

'For the record,' Arlene asked, 'which of you made the phone call to the bank to transfer the money to the Isle of Man account?'

'I did,' admitted Helen.

I gave Arlene a told-you-so look.

'Say *film*,' I said to Nadya.

'*Fillum*,' she said.

Under cover of Nadya's bemusement at my instruction, Arlene poked her tongue out at me. 'Smartass,' she mouthed.

Arthur cleared his throat. 'Excuse me for asking,' he said slowly and, I suspected, playing catch-up, 'but what difference does selling the shop make? Ali Khan's got his money – well over the odds too, going by what you told me, Nick. He can give the kids their dowry, Helen can pay back the stolen money and, Bob's your uncle, everybody's happy.'

'Including bleeding Blackstone,' I said. 'The damn scam that Norman and I came up with was perfect. Too bloody perfect, in fact.'

Norman clutched his forehead. 'You don't mean . . .'

293

'Yes, Oldbrook *is* ripe for development. The limit has been reached in areas like Highbury and Islington, no land left, hardly a property that hasn't been converted into bijou maisonettes or taken over in its entirety by the nouveau riche; Docklands, as we know, is fine for those who can spend all day in their dream homes and don't have to face the nightmare of actually travelling anywhere. Oldbrook, my friends, is poised to move up-market. Am I not right, Helen? Isn't that why you were prompted into executive action two weeks ago, even though Nadya wasn't due to be married until next summer when she had finished her degree?'

'I was approached by a firm of developers,' she said. 'They were sounding me out unofficially to learn how the council might react. They wanted to acquire the site on which the shop occupies the central position, demolish everything and erect a big new building – shopping precinct on the first two floors, offices above. In return for the planning permission, and the council selling them a further parcel of private residential land, they were willing to pull down the surrounding council houses and build a new estate of more and better ones. It made sense for them to improve the neighbourhood – a better environment for their new venture. And with the money we as a council would get, we could improve facilities throughout the borough; refurbish blocks of flats, build a new sixth-form college for the likes of Saeed, a leisure centre, the list was almost endless. Everyone would gain.'

'And now,' I said petulantly, 'bloody Blackstone has the lease on the major, and pivotal, part of the prime site.'

'Then we must buy it back,' she said as if it were the most simple thing on earth.

'Which will not be easy,' I pointed out, 'since Blackstone is rightly convinced he is sitting on a gold mine. He thinks he can sell it for a million.'

'Which we haven't got,' Helen said gloomily.

'But I have a plan,' I said, ignoring Norman's not-another-one look. 'If Mrs Crabtree will agree to help.'

'How can I refuse,' she said, 'seeing that I am partly responsible? What do you want me to do?'

'And then everything will be all right?' Arthur asked, when I had finished going through the details.

'Unfortunately not, Arthur,' I said with a reinforcing shake of my head. 'Ask Mr Collins. For while we may solve one problem, we are left with a much bigger one; one with far-reaching ramifications; one which would put an end to Ali Khan's aspirations after all, and force Helen to resign from her job, with no hope of working in local government ever again.'

Collins put down his whisky glass and prepared to speak. At last, I could see him thinking.

He should have acted more quickly. Before he had a chance to open his mouth, Helen jumped in.

'If you're talking about the two frauds you've discovered,' she said, causing Nadya's eyes to open wide and bringing a silently mouthed 'Wow' from Saeed, 'the ones you discussed with Stuart McCready this morning, I don't see that those can have such far-reaching consequences. We will suspend the staff while you finish your enquiries and then no doubt we will have to sack them. It will grab a few column inches in the local press for a week, maybe two, but will soon blow over.'

'Madam,' Collins said firmly, 'you will take no action until after the Festival. That is our deadline. And I deliberately stress the first syllable.'

Collins finally had the floor, and everyone's attention.

'I spent all day yesterday with colleagues from the local police and from Special Branch.' He turned to look challengingly at Ali Khan. 'I understand that you are going ahead with this Festival against the advice of both.'

'We will not be dictated to by a bunch of small-minded racists,' Ali Khan replied.

'Not even if it means putting in jeopardy the lives of the good citizens of your borough?'

'The police will protect us. It is their job.'

'You overestimate their powers – the best they can do is to act after the event. There will be a police presence, of course, but it will be low key – in line with your demands. When the trouble starts,' he said, in his certainty not bothering with *if*, 'the police will move in as swiftly as they can, given the traffic chaos the Festival will create, and in force. All we can hope is that it will not be too late.'

'I have great faith in law and order.'

Collins rolled his eyes. 'Faith can't always move mountains.'

'In any case,' Ali Khan said, demonstrating the selective hearing of a true politician, 'we did not want to create a media opportunity for OWN.'

'No,' I interjected, 'you wanted that reserved entirely for the borough and yourself. Greedy, Mr Khan.'

'Maybe one error of judgement could be forgiven,' Collins said. 'But I'm afraid there is a second. You have all underestimated OWN. And that is very dangerous.'

'Crackpots,' Ali Khan said dismissively.

'Crackpots with money,' Collins said.

'I'll vouch for that,' Arthur said. 'They're buying a crowd for Friday. Five hundred pounds a head.'

'How do you know?' Collins asked, surprised at Arthur's intelligence.

'I'm a fully paid-up member of OWN,' he said.

There followed an oppressive silence. You could have heard a pin drop; although the more likely sound to listen out for was knives being sharpened.

'Well,' he added quickly, 'not really paid-up. Because you don't have to pay any dues.'

He wasn't exactly winning over the opposition. Waves of hostility were still rolling towards him.

'And not a member either,' he said, in further qualification. 'But I've been recruited.'

'Let me explain,' I said, before the lynch mob started tying a knot in the rope and estimating Arthur's height for the required drop. 'We have been pursuing another line of enquiry. This has given Arthur an opportunity to insinuate himself into the ranks of OWN. The key point, as Mr Collins said and Arthur has verified, is that these are crackpots with money. And the irony of it is, it's *your* money.'

'My money?' Ali Khan shook his head and gave a little laugh. 'And you were doing so well up until now, Shannon.'

'Oldbrook's money,' I corrected. 'OWN is being financed by Oldbrook Borough Council.'

'Can you prove this?' Helen said, while Ali Khan stared sightlessly into space like a victim of catatonic shock.

I looked across at Norman.

'Almost,' he said, pulling a sheaf of papers from his inside pocket.

'The background,' I said, while Norman was marshalling his research, 'is that OWN came into existence at the same time as Oldbrook was formed. We do not believe that is a coincidence. Our theory is that OWN is being bankrolled through a series of frauds within the council. The frauds revolve around the privatisation of services.'

'It isn't possible,' Helen said, relaxing slightly. 'You've seen the system, Nick. We explained it to you. It's . . .'

'I know,' I said, sighing, 'it's foolproof. But not *thiefproof*.'

'To date,' Norman said, 'you have awarded twenty-seven contracts for the supply of services to the council.'

'To twenty-seven different companies,' Helen countered. 'Surely that proves my point. How can there be a series of frauds when every tender has been won by a completely separate company?'

'Just because they have different names,' he replied scornfully, 'it does not mean they are not linked. Mrs Crabtree and I have spent the day at Companies House, slaving over a hot microfiche reader. And straining our eyes to boot. But not straining our credulity. All twenty-seven companies are in turn owned by the same holding company: name of WhiteFire.'

The name itself seemed proof enough – rich in connotations of racial violence, with echoes of Whitewater too.

'Registered where?' I asked.

'Jersey,' Norman said. 'So that's where the trail stops. Except the company does have a postbox address in London. That may lead us somewhere.'

'But how?' Helen asked. 'How can what amounts to the same company win every tender?'

'Because it has inside information,' I said. 'Take the privatisation of refuse collection and disposal. A set of pertinent information goes out with the tender documents. It gives all the details of your current operation, most notably the size of the workforce, wages and salaries paid, vehicles owned, their written-down value in the books and so on – in case the bidder wants to retain the employees or acquire those assets. And also to ensure that all bidders play on the same level playing field. Except that someone knows the true picture. For instance, that two trucks aren't the scrap they're supposed to be; and that the service is operating with just half the number of men on the books. So the WhiteFire subsidiary company can put in the best bid. Can't fail to win the contract. It's been going on since the very first contract – catering. Remember the problems pre-privatisation with hygiene and so on?'

'So who is feeding WhiteFire the information?' Helen asked.

'That's easy,' I said. 'Even Adam can tell you that. What do you reckon, Adam? To set out to win every contract: what's that?'

'Greedy,' he said.

'Exactly,' I nodded

CHAPTER THIRTY-FOUR

'If you hadn't stolen the four hundred thousand pounds,' I said to the distaff side of the table, 'I would have worked it out sooner. But, then again, I suppose I wouldn't have got involved in the first place. Which would have saved us all a lot of aggravation.'

'Not to mention,' Arlene said bitterly, 'our home and offices being trashed.'

Helen gave her a puzzled look.

'You see,' I said, leaning back in the chair at the head of the table, 'ever since I have been on this case, someone has been trying to persuade me to drop it. First, the attack at Ali Khan's shop: *I* was the intended victim. Then a bunch of thugs vandalise our premises and nearly kill one of our kittens. And finally, this morning, the bin men tried to take me out of action for good.'

Arlene frowned at me.

'Thanks to Arthur's intervention, I escaped with just a split lip.'

'Sorry,' he mumbled, confusing everybody.

I shrugged. 'Could have been a whole lot worse, Arthur.'

'How do you know it's McCready?' Nadya piped up, her natural instincts for accounts awakened at last.

'Whoever set up the attack at the shop,' I explained to her, 'had to be aware that I would be there. That's why I thought Helen was behind it – she knew I would be coming in with Ali Khan that morning. But, I presume, Helen told McCready.'

'There didn't seem to be any reason not to,' she said.

'When I first stepped into McCready's office, he was surprised – no, shocked – to see me. I put it down to him being confronted by a convicted murderer – it's a reaction I've encountered before. I assumed that he'd recognised me from the pictures in the papers or on the television. But he couldn't have. Even I wasn't famous enough to be a hot news property in South Africa – and that was where McCready was at the time. My appearance made him jump simply because I was never supposed to arrive at the offices. He was expecting his thugs to put me in hospital, or at least scare me into dropping the case.'

I lit a cigarette; paused to give them a chance to absorb one deduction before gradually leading up to the worst of McCready's crimes.

'When that didn't work, he arranged for the same thugs to trash our premises.'

'And all to keep you from investigating the Treasury accounts?' Nadya said. 'In case you uncovered his fraud?'

'More than that,' I said gravely. 'I think McCready was responsible for Rashid's death.'

'Fraud is one thing,' Helen said, struggling to cope with the accusations about someone she had worked with for years, 'but murder is another.'

'I don't know if Rashid's death was a deliberate and premeditated act. Arlene once said to me that the first reaction of a human being in a crisis is to panic. I think it's more likely that McCready just wanted to frighten him; make sure he kept his mouth shut.' I inhaled deeply and blew a reflective stream towards the ceiling. 'Treasury, as Adam informed me, operates on a system of double-check. It was part of Rashid's job to check McCready's work. I think Rashid guessed what McCready was up to. And since Rashid didn't do anything about it, my guess is that he blackmailed McCready into buying him off or cutting him in. Which worked fine until McCready told him an outsider was coming to look over the books. Rashid died of a case of cold feet.'

'But this is all assumption on your part,' Helen said. 'You can't prove that this WhiteFire company is a vehicle to fund OWN – although I have to admit that does seem highly likely – or that McCready is behind the frauds and Rashid's death. Anyway,' she tilted her head to one side and frowned, 'it takes money to set up a company that can handle a big contract. How did McCready get his hands on that sort of money? He can't possibly have been stealing from our bank accounts. We've had plenty of audits, both internal and external, since Oldbrook was formed. Someone would have spotted something.'

'He borrowed the money to set up the first company,' I said.

'Thank goodness for that,' Helen said.

'Don't relax yet, Helen,' I warned. 'He borrowed the money from the council.'

'Impossible.'

'In McCready's office, there are ten folders for holding bank statements. The council only has nine accounts.'

'We set up the tenth account for our transfer,' Nadya said. 'Remember?'

'Forgive me for scoffing,' I said, 'but I haven't yet come across a bank that sends out a new folder that swiftly. The tenth folder is for something that is outside the scope of your normal council audit – internal and external. It's for something, in fact, that few of us give much thought to.'

Norman nodded wisely. He thought like an old fraudster and was consequently ahead of me.

'McCready set up the first company shortly after the borough was formed. What assets did you have on start-up?'

'The first tranche of our Government grant,' Helen said, thinking back. 'Plus a short-term Government loan for cash-flow purposes. Then we took over the rents and other income from the surrounding councils. But all those go through the council's books. They're all subject to audit.'

'Where were you on Friday afternoon?' I asked Helen. 'Before your conversation with Adam in the car park when you told him of his father's accident that day.'

'At the retirement party,' she said. 'But what does . . .'

Her face dropped.

So had the penny.

'McCready,' I said, 'used money from the Pension Fund to set up WhiteFire. I called the bank manager – he went through the fund's bank statements and verified it. The money, plus a return on the capital, was repaid a year later when the company was in profit. Smart move. To the trustees of the fund it would look like a genuine investment. So, effectively, the council has bankrolled WhiteFire from the very beginning.'

'This gets worse and worse,' she said.

'If it's any consolation, that's the end of the bad news.'

'But what are we going to do?'

'We are going to set a trap for McCready. And when he takes the bait, we will have our proof. Mr Collins will present the authorities in Jersey with a Mareva order freezing their assets. OWN will be starved of funds. And totally discredited. Quite a story to lay before the media. Think about the day when you can tell them of your suspicions, and how you all pretended to steal four hundred thousand pounds as an excuse for an undercover operation by yours truly.'

'Very clever,' Ali Khan said with a big smile. 'What is this trap?'

'*That* I am not prepared to reveal until you, Mr Khan, agree to do something for me.'

The smile faded.

'We have a police officer present,' he said. 'I hope you're not trying to extort money from me.'

'We have a contract with the council. I expect that to be honoured. Our agreed commission is the only recompense I want.' I stubbed out the cigarette with a slow and relentless grinding motion. 'No, I don't want money from you, Mr Khan. I want blood.'

'What?'

'I want a uniting of blood: Nadya's and Adam's. You will announce their engagement when you make your speech to open the Festival.'

'I will do no such thing.'

'Shame,' I said. 'It would have been another media coup for you. Instead you'll have to make do with a débâcle.'

'What are you on about, Shannon?'

'If you play it my way, the council can quietly spirit away the fraudsters in Social Services and Commercial Services. Mr Collins will agree not to prosecute in view of the political implications.'

'And if I don't agree?'

'I will tell the media everything; let them know about your funding of OWN for a start. And then make them aware that Oldbrook is a hotbed of corruption. But what could one expect? Especially when one sees the example that comes from its leader. Someone who buys votes by running a supermarket at a loss. That *is* what you admitted to me when we were discussing the price of your shop?'

'Shannon, you are totally unprincipled.'

'Just the reverse, Mr Khan. My principles, unlike yours, are unbending. *I* do not preach equality and then subjugate my daughter; force her to marry against her will, even though she loves someone else. Of course, the fact that her one true love is white, well . . . You can see how bad that will look.'

'This is blackmail,' he spluttered.

'But beautifully executed, you must admit.'

He stared angrily at me.

Oh well, I suppose beauty is in the eye of the beholder.

'Please, Father,' Nadya pleaded, turning those doe eyes on him.

'Ali,' his wife said, 'you know Shannon is right. Let her lead her own life. Aren't we a mixed marriage – Hindu and Muslim? We are happy. They can be happy too. If only you'll let them.'

'Very well,' he said, giving in grudgingly to the weight of opposition. Or maybe he was at last realising the benefit to his image – white and brown joined in holy wedlock, rather than deadlock. 'I agree to your demands.'

Nadya and Adam looked into each other's gooey eyes. Adam put his arm around her and squeezed her tight. Any minute now he'd go, 'Oh, Nadya,' and she'd say, 'Oh, Adam,' in a breathless voice.

'I hadn't finished,' I said. 'There's more.'

'You try my patience, Mr Shannon.'

'I have that effect on a lot of people,' I said with a wink at Mrs Crabtree. 'Mr Khan, you will let Nadya join a firm of accountants, and not try to force her into your business.'

He nodded.

'Lastly,' I said, 'the dowry. When we get the shop back from Blackstone, you will give it to the happy couple. After all, that was your original intention. And it will give Adam a chance to prove himself as an entrepreneur. Who knows, it might be the start of a new empire. That would be fitting, wouldn't it, Helen?'

She shook her head uncomprehendingly at me.

'It would mean, Helen,' I said, suppressing a giggle, 'that yours could be the face that launched a thousand shops.'

CHAPTER THIRTY-FIVE

Day Nine

Sorry may well be the hardest word to say, but waiting is without a shadow of a doubt the hardest game to play. At this very moment, Mrs Crabtree would be acting her heart out (with Collins in attendance in the infinitely easier role of mini-cab driver – all tooth-sucking and 'I don't know about that, Guv. Not at this time of day.'). Saeed should have made his delivery and, hopefully, was now riding pillion on a friend's scooter through the streets of London. Norman would be doing the rounds of the other tenderers bidding for the refuse disposal and collection contract, levelling up the playing field. Meanwhile, I was oscillating indecisively between finger drumming and finger crossing, having discovered it was impossible to do both at the same time.

I was sitting in Helen's office, drinking coffee and making the simple calculation of distance to be travelled divided by the average speed of a Rolls-Royce driven by a goon with his foot to the floor. It came out at thirty minutes before Blackstone would burst on to the scene. Last time the answer had been thirty-two minutes – the two results didn't differ due to changes in assumptions on the variables, but because of the time gap in between making the two calculations.

'More coffee?' she said, looking up from her notes.

I shook my head. 'No, thanks. I'm so high on caffeine that another cup will send me floating up to the ceiling.'

'I'll have another,' said Detective Inspector Walker. 'I always said I could drink you under the table, Shannon.'

'It's just that when I'm finally confronted by Blackstone and his two bodyguards I don't want my brain fogged. I want to keep my wits about me.'

'I can see your problem,' she said, nodding her head wisely. 'Especially when you've got to locate them in the first place.'

'You must forgive Walker,' I said wearily to Helen. 'She has a personality defect. Nothing specific, you understand, just the personality in general.'

'Do you two always go on like this?' Helen asked.

'Only because Walker is so argumentative,' I said.

'No, I'm not,' she said

'I rest my case.'

She sighed.

I blew her a kiss.

She glared.

Another minute ticked off. What next?

Walker turned her back on me.

'Tell me about Nadya,' she said to Helen. 'Pretty hot stuff, I hear.'

Hot stuff! Walker would have crucified me if I'd used that term about her. Well, after she'd picked herself up off the floor, that is.

'She has three of the top accountancy firms bidding for her,' Helen said proudly of her future daughter-in-law.

'Can't interest her in the Fraud Squad, I suppose? We need more good young women.'

What do you mean, *more*?

'Who knows?' Helen said. 'She has the right type of mind. It *was* Nadya who thought up the plan for, er, borrowing the four hundred thousand pounds.'

'Maybe I'll have a chat to her,' Walker said. 'Now what about the wedding? Have they set a day?'

I got up from the table and wandered over to the window. Stared down into the street while two of London's power-laden women cooed over dresses and flowers and bridesmaids and going-away outfits and . . .

'Game on,' I said, as they reached the honeymoon stage. 'Blackstone's car has just pulled up.'

'Mr Blackstone,' I said, looking away from his face (purple with anger and veins visibly pulsing on his forehead) in order to cast nervous glances around Reception and then at the two goons by his side. 'I didn't expect to see you today.'

'Or any other bloody day, I imagine, Mr Bannerman. Except it isn't Bannerman, is it? It's Shannon.'

I gave Jakki a wonders-never-cease look and edged away from her desk, moving deeper into the atrium.

Blackstone and his goons followed me.

'We need to have another of our little chats,' he said. 'Let's go for a ride.'

'Not today,' I said. 'There really is nothing to discuss.'

'Don't make my life even more difficult,' he said, stabbing me with his finger. 'Start walking, Shannon.'

'Stroll on, Blackstone.'

'Pick him up and carry him outside,' he ordered.

I stood there with a shocked expression – pretty good acting, I thought, even though this was exactly what we had expected – and put up a perfunctory struggle as the goons grabbed my arms and lifted me into the air. Then I created merry hell.

'Get your hands off me,' I shouted at the top of my voice. 'Call security, someone. I'm being kidnapped. Help!'

'What's going on here?' Helen said on cue and in her best authoritarian voice.

'Nothing to interest you, love,' Blackstone said.

'Everything that goes on here interests me,' she replied. 'And I am not your *love*. I am the Chief Executive of this borough.'

'Well, go and execute somewhere else.'

'Put Mr Shannon down this instant.'

'Take a hike.'

'Well, really,' Helen said.

'Perhaps I can help, Helen,' Walker said, digging into her shoulder bag. She flashed her warrant card. 'Inspector Walker. Metropolitan Police.'

Blackstone stared, not knowing whether to believe his ears or his eyes – how could this Naomi Campbell lookalike in a figure-hugging grey suit be a copper?

The bodyguards' brains seized up.

I dangled.

'May we use your office?' Walker said to Helen. 'Or,' she said to Blackstone, 'would you rather accompany me to the station?'

He paused for thought. Not to weigh up the alternatives but, hopefully, to explore the unexpected opportunity of using Walker against me in the battle to get his money back.

'The office sounds fine to me. And anyway, I've done nothing wrong.'

'Then *you* come with me,' she said to Blackstone, before turning to the two bodyguards. 'And you two will leave the premises now.'

They looked at their boss, received a nod, and trooped from the building. The remaining four of us trudged through the atrium, into the old building and along the corridor to Helen's office. All the way Helen kept thanking Walker for her presence and saying things like, 'I'm just so glad you were here for our meeting. I can't think what we would have done without you. What a stroke of luck.'

Walker took Helen's seat at the desk, cleared some space by ostentatiously brushing aside a folder freshly labelled with 'Police Liaison – Oldbrook Festival' in bright red capitals, placed her elbows on the desktop, interlocked her long slim fingers and leaned forward.

'Sit down, the two of you,' she barked.

Blackstone and I sat down opposite her. Helen pulled across a chair next to, and a little behind, Walker.

'Who are you?' she asked me. 'And what is this all about?'

'Nick Shannon. I'm working here for a while in Treasury. Isn't that right, Helen?' She gave a nod. 'And I have no idea what is going on.'

'He's a con man,' Blackstone said, smiling sweetly at Walker. 'He took me for nearly five hundred grand.'

'That's a serious charge, Mr Shannon. What do you have to say?'

'He's mistaken,' I said, shrugging.

Walker turned to Blackstone. 'Can you substantiate this accusation, Mr . . .'

'Blackstone. Yes, I can. I want him arrested. After you get him to hand over my money, that is.'

Walker shook her head slowly.

'I'm afraid I need a bit more than your say-so to arrest someone,' she said. 'If you want my help, you'll have to give me details, Mr Blackstone.'

'Well,' he said, hesitating for a second before deciding to bite the bullet. 'First, he conned me into giving him thirty grand for the address of a property. Then . . .'

'Excuse me,' Walker interrupted, 'but why would you pay thirty thousand pounds for an address? You can buy the whole Yellow Pages for a fraction of that.'

'You don't understand,' he said, clenching his fist in frustration. 'It was supposed to be the address of a site that some developers were after.'

'What developers?'

'I don't know.'

'Really,' said Walker, imbuing the word with utter disbelief.

'Look, he didn't say. He pretended to be a bloke called Bannerman who worked in the Planning Department.'

'Is this true?' she asked me.

'I never said I was called Bannerman,' I said. 'Did I, Mr Blackstone?'

'No, but the girl on reception did.'

'Must have been confused. Easy to do, I imagine. She must have hundreds of visitors each day. Bound to get the odd name wrong.'

'But what about this thirty thousand pounds, Mr Shannon?' Walker asked.

'It was Blackstone who approached me,' I said. 'Wittered on about developers and wanting an address. I didn't know what he was talking about, but it seemed too good an opportunity to miss. I mentioned a figure of thirty grand and he agreed. He got what he asked for, and so did I. He didn't complain at the time.'

'Is that right?'

'Yes,' Blackstone was forced to admit. 'But that was before I realised it was a con. You see, Inspector, a man called Simpkins asked me to buy a property for him. He said I would probably get it for only four hundred grand and he'd buy it back off me later for half a million pounds.'

'So you made a hundred thousand pounds,' Walker said. 'What's your complaint, Mr Blackstone?'

'No I didn't,' he protested. 'Instead I spent four hundred and twenty-five thousand on a property worth God knows how little.'

Walker clutched her forehead. 'So this Simpkins didn't pay you the money?'

'Well, no. I decided not to go along with his deal.'

'You turned down the chance to make a hundred thousand pounds?'

'I keep telling you, it was a con. A bloody scam. I would never have tumbled if that old biddy Crabtree hadn't come along to crow.'

'Crabtree?' Walker said, while Blackstone flushed at his slip. 'This is very complicated, Mr Blackstone. Who is Crabtree? And how does she fit in?'

'Just someone who did a little business with one of my companies,' he said, waving his hands in the air to dismiss the matter as of no consequence.

'And?' Walker probed.

'Unfortunately the company had a liquidity problem and was forced to go into voluntary liquidation. Crabtree was a creditor. Mistakenly thought the debt was my responsibility.'

'I see,' Walker said ominously.

'I did nothing illegal. But Mrs Crabtree decided to take the law into her own hands. Hired Shannon here to swindle me out of the money she reckoned I owed her.'

'Some debt. Nearly half a million. Wasn't that what you said?'

'Yes. I mean no. Mrs Crabtree and her friends only lost twenty-five thousand.'

'Only?'

'You're missing the point,' he said, both fists clenched tightly now. I fought back a smile, indulging myself in a spot of *schadenfreude*. 'Shannon and Simpkins . . .'

'I don't know any Simpkins,' I interrupted. 'I told Blackstone at the time. Never heard the name, I think were my words.'

'Only because Simpkins is Timpkins,' Blackstone said.

'So Simpkins is Timpkins now?' Walker said with a shake of her head.

Blackstone banged his fist on the table. 'Timpkins is Shannon's business partner. That's what Crabtree says. She asked them to get her money back and teach me a lesson. Have you got it now?'

'There's no need to shout, Mr Blackstone.' Walker looked at me with narrowed eyes. 'Is this true, Mr Shannon?'

'What if it is? I didn't approach him, it was *he* who came to me. I simply gave him an address – for which he paid me thirty thousand pounds. Then he went off and bought a property. To echo Blackstone's words, I did nothing illegal.'

'Unfortunately, Mr Blackstone,' Walker said, tutting loudly, 'I'm afraid he's right.'

'But that's not fair.'

'No,' said Helen. 'I agree.' Her face went stern. 'Mr Shannon, you may not have acted illegally, but what you have done is to abuse your position here. We hired you in good faith and your actions may well bring this council into disrepute. If you want your contract with us to continue, you will give Mr Blackstone his money back. Starting with the thirty thousand pounds.'

'I can't,' I said. 'I handed it straight to Mrs Crabtree, less our expenses, of course. Compensation for what Blackstone swindled out of her and the other poor little old ladies.'

'And what about the money from the sale of the premises? Who has that?'

'Ali Khan.'

'Ali Khan!' she thundered. 'You involved the leader of the council in this scheme of yours. My God!'

'I didn't involve him,' I said quickly. 'He doesn't know anything about this. He just happened to have a property that fitted the bill.'

'Inspector Walker,' Helen said, frowning deeply. 'I must speak to Councillor Khan. This has serious ramifications. Would you keep these two here for a little while?'

Walker nodded. Helen made a swift and serious exit; went for a little stroll and reappeared five minutes later bearing a single sheet of paper.

'Councillor Khan is most embarrassed,' she said. 'He is anxious to put things right, straight away. Would that be agreeable to you, Mr Blackstone?'

'He'll buy back the shop?' Blackstone said, brightening up.

'Yes,' Helen said. 'There is just one problem. He has already spent some of the money.'

'How much?' he asked gloomily.

'I'm afraid he only has four hundred thousand pounds left.'

'But I've already lost the thirty grand I gave to Shannon.'

'Put it down to experience,' Walker said. 'Unless, of

course, you want a costly legal battle. It would have to be a private prosecution. The CPS wouldn't take the case to court.'

'But I'm going to drop another twenty-five grand.'

'Councillor Khan,' Helen said, 'told me the property is only worth two hundred thousand. He said that if we couldn't straighten things out right now, it would be too late – what with the by-election imminent.' She frowned thoughtfully. 'I suppose you could always keep it. Do you have any experience of running a supermarket?'

Blackstone seemed aghast at the thought.

'Okay,' he said, sighing heavily. 'But I want cash.'

'You have the original Bill of Sale?'

He took the papers from his inside jacket pocket; passed them to Helen to examine.

'If you would like to come with me, Mr Blackstone, I will take you to Councillor Khan and then on to the bank.'

Blackstone stood up. He wasn't exactly over the proverbial moon at the outcome, but neither was he as sick as a parrot – he had managed to save some face and recover most of the money.

'If you could just sign this,' Helen said, passing him the single sheet of paper. 'It is an agreement not to mention this matter to anyone. And an indemnity, should you do so, for any loss the council may suffer as a result. It saves us from all the bother of a libel or slander action, you understand.'

'I'm not signing anything,' he said.

'What's your first name?' Walker asked him.

'Why?' he said.

'So I can read you your rights. I am going to arrest you on charges of causing an affray and attempted kidnapping.' She took the printed caution from her bag. 'First name, please.'

Blackstone studied Walker's face. I imagined the words of the caution running through his mind; maybe in the variant that goes, 'Anything you say will be twisted and turned and used against you.'

'Oh, very well,' he said with a resigned shake of his head. 'Where do I sign?'

What was it Norman had once said? 'It's only right that people with lots of money and no brains should hand it over to people with lots of brains and no money.'

It was a little after three when Saeed showed up at the council offices. One look at his face told me his mission had not been a total success.

'Here's your camera back,' he said.

'How many pictures did you take?'

'Just two,' he said, hanging his head. 'I'm sorry. We lost him.'

'But you made the delivery?' I said.

'Yes,' he said. 'We bought the poster first thing this morning and . . .'

'Which one did you buy?' I asked, as if it made any difference.

'One of the really big ones, like you said. The girl playing tennis. You know, the one where she's scratching her . . .'

'I think I know the one,' I said.

'The shop put it in a long cardboard tube. We stuck on the address label, put the bright orange tape around each end and took it to the postbox accommodation address.'

'So far so good. Then what happened?'

'It was a motor cycle courier. We took one photograph of him coming out of the building, carrying the tube – our tube – and another of it sticking out like a giant lollipop from his saddle-bag. Then we followed him.'

'And?'

'He headed out through the East End and we stuck to him like glue, till he joined the Eastway. We couldn't keep up. As soon as he was on the dual carriageway, he put his foot down. Must have been doing eighty or ninety. Maybe more.'

I wondered, after allowing for the exaggeration and

imagination of the teenage mind, how fast the courier really had been going. Even at sixty miles an hour though, the following scooter would have been struggling to keep up. It had a much smaller engine than the courier's bike, and was carrying two passengers to his one.

'Don't worry,' I said. 'It was the delivery that was the important part of the mission – getting the poster into the system and on to its final destination. You accomplished that. A photo of it arriving would simply have been a bonus. You did a good job, Saeed. Really, you did.'

He shrugged.

'I'm sorry,' he said again. 'I let you down.'

'No, you didn't.'

'Yes, I did.'

I put my arm round his bony shoulder.

'Why don't we skip the pantomime double act?' I said. 'Any minute now one of us will be shouting out, "Behind you!" How about we take a walk? I could do with some fresh air. Maybe we could treat ourselves to an ice cream. What do you say, buddy?'

'No, thanks,' he mumbled. 'I've got to get back. People to see.'

'Okay,' I said. 'See you Friday at the Festival. And, Saeed, thanks again for your help.'

'Some help!' he said, before slouching off.

At the entrance to the building, he turned around.

'I'll make it up to you, Nick,' he called back to me. 'I promise.'

CHAPTER THIRTY-SIX

Day Ten

'Do I get to keep the money?' Arthur said out of the blue.

We – Arthur, Arlene, Norman, Collins and myself – were sitting in Toddy's enjoying a welcome respite from the confines of Arthur's flat, where our activities seemed to consist of tripping over each other's feet and debating what type of earplug would be most effective at blocking out Sindy's rendition of the old Rolling Stones hit 'I Just Wanna Fake Love To You'. Collins and I had just begun reporting on our meeting with Oldbrook's bank manager (not the happiest of bunnies, one might say) when, by some convoluted and tangential thought process, Arthur had popped up with his question.

'What money?' I asked, reaching for my red wine in a pre-emptive measure to deaden my brain against Arthur's circuitous logic.

'The money OWN is paying me,' he said with a protracted sigh, as if it were I who had turned over two pages of the script. 'For being at the Festival tomorrow. You remember. I told you about it the other day.'

'Silly me,' I said. 'Fancy forgetting. What with having so little on my mind too.'

'Never mind,' he said magnanimously. 'But what I want to know is does it have to go into the business, or is it mine?'

'Five hundred quid, wasn't it?' said Norman, politely interested but not overexcited by the sum.

'Yeah. I got the first half today, along with the uniform. Although it's not much of a uniform: just a pair of black trousers, a black T-shirt printed with the white lightning fork logo and an itchy black wool balaclava. I get the rest of the money when I show up for duty tomorrow afternoon.'

'It's not the sort of income,' Norman said with a curl of his lip, 'that we would want to show in the books: "Payment received for services rendered to racist organisation." That would really endear us to the Inland Revenue and Customs and Excise. You'd better keep it,' he concluded generously. 'On the other hand, you could pick up tonight's tab. I'd hate to think of you tossing and turning at nights because your conscience was bothering you.'

'And,' I added, 'I'd hate to think of Norman lying awake thinking of you tossing and turning because your conscience was bothering you.'

'And I . . .' Arlene began.

'Okay. Okay. I get the picture,' Arthur said, holding his hand up to ward off any further contributions. 'Looks like it's my treat then.'

'What exactly do you have to do to earn this money?' I said, while Norman was signalling the waiter to open another two bottles of his special Pomerol.

'Form a picket line,' Arthur said. 'Block the route of the procession. Stop the floats from getting through. "They shall not pass."'

'Motto of the England football team,' I said. 'No, on second thoughts, that was "They cannot pass."'

Collins gave me a withering look – must have picked it up by working in close proximity to Walker.

'How many of you on this picket line?' Collins asked, presumably intending to pass on the information to his contacts in Special Branch.

'A hundred,' Arthur shrugged. 'Maybe more. You know how blokes exaggerate when they get talking.'

'I can imagine,' Arlene said, tossing her head.

I watched the swing of her auburn hair as it caught the light and brushed across shoulders exposed in all their beauty by the spaghetti straps of her dark red silk slip-dress. I took her hand. Looked deep into her hazel eyes.

'I don't think you should come to the Festival tomorrow,' I said.

'What! And miss all the fun? You must be joking, honey.'

'I couldn't be more serious,' I said. 'If this Rent-a-Mob gets out of control, it could turn into a full-scale riot. It's far too dangerous.'

'In that case I'd rather be at your side than sitting somewhere nervously biting my nails while waiting for the phone to ring.'

'What if I said I forbid you to come?'

'I'd laugh,' she said. 'Call you a male chauvinist pig. And still come.'

'Bribery?'

'A better tactic,' she said, nodding thoughtfully. 'But it won't work this time.'

'Why not? Has my charm deserted me? Am I losing my fatal attraction?'

'No,' she said. 'If you were, I'd stay away. Wouldn't I?'

'I suppose there's a certain logic in that,' I said uncertainly. 'But it doesn't help much. What if I said pretty please?'

She shook her head.

'Pretty please with chocolate sauce on?'

'Might depend,' she said impishly, 'on precisely what the chocolate sauce is on.'

'In that case . . .'

'No,' she said resolutely. 'No deals. And anyway, you're too late. I've already told Mrs Crabtree I'd go.'

'Mrs Crabtree?' I gasped. 'Where the hell does she fit in?'

'She's the one who made all the arrangements, honey. There's the coach . . .'

'What coach?'

'The one she has booked to take all the ladies to the Festival.'

I slapped my head with the palm of my hand. 'Jesus Christ,' I said.

'Do I take it, Nick,' she said sweetly, 'that you're not totally enamoured by the arrangements?'

'I can't hide anything from you, can I?'

'We Americans are very perceptive.'

'Glad to know that I didn't have to go to all the bother of getting up and banging my head against the wall.'

'It'll be all right,' she soothed. 'Mrs Crabtree spoke to Ali Khan. Used the fact that she had been instrumental in the buying back of the shop to – how can I put it? – persuade – yes, persuade – him to set aside a special area for us. We have ringside seats.'

'I wish you hadn't used that phrase,' I said, closing my eyes in silent prayer. 'Let's hope it doesn't turn out to be prophetic.'

CHAPTER THIRTY-SEVEN

Day Eleven

Half past eight in the morning and I had to reverse out of the car park at the council. There wasn't even room enough to turn round. All the spaces around the edge had been taken. An extra-long low-loader truck sat inconveniently in the exact centre. Encircling it was an army of volunteers (their description) or a leaderless, unruly mob (mine) milling around and getting in each other's way as they went about the task of building the float. I watched as a giant *papier mâché* globe was lifted on to the back of the lorry and rolled along to a raised turntable at the front; smiled with amusement as a small chunk broke off, widening the English Channel and leaving the whole of Normandy lying on the wooden deck – and the world mourning the loss of its supply of calvados (but, the xenophobes would say, a small price to pay). Crêpe paper blew in the breeze, curling itself around the flailing hands of those trying to fix it along the sides of the truck with what appeared to be blunt-headed drawing pins. Someone stepped into a pot of red paint and swore loudly. The final preparations for the Festival of Oldbrook had begun. And I had a terrible premonition that the day would continue in a state of organised chaos.

I parked the car in a side street half a mile from the offices and walked back past vendors setting up food stalls. Blackboards advertised flying fish sandwiches and rum punch, assorted curries and rice, various stir-fries (were they free? – all wok and no pay) and Hong Kong beer, and tacos, chilli, guacamole and tequila sunrise. An enterprising Spaniard was doing a roaring trade over an equally roaring gas stove, selling churros in twists of paper. I bought a large cone, forgot to say when as the sugar was added and enjoyed every melting mouthful as I strolled in the warm sunshine.

Entering the old building, I made my way along the corridor to what had once been the ballroom of the grand house and was now the Council Chamber. The heavy double doors had been covered in dark red leather and decorated with shining brass studs in the shape of a phoenix. Inside was a raised dais with a long oak table and nine high-backed chairs in the same shade of clotted blood leather as the door and with more brass studs along the perimeter of the seat frames. It looked like the interior designer had watched too many movies of Tudor kings eating off trenchers and lobbing chicken bones over their shoulders for the servants to fight over. The main body of the hall was taken up by six rows of semicircular benches – yet more leather and studs, consistent if nothing else – on either side of a dividing walkway. At the back, on a railed-off minstrels' gallery were tables and chairs for the use of representatives of the media during council meetings. The ceiling was stuccoed, heavy velvet drapes were drawn tightly across the windows, chandeliers glimmered in the gloaming. The only discordant note in these confused historical flashbacks was provided by the anachronistic microphones dangling conspicuously from black wires and the four speakers, so big they might have come from an Emerson, Lake and Palmer concert at Wembley Arena.

And in all of this vast room there were just six of us.

Normally, being chosen to witness the opening of tenders would have been an ideal start to the day for most staff – a chance for the *hoi polloi* to hobnob with the exalted likes of Helen and McCready, drink real coffee and while away an agreeable thirty minutes or so. Today, the three staff randomly picked from the telephone list the previous afternoon appeared edgy and frustrated, as if anxious to get back to their desks, clear them, join in the excitement, savour the anticipation and leap into costume. A young lad sat on the first row of benches biting his nails and willing the hands of the clock to move more quickly to the appointed hour of nine o'clock. A woman in her fifties was knitting a pair of pink booties with the fervour that usually comes with the news of an imminent or premature birth. A grey-haired man peered myopically at the racing pages of one of the tabloids with pen poised hesitantly. Only McCready seemed relaxed.

But why shouldn't he be? Where was the thrill of the unknown for him?

He stood on the dais, the four thick manila envelopes containing the tenders spread out on the table in front of him. I grinned up at him and he did his best at forcing a smile on to lips I could barely see through the under-growth of moustache and beard. Climbing the short flight of steps, I smiled genuinely at a tense Helen and approached her and the welcome cup of coffee she was holding out towards me.

'Gather round everybody,' McCready said, his voice echoing in the near-empty room.

The others joined us on the platform.

I sipped my coffee, sighed appreciatively and gave Helen a reassuring wink.

She was wearing a plain, dark grey suit, white blouse and two-inch-heeled black suede shoes. All very sober and professional, and perfect for the events of the morning and early afternoon.

McCready, on the other hand, wore a dun-coloured woollen suit flecked with yellow: what it was perfect for, apart from burning or maybe camouflaging oneself in a field of mustard where loose-bowelled cows had grazed, I couldn't guess. The suit might have been made-to-measure: if so, it had been for someone with longer arms than McCready. The sleeves of the jacket came halfway down

322

his hands, covering the cuffs of his dark green shirt and his wristwatch.

'I'd like you all first,' he said, 'to look at the backs of the envelopes and examine the flaps. Across the seal you will see two signatures. These were written by Helen and myself at the moment the tenders were delivered to these offices. Please step forward and verify that the seals are intact.'

The three members of staff picked up the envelopes and stared at the seals. The woman and the grey-haired man nodded; the young lad shrugged.

'You too, please,' McCready said to me. 'Since you wanted to witness this ceremony, I think you too should subject the envelopes to scrutiny.'

I felt like someone press-ganged out of the audience to assist a magician with his act – check the padlocks, test the chains, tug on the buckles of the strait-jacket, stare inside the tank filled with water in which he would immerse himself. I picked up the envelopes one after another; looked exaggeratedly at the signatures; carefully placed a finger under the sealed flaps. I even held them up to the light.

'Satisfied?' McCready said, when I had replaced them on the table.

'Nothing up your sleeve?' I asked.

The young lad sniggered.

McCready shook his head – more in pity than denial, I suspected.

'This is the procedure,' he announced. 'One of you, I don't mind who,' – how magnanimous – 'will open an envelope and turn to the last page of the document where the price is given. This is the amount the council will have to pay that company, if the contract is accepted, for providing the refuse collection and disposal service. You will enter the price on this sheet of paper – demonstrative wave of paper in air – 'next to the name of the relevant bidding company. You will append' – *append*, can't they just sign? – 'your initials in the column next to the price. The rest of you will check the price and, likewise, initial the paper. The procedure will then be repeated for the other three envelopes,' – yawn from Shannon – 'and the completed sheet passed to myself and Helen. Is that clear?'

'And you always go for the lowest price?' I said, seeking confirmation.

'Although price is not the only consideration,' he replied with a sly smile, 'let us simply say there has never been an occasion yet when we have not chosen the lowest.'

'So there's no rule,' I said, nodding my head to show total comprehension. 'And you've never broken it.'

He sighed. Looked up at the clock. 'Nine o'clock precisely,' he said. 'You may begin.'

It was like being back at school or in the Examination Hall at university. The young lad broke first, his conditioning being the most recent. He snatched at an envelope and ripped it open; rifled through to the back of the document; grabbed the sheet of paper; wrote down the figure, his tongue poking out in concentration, and signed.

I joined the queue of counter-signatories; penned my initials with a flourish, as the lad moved on to the next envelope.

The whole procedure, lasting as it did only a minute or two, might have been an anticlimax, but for the look on McCready's face as the completed sheet was passed across the table to where he and Helen sat. He stared down incredulously at the figures. This couldn't be happening, his hanging jaw seemed to say.

'A close-run race,' Helen said.

'Aye,' he mumbled. 'Very close.'

Suspiciously close?

'I declare,' Helen announced with unaccustomed pomposity and unbridled satisfaction, 'that the contract is hereby awarded to Eastern Refuse Limited.'

Which was one of the three names McCready did not want to hear.

He dragged his eyes reluctantly from the sheet of paper;

turned them in my direction; hit me with an expression of anger and loathing.

I gave him a broad grin; went over to the windows; drew back the curtains; let the sun shine in; whistled loudly. *Oh what a beautiful morning, oh what a beautiful day. I got a wonderful feeling . . .*

Funny though, McCready didn't join in.

'Well?' Helen said, when we were alone.

'Yes,' I said. 'Very well. I thought it went very well indeed.'

'If looks could kill,' she said, shaking her head and sucking air through her teeth.

'I wouldn't be here now,' I shrugged. 'I'd be pushing up the daisies. I might not have any mittens, but this cat has nine lives.'

'And how many have you used so far?'

'I wish you hadn't asked that question. It reminds me of my mortality. I think the count is seven to date.'

'Well, it was only a metaphor,' she said, attempting re-assurance.

'Sticks and stones may break my bones, but metaphors can't hurt me.'

Not unless they're written on a piece of paper wrapped around a blunt instrument.

'So will it work?' she asked. 'Will McCready follow the direction of your heavy-handed shove?'

'Does Max Clifford like publicity? Does Jeremy Beadle like practical jokes? Does Lester Piggott hate the taxman? Does . . .'

'I think I get the picture,' she said.

'McCready, like the rest of the human race, cannot go against his nature. We are what we are – leopards who cannot change their spots.' I shrugged helplessly. 'Anyway, philosophy aside, McCready knows by now that I have rumbled him. He must realise that this is the end of the road. He'll want to exit stage left in a blaze of glory. One last hit and flee the country. This morning your fortnightly tranche of Government grant wings its way into your bank account; a tempting eight million smackers sitting there blowing kisses at him. The bait is irresistible. And the pressure is too great.'

'You sound very sure about everything.'

'Yes,' I said. *Sound*. 'What are we going to do to kill some time?'

'*I'm* going to give moral support to the troops working on the float. What about you? How are you with a hammer?'

'Lethal,' I said. 'DIY is not one of my strong points. And anyway, I suspect it would be a case of another cook spoiling the broth. I think I'll seek out Collins. I have a question for him.'

One he had avoided answering the first time I had asked it.

'How did you get on to Leyton?' I asked Collins as we sat in the snack bar drinking coffee. 'All you said in the hospital was good old-fashioned police work.'

'You don't want to know,' he replied.

'You've just confirmed my fears,' I said. 'So you might as well tell me the worst.'

'It's your funeral,' he said with a careless shrug.

'That's what I'm worried about.'

'The hit-and-run occurred in the area covered by Mid-Anglia Police. The assumption, therefore, is that the boot print belonged to one of their people. Right?'

I nodded.

'So I needed to get hold of their personnel records – or at least a list of those who had undergone special training and been issued with the ultimate in footwear. I bribed a civilian clerk.'

'And that's good old-fashioned police work?'

'A smart detective cuts a few corners.'

Cutting corners was one of Collins's many habits that had not earned the undying respect of his superiors.

'And Leyton?' I pressed.

'I also got the clerk to check on who was in charge of CID at the time. Someone had to remove the piece of vital evidence from the file. Someone high up, that is. I tracked Leyton down to the hospital and had a little chat.'

'But he didn't confess straight away?'

'Who does?' Collins replied. 'He took a day to mull it over, then contacted me. That was when I sent for you.'

'And he confessed solely to protect someone.'

Collins nodded and stared out of the window, feigning great interest in the last-minute activities of the food vendors before the lunch-time rush begun.

'In which case, we can safely assume that he spoke to that person.'

'Very probably,' Collins admitted.

'Who is now aware of your interest.'

'You can't make an omelette . . .' Collins said.

'It's not eggs being broken that I'm worried about. It's legs. Or necks. Someone has tried for nine years to keep my sister's hit-and-run from being investigated. I doubt that whoever is the culprit is going to let you open the can of worms without putting up a fight. You have put yourself in jeopardy. And me too.'

'How do you work that out?' he said innocently.

'Because said culprit is a policeman. And he will check up on you; discover that we worked together at the Fraud Squad. After that, he has to play safe; work on the theory that you would tell me everything.'

'Maybe in the future you'll listen when I say you don't want to know.'

'If you don't report Leyton's confession and formally close the case, the killer will realise you didn't buy it. Then he'll come after us.'

'Don't worry, Shannon,' he said. 'I have a plan.'

'This time, Mr Collins,' I said, 'I really don't want to know.'

CHAPTER THIRTY-EIGHT

The bank manager bore his impotence with ill grace, but maybe that's all one can bear under the circumstances. Confronted by a superintendent from the Fraud Squad, the Chief Executive of his most important client, a dictum from Head Office, and a hyperactive Shannon who was busy rearranging his office and tampering with much that it contained, what else could he do but moan?

'Do you realise,' he said in a morose monotone, 'the number of complaints we have had already?'

To emphasise his point, seemingly unable to do so by vocal inflexion, he took off his glasses and stabbed them in my direction.

'Look on the bright side, Mr Matlock,' I said. 'It would have been even more if we hadn't banned the use of the telephones.'

'*That* is the reason we are receiving the complaints,' he pointed out.

Some people you just can't please.

'It's all in a good cause,' Helen said in a vain attempt to pacify him.

'Surely there must be some other way to catch the man?' he asked. 'Something slightly less likely to cause mayhem in my branch.'

'Well,' I said, fiddling distractedly with his wall clock till it was perfectly vertical, 'maybe if you issue a personal invitation to McCready to join you for a glass of sherry and . . .'

'Yes?' he said hopefully.

'We replace all your staff with police officers and . . .'

He winced at the thought of the consequences: irreparable damage to his customer base, computer systems fouled, tills impossible to reconcile, whisky stains and cigarette ash all over the paperwork.

Helen shot me a reproving glance. Collins hid a smile – he'd suffered at the hands of many an uncooperative bank official in the past and was enjoying my bear baiting.

'If you could move, please,' I said to Matlock, while standing in a predatory fashion ready to take his seat behind the desk.

'But you've checked everything already,' he protested.

'And now I'm going to check it all again. You can't be too careful. Isn't that what we say, Mr Collins?'

'You can't be too careful,' he echoed, his hand placed strategically in front of his grinning mouth.

Okay, so maybe I was milking the situation; teasing Matlock unmercifully for my own self-gratification. But I had to do something to cheer myself up after my conversation with Collins.

I sat down; swivelled in the big leather chair, experimenting to see whether it filled me with the awesome power to strike fear into the hearts of grown men. No joy. I leaned forward; checked the microphone clipped out of sight to the back of a plastic cylinder containing a collection of pens and pencils; traced the wire into the top drawer, covering it with an orange folder when I was satisfied. I pressed the jack plug firmly to secure the connection and went through the standard routine of 'Testing. Testing. One, two, three. Now is the time for all good men', and so on.

I played it back. It was fine, except that it was obviously someone else's voice.

'Before McCready enters,' I said, 'all you have to do is depress the red button.'

Hello, red button, I imagined him saying in his normal, downcast tone.

'I think I can manage that,' he said.

'And act natural,' Collins added.

Matlock nodded, not quite so confident now. He tugged at the sleeves of a dark grey suit and inspected the length of white cuff on show. As if McCready, of all people, was going to award him marks out of ten for sartorial elegance!

'We,' Collins said, 'will be waiting in your assistant's office with our ears up against the connecting door. As soon as McCready asks you to make the transfer, we will burst in.'

'Shouting *aha* at the tops of our voices,' I said.

'And when will he arrive?' the bank manager asked, anxious to get his part over and done with and the branch back to normality.

'It will be some time before three-thirty,' I said, 'since that is the close of banking business and therefore the deadline for making the transfer. Other than that, we really don't know.'

He looked at his watch to see how much time remained, then sighed.

'Right,' Collins said decisively. 'We'll take our positions. I'll leave the door slightly ajar until we hear the knock that signals McCready's arrival.'

We trooped next door. Unlike the bank manager's office with its space for the long wide desk, four chairs, three filing cabinets and bookcase, the room was so small that a cat-swinger would have had trouble practising his perverted hobby.

'Mobiles off,' Collins said, setting us an example. 'We don't want any untimely interruptions.'

When we had followed suit, he offered Helen the only chair that looked remotely comfortable, then dragged a hard, grey plastic chair over to the window, threw it open, sat down, stretched out his legs and lit a cigarette. I joined him.

'Keep out of sight, Shannon,' he barked unnecessarily.

'Spoilsport,' I said. 'Just when I was looking forward to

poking my head out of the window and shouting, "Free samples."'

'And keep your mouth shut. When the waiting is over, I want to be still sane.'

'What do you mean *still?*' I said.

Helen tilted her head. Gave us both a strange look. Took a book from her bag. Buried her nose inside. The words *Men are from Mars* glared accusingly in our direction.

The time passed slowly. And no one was interested in playing 'I-Spy'.

At three o'clock the knock came.

The bank manager cleared his throat nervously.

I shut the door.

We jockeyed for position behind it.

And held our breath. Which was good news for Helen and me. Inhaling Collins's second-hand whisky fumes would have prevented us driving for the rest of the day.

McCready gave a grunt of greeting and then went straight for the bank manager's throat, angrily lambasting him because he'd been unable to get through to the bank on the telephone. Matlock, trained in defusing tricky situations involving irate customers, remained silent until McCready's spleen had been fully vented.

'All I can do is apologise most profusely, Mr McCready,' he said eventually, so very *''umble'*. 'Although it is not our fault. British Telecom thinks the problem must have something to do with the preparations for the Festival.'

'Damned Festival,' McCready hissed.

'So how can I be of assistance?'

'In spite of the Festival, life must go on. There is the usual daily list of transfers to make. I have all the details here.'

There was a pause as McCready presumably passed over a detailed list of transfers from the council's various accounts to whatever vehicle he had chosen for his fraud. I had only two questions: would the money be going to OWN or into some private account of McCready's? And would he go for the whole amount – clean out the council in one fell swoop? I gave up on the answer to the first, and settled on a fairly safe *yes* for the second.

'This all seems quite clear,' said Matlock, raising his voice a fraction. 'You wish all these transfers made today?'

'Of course I do,' McCready almost screamed. 'Immediately.'

We all drew our ears back from the door at the unequivocal instruction. Collins turned the handle silently; threw open the door. And we burst inside.

'Aha,' I shouted, keeping my promise.

'Shannon,' McCready groaned. 'And Helen.'

'And Detective Superintendent Collins of the Fraud Squad,' the last member of our trio introduced himself.

McCready clutched his briefcase tight against his stomach and stared transfixed at Collins, an expression of stunned horror peeping out from the ginger beard and moustache.

I stepped past the moving little tableau – if that is not a contradiction in terms – and picked up the sheet of paper detailing the transfers. McCready had gone for the lot – Greedy by name and greedy by nature. The final sum was a little under nine million pounds. His instructions were for transfers out of eight of the council's accounts into the final one, and then one transfer from that. To WhiteFire. There's altruism for you.

'Can we answer the telephones now?' Matlock asked single-mindedly.

'Yes, Mr Matlock,' I sighed. 'Business as usual.'

'Not quite,' McCready said, taking a gun from his brief-case and waving it in the air. 'Everyone up against the wall.'

Helen and Collins stopped dead in their tracks. Matlock whimpered. McCready wore an expression of deep concentration as he presumably tried to think of a way out of the situation, and the office.

'Do as he says,' Collins ordered, taking charge.

I helped Matlock out of his chair and led him back to the wall where Collins and Helen were now standing. Collins shot me a look. You've done it again, Shannon, it said.

Bloody cheek. It was normally *he* who landed *me* in trouble. And how was I to know McCready would have a gun? And a very strange one at that.

It was a large, heavy weapon – revolver, *circa* nineteen-fifties or sixties, I reckoned. Although, I must admit, my knowledge of guns was pretty limited – to staring down a barrel usually. Anyway, it seemed to me as if it probably went out of production about the same time as crêpe-sole brothel-creepers. The gun even had a metal ring at the base of the grip where a lanyard could be attached. Chances were it was so old it would probably misfire. Maybe.

'Come on, McCready,' I said scathingly, 'this is the end of the line. You're finished. Now, be a good boy and put the gun away.'

He shook his head. Pointed the gun at Helen. Took a quick glance at the clock.

'Not the end of the line, Shannon. Just a change of trains.'

Was this how it would end? Death by an excess of corn?

'There's still time to make the transfer,' he said. 'And to make my escape. Of course, I won't be able to risk attending the Festival. Shame about that. I was looking forward to putting a bullet between Ali Khan's eyes.' He shrugged. 'But who knows? Maybe someone else will take my place. There are plenty of others who share my loathing of the man.'

I had to stall him. Buy some time. For thought and then action.

'Why, McCready?' I said. 'Why did you commit the frauds? And why must you kill Ali Khan? Is Rashid's blood on your hands not enough for you?'

'I needed the money for the cause,' he said. 'For OWN.

And Ali Khan? He gives people ideas above their station. That can't be permitted, Shannon. As for Rashid, he wasn't meant to die. Though I can't say I shed any tears. I couldn't trust him to keep his mouth shut. He was a black-mailer. Had no backbone. Like all of his kind.'

'Is that the root of it? He wasn't white, so what did his life matter?'

'Very perceptive, Shannon. But then I expect no less of you. This trap was your idea, I take it? I see it all now. The visit to the dump. The trick you pulled on the tenders. The poster you sent me. All merely intended to panic me into action. It almost worked too. But almost isn't good enough.'

'Neither is that gun by the looks of it. Been raiding the rejects on the *Antiques Roadshow*?'

'This is a treasured possession, Shannon. Don't knock it. This gun has shot many a black man in South Africa. I couldn't be parted from it when I was forced to make a dis-creet exit – things were getting just a little too hot for me – and return to this country. Packed it in the container with my furniture. Since then I've cleaned it, oiled it every week without fail. I guarantee it will function perfectly. As you will no doubt find out in a little while. Matlock will execute the transfer just before half past three – so that the instructions cannot be rescinded when I leave – and then I'll execute you. Nigger lover.'

'I can't believe you were always this evil, McCready,' I said, although maybe I could. 'What happened in South Africa? What pushed you over the edge of sanity?'

'I'm not mad, Shannon. Just see things more clearly than you short-sighted lily-livered liberals.' His left hand drifted to his beard and scratched at his chin. 'But then again,' he said, 'my eyes were forced open.'

I glanced to my side while he paused for breath. Saw a white-faced Helen, a bank manager close to catatonic shock and Collins with a cool and calculating expression.

'I was working in the Transkei,' McCready continued,

his eyes seeming to blaze with fire. 'Good job. Nice house. Swimming pool. Three servants. The lot. Couldn't have wished for more. Except for the blacks, of course. Damn blacks everywhere.'

What the hell did he expect? Eskimos?

'Filled with envy, the ungrateful blacks were,' he said, shaking his head at the incomprehensibility of the world. 'Weren't satisfied with what they had. And as they weren't mentally capable of earning the money they craved, they had to steal it. A bunch of the buggers burgled our house. I was at work. But my wife and daughter were at home. The blacks killed them, but not until after they had raped them. My daughter was only twelve, Shannon. And you wonder why I hate the bastards?'

Matlock started to sway. Come to that, I wasn't feeling too great either. I could almost picture the scene. Could understand the trauma which poisoned McCready's mind. But couldn't for the life of me find a way of justifying his distorted philosophy or his callous actions. Vengeance is a whole world apart from justice.

'You'd better sit down, Matlock,' McCready said. 'I can't afford for you to pass out on me. Not now. Only ten minutes to go. Time you began the preparations for the transfer.'

Matlock staggered over to his chair and sat down heavily. His face had drained of blood. A fraudster caught red-handed in his office; a tale of murder and rape; a gun being waved about. He could dine on this story for years to come. If he survived.

'Pick up the phone, Matlock,' McCready said firmly, 'and contact whoever will action the transfer. Read over the instructions exactly as they are written. And, don't forget, I'll be listening to every word. No tricks.'

It was an unnecessary warning. I didn't think Matlock had a trick left in him.

'But . . .' he began.

'Do as he says,' I interrupted. 'Pick up the phone.'

He looked at me helplessly, but stretched out a shaky hand for the telephone; tapped out a four-digit extension. In a trembling voice, he announced himself, said, 'I want you to make the Oldbrook transfer.'

There was a pause while the person at the other end spoke. Then Matlock raised his voice and said, 'I don't care. Do as I say. This instant.'

He read out, slowly and clearly, the first item on the list. McCready checked the clock again. Collins caught my eye. I could tell what was going through his mind. He wasn't the world's most patient man. Probably wasn't even in the first twenty billion, come to that. He would be itching to act; planning some move. Surely.

Matlock continued to drone on, working his way towards the bottom of the list. If I were him, I'd be taking my time too. The moment he finished issuing the instructions he would be expendable.

The gun still pointed directly at Helen. She was half-standing, half-leaning against the wall, Collins on her right, myself on her left. I noticed Collins move fractionally away. I, in turn, edged slightly to widen the gap between Helen and me. If Collins was thinking what I thought he was thinking, he was about to take a big chance.

Matlock replaced the handset.

McCready smiled.

'Well, Shannon,' he said. 'Thanks for setting the trap. Too bad it sprung without me being inside. Oh, and thanks for alerting me to the fact that you were on to me. I wouldn't have dared risk everything otherwise. Still, fortune favours the brave, eh? I appear to have hit the jackpot.'

'Will you tell him?' Collins said to me. 'Or shall I?'

'Let me, please,' I said. 'You know my wicked sense of humour. Don't deny me the pleasure.'

'Go on, then. Spoil yourself, Shannon. It's about time.'

'How droll,' I said, taking a small pace forward and to my left. There was only – still? – three large strides to go to reach McCready. 'You see, Stuart — I can call you Stuart, can't I? — you don't mind?'

'Actually,' he said with distaste, 'I like a little more respect. I never did support this damned nonsense of only using first names.'

'Okay, Mr McCready — or do you prefer Bwana? Collins was right on the button, you see. It's about time. Let me demonstrate.'

I took a step towards the clock on the wall, glimpsing from out of the corner of my eye Collins preparing himself.

'Stay where you are,' McCready shouted.

'Very well, then,' I sighed. 'Perhaps you would be so kind as to look at your watch.'

'I know what the time is, Shannon. Time for me to kill you all and go.'

'Look at your watch,' I said, balancing myself to spring, 'and you'll see that it's later than you think. Before you entered the room, I moved the hands on the clock back by ten minutes. I like to have time on my side. Your transfer, McCready, never happened. You were too late.'

He examined my face. Must have known by my self-satisfied grin that I was telling the truth. But he just had to make sure.

He pulled at his sleeve, the gun perforce at last moving away from Helen.

'Now,' shouted Collins.

We leapt forward together, Collins to McCready's extreme left, myself from wide right, both of us diving headlong towards the gun.

McCready swung the gun round.

Hesitated for a fraction of a second over which of us to shoot.

And then it was too late.

I had my hand on the gun. Collins had his wrapped tightly round McCready's throat.

The chair overbalanced with the combined weight of three bodies, two of them carrying a lot of forward momentum. We lay there in an untidy heap that failed to do justice to our actions.

'Throw the gun to Helen,' Collins snapped at me while we all struggled.

I wrenched the weapon from McCready's grasp, weakened as it was by the constriction of his windpipe. Slid it gingerly along the floor. Watched as Helen placed a foot over it.

'Help me get him up,' Collins wheezed breathlessly. 'Then face down over the desk.'

We pulled him up. Spun him round. Slapped his head down on the top of the desk. Collins took hold of one arm and bent it behind McCready's back.

'Matlock,' Collins hissed. 'Make yourself useful and call the police.'

I continued to press down on McCready's back, determined he wouldn't move an inch until reinforcements arrived and slapped him safely in handcuffs.

'Christ, you were pushing your luck,' I said to Collins. 'What if he hadn't hesitated? What if he'd shot you?'

'A calculated gamble,' he replied calmly. 'He couldn't shoot both of us in the fraction of a second he had available. So, either he would hesitate, which would give us the time to act, or . . .'

'Or what?'

'Or he'd make a snap decision on which of us to shoot. And, let's face it, Shannon,' he said with a casual shrug of his shoulders, 'it was never going to be me who would be his first choice.'

CHAPTER THIRTY-NINE

Five minutes to go before Ali Khan's speech to open the Festival and signal the birth of a new Oldbrook. Five minutes before he announced the engagement of his daughter to Adam Schroeder and welded together two faiths. Five minutes to manoeuvre Helen through the crowded streets so that she could stand by her son's side and beam with pride. The three of us burst through the door of the bank. Then stood there staring around us and at each other.

You didn't need to possess the deductive powers of Sherlock Holmes to know that something wasn't quite right. The silence was eerie – the dog, yet again, wasn't barking. There was no laughter, no singing, no chitter-chatter hum of anticipated excitement. The food vendors were packing up their stalls. And then there was the crowd – the expressions of fear bordering on panic on the faces of the fast-moving tide. Fast moving in the wrong direction too. Away from what should have been the focal point. The magnet that was the start of the procession was repelling rather than attracting.

We broke into a stuttering run, the best we could manage against the oncoming sea of troubled people. Collins and I thrust out our hands and pushed out our elbows to carve a path for Helen to follow. Jinking and swerving like rugby players heading desperately for the try line in the dying moments of a tied game, we neared the raised platform where Ali Khan stood. Open-mouthed, speechless – what bigger omen could one need? – he was looking around helplessly.

Helen mounted the steps, Collins and I following close behind. From the vantage point above the heads of those who still remained – either because they could not leave or chose not to do so – I could view the whole scene. TV cameras on gantries to right and left; Mrs Crabtree, her old ladies, Norman and Arlene in a specially roped-off area below; opposite me, Saeed Khan with a group of thirty or forty of his college friends; in the middle of the road, the Oldbrook Council float, flag flying over a mass of costumes and colours. And directly ahead of it, a wall of black – the massed ranks of OWN.

I estimated the numbers as close to a hundred: four lines deep, faces covered by balaclavas, arms interlocked. From the middle of the front rank, one figure stood head and shoulders above the rest. It turned to look up at me.

'Wait,' I mouthed at Arthur.

'Move back,' Ali Khan commanded, finding his voice and sending it booming out from the speakers. 'Clear the road, please.'

Helen turned to Collins. 'Why don't the police *do* something?' she asked.

'Afraid of starting a riot they won't be able to contain,' he replied. 'You wanted low-profile police presence. That's why all you've got is a handful of beat bobbies who came here on the look-out for the odd pickpocket, argumentative drunk or voluptuous dark-skinned maiden with whom to boogie for the cameras. Frankly, there aren't even enough of them to clear the road let alone cart off the opposition, bearing in mind its size and their violent intentions. With a bit of luck, reinforcements have been summoned. When they manage to force their way through the crowds, maybe then they'll act.'

If Walker were here she would be saying *maybe not*; that maybe some of the police would prefer to be reinforcing the wall than breaking it down.

'Keep talking to them,' I said to Ali Khan, noticing a movement in the crowd. 'Plead with them. Say anything you like, but stall them.'

Saeed had ducked under the red tape, all the barrier there was separating the crowd from the intended route of the procession. His teenage friends – the new Black Panthers – followed him as his short thin frame held itself erect and walked purposefully to the front of the float.

'Stupid bloody kid,' I hissed, watching them form their own feeble line.

I placed my palms on the wooden handrails of the steps, swung myself down the whole flight, spun round quickly to face the road, pushed my way to the kerb, ducked under the barrier and strode towards Saeed.

As I approached, he smiled at me like a proud puppy dog who had just delivered the evening paper.

'I told you I would make it up to you,' he said. 'For messing up by not getting the photographs.'

'A box of chocolates or a bottle of wine would have done. Come on, Saeed, move your friends back. You'll only provoke the enemy. And we're hardly equipped to deal with them at the moment.'

'I took your advice,' he said.

'And what the hell was that?' I said, groaning as I watched orders being relayed among the body of black T-shirts with their white lightning-flash logos.

'I've been reading about Martin Luther King.'

'Jesus Christ,' I said, understanding his intentions and cursing the size of my mouth and the foot which had been planted firmly inside it.

'We shall overcome,' he said with the dangerous fervour of a convert. 'Just like you said. Passive resistance. No violence. We will conquer. Won't we, Nick?'

He gazed up at me, doe-like eyes seeking support for his determination and reassurance for his doubts.

'Oh, yes,' I said, shrugging my shoulders. 'In the long run, you'll conquer. That is, if you survive the short run with its high probability of getting your heads kicked in.' I put an arm round his bony shoulder. 'Come on, little brother, let's all move back. Discretion *is* the better part of valour, Saeed.'

'No,' he said, clenching his fists. 'Someone has to make a stand.'

'Why you?'

'Look about you. Can you see anyone else who is prepared to?'

'That's because they're scared. Like you should be.'

'I am scared,' he whispered.

'Don't you read the papers, Saeed? I'm the one who is the resident hero around here.'

'Then stand with us.'

It would have been easy to pick him up and carry him bodily to the other side of the barrier; to humiliate him in front of his friends; to shatter the glass that reflected a rose-tinted image of Nick Shannon and substitute in its place a distorted fairground mirror with an image that was all mouth and no trousers.

'Hell, Saeed,' I said, 'whatever happened to freedom of choice?'

He gave a wide smile.

'Thanks, Nick,' he said. 'Now what do we do?'

'Make them think,' I said.

OWN's order having been transmitted, their front line took a pace forward.

I nodded to Arthur and tossed my head back, beckoning him.

He broke ranks and stepped towards us.

Saeed, at my left side, tensed.

'Relax,' I said. 'He's one of us.'

Arthur peeled off his balaclava, grinned and took his place at my right hand.

'Bleeding hot inside that thing,' he grunted.

'Not as hot as it's going to get,' I said.

'Bunch of hired thugs, most of them. No real conviction or commitment. Probably turn and run as soon as we throw the first punch.'

I shook my head and sighed.

'No punches, Arthur,' I said. 'No forearm smashes, kicks

342

or strangleholds. The kid is now a believer in passive resistance. Let's not disillusion him.'

'You're joking,' he said.

'Not this time.'

'Bloody hell,' he groaned. 'I don't know if I can handle that. Goes against my nature. Standing still while someone beats me to a pulp, that is.'

'Just look frightening and hope for the best.'

'Typecast as ever,' he mumbled.

He stripped off his black T-shirt. Ripped it in two. Threw it to the ground. Flexed his exposed bulging muscles at the enemy. Glared menacingly along the front rank.

'Get your friends in a line behind us,' I said to Saeed.

Ali Khan's voice, steady and controlled, bellowed out of the speakers. 'Today is a very special day,' he said.

He was finally going to make his announcement. As a stalling manoeuvre, it had a lot going for it. The same went as an incitement to riot too.

I watched Saeed marshal his little band of acne-faced warriors. Heard the clicking of heels behind me. Turned to see Arlene hurrying across the road.

'What are you doing?' I said aghast. 'You should be getting as far away from here as possible. This is liable to get nasty. Very nasty.'

'If *you're* staying,' she said, grabbing my arm, 'then my place is at your side. And, anyway, someone has to represent the Puerto Rican half-breeds.'

'Whatever happened to the creed of keeping out of danger?'

'I can't change you, Nick. I realise that now. You are what you are. And I love you for it.'

I bent my head down and kissed her.

'Not now, Shannon,' Collins said, suddenly putting in an appearance. 'The TV cameras are rolling and it's not yet the nine o'clock watershed.'

Our front line rearranged itself to accommodate the extra numbers. Arthur moved to the right flank. Collins, who had always had a soft spot for Arlene, placed himself protectively next to her.

Ali Khan finished his announcement. Nadya and Adam gave embarrassed bows. There was a burst of stiff-fingered applause from the roped-off area and a muffled cheer from the crowd – was it my imagination or did it seem to be growing bigger? Helen hugged her son and future daughter-in-law. Adam said something to his mother and she frowned. He kissed her on the cheek. Climbed down the steps. And walked towards me.

Nadya ran after him.

So did Helen.

Ali Khan stood alone on the platform. He looked across at us. The light of the sun flashed off the lens of one of the TV cameras as it swivelled to zoom in on his thoughtful expression. He took a deep breath, puffed up his chest and, head held high, descended the steps.

He joined us, moving to the central position of our growing line and drawing his son and daughter close to him.

'Time to form two rows,' I said. 'Ali, Saeed, Nadya, move one pace back.'

'What is this?' Ali Khan said. 'Trying to steal my lime-light?'

I could have pointed out that *I* was here first. Instead I said, 'This is positive discrimination, Ali. Maybe they'll hesitate to come through us to you. White against white doesn't make for such good headlines.'

'My rightful place is . . .' he began, before stopping to stare.

I stared too, jaw hanging low.

There was Norman.

And the cavalry.

Mrs Crabtree's arthritic army – zimmer frames, wheel-chairs and all. Wobbling unsteadily to form a new line. At the very front.

It was then I knew we couldn't lose.

And everyone else present sensed the same.

There was a cheer. The crowd surged, moving to the small gap behind us and ahead of the float, and pressing us forward.

So it was that we advanced: a bunch of little old ladies; a trio of ex-convicts, one ex-Martinez, a detective superintendent, the Chief Executive of a London borough and her handsome son; the Khans, at last united; Saeed's hormone-surging, spotty-faced teenage idealists; and the good citizens of Oldbrook.

OWN's line broke. The five-hundred-pound-a-head mercenaries assessed the odds, backed away from the nightmare march of their mothers and grandmothers, and scattered.

The diesel engines of the floats spluttered into life.

The procession rolled forward.

The Festival of Oldbrook had begun.

POSTSCRIPT

All the frauds/scams in this purely fictional novel have been committed in the past in some form or other, or could with relative ease be committed in the future – unless, of course, the gaps exposed in *The Money Race* are plugged.

I would like to thank Essex County Council, its officers – past and present – and particularly those in the Treasury Department and the Press Office for their invaluable help in providing background, for verifying the frauds I initially proposed and for suggesting others. I hasten to add that ECC bears no resemblance to my London Borough of Oldbrook in any shape or form – although I have used a liberal spoonful of artistic licence in adapting their premises! Equally, no connection should be made between its staff and the many scoundrels of Oldbrook.